He leaned on the shovel.

"What's this?" he muttered, frowning as he jabbed at the loosened dirt.

"Paul? What are you looking at down there?"

"Well, I wanted to dig a little deeper to see what kind of soil bed you were going to have for your garden, but I'm coming onto something...."

"What is it?" She leaned forward.

He prodded experimentally with the shovel. "It feels like...I'm not sure."

"A treasure chest?" she asked hopefully.

"I'm afraid not. More likely a buried pet. That's what I'd guess, anyway. It feels like a bundle of bones wrapped in some kind of plastic tarp."

Jackie felt a stirring of uneasiness in her stomach, accompanied by a cold chill of fear. She walked across the freshly dug sod to peer into the furrow. At the bottom of the trench, partially exposed in the dark soil, was a blue plastic tarpaulin. The rotting fabric had been wrapped tightly around something that formed a faded cocoon about five or six feet long.

Paul and Jackie exchanged a glance. "You know what?" she muttered. "It looks like..."

"It sure does," he said when she fell silent. "So what should we do now, Jackie?"

"Dalton offers a graphic, well-researched look into the world of police procedure and forensic medicine...."
—*Publishers Weekly* on *Third Choice*

MARGOT DALTON

Fourth Horseman

RECYCLED PAPER · RECYCLED PAPER

ISBN 1-55166-522-0

FOURTH HORSEMAN

Copyright © 1999 by Margot Dalton.

Visit us at www.mirabooks.com

Printed in U.S.A.

This is entirely a work of fiction. There is no Northwest Substation presently associated with the Spokane Police Department; nor are any of the characters in this book based on real people. Apart from a basic effort to portray the work of an investigating officer with some accuracy, a number of liberties (mostly related to administrative and procedural matters) have been taken for the sake of the story.

Many thanks to Sergeant James Earle of the Spokane Police Department, and to Sergeant L. K. Eddy (retired) of the RCMP for their generous assistance. Any errors or discrepancies in this work are not theirs, but the author's.

"And when he had opened the fourth seal... I looked, and behold a pale horse: and his name that sat on him was Death, and Hell followed with him."
—*Revelation* 6: 7–8.

1

Rain fell during the night, a cold spring downpour that pattered in the bare tree branches and washed the last snow from the prairie. By morning the streets of Spokane smelled fresh and clean, with a tang of damp sage carried on the west wind and a scent of new grass pushing through wet soil.

Jackie Kaminsky stood at the curb in a quiet residential neighborhood, leaning against her police car, hands jammed deep in the pockets of her jacket. She was a tall woman, still slender and athletic though her body bulged with pregnancy. Her hair was black and short, and her attractive face showed traces of a mixed ethnic background in its dark eyes, high cheekbones and pale coppery skin.

She looked intently at a small two-story house standing back from the street behind a peeling white picket fence. The house was covered in white siding with dark green trim and shutters, and had a green shingled roof. At one side, a wooden trellis thatched with a network of vines stood above a gate that led to the backyard. The house was encircled by a tall hedge, just beginning to show a drift of new green leaves.

Jackie took a deep breath and pressed one hand automatically against her abdomen. By now, nearing the eighth month of her pregnancy, she was certain she could actually feel the outline of little feet as they pressed into her sides.

"Do you like it?" she whispered to the tiny person who rested snug and unseen within her body. "Do you like this house? Because it's probably going to be ours, you know. I think I'm going to buy it for us."

Hearing the words spoken aloud in the quiet April morning made her suddenly fearful. She glanced around nervously, then straightened and moved away from the car as another vehicle pulled up and parked behind her.

A woman got out, hauled a briefcase from the back seat and bustled toward Jackie. She was heavily built, probably in her forties, wearing a long black coat and dark nylon stockings, her plump feet jammed into high-heeled pumps. Her hair was an unlikely shade of bright auburn, and she had a green paisley shawl draped over her shoulders.

"Hello," she said, extending her free hand. "I assume you're Ms. Kaminsky? I'm Lola Bridges."

"And I'm Jackie." They shook hands, taking the measure of each other.

"Well, good morning, Jackie. Nice to meet you." The woman rummaged in her coat pocket. "I'll just find the key, and we can..."

A vehicle drove past them and braked, then swerved and backed expertly into the spot in front of Jackie's car. She tensed and felt her mouth go dry.

The new arrival was a big ranch truck, its undercarriage caked with mud, bits of straw clinging to the dusty metal sides. As the two women watched, a man climbed down from the driver's seat, slammed the door and strode toward them.

He was tall and bareheaded, the pale sunlight glinting on his smooth blond hair and blunt cheekbones. Even in faded jeans, work boots and a worn denim jacket lined with sheepskin, he moved with lithe grace and the air of contained power that always stirred Jackie.

She watched him draw closer and felt almost sick with love. Her first reaction was to hug him and burrow close. But, as always, Jackie's fear of this emotion rose up and overwhelmed her. So instead she held herself stiffly and gave him a cautious smile.

His dark gaze raked over her, studying the bulge of her abdomen, then her face, with a hungry yearning that took her breath away. But as soon as he caught her eye, he masked his expression and turned to nod politely at the woman with the briefcase.

"This is Paul Arnussen," Jackie said to the real estate saleswoman. "He's a…friend of mine who's going to have a look at the house for me and see if everything's okay with the foundation and construction. Paul, this is Lola Bridges."

He shook the woman's hand while she gaped up at him with a look of stunned admiration, her plump cheeks and parted lips making her seem like a goldfish with makeup. Jackie hid a wry smile and moved away from them toward the house.

"Well, let's get started, shall we?" she said over her shoulder. "I'm just on a coffee break. I'll have to get back to work soon."

The saleswoman gathered herself together and

trotted up the walk next to Jackie. Paul followed, squinting thoughtfully at the exterior of the house.

"I understand you've already viewed the property," Lola Bridges said.

Jackie nodded. "I came over here yesterday afternoon for the open house, and spent almost an hour looking around."

"Oh yes, my assistant was here for the open house. He said it was busy all afternoon." Lola gave her bright, professional smile.

"It was pretty busy. Apparently a lot of people are out looking at houses these days."

Jackie stood aside while Lola unlocked the front door, uncomfortably conscious of the man standing close behind them on the tiny front veranda.

As always when Paul was nearby, the baby seemed, mysteriously, to be excited by his presence. The baby was moving and surging with buoyant energy. Jackie winced as it turned and kicked lustily.

They walked into the house, paused to take off their boots and left them on the entry mat, while Lola hurried through the house switching on the lights. Alone with Paul, Jackie sighed and pressed both hands against her stomach.

"I think this kid is turning somersaults," she said. "All the thumping around is practically driving me crazy."

He glanced down at her, then moved closer and pulled her jacket aside to lay a callused palm on the bulge of her abdomen. When the baby stirred and kicked against the pressure of his hand, Paul's face relaxed into one of the rare, shining smiles that always transformed him, making him look boyish and young.

But the warmth vanished as soon as it came. He withdrew his hand and studied Jackie's face.

"Are you feeling all right?" he asked. "You're not getting too tired?"

"I'm fine. These days I'm eating spinach and liver, even though it makes me sick," she told him with forced lightness. "And swallowing tons of vitamin pills and folic acid. This is probably going to be the healthiest baby in the world."

He seemed on the verge of saying something else, or reaching out to touch her again. To Jackie's relief, the real estate agent came back with a folder in her hands.

"It's pretty straightforward," Lola said, glancing curiously at the two of them as they stood together in the foyer. "Just a lovely, cozy little house with everything a young family needs. A perfect starter home. Clear title, no existing mortgage. Too bad it's empty at the moment," she added. "The last occupants had it furnished so nicely."

"I'll go down and check the basement, if you don't mind," Paul told her. "I'd like to have a look at the foundation."

The agent indicated a door behind her and he moved away, looking big and broad-shouldered in the narrow hallway.

Lola watched him go, then cast Jackie another questioning glance.

"I'll need to know what the property taxes are," Jackie said. "And the average monthly utility bills."

"I have all that information right here. We can sit down and go over the numbers after you and your..." Lola hesitated, looking down at the papers in her hands. "After both of you have had a chance to look around," she concluded awkwardly.

"Thank you." Jackie moved into the small living room and studied the brick fireplace with its old-fashioned gas heater and oak mantel.

Beyond the window she could see the veranda and the branches of a tree that drooped across the railing.

"That's a mountain ash," the woman said, following her glance. "In the summer it shades the whole front of the house and makes it quite dark."

Jackie pictured the bower of sheltering green leaves, the berries and flocks of birds. She turned away to hide her expression and ran a finger along part of the oak chair rail that encircled the room.

"Such overdone woodwork," the saleswoman commented. "I've never thought it really suited a modest house like this."

Her manner seemed oddly negative. Jackie wondered suddenly if perhaps Lola Bridges had another buyer for the house.

"It sounds like you know a lot about the place," Jackie said, trying to sound offhanded.

"Well, as a matter of fact, I do." Lola waved a hand toward the front window. "My father lives next door. He's been there for almost twenty-five years. That's how I got the listing, actually. My father was quite friendly with the young couple who own the house."

"No kidding," Jackie said. "So you grew up in the neighborhood?"

The woman smiled wryly. "Well, thank you for that nice compliment, Jackie, but I'm afraid not. I was already in college when Dad moved here."

Jackie heard Paul's footsteps as he came back up

from the basement and mounted the stairs to the second floor. She waited tensely, listening while he moved around overhead, then came down.

He leaned in the arched living-room entry, watching her.

"Well?" she said at last.

"It looks fine. I found a few cracks in the basement walls, but that's to be expected in a house this age. And they're all vertical cracks, so they aren't likely to be a problem. It's the big horizontal cracks that wind up costing you money."

Jackie felt a surge of relief.

"Could you excuse us for a moment?" Paul said to the saleswoman.

He nodded to Jackie and started toward the kitchen, padding softly in his heavy work socks.

She followed him through the door and stood by the sink, looking down nervously.

The silence lengthened between them, growing tense and uncomfortable.

"You're sure about what you're doing, Jackie?" he asked at last. "This is really what you want?"

"Paul, I don't want to get into all that again. We've talked about it a hundred times and we never get anywhere."

"That's because you won't..." He clenched his jaw and stared out the window at the backyard, his profile etched with a pale wash of silver.

Suddenly, Jackie was overtaken by another stormy wave of sexual desire. Again she longed to touch him, to nestle in his arms and hold him close, to smell his clean male scent and taste his mouth. It was a struggle to bring the wayward emotions under control and keep him from seeing her weakness.

"I'm not prepared to move out and live at the

ranch with you," she said. "And I'm not sure if I ever will be."

"Why not?" He looked at her steadily. "You keep telling me how much you like the ranch."

"Don't be dense, Paul. You know the ranch isn't the whole issue. It's—"

"Commitment," he said when she stopped abruptly. "Oh yes, I know how scared you are of committing to a life with me, Jackie. God knows we've fought about it often enough. I just never thought you'd carry it this far."

"How far?"

"Choosing to raise your child without a father."

"I'm not raising this baby without you!" she said, stung. "You'll be able to see the baby whenever you choose."

"That's always nice to hear," he said dryly. "Visits every weekend. Maybe a phone call in the evening when the kid gets older. Sounds like a great life."

Jackie ignored the sarcasm, since this was an argument they'd had many times before. "But I also don't want to raise my baby in an apartment," she went on as if he hadn't spoken. "That's why I think a little house like this is the ideal solution."

"Well, I still believe it's a huge mistake. I think you should be living with me, both of you. I want this baby to grow up in my house. I want to marry you, Jackie. It's what I've always wanted, and I always will."

"Look, I really don't think we should be—"

"I know," he said wearily, waving a hand to cut off her words. "I know what you think. And I'm tired of arguing with you. I'm tired of these fears and demons you haven't been able to shake since childhood. I wish you'd give me a chance to show you how secure I could make you. Why can't you try it, Jackie?"

For a moment she pictured herself giving in, moving out to the ranch with him where they'd sleep together every night and share their child.

But the seductive image was washed away almost immediately by a cold, familiar wave of fear.

Jackie Kaminsky had always been a loner. If she was alone, she could look after herself without risk of being left or abandoned. The thought of putting her life into the hands of anybody, even this man she loved, was too terrifying to be contemplated.

"Paul, let's not do this," she pleaded, turning away from his intent gaze. "Let's just talk about the house, okay?"

"Sure, fine," he said coldly. "It's a nice little house, Jackie. If you want to buy it, go ahead. For the money, you're probably getting a pretty good deal."

He turned and left the kitchen. She followed him and waited while he said a brief farewell to Lola Bridges, then pulled on his boots and strode down the walk to his truck.

"Oh, my goodness. What a handsome man that is," the saleswoman breathed, watching through the front window as he climbed behind the wheel. "He's a...friend of yours, you said?"

"He's my baby's father," Jackie said. "Now, can we go somewhere and talk about this deal? I don't have much time."

They sat outside the house in Lola's car with listing forms and papers spread on the seat between them. Lola asked questions, punched numbers on her calculator and scribbled busily on a sheet of paper.

"Now, what's your place of employment, Jackie?" she asked.

"I'm a detective with the Spokane Police Department."

"Really?" The plucked eyebrows shot up. "How long have you had that job?"

"I made detective four years ago, but I've been in the police force for almost fourteen years, since I was twenty."

"All of that time in Spokane?"

Jackie shook her head. "I started as a patrol officer in Los Angeles, where I grew up. After about five years I moved to Spokane."

"Well, that's just fascinating," Lola said. "What would your annual salary be? I need to know," she added when Jackie hesitated, "so we can calculate your eligibility for the mortgage."

"The base salary is forty-one thousand a year, but overtime bumps it up quite a bit. I usually net about twenty-five hundred a month after deductions and my pension contribution."

"And how much can you bring forward as a down payment?"

"I have eleven thousand saved, but I'll want to keep a couple thousand of that in reserve to buy things I'm going to need when the baby comes."

"Of course. Nine thousand is more than adequate." Lola scribbled busily on her notepad. "So, if we can get them to come down a little on their price, that would mean a mortgage of...say, eighty thousand dollars. At current rates, with interest and taxes included, the monthly payment would be about seven hundred a month, or a little more than twenty-five percent of your net income.''

"Will the bank be willing to go for that?''

"Oh, I'm sure they will. In fact, you could almost certainly qualify for a higher mortgage if you wanted a house that was a little—'' Lola paused tactfully. "A little newer,'' she said at last.

Jackie felt a flood of relief. "I don't want a newer house,'' she said. "I want this one.''

"Are you sure?'' Lola cast her a thoughtful glance. "It's not wise to underbuy, you know. And with your salary and available down payment, I could show you a lot of very nice properties.''

"This is the house I want.''

The woman frowned briefly and seemed on the verge of continuing the argument, then gave Jackie a bright smile. "I see. Well, then, we'll just have to write up an offer and see that you get it, won't we?''

"I guess we will.'' Jackie looked out the window at the little green and white house, annoyed by the saleswoman's patronizing manner.

But she was afraid to antagonize Lola Bridges. For the moment, at least, Jackie had the uncomfortable sense that this woman held her future, and the baby's, in those pudgy hands sparkling with rings.

"When should I talk to the bank?'' she asked.

"As soon as possible. Today, if you can. We'll need confirmation on acceptance of the offer that you can come up with the funds.''

Anxiety gnawed at Jackie, a result of the lifelong insecurity over money that was a legacy of her impoverished childhood.

"You're sure there won't be any problem with the mortgage?"

"Nothing that I can see at the moment. Unless you have a lot of other debts and fixed payments?"

"Just my car loan at three hundred a month, and it's almost paid off. There's another four or five months to go, I think."

"No outstanding credit card balances?"

Jackie shook her head. "I only have one credit card, and I pay it in full every month. I'm very disciplined with money," she said.

Well, that was certainly true. In fact, the one extravagance in Jackie's life was the money she sent on a more or less regular basis to her grandmother in Los Angeles.

God only knew what those checks were spent on.

Irene Kaminsky swore she wasn't drinking anymore, that the money went straight into the bank and was used to buy food, pay medical bills and make life a little nicer for herself and Jackie's ne'er-do-well cousins, Joey and Carmelo, who still lived with Gram though they were in their mid-twenties by now.

Jackie, too, had grown up in that squalid apartment in south L.A., after her father ran off and her young mother died of a drug overdose when Jackie was little more than a baby. Irene Kaminsky had the care of a number of her grandchildren, a group of cousins whose unruly antics had made the old woman's cranky nature even more sharp and irritable.

On Jackie's rare visits to her grandmother these days, she never saw any evidence of the money she sent. A couple of the ancient appliances were usually malfunctioning, and a front windowpane that had been shot out a couple of years earlier was still covered with weathered plywood.

No doubt Gram spent the money on vodka and bingo. But if Jackie went too long without mailing a check, she was sure to get an abusive, accusatory phone call from the old lady, and after all these years she still couldn't withstand Gram's verbal attacks.

In fact, that was another of the things she and Paul fought about...

"Hmm?" she asked with a start, realizing that Lola was saying something to her.

"I just wanted you to sign the offer. Right here, and on this line, too."

Jackie looked at the form. Her heart beat faster and she felt suddenly terrified by what she was doing.

Jackie Kaminsky, about to become a home owner. What a concept.

She kept her face deliberately expressionless, took the pen and signed the real estate form.

"Well, that's just excellent," Lola said with satisfaction, tucking the sheet into her briefcase. "Now I'll run back to my office and present this to the vendors before lunch. I'll call you as soon as I can with their reply."

"Thanks. I'll be waiting to hear from you."

"That man...your friend..." Lola fingered the gearshift lever.

"Yes?"

"I'm curious. You said he's the father of your baby, didn't you? But I take it you're not planning to live together."

"That's right." Jackie watched a thin black cat as it slipped under the trellis beside the house and walked up onto the veranda, then squeezed back through the railing, jumped lightly to the ground and vanished into the lilac hedge.

"Why not, if you don't mind me asking?"

But I do mind, Jackie thought, startled. In fact, I mind a whole hell of a lot.

She looked at the woman's heavy makeup, her dyed hair and consciously dramatic clothes, and marveled that anybody could ask such a question.

People were so amazing...

"Because you know, if I had a man like that," Lola said wistfully, "believe me, I wouldn't let him out of my sight for a minute."

Jackie glanced again at Lola's left hand. Despite all of the rings on those plump fingers, there was no evidence of a wedding band.

Her annoyance gave way to reluctant sympathy. Lola Bridges sounded like a lonely person, and Jackie knew all about loneliness.

"Paul and I have a lot of differences," she said at last. "He owns a ranch out by Reardan, and living that far from the city would be difficult for me given that I work odd hours and have to be on call. Besides, he's not thrilled about being married to a police officer. He thinks the job's too dangerous. If we lived together, he'd start pressuring me to quit. Especially," she added, "now that I'm pregnant."

"But you're still friends?"

Jackie thought about Paul's look of hungry intensity, quickly masked, his obvious anger over her purchase of this house and the tension that always hung between them these days.

She wondered if it was possible to make anybody truly understand the complexity of a relationship, the powerful attraction that drew a man and woman to each other and the disagreements, fears and insecurities that made it impossible for them to live together.

"Sure," she said at last. "We're still friends."

Lola sighed. "I think that's so romantic."

"Romantic?" Jackie smiled without humor. "I'm not sure that's the exact word I'd use to describe our relationship."

"But he loves you so much," Lola said. "The man's crazy about you. Anybody can tell that by the way he looks at you."

"I have to get going." Jackie glanced abruptly at her watch and reached for the door handle, then paused.

"Do you think you could let me have the key, just for now? I'd like to go through the house once more by myself."

"Well, it's not usually allowed until the deal is concluded. But tell you what." Lola gave her a conspiratorial smile. "I'll let you into the house before I go, and you be sure to lock it up when you leave, all right?"

"Thanks," Jackie said gratefully. "I'd really appreciate that."

She followed the woman back to the house, stood in the doorway watching as Lola drove off, then went inside.

The baby moved and kicked, and Jackie smiled.

"Well, it looks like this is really going to happen, kiddo," she said to her bulging smock. "And you know what else? I think maybe we already have a cat.''

There was no sign of the black cat at the moment, but she'd detected a certain proprietorial manner in the way he'd slipped under the trellis and marched up onto the veranda.

Although a black cat was supposed to be bad luck, wasn't it?

Jackie remembered her grandmother, with her harsh superstitious nature. *''A black cat's a terrible omen, Jackie. If you see it when you're starting something new, you'll surely fail...''*

She shrugged off her memory of the bitter old woman and moved through the rooms of the little house with a growing sense of euphoria.

It was really, truly happening. She was going to buy this place. For the first time in her life, she'd be a property owner.

That hinged oak window seat in the living room, the flower-sprigged wallpaper, the bathroom with its big claw-footed tub and the mountain ash in the front yard—all would be hers.

Already she loved the place.

Jackie climbed the stairs to the room on the second floor she'd designated in her mind as the nursery. The wallpaper was faded and dull, peeling away from the oak baseboard in places.

She and Paul had done a lot of wallpapering together while he renovated the old house on his ranch. Maybe she could ask him to help. They worked efficiently as a team, and it was so much easier than wrestling with wet sheets of paper all alone.

Then she remembered his attitude that morning,

his look of disappointment and taut anger as he'd left the house.

"I'm afraid we're on our own, sweetie," she said ruefully to the baby. "Your daddy isn't crazy about us having this house in the first place. It's hardly fair to ask him to hang wallpaper for us."

She moved around the little room, picturing where she'd place the crib, the changing table and the little dresser she'd already purchased, with its rows of whimsical teddy-bear knobs on the drawers.

Near the window she felt a sudden chill, like an icy breath on the nape of her neck. Jackie paused and examined the window, which was closed and locked. Tattered lace curtains hung limply across the glass.

Again she felt the coldness, and a wholly irrational sense of dread, as if she were in the presence of something evil. She moved forward and put her hand out to see if air was coming in around the window frame. But she could find no evidence of a leak.

At that moment the curtain lifted and stirred in the morning stillness, as if a breeze tugged at it gently.

"When a curtain moves and the window's not open," Gram's voice said in her memory, *"it's terrible bad luck, Jackie. It means somebody's going to die soon in that room..."*

Jackie was stunned by her clammy rush of terror. She'd never paid the slightest attention to her grandmother's drivel in the past. Pregnancy must be making her come unglued.

She left the small bedroom and went back downstairs, walking with a firm tread and resisting the nervous urge to look over her shoulder.

But she kept a protective hand over the warm swell of her abdomen, and she couldn't quite shake the unreasoning sense of dread, even after she'd locked the door and walked back outside into the thin April sunshine.

2

At noon, Jackie entered the Northwest substation, carrying two sacks of food into the detective squad room.

Brian Wardlow was at his desk in shirtsleeves, with a suit jacket and green-striped tie slung over the chair back, a leather shoulder holster strapped under his arm. Messy stacks of files lay open all around him, and his normally cheerful face looked so pale with fatigue that the freckles stood out in sharp relief.

"I brought lunch," Jackie told him, unloading the burgers and fries she'd picked up at a fast-food place onto his desk.

He nodded absently and unwrapped one of the burgers while he continued to pore over a file.

"Your gratitude is really overwhelming, Brian."

Jackie sat down and opened the salad container, picked up a little plastic fork and turned on her computer.

Wardlow said nothing, just went on munching and reading, his curly head turned away from her.

With a surge of impatience she reached over, closed his file and took it from him.

"Hey, Kaminsky!" he protested. "What the hell are you doing?"

"It won't hurt you to take few minutes off for lunch. You've probably been here since...what? Five o'clock this morning?"

"But I still have to check on—"

"Shut up." Jackie went across the room to the coffeemaker, poured him a mug and stopped to get herself some water.

Wardlow sighed and stretched, extending his arms over his head, then picked up a handful of fries. "I hate this goddamn job."

"Well, you're not likely to get any sympathy from me, Cupcake."

He grinned impudently and began to look more like his normal self. "Getting a little bit cranky about the desk work, are we?"

She glared at the pile of papers near her computer, then sighed. "It's been three months since I last worked outside the office."

Wardlow took another handful of fries and gulped some coffee. "You're the one who went and got pregnant," he pointed out.

"But this is such a stupid, archaic policy, putting a female officer on light duties as soon as she starts to show. Would it really hurt anybody to have a pregnant detective doing an investigation? I'm sure the public knows where babies come from."

Wardlow shrugged, looking bored.

He'd heard all these same complaints from Jackie at least a dozen times since their sergeant, Lew Michelson, had removed her from active investigative duties in the fifth month of her pregnancy.

"Thanks for the food, Kaminsky." He unwrapped a second hamburger.

"You're welcome," she said dryly.

"So, where were you this morning, anyhow?" he asked with his mouth full. "Adrienne was trying to get a hold of you."

"Adrienne?" Jackie set her fishburger down and stared at him, wiping mayonnaise from her chin, then reached hastily for the phone. "Jesus, Brian! Why didn't you tell me?"

"Don't panic, it's nothing urgent. She just wanted you to stop by for milk and cookies later today if you had a chance."

"Oh." Jackie relaxed, put the phone down and went on eating.

Her friend Adrienne Calder was hugely pregnant, ready to deliver at any moment. Jackie waited tensely for word that she'd been taken to the hospital, increasingly nervous because Adrienne, too, was pregnant for the first time and in her late thirties. But Adrienne moved serenely through her days, glowing with happiness.

"You'll be getting out of the office for a while this afternoon, won't you?" Wardlow asked, taking another thirsty gulp of coffee. "I thought you had to go to court on the Darla Drake murder."

"I do. I'm scheduled to testify at three o'clock. But that's not much fun either. In fact, I think I'd rather stay here and do paperwork."

Her partner grinned. "There's just no pleasing the woman. So," he added, "where were you this morning?"

"I bought a house." Jackie opened one of the files she'd prepared for her afternoon court appearance and squinted at a crime-scene photo of a young woman's corpse lying in a congealed pool of blood.

"Kaminsky!" He turned to stare at her. "Are you joking?"

"No, I'm terrified."

"You really bought a house?"

Jackie nodded, leafing through the file. "It's up in Corbin Park. In fact, it's just down the street from where Maribel Lewis used to live. Do you remember the neighborhood?"

"How could I forget? That was our very first homicide, you know. And I met Chris up there, too." He looked wistful. "We've had some fun at this job, haven't we, Kaminsky?"

She glanced up, startled by this uncharacteristic sentiment.

"Yeah, Brian," she said. "We've had some fun, all right. I can't wait to get back to doing real police work again."

"Maybe I won't take you back. After you've had your damn maternity leave, and Pringle and I get a chance to bond, I might want to keep him as my partner. The guy's a barrel of laughs, you know."

Jackie chuckled and reached out to punch his arm. "You'll take me back," she said.

Dave Pringle, who'd started as a patrolman with the substation, had recently passed his detective exam and been assigned to Wardlow while Jackie was out of commission. The young officer was competent enough, but notoriously lugubrious and silent.

In fact, Pringle never spoke unless somebody addressed him first. His plodding nature often frustrated the ebullient Wardlow.

"So tell me about this house," Wardlow demanded.

Jackie described the little green and white house in fond detail.

"And you've actually made an offer on the place?" he asked.

"I signed on the dotted line about an hour ago. The real estate lady should be calling back this afternoon to let me know if they accepted my offer. And I'll have to go to the bank after work to make sure I can qualify for the mortgage."

"You'll qualify," Wardlow said comfortably. "For a little place like that? No problem."

"Well, that's encouraging, since you're now an expert on all this financial stuff."

Jackie's partner, too, had recently bought a new home. Wardlow and his girlfriend, Christine Lewis, were getting married in the fall, but they had already pooled their resources to purchase a small acreage on the outskirts of the city where Chris and her young son could keep a few horses.

"I wouldn't want the mortgage payments you're going to be paying," Jackie said.

"Chris and I both have good jobs." He reached out with a freckled hand to pat Jackie's bulging abdomen, then grinned at her. "As long as I can keep this from happening, we'll have no trouble paying the mortgage."

"Don't you ever want to have kids?"

"Sure I do." He sobered and drank the last of his coffee. "I was just teasing you, Kaminsky. Has somebody checked this house over? Foundation and gutters and all that stuff?"

"Paul came in this morning to have a look at it."

"Paul did?" He stared at her. "You're kidding."

"We're still friends," she said a little stiffly. "It's his baby, too, you know."

"Sure it is, but the guy can't be happy about you buying a house. This pretty much takes away his last shred of hope, doesn't it?"

Jackie shifted her bulk uncomfortably in the chair. "I don't want to talk about Paul. Dammit, you're as bad as the real estate agent. She asked me why we weren't living together."

Wardlow chuckled. "I hope you told her it was none of her business."

"I wanted to, but she was filling out my offer at the time. I was totally intimidated by her."

"Impending motherhood has made you a softie, Kaminsky. In the old days you'd have taken the woman's head off."

"I probably would have." Jackie grinned at her partner, then handed back the file he'd been studying when she arrived. "How's this going, anyhow?"

He sighed. "You know, it's the damnedest thing. Four jewelry stores broken into, all of them cleaned out of their most valuable inventory. That's almost half a million dollars' worth stolen so far, and not a trace of forced entry. The guy's getting in and out without leaving a sign."

"So you think these are inside jobs?"

"Well, they'd have to be, right? But we can't find any kind of connection or common thread among the staff at the four stores. It's driving me crazy."

Jackie looked wistfully at the file, then at the pile of paper on her own desk. All of it was tedious and repetitive busywork, the kind of job any beginning officer could do.

"Let me see what you've got." She glanced at

her watch. "Technically it's still my lunch break. I can give you a few minutes."

"Hey, Kaminsky," he said gratefully, "could you? Dave Pringle isn't exactly a fountain of ideas when dealing with something like this."

She waved her hand in dismissal and studied his file, intrigued by the problem.

"I'd love to be on this case with you," she said with a sigh. "If we were both out there talking to the store owners and employees, I'd have a whole lot better picture of what's going on."

"Better than Pringle, that's for sure," Wardlow muttered darkly, making her chuckle.

Frowning in concentration, she read the files of the four break-ins, including detailed reports from the crime-scene technicians, then glanced at her partner.

"Has anybody checked the roof?"

"The roof?" he asked blankly.

"Maybe it's not an inside job. These are all single-story buildings. What if this guy's cased the stores in advance to know exactly what he's looking for, and he's coming in from the top through an air-conditioning duct or something, not leaving any sign of forced entry?"

Wardlow stared at her, his eyes widening, then leaped to his feet, put on his tie and jacket and stuffed the files into his briefcase.

"Kaminsky," he said, heading for the door, "you're a goddamn genius!"

"Yeah, sure I am," she muttered.

But she felt a glow of pleasure that lasted until she brought up a computer file and settled in to enter the endless, tedious pages of traffic logs.

* * *

At midafternoon Jackie went downstairs to her locker, then to the female officers' room where she changed out of her roomy plaid top and comfortable corduroy slacks and put on the only dressy outfit she was able to wear at the moment. It was a pair of trim black woolen slacks with a maternity panel, topped by a gray tunic with a fine black pinstripe. She adjusted the waistband of the slacks, then frowned at her reflection in a long mirror next to the toilet cubicles.

After Michelson had taken her off active investigations and relegated her to a desk job, Jackie stopped carrying a weapon in the line of duty. But still, even several months later, it was an odd feeling to go out in public without the comforting bulk of the leather holster and handcuff pouch at her belt.

Not that she didn't have a whole lot of bulk at her waistline these days...

She brushed her hair, put on a dash of makeup and hurried over to the courthouse, knowing that, after all this rush to be on time, she'd probably still be forced to sit and wait until she was called.

As it turned out, she cooled her heels in the witness room for almost a full hour, feeling more annoyed all the time.

Police departments around the nation spent millions of dollars paying officers who wasted precious time waiting to testify in court on cases that were as often as not canceled or rescheduled at the last moment.

Then, to make matters worse, the cops had to work expensive overtime so they could get their regular jobs done.

This creaking, overloaded judicial system was, in Jackie's opinion, one of the most senseless money pits in the world.

She felt irritable, hot and itchy in the woolen slacks by the time she was finally called to the witness stand and sworn in.

The state's attorney took a ridiculously long time to establish Jackie's identity and credentials, as if she were going to be giving the testimony of an expert witness, not an attending detective.

But this was a high-profile case. They were probably trying hard to avoid mistakes that could come back to them on appeal.

While Jackie answered calmly and impassively, Jason Burkett, former congressional candidate and the accused in this action, sat in front of her at a table with his team of lawyers, looking puffy and listless. The courtroom was crowded, but there was no sign of Burkett's glamorous young wife.

Jackie had heard that Norine Burkett was already moving on with her life, and had recently formed an attachment with another powerful man on his way up the political ladder.

She testified to events leading to that snowy evening the previous December, when she and Wardlow had discovered Darla Drake's body, and what they'd observed at the crime scene and later at the autopsy.

By that time, court was ready to adjourn for the day, and they hadn't even begun to talk about the really awful part of the case. She would have to come back tomorrow and tell the court what happened out in that isolated cabin on the Spokane

River, the gunfire and blood and sheer, gut-wrenching terror...

Jackie was excused for the day and left the witness stand, moving as gracefully as she could through the courtroom.

As she passed the team of defense lawyers, Jason Burkett caught her eye with a look of pleading and despair. Jackie turned her head away from him quickly and kept walking.

Outside the courthouse, those images of remembered horror filled her mind, making her feel fragile and a little nauseated, though the worst of her morning sickness had ended months ago.

She checked her watch, and saw that it was almost four-thirty.

Jackie hesitated, frowning. The last of the day's busywork had been filed before she left her desk. Not much point in going all the way back to the substation to close out fifteen minutes of her shift. And since she was all dressed up anyway...

She took a deep breath, got into her car and headed down the street to the bank, where she parked and looked at herself critically in the rearview mirror. Then she got out and walked into the bank carrying a briefcase full of papers, including old salary stubs, tax forms and other documentation of her income, as well as copies of the real estate listing form and her signed offer on the little house.

She sat in an alcove near an artificial rubber tree, waiting to be seen by the loan officer, and gripped the briefcase so tightly in her lap that her knuckles hurt and her palms were slick with sweat.

When she was called to the office, the person in charge of dispensing mortgages turned out to be a fresh-faced young man with a crew cut, probably five years younger than she was, who wore a pair of running shoes with his business suit.

"I play squash before work," he confessed, looking a little abashed when she glanced at the sneakers. "Forgot to bring my other shoes with me. Sorry."

Jackie smiled and felt herself relaxing. "Hey, don't apologize. I think it's a nice look. Casual but sophisticated."

"That's a nice look, too," he said, nodding at her bulging tunic.

Jackie glanced up, startled.

"My wife's six months pregnant." He smiled shyly. "I think she's never been so beautiful. I can't stop looking at her."

"Well then, she's a lucky person. You both are." Jackie opened her briefcase. "I'm not sure how to begin on this…"

"Just show me what you've got. They pay me to know all this stuff," the young man said cheerfully.

And he was right. As soon as they began, the casual tone dropped away and the loan officer was all business, checking though numbers and payment schedules, working out a formula to determine what Jackie could afford.

After all her anxiety, she found the process relatively painless, almost enjoyable. By the time it was over, she had bank approval on an eighty-five-thousand-dollar mortgage and felt like a woman walking on air.

Her cell phone rang on the way to the car. "Yes?" Jackie said, settling behind the wheel.

"It's Lola. Looks like we have a deal if you're

willing to come up with another nine hundred dollars. How about it? This seems to be pretty much their bottom line, I'm afraid."

"That's fine with me," Jackie said. "I just got mortgage approval to eighty-five thousand. I'm leaving the bank right now."

"Good. I'll make the changes on this offer and bring it over tonight for your initials. Can you give me your home address?"

Jackie waited while Lola wrote down the address. "I'll be at home..." She glanced at her watch again. "Anytime after six," she said. "Thanks so much, Lola."

"Thank *you*. I think you just bought a house. How does it feel?"

Jackie gripped the steering wheel with her free hand, staring at the pastel swirls of color above the treetops. "It feels wonderful," she said, taking a deep breath. "Damn wonderful."

Lola chuckled and Jackie found herself liking the woman a lot more. She was actually sorry when Lola terminated the conversation, saying she was late for another appointment.

Jackie grinned and put the phone away. Then she sighed.

Though she usually enjoyed solitude, for some reason she didn't want to be alone just now.

She had a wistful image of the ranch, the way the sprawl of weathered buildings always looked soft and ashy at this time of day against the pearl-tinted sky. And the air out there felt different in the early evening, too, with a cool edge of mystery and enchantment. The wind would be freshening, while shadows filled the little hollows on the prairie like bowls of liquid silver. Coyotes were probably beginning to sing in a ragged chorus along the brush-covered coulees.

Paul would be finishing his afternoon chores soon, and going into the house to cook a solitary dinner. He'd eat at the kitchen table in his plaid shirt and work socks, with miles of darkness all around him and a book propped against the coffeepot...

She ached for him suddenly. It wasn't the same kind of fleeting sexual urge she'd felt that morning, which assailed her from time to time during her pregnancy. Those occasional impulses she chalked up to hormones sent awry by all the other changes in her body.

Tonight she just missed him, wanted to talk and laugh with him, maybe sit by the fire and play a friendly game of chess as they'd done so often, and talk about the baby and the future and the dreams they both had for this unborn child.

But, of course, none of that was possible. If she didn't want to live with the man, it certainly wasn't fair to use him for company on the occasional night when she felt lonely.

3

The next six weeks were busily occupied with the myriad intricacies of home ownership, as well as preparations for moving and a new baby.

About three weeks after Jackie closed the deal on her house, Adrienne Calder gave birth to an eight-pound baby boy.

Jackie went to visit her friend in the hospital the day after the birth, and came away feeling both excited and frightened by the reality of motherhood.

Hers had not been a planned pregnancy like Adrienne's. In fact, in the months since discovering what was happening inside her body, she'd struggled to understand and accept the reality and responsibility of a newborn life. For a person who had been essentially solitary for more than thirty years, this was not an easy adjustment to make and the winter months had seemed to drag by.

But when Jackie entered the final months of her pregnancy and signed the deal on the house, time began to fly.

In the daytime she was still busy with her job, which she intended to keep until the final weeks.

She had also banked overtime and quite a few holidays to add to her three months of maternity leave, which would allow her to stay home with the baby until the coming Christmas.

At the moment she had no desire to plan any further ahead than that.

Instead, she craved action, something that would move time forward and bring her closer to the weekend when she could finally move into her house, and the day soon afterward when the baby would be born.

On a Saturday afternoon in late May, three weeks after the birth of Adrienne's child, Jackie packed baby clothes in boxes and thought about Paul and her problems with the relationship.

Adrienne was right, up to a point, when she said Jackie feared both intimacy and abandonment, and that those terrors made it impossible for her to commit to a relationship.

But it was actually the final step that appalled Jackie, the moment when she would have to fling herself out into an emotional void, trusting another's arms to catch her. Nothing in her life had ever prepared her to believe she would survive the fall.

Jackie folded a soft blanket patterned with balloons and kittens, putting it in the box along with a stack of cotton diapers.

When it came to this relationship, though, she was privately inclined to blame something that everybody else seemed to miss.

Part of the blame, she attributed to Paul. In fact, he had a lot of the very same emotional hang-ups. His mother, too, had died when he was a small child, and he'd been raised by a drunken, careless father who gambled away their ranch, died in a truck accident and left Paul to fend for himself as a teenager.

Psychologists claimed that people were attracted to others who shared their own character flaws, thus forming a bond that was certain to destroy both of them. If that was true, Jackie Kaminsky and Paul Arnussen were a classic case of a couple destined for mutual destruction. They would be better off saying goodbye and living apart than tearing each other to pieces.

But now this baby held them together; it was part of both of them.

She folded a yellow terry-cloth sleeper, laying it briefly against her cheek, then picked up a tiny cotton shirt, cleverly designed with attached underpants and held together by a row of snap fasteners across the stomach. It had taken Jackie quite a long time to figure out how these little garments worked, practising on a teddy bear that had been given to her on Valentine's Day by Alex Gerard, Adrienne's teenage foster daughter.

She smiled dreamily and sat on the bed, where the teddy bear rested against the pillows. Jackie pushed one of the bear's arms into the shirt, fitted the pants over his plump bottom and fastened them, then held him up and grinned. From the back he looked like a fat, furry infant, his arms and legs dangling.

She hugged the bear, patting him tenderly. Within her body the child stirred, and she felt a flood of love so intense that it was almost frightening.

This was something else she was going to have to deal with, the sheer terror of loving somebody so much. It was an emotion that made you dangerously weak. How could you walk through the world with courage when there was another person whose very existence rendered you so intensely vulnerable?

She glanced at her watch in sudden alarm and began to hurry around, changing into clean jeans and a baggy sweatshirt. Then she grabbed her keys and left the apartment, driving across the city toward Adrienne's home. Traffic was sparse and the late-afternoon sun filled the sky with gold.

Harlan answered the door. His pleasant, bearded face looked exhausted, and Jackie felt a quick pang of sympathy. Harlan Calder was in his fifties, going through new parenthood for the first time. This couldn't be easy on him.

He led Jackie into the family room where Alex sat cross-legged on a leather ottoman. She wore nylon bike shorts and a T-shirt and was practising the flute. Her golden braid fell over one shoulder and her profile was austere and beautiful. The soft notes of her flute filled the quiet room, one of the lilting Gaelic airs that Jackie loved and had struggled without success to learn.

But Alex, though only sixteen, was a musical genius. She was also a lovely, sensitive girl whose life had been on the brink of ruin two years earlier when Jackie had found her working as a prostitute on a downtown street, and brought her to Adrienne and Harlan.

"Hi, kiddo." Jackie sat next to the girl, slipping an arm around her. Alex put the flute down and burrowed into Jackie's shoulder.

"Hey, what's all this?" Jackie drew away to look at Alex, who kept her blond head lowered.

"Nothing," she murmured. "It's nice to see you, that's all."

Jackie glanced at Harlan, who sprawled wearily on the couch, his legs extended.

"Come on, honey, keep playing," she said. "Those old songs are so pretty."

Alex picked up her flute and began to play again, frowning in concentration as the sweet notes rippled through the evening stillness of the big house.

Jackie exchanged another glance with Harlan, feeling increasingly troubled.

"Adrienne's in the kitchen," he said. "She's feeding the baby."

"Is it okay if I go up?"

"Of course. She'll be glad to see you."

He rested his head against the back of the couch and closed his eyes. Jackie rose, and paused to drop a hand on his shoulder, then left the room and went upstairs, the soft notes of the flute drifting behind her.

Adrienne sat on a straight-backed chair in the kitchen, holding the baby. Her dark hair was tousled, her face looked drained and surprisingly old. She'd unbuttoned her shirt and her infant son nuzzled drowsily at her breast.

A couple of years earlier, when Jackie had investigated the kidnapping of Adrienne's little nephew, she would never have imagined such a warm friendship developing between herself and the elegant, haughty woman that Adrienne had been in those days.

But under the veneer of education and sophistication, Adrienne Calder had quite a lot in common with Jackie Kaminsky. Each woman had suffered through a troubled adolescence, raised by family members who were either indifferent or hostile, and their self-destructive rebellions against authority had almost ruined both their lives.

Those unhappy times in the past now forged an unspoken bond between the two women, something that helped to deepen and enrich their friendship.

Jackie sat nearby and leaned forward to look at the baby when Adrienne held him out for inspection.

Little Matthew Calder, aged three weeks and four days, had a round face, slate blue eyes and a head of black hair that stood on end like a brush.

"Oh," Jackie breathed, feeling the same rush of tenderness she always did when she saw him. "He's such a darling, Rennie. I swear he gets cuter every time I come here."

"And he's hungry every ten minutes," Adrienne muttered. "Around the clock. I'm beginning to feel like a broken-down old milk wagon."

Jackie looked at her friend in concern. "Are you still tired?"

"Anybody would be tired," Adrienne said with uncharacteristic peevishness, "if they never got to sleep more than an hour at a time."

"Maybe you should wean him and put him on formula," Jackie suggested dubiously, watching as little Matthew's eyes drooped shut. He folded one fist and curled it under his chin in a gesture so endearing that, impulsively, she reached out for him.

Adrienne surrendered him with obvious relief and fastened her nursing bra, then did up the buttons of her shirt and leaned back in the chair.

"If I wean him," she said, "I'll be acknowledging failure within the first month. Not that I didn't know I was going to fail." She got up restlessly and opened the door of the fridge to peer inside. "I never had any kind of decent mothering, Jackie. What made me think I could do this?''

Jackie stared at her friend, alarmed by the note of bitterness and defeat in her voice. ''But you're a wonderful person, Rennie,'' she said. ''And you've always been such a terrific mother to Alex. What on earth are you talking about?''

''Nothing.'' Adrienne took a pitcher of orange juice from the fridge. ''Forget I said it. What would you like to drink? Is this okay?''

She put the pitcher on the counter and began to search for glasses, then shook her head.

''If I drink any citrus, he gets diaper rash the next day. Oh, shit, Jackie!'' Her face twisted. She slammed her hands on the counter in obvious despair. ''I just can't seem to—''

Harlan appeared in the doorway and Adrienne stopped talking abruptly, then forced a smile.

''I have to go and empty the dryer,'' she told her husband. ''Can you find Jackie something to drink?''

''Of course.'' Harlan came nearer to gaze at his son, now cuddled in Jackie's arms. The baby's eyelashes fluttered and his pink mouth worked rhythmically, as if he were still nursing.

Harlan beamed, but the smile faded when he looked at the doorway where his wife had disappeared.

''She'll be fine,'' Jackie told him, feeling awkward. ''She's just tired, Harlan.''

''I know.'' He took a couple of crystal tumblers from an upper cabinet and poured two glasses of orange juice. ''I know how tired she is.''

He sat at the table next to Jackie and they sipped their juice in silence while the baby slept.

"He's such a sweet baby," Jackie told Paul. "Really fat and cuddly and good-natured."

It was a week later and she was in the small upstairs room at her new house, watching while Paul put the crib together.

He stood erect and tugged at the bars, squinting as he lined them up. "What did you say his whole name was?"

"Harlan Matthew Mellon Calder. But they're already calling him Matt."

"Matt Calder." Paul picked up a wrench. "I like that. Sounds very rugged and manly, doesn't it?"

Jackie shifted her body slightly.

Her moving day had finally arrived, and she was sprawled on the brass-bound footlocker she'd been hauling around ever since her early days with the LAPD. The trunk was navy blue, very battered and stenciled with her old badge number. Jackie planned to cover it with a cotton afghan and use it as extra storage for baby clothes.

"So how's Harlan adjusting to fatherhood?" Paul asked.

"He's wonderful with the baby. In fact, right now he's probably more patient than Adrienne. She's still really worn out, I think. It was a hard birth, especially for a woman who's over thirty-five."

He gave her a quick, thoughtful glance. "You sound worried."

"I guess I am, a little bit. Rennie doesn't seem like herself at all."

"But Harlan's good with the baby?" Paul tightened a couple of bolts at the side of the crib, then fitted a set of rails in place and tested the action that raised and lowered them.

"Yes, he really is." Jackie watched the crib rail. "Isn't it neat the way that works?"

"It's very neat." Paul glanced at her briefly, then returned his attention to the crib. "You know, it surprises me that you'd choose to raise a baby alone, after going through your own childhood without a father."

Jackie tensed, startled by his words.

But fathers can disappear, she thought. They can go away and leave you all alone, and nothing in the world hurts more...

She looked down at a stack of diapers on the floor near the trunk. "What do you mean, raise the baby alone?" she said, keeping her voice light. "Are you planning to go somewhere?"

"I'm not going anywhere. You know what I mean, Jackie."

He stood waiting for her answer. Jackie bent and picked up one of the white squares of cotton, smoothing it on her knee.

"Paul, have you ever seen that trust exercise they do in therapy groups? The one where people close their eyes and fall backward, and their partner, standing behind them, is supposed to catch them?"

"I've seen it."

"Well, I think it would kill me to do that. I can't imagine anything more horrible. What's more," she added, looking up at him, "I'll bet you feel the same way, don't you?"

Paul studied her so intently that her cheeks warmed with discomfort. But he made no response.

Instead, he bent and packed his wrenches away in an old metal toolbox, then stood.

"Don't you?" she persisted.

"I thought we agreed we'd stop analyzing each other all the time."

"But if we don't talk, how can we ever resolve our problems?" she asked.

"You don't want to resolve anything, Jackie. You want to use all this psychobabble to keep me at arm's length even though you're about to bear my child."

"Oh, for God's sake," she began with rising annoyance. "If you won't even answer a simple question..."

"There's no safe way for me to answer one of those questions. If I said I felt genuine trust, you'd tell me I was in denial. If I admitted I was just as scared as you are, you'd take it as an indication we shouldn't be together."

Jackie frowned. "Come on. You really think I'm that unreasonable?"

"Anything else up here that needs fixing?" he asked brusquely. "I might as well tend to everything while I'm here."

Jackie stared at him with narrowed eyes, then shrugged in defeat. "Sure, Paul," she said. "Whatever you say. In fact, maybe you could take a look inside the closet at those shelves."

He opened the closet door and tested a rack of unpainted shelves, which had clearly seen a lot of hard usage over the years. Several shelves hung loose, slanting crazily, with bent nails sprouting from the ends of the boards.

"I don't think they can be fixed," he said. "The

uprights are in pretty bad shape, too. I should probably build some new shelves and replace these altogether.''

"That's all right," Jackie said coolly. "No need for you to spend all that time. I'll pull the shelves out myself if you don't think they can be salvaged."

"I don't mind building new ones, Jackie. Anything else?"

"A few little chores out in the yard and garage, I guess. I'd really like to get that flower bed dug today. But let's have a glass of milk first, all right?" Jackie heaved herself to her feet. "You must be getting sick of all this handyman stuff."

"I'm enjoying it. There's nothing I'd rather be doing with my weekend."

She gave him a suspicious glance, but his voice was casual as he paused to test the crib rail again, and he didn't follow up on his statement.

It seemed to be a new tactic on his part, this attitude of calm noninvolvement. Except for his brief question about fathers, Paul had made no reference all day to their awkward living situation.

Maybe his strategy was not to press her anymore, hoping she'd come around and see things his way if he stopped pursuing.

Or perhaps he was secretly relieved they wouldn't be moving in together and he could enjoy the pleasures of weekend fatherhood while living in comfortable privacy out on his ranch....

Jackie shivered briefly and hugged her arms. "Paul, do you feel anything strange about this room?" she asked abruptly.

"Strange? What do you mean?"

"Just sort of...creepy, somehow. I get a feeling

from time to time, like there's a draft in here somewhere, even though I know there can't be. I wondered if you noticed anything."

This wasn't just an idle inquiry. Paul Arnussen was more attuned to unseen vibrations than anyone Jackie knew. In fact, that was how they'd met a couple of years earlier, when one of his psychic visions had helped the police find Adrienne's nephew.

Paul was embarrassed by this strange gift and never spoke of it voluntarily. Now he bent and lifted the toolbox, his tanned biceps rippling under the sleeves of his T-shirt.

"That hardly ever happens anymore," he said. "And when I do feel things, it always relates to somebody who's hurt or in pain. I don't see ghosts or bend spoons with mental energy."

"Well," Jackie told him with an awkward smile, "I can't bend spoons, either, and God knows I'm the last person in the world to see ghosts. But sometimes in this room I get the most awful feeling."

"Like what?"

"I don't know how to describe it," she said slowly. "As if the air's all filled with coldness and misery, I guess. An evil kind of feeling. It scares me."

His dark eyes rested on her in concern. "I thought nothing scared you, Jackie."

"I'm not afraid of things I can see."

"Then what else is there?" he said reasonably. "Come on, this isn't like you. It's probably just because you're pregnant and feeling vulnerable." He opened the closet door again and turned to grin at her over his shoulder. "See? No monsters in here. Nothing lurking inside the walls or behind the woodwork. When the rest of the baby's things are in here, you'll love this room.''

''I know. You're right.''

''I've heard,'' he told her seriously, ''that pregnant and nursing women can get a little psychic, even ones who've never had any leanings in that direction. It's some kind of primitive, elemental thing.''

''So I'm not crazy?''

''No more than usual,'' he said with a smile.

She followed him down the stairs, comforted by his understanding, as well as the thought of the cuddly baby clothes, the toys and the new crib with its side rail that raised and lowered so smoothly.

4

Emma Betker was having a good day. She sat by the leaded-glass window in a soft armchair, holding Frosty on her lap. The cat, a big white Persian with yellow eyes, was overweight, slow-moving and old.

Like Emma, Frosty had settled down with advancing years. Both of them now had more good days than bad ones, long spells of peacefulness when they sat blinking contentedly in the sunshine and weren't troubled by anything.

Especially when it was springtime. Emma loved the warmth, the green growing things and the feeling that another winter had passed and she hadn't died. She could stop being afraid for a while.

In the adjoining yard, which she could see over a low picket fence, lilacs would soon bloom in the hedge and fill the air with perfume.

Emma had always loved the lilacs....

"So pretty, Frosty," she murmured to the big cat, smoothing his ears with her gnarled hands. "We love the pretty flowers, don't we, Frosty?"

Emma was in her late sixties, a tiny, dainty woman with flyaway silver hair and a delicate face. Her eyes were wide and blue, set above finely molded cheekbones. Even when all alone, she had a vaguely timid air, an uncertainty in the way she handled the cat or reached up to draw the curtain aside and look out.

Two people came out of the neighboring house and into the backyard. Emma watched them in sudden alarm, gripping the cat so tightly that he squirmed in discomfort and she had to whisper a quick apology.

The people didn't seem to be anybody she knew. These days it was harder than ever for Emma to remember faces and make sense of what people did, but she was fairly certain the last people who'd lived in the house next door had been small and dark-skinned, a man and woman with a couple of shy, pretty children.

These two were different. The man was big and broad-shouldered, with hair that shone like spun gold. The woman looked almost as tall, but had black hair and was very fat.

Emma frowned and bent forward to watch as they stood in the yard, talking and gesturing.

The woman turned, pressing her hands into the small of her back, then indicated a patch of grass beside the fence. Vaguely, Emma realized the black-haired woman wasn't fat, after all, but heavily pregnant.

She felt a sudden remembered horror and a creeping sense that something dreadful was about to happen all over again.

When the man strode into the old garage and reappeared carrying a shovel, the shadows gathered and beat like dark wings inside Emma's head, trying to get out. She moaned, covering her face with her hands, then slumped forward and clutched the cat tightly.

Frosty squealed in pain and wriggled from her grasp, jumping to the floor. For a moment he paused to glare up at her indignantly, then marched out of the room with his tail high and stiff.

Eleanor Betker appeared in the doorway, hands on hips, and frowned at her sister.

The two women were almost comically dissimilar in appearance. Eleanor was the elder by three years, tall and sturdy with a clipped shock of iron-gray hair and large capable hands. She'd retired a few years earlier from her job as an operating-room nurse, and now spent all her time looking after Emma.

"What's going on?" Eleanor said impatiently, coming into the room and towering over her sister's chair. "What have you done to the cat?"

Emma waved a shaking hand at the window, toward the dreadful scene in the neighboring yard. "They're…it's awful," she whispered. "Look, Ellie, it's happening again. Just like that time when…"

Eleanor put a big hand on her sister's head, stroking the thin hair with a soothing, automatic gesture. She watched the blond man through the window as he thrust the blade of the shovel into the grass, lifted a clump of sod and tossed it onto a wheelbarrow.

"That woman is our new neighbor," she told Emma. "Lola Bridges says she works for the police. And I suppose the handsome man is her boyfriend. He looks too blond to be a relative."

"The—the police?" Emma whispered, looking up fearfully.

"Yes, she's a detective. Apparently she's been quite the local heroine, involved in some famous cases over the past couple of years. Her name's Jackie Kaminsky.''

But Emma wasn't listening anymore. She began to whimper in distress, plucking at the sleeves of her cardigan and the velour slacks that covered her skinny legs.

Sighing, Eleanor bent and lifted her sister out of the chair as if she were a child, carrying her off to the kitchen.

''There's nothing to be afraid of,'' she said firmly. ''Whatever's bothering you, just forget about it. Do you hear me?''

Emma sobbed and buried her face in Eleanor's shoulder.

''Do you hear me, Emma? Stop this!''

The little woman nodded jerkily at her sister's fierce tone. She allowed herself to be settled into a chair by the table and given a plateful of oatmeal cookies and a glass of chocolate milk, which was her very favorite.

But she couldn't forget the dreadful image of those two people in the backyard, with their shovel and the clumps of soil rattling into the wheelbarrow with a hollow thumping sound.

''Eleanor,'' she whispered, her lips trembling. ''It's just like…''

''Here, have another cookie,'' Eleanor said briskly, wiping a dribble of milk from her sister's chin. ''And then we'll go for a nice drive. Would you like that, dear? We'll go over to the park and sit by the river to watch the ducks.''

Emma nodded eagerly, grasping at the image of the pretty green-headed ducks waddling in single file along the cinder path. "Can—can I feed the ducks, Ellie?" she asked.

"We'll take them a whole bag of stale bread," Eleanor said.

Emma clapped her hands like a child and her sister smiled at her tenderly.

For a moment the dark wings trembled at the edge of Emma's mind again. She tried to remember what had upset her.

A shovel, and somebody digging...

But Eleanor was bundling her into her coat, still talking about the ducks in the park, and the unhappy memories wouldn't stay in place long enough for Emma to grab hold of them.

"I feel as if we're being watched," Paul said, continuing to spade up clumps of sod and toss them into the wheelbarrow. "It's like an audience of thousands is following our every move."

Jackie laughed and settled herself on a pile of bricks near the garage. "There are quite a few elderly people living around here," she said. "I think they spend a lot of time peeking out their windows and keeping track of the neighbors."

"Well, that's good." His arm and back muscles strained as he plied the shovel. "Watchful neighbors make for good security, right?"

"I suppose so." Jackie lifted her face to the sunlight. "But it's really strange, you know, being in a house. You actually have more privacy when you're in an apartment with other people living just a few feet away from you. Here, I feel as if all my comings and goings are being monitored."

He straightened and wiped an arm across his forehead, glancing around. "Who lives on each side?"

She indicated a small yellow house that was barely visible through the screen of lilacs. "That's John Caldwell next door. Lola Bridges's father."

"And who's Lola Bridges?"

"The real estate lady," Jackie told him patiently. "Remember the day you came to check the house for me before I bought it? Poor Lola was so smitten with you, it took her quite a while to get over it. She kept asking questions about you and about…our relationship." Jackie flushed, suddenly embarrassed.

She bent forward and plucked a dandelion from the grass near her feet, blowing on it to hide her nervousness.

"So what's her father like?" Paul asked.

"John? He's a nice little man. Very quiet, bald and chubby. He sits on the back porch wearing slippers and reading the Bible. Sometimes he knits."

"He knits?"

"John's a much better knitter than I am." Jackie smiled at the yellow house. "And we share a cat," she added.

"That skinny black one?"

Jackie nodded. "I call him Shadow. He hangs around here a lot. I saw John feeding him one day and thought it was his cat, but he says Shadow's just a stray who visits from time to time. John's only been giving him dry cat food, but I'm trying to entice him with Fancy Feast and cream."

Paul chuckled, then looked around at the area already cleared of sod. "So, how big do you want this flower bed to be?"

"Just a few more feet to the left, where the edge

lines up with the sidewalk. But you don't have to finish it all today, Paul. I can dig the rest myself if you get most of the sod out."

"I don't think shoveling is a good thing for you to be doing right now." His eyes rested thoughtfully on her swollen abdomen. "Do you know anything about planting flowers?"

"Not a thing," Jackie said cheerfully. "But Harlan says it's really easy. You just have to buy the bedding plants and dig holes to set them in, then water them and they'll grow."

"What kind of flowers are you going to buy? There's a huge variety of bedding plants, you know."

She shrugged. "When I go to the store, I'll ask them for advice. How hard can it be? Look at all the flowers around here, Paul. Somebody planted them, and they're growing just fine."

He laughed again. She joined him, feeling relieved, almost grateful. It really was good to see him relaxed like this, especially after the kind of emotional intensity they'd weathered in recent months.

If she and Paul could just be friends and get along together for the baby's sake, her life would be much less complicated...

"That's very typical of you," he said, leaning on the shovel. "You have so much confidence in your ability to deal with any situation."

"Not necessarily backed up by reality?" she asked dryly, digging the toe of her running shoe into the soft grass.

"Almost always backed up by reality. You're a very capable woman, Jackie." He smiled at her. "You look nice, sitting there in the sunshine. I think you're prettier right now than you've ever been. Pregnancy really suits you.''

His direct, admiring expression made her uncomfortable, not least because of a thrill of warmth it brought, the kind of shivering, delicious trickle of sexual excitement that was such a source of discomfort to her these days.

Anybody would think that when a woman's body was so misshapen and bulky, it wouldn't have room for lustful impulses. Apparently, that wasn't the case at all.

To change the subject, she waved a hand at the house on the other side of them, a narrow Victorian mansion complete with turret, cupola and masses of gingerbread trim. Its grounds were so impeccably maintained that the blades of grass might have been trimmed individually by hand and the shrubbery carved out of plastic.

"Speaking of neighbors," she said, "Lola's told me quite a bit about mine, especially the two who live over there."

"Married couple?" he asked, returning to his digging.

"No, they're sisters, never married, and they've both lived in that house ever since they were born. Their grandfather owned one of the first railroad lines to come through the Northwest."

"No kidding." Paul squinted at the big house. "Great Victorian architecture," he commented. "Either somebody's restored all the gingerbread trim, or taken really good care of it."

"Eleanor takes care of everything. She's a retired nurse, a big strong woman with muscles like a man.

She wears bib overalls, does the carpentry, tends to all the yard work and looks after Emma.''

"Who's Emma?"

"That's the younger sister. She's probably about sixty-five or so, just like a little bird or a kitten. I talked to her over the fence once when Eleanor put her out in the yard for a sunbath. I think she must have Alzheimer's or something because her mind seems pretty fuzzy, but she has such a sweet nature, Paul.''

He scanned the quiet, shaded neighborhood. "This would have been a pretty upscale location at one time, with some nice big houses. Are any of the other neighbors longtime residents?''

"A couple. Old Mrs. Weitzel across the street has lived here since she was a young bride, and a couple of the other immediate neighbors have been here at least thirty or forty years. I think Lola told me her father moved in about twenty-five years ago, when she was going to college.''

"Poor guy's just a newcomer." Paul gave her a teasing smile. "Still getting the feel of the place.''

Jackie smiled back at him, then sobered. "If he's a newcomer after twenty-five years, what does that make me? No wonder they all seem standoffish when I try to chat with them.''

"You're always so impatient," Paul said, but gently enough that it didn't sound like a criticism. "You want everything in your life solved, sealed and settled within the first two days. It takes time to become part of a neighborhood. You can't expect it to happen overnight.''

"I've never lived in a house before. Did you know that, Paul? First I lived in Gram's dumpy apartment, then…'' She poked at the grass again. ''Then a couple of fun-filled years in juvenile detention, then the police academy while I was in training. And I've always lived in apartments during my service.''

''You've lived in my house sometimes,'' Paul said, digging without expression. ''But I guess that was never long enough to classify as a lifestyle.'' He tossed a clump of sod onto the wheelbarrow. ''Those were more like visits, weren't they, Jackie?''

She tensed, afraid of what he might say next. But he leaned on the shovel and watched her gravely.

''Is this what it takes to make you happy?'' he said at last. ''A little house with a brick fireplace and some flower beds. Is that really going to do it for you?''

He didn't seem to be challenging her this time, just expressing interest. She took a deep breath and pressed one hand against her abdomen, where the baby turned and kicked.

''You know, I think it is,'' she said. ''I really need to have this experience. I want to be the owner of my private bit of the world, and be confident that it won't disappear if I turn my back. I need the kind of permanence I've never managed to find.''

''And you can really find your security in some wood and concrete, and a few bits of grass?''

Jackie looked around at the surrounding neighborhood. ''Some of these people have lived here for seventy years. That's the kind of security I want to have. And I want it for the baby, too. I need to feel that sense of things continuing, of permanence and stability. My life has been so—''

"What's this?" he muttered, frowning as he jabbed at the loosened dirt.

"Paul?"

He looked up briefly. "Sorry, I didn't mean to interrupt."

"What are you looking at down there?"

"Well, I wanted to dig a little deeper to see what kind of soil bed you were going to have for your garden, but I'm coming onto something..."

"What is it?" She leaned forward. "Have you struck oil? We'll all be rich. Maybe I can use disposable diapers, after all."

He prodded experimentally with the shovel. "Not oil. Feels like...I'm not sure."

"A treasure chest?" she asked hopefully.

"I'm afraid not. More likely a buried pet. That's what I'd guess, anyway. It feels like a bundle of bones wrapped in some kind of plastic tarp."

Jackie stared at the loosened soil and the narrow pit he'd excavated. Suddenly, she felt a stirring of the familiar uneasiness in her stomach, accompanied by a cold chill of fear.

"Whatever it is," she said sharply, "I don't want it in the middle of my flower bed."

He poked the tip of his shovel along the trench, then frowned. "What the hell?" he muttered.

Jackie heaved herself erect and walked across the freshly dug sod to peer into the furrow. At the bottom of the trench, partially exposed in the dark soil, was a blue plastic tarpaulin. The rotting fabric was riddled with holes from which frayed threads bristled, and had been wrapped tightly around something that formed a faded cocoon about five or six feet long.

Paul and Jackie exchanged a glance. "You know what?" she said. "It looks like…"

"It sure does," he said when she fell silent. "So what should we do now, Jackie? You're the expert in situations like this."

She knelt awkwardly, reaching out to touch the brittle fabric. "There's no reason to suspect this is human remains," she said. "Any number of things could be wrapped in a bundle this size."

"Like what? A dead Russian wolfhound?"

Jackie found a loose edge of fabric and tugged gently, then with more force. Bits of the old tarp frayed and pulled apart in her hands.

"It's all stuck to itself," she muttered.

"Why?" Paul knelt beside her, staring into the pit. "Could somebody have glued it?"

"Not necessarily," she told him. "Decaying body fluids would also cause the plastic to stick and fuse like this. But I can't smell anything at all, so if there's a body in here, it's been buried a good long time."

"Well," Paul said grimly, "that's comforting, isn't it?"

He reached into a small pouch at his belt and took out a black-handled case knife, flicking it open to reveal a shining blade.

"Here," he said, handing it to Jackie.

She took the knife, then hesitated. "Technically, we shouldn't be doing this. We should call Ident and get them out here to take some pictures before we—"

"Come on," Paul said, touching her shoulder. "I think you're overreacting. You've been on the police force in Spokane for ten years, right?"

She nodded.

"And in that time, have you ever heard of a murder in this neighborhood besides Maribel Lewis?"

She shook her head.

"So the chances of this being a human body are pretty remote. More likely what's under this tarp is somebody's pet dog, or a litter of unwanted puppies wrapped in old gunnysacks."

"You're probably right," she said reluctantly.

"Of course I am. So let's see what it is before we have police cars all over the place and wind up terrifying the neighbors. Do you want me to cut the tarp open?"

"No, I'll do it, just in case there might be any questions later."

Paul grinned. "Always a cop, even off duty."

Jackie ignored him, placing the knife carefully into the chrysalis of faded blue plastic and slicing downward for a couple of feet. After she got it started, the blade moved easily.

She set the knife aside, grasped the cut edges of the plastic and pulled them open, then gasped.

A human skull grinned at her from the shadows. It was darkly stained, with clumps of dirt lodged in the eye sockets.

A stale, fetid gush of air came from within the blue wrappings and vanished on the afternoon breeze. Apart from that, there was no smell of decay.

Paul knelt and pressed close to her, staring in fascination at the skull. "What's that stuff?" he asked, pointing. "It looks like dried grass or something."

"Probably hair," Jackie muttered. "Human hair will survive a long time underground after all the body fluids and tissues are gone. It even outlasts cartilage.''

She nerved herself to pull the plastic wrapping aside and looked more closely.

The skeleton was mostly bare and clean. The bones seemed to have sustained some kind of trauma and were strangely jumbled within the torn cocoon. Here and there she saw traces of a mottled, papery substance that could be the remnants of clothing.

She tried to think clearly, to remember the procedure for cases like this. But as she studied the clutter of bones, horror began to mount in her brain, screaming at her and making her dizzy.

''Jesus, Paul,'' she murmured, turning to lean against him.

''Jackie?'' he asked. ''What is it?''

She choked and swallowed a sob.

''Jackie, you're shaking.'' He put his arms around her and moved closer on his knees to hold her awkwardly.

She sniffled and took herself in hand, pulling away from him to swipe an arm across her damp face.

''Look,'' she told him, pointing. ''Look there.''

Amid the jumble of bones was a small, rounded object. Jackie turned it over with a shaking forefinger.

Paul gasped, then went pale beneath his tan.

The little globe was a baby's skull.

He clutched Jackie's arm so tightly that it hurt.

''It's a baby,'' he muttered. ''And somebody made a hole in its head.''

Jackie shook her head, still gripped by irrational,

shuddering terror. She touched the place where her own baby kicked placidly in its safe, watery world.

"That's not an injury," she said. "It's a fontanel. What people call the soft spot." She glanced briefly at Paul. "This was a newborn baby."

He settled back on his heels, looking at the two grinning skulls. "Maybe it was a natural death. She could have died in childbirth."

"She could have," Jackie said. "But it doesn't look like it."

Jackie struggled to get up, finally accepting the hand he offered, then bent to brush off the knees of her jeans.

"I have to call somebody," she said over her shoulder as she walked toward the house. "The one thing I'm sure of is that she damn sure didn't bury herself in the backyard."

5

Jackie began her maternity leave haunted by the image of those two grinning skulls within their tarpaulin wrapping. Her sleep was broken by nightmares that brought her awake with clammy, shuddering terror. But afterward, when she lay alone staring at the shadows on the unfamiliar walls and ceiling, she couldn't recall any details of her dreams.

By now birth was imminent and it seemed increasingly difficult to find a comfortable sleeping position, even with banks of pillows propped all around her swollen body. The baby moved sluggishly and sporadically, which worried her, though the doctor said it was a normal sign of impending childbirth.

Jackie would have liked to drop by and have a long talk with Adrienne about all the things she was thinking and feeling. But for the moment, at least, her friend remained unavailable to her. Normally blunt, cheerful and wittily profane, Adrienne was still drained with fatigue these days, and so miserable that she seemed totally unlike herself.

Now that Jackie no longer went to the office, she spent her time working to organize things in her new house and yard, moving slowly as her size increased.

On Thursday afternoon, four days after their discovery of the two skeletons, she was outside in the backyard again. Wearing shorts, a smock and a big sun hat, she squatted on the grass and set out bedding plants, digging holes in the new flower bed that Paul had finished spading and raking the previous weekend.

The sun shone warm on her back, and the air was fragrant with the scent of freshly mowed grass and lilacs in bloom. Even the baby seemed lively and happy today, kicking hard enough at her rib cage to make her gasp for breath.

"Planting some petunias, are you?" a voice said nearby.

Jackie looked up and smiled at her neighbor, John Caldwell, who leaned over the picket fence with a rolled newspaper under his arm.

"Trying to." She freed the roots of a ruffled white blossom from its little pot and set it in one of the holes she'd dug with her trowel. "Actually, I don't have a clue what I'm doing."

He studied the flat of bedding plants, already a mass of colorful blooms. "You'd have been better off picking ones that weren't flowering," he told her. "If your plants are too advanced, they take a big setback after you set them out."

"You're kidding." Jackie sat back awkwardly on her heels and looked at the little plants in dismay. "The man at the nursery said this was the best way to have an instant garden."

Her neighbor grinned, displaying the even whiteness of dentures. "They always try to get rid of the flowering ones. Hardest to sell, you know."

"Unless somebody really gullible comes along," Jackie said ruefully. "Right, John?"

"There was no way for you to know. Lots of things just have to be learned by experience."

John Caldwell was probably about seventy, and wore a long-sleeved blue shirt, despite the early summer heat, and old dress trousers held over his ample waist by a pair of suspenders. A fringe of white hair encircled his bald head, and his face was as round and affable as a baby's.

He gestured with his newspaper. "I see that you folks found something a little strange in your backyard the other day."

"Was that in the paper already?" Jackie said. "I haven't had time to do much reading lately."

"Just a little article in the back of yesterday's edition. It said you found some bones that were believed to be of human origin."

"Oh, they're human, all right," Jackie said grimly, remembering the two skulls. She dug another series of holes and frowned at her box of plants, trying to decide whether the colors should be random or arranged in some kind of pattern.

John leaned on the fence with a confiding air. "So what were they? Remains of some old native burial ground? I recall they found one of those over in Coeur d'Alene a few years ago."

"We're not sure what they are," Jackie said. "The police department is flying in a forensic anthropologist from Chicago to have a look at them."

"Well, now, isn't that interesting. All the way from Chicago!"

Jackie glanced at her watch. "He was supposed to be here sometime today, I think. But the pathologist at the hospital didn't think the bones were that old. His guess was not more than a few decades."

John Caldwell's gray eyebrows shot up. "Really? I've been living here for twenty-five years myself, you know."

"Lola told me that." Jackie squinted at him against the sun. "So, have you ever noticed anything strange going on over here, John?"

He frowned, clearly thinking hard, then shook his head. "Nothing along those lines, that's for sure. When I first moved here, an old couple named Karl and Wilma Gottfriedson lived next door. They were already in their seventies, and Karl died a few years later. Wilma stayed another fifteen years until the kids finally had to move her into a nursing home."

"Had they been here long?"

"I don't think so. Maybe a year or two, after they sold their farm. Not like the Betkers," he said with a grin. "Over there in their castle since the beginning of time. Or Mrs. Weitzel, who moved in across the street more than fifty years ago."

The little man sobered and frowned again while Jackie waited.

"I think Karl told me the place had been rented before he bought it," John said. "I remember there was quite a lot of damage that he had to repair. And then, after Wilma moved away, the house changed hands a few times before you bought it."

"But there was never any gossip in the neighborhood about the Gottfriedsons, or any of the people who lived here before them?"

"Not that I recall. Of course," he added, leaning cozily against the fence, "I've never been much for gossip."

Jackie gave him an indulgent smile. "I can see that, John."

But her neighbor missed the gentle irony, turning away to look over his shoulder. His daughter was approaching along the flower-lined path with a briefcase in her hand.

"Hi, Lola," Jackie said. "How are you?"

"I'm fine." The saleswoman joined her father near the fence. She wore flat shoes and a patterned cotton dress and looked younger than Jackie remembered, though still heavily made-up.

"Jackie's planting some flowers," John Caldwell told her.

"I can see that, Daddy." Lola made an impatient gesture, then turned her attention back to Jackie. "So, are you settling in all right? I've been meaning to call, but things are crazy these days. Any problems?"

"None at all."

"Except for finding horrible things in the backyard," Lola said dryly. "I read the paper yesterday, and couldn't believe my eyes."

"Well," Jackie said, "I'll admit that was a bit upsetting."

"So, will you be on the case?" Lola asked, leaning on the fence next to her father. "Will you find out where those bones came from, and who put them here? That would be so exciting."

Jackie shook her head, amused by the public's insatiable and baffling absorption with anything related to police work.

"It's not all that exciting," she said. "Especially when it involves following such an old trail. Anyway," she added, "I'm on leave now. Whoever gets the case, it won't be me."

"When's your baby due?" Lola asked.

"Anytime now, I guess. My official due date is the tenth of June but the doctor thinks the baby could come a little early."

Lola stared at her, clearly fascinated. "Aren't you terrified?"

Jackie considered the question, startled and a little touched as she often was by Lola's occasional moments of childlike frankness.

"No," she said at last. "I'm not frightened at all by the prospect of childbirth. I just want to get it over with."

Lola shuddered. "I can imagine."

"I am a little scared about the thought of being a parent," Jackie said, thinking of Adrienne's current struggles. "But I guess I'll have to cross that bridge when I get there, won't I? Because it's a little late to back out now."

"Well, let us know if you need anything," Lola said, while her father nodded his bald head in silent agreement. "Anything at all."

"Thank you," Jackie said, moved by their concern. "Both of you."

She set out the last of the flowers and heaved herself upright, feeling awkward because Lola and John were still watching her.

"I'd better go in and clean up," she said. "Paul's coming over to bring some groceries and cook dinner for me tonight. He finds an excuse to check on me every day now, it seems."

At the mention of Paul, Lola's face took on a soft, avid expression. "That man is so gorgeous," she said. "Jackie, I just can't imagine why you—"

But at a murmured word from her father she stopped abruptly and turned aside, taking his arm.

"Come on, Daddy," she said brightly. "Let's go inside and have some tea, and quit bothering Jackie. She has lots to do if she's going to be entertaining a dinner guest in a few hours."

John turned away obediently and followed Lola's bright cotton dress up the walk to the house. Near his back door he paused.

"Say, Jackie, have you seen that black cat of ours lately?"

"He's not around much," Jackie said evasively, plodding across the lawn to her own house. "He just drops by sometimes in the morning for a snack, but I hardly ever see him otherwise."

John nodded and disappeared into the little yellow house with his daughter.

Jackie opened the door to her porch and stepped inside, where the black cat lay in a square of sunlight on the wooden floorboards. At her entry he looked up and purred, then rolled into a sinewy ball with his nose tucked between his front paws.

"See what you've done?" Jackie told him. "You've made a complete liar out of me, and with my nice new neighbor, too."

She stooped to scratch his ears while he writhed in pleasure.

"If you'd just quit your philandering and make a real commitment to me, I could go public with our relationship," she said. "But the way you keep wandering around this neighborhood, who even knows where your heart is, you bad cat?"

He rolled over and waved his paws lazily. Jackie stroked his furry stomach, chuckling.

On Friday morning Jackie stopped in at the Northwest substation after her weekly doctor's ap-

pointment. She used her security key and slipped in
through the back door to avoid being fussed over by
the receptionists, then made her way through tiled
corridors to the squad room.

The place was quiet and deserted, a sure sign that
everybody was busy. She looked around at the battered wooden desks with their rows of computers,
the empty coat trees, the overflowing work baskets.
Somebody, probably the department secretary, Alice
Polson, had placed a big jar of lilacs on one of the
tall metal file cabinets, and they flooded the room
with fragrance.

Jackie sniffed the air and felt a stab of loneliness.
She'd only been on maternity leave for a week, but
already she felt a sense of exclusion, of being
pushed aside.

After a moment she made her way across the
squad room to the glassed-in sergeant's office where
Lew Michelson sat behind a desk with his reading
glasses perched on his nose, leafing through a stack
of files.

The bluff, gingery sergeant had recently lost a fair
amount of weight and looked trim, almost handsome, in his dark blue uniform. Jackie knocked on
the opened door and smiled at him, then noticed
Brian Wardlow sitting in one of the visitor chairs.

"Am I interrupting something?" she asked.

Michelson waved a hand toward the other chair.
"Come on in. We were just talking about you. How
are you feeling?"

Wardlow watched in awe as she settled into the
chair. "My God," he muttered. "You look posi-

tively dangerous, Kaminsky. It's like you could blow at any moment."

Jackie glared at him. "Is that so? You wanna try carrying this around for a while?"

"No way," Wardlow told her fervently. "No bloody way."

"So, is everything going all right?" the sergeant asked.

"I'm fine. Just came from the doctor's office, and he says I'm right on schedule. The baby could arrive any time now."

Michelson smiled at her. "We're all looking forward to it."

Jackie shifted in the chair, trying to find a more comfortable position. "I stopped in to see what you found out about my skeletons."

"Your skeletons," Wardlow muttered. "I should be so lucky."

Jackie grinned. "I take it you've been assigned the case, Brian?"

"I'm buried here," Wardlow complained. "We have a biker gang trying to get established in the city, two homicides at a convenience store on Tuesday night and this damn string of jewelry store robberies on top of all the regular shit. Pringle takes about four hours to type up a witness report, so he's not much help. And now I have to run around trying to track down leads on a thirty-year-old murder."

"Is it definitely thirty years?" Jackie asked. "They've confirmed that?"

"The bones are less than thirty-two years old," Wardlow said, consulting a file.

"Wow." Jackie's eyes widened. "I had no idea they could be so precise."

"They weren't," Wardlow said. "But the city trenched new water lines into that whole block of houses in 1965, and yours runs right underneath the spot where Paul found the skeletons. So they had to have been buried later than that."

Jackie beamed at the red-haired detective, then leaned over to pat his arm. "Hey, good work, Brian. I'm really impressed."

Wardlow scowled briefly and returned to the file.

"The larger skeleton is a woman, probably under twenty-five years old."

"How can they tell that?"

"Some kind of ridge detail on the pelvic bones that only starts to develop around the middle of the third decade of life. None of these ridges were present on the skeleton."

"Did you find any missing-person's reports from the same time?"

Wardlow shook his head in disgust.

Michelson took off the reading glasses to rub his eyes. "Nothing local at all. Not a trace. We're running it through the FBI to see if there's anything national, but this is pretty old stuff, Jackie. A lot of those back files have never been entered into their database, so it takes a long time to search, and this is low priority."

"She was hacked to pieces, probably with an ax," Wardlow said. "Dismembered and decapitated. An especially gruesome murder."

"You're kidding." Jackie stared at him, suddenly dismayed by a touch of the same clammy chill that often assailed her in the small upstairs bedroom at her house. "She was decapitated?"

"The forensic anthropologist showed me the cuts

on the bones. You could see where the ax sliced right through one of her neck vertebrae, and the bones in her arms and thighs. There was damage to the rest of the skeleton, too. Somebody spent a lot of time whacking away at her.''

"God.'' Jackie rubbed her arms and glanced out the window, where the trailing branches of a willow tree swept the lawn. "How about the...'' She paused, nerving herself to continue. "The baby... was it cut up, too?''

"No ax marks on the baby,'' Wardlow said. "In fact, no trauma at all. The skeleton was still perfectly articulated. They figured it probably died of suffocation and was buried carefully. Or it could even have been buried alive. The specialist said it was a newborn.''

"I thought so. Isn't it strange,'' Jackie murmured, "that the killer would be so savage to her, but not chop up her baby?''

"We're not even sure it was her baby,'' Wardlow said. "There's no actual sign that this woman had ever given birth.''

Jackie looked at the two men in confusion. "Can't they tell something like that?''

"Actually, it was pretty interesting,'' Wardlow told her. "They had this skeleton all laid out on one of Dr. Klein's tables in the morgue. He said to say hello to you, by the way.''

Jackie smiled, thinking of the plump little pathologist who loved his job and made autopsies so interesting for the attending police officers.

"Anyhow,'' Wardlow went on, "they'd pieced her together like a jigsaw puzzle, and Klein and the anthropologist could practically tell what the woman had eaten for breakfast, just by looking at those old bones.''

"I wish I'd been there,'' Jackie said. "You should have called me.''

"Hey, this isn't your case, Kaminsky,'' her partner reminded her. "Even if you did dig up the bodies in your backyard.''

"So, tell me about this woman. What makes them think it wasn't her baby?''

"I didn't say that.'' Wardlow looked at his file again. "The skeleton showed evidence of some kind of long-healed pelvic injury. Dr. Klein said the woman probably would have walked with a limp. Apparently, the nature of this injury makes it impossible to determine if she'd experienced a normal pregnancy, but they could definitely tell that she hadn't given birth. The pelvic bones weren't sprung apart far enough.''

"So, it wasn't her baby, then? I'm not sure what you're saying, Brian.''

The two men exchanged a glance, and Michelson cleared his throat.

"There are other ways to give birth besides through the pelvic canal, Jackie,'' the sergeant said.

"Especially if somebody in the room's got an ax,'' Wardlow added.

Jackie winced and clutched her abdomen involuntarily. "Jesus, Brian,'' she muttered.

"Sorry, Kaminsky.'' He waved the file folder. "I sent Pringle out to talk to a few of your neighbors yesterday, but we got nothing from them at all except some vague memories about an old couple who used to live in the house.''

"That would be the Gottfriedsons,'' Jackie said.

"They bought the place in the early seventies when they retired from farming."

Michelson put his glasses on and peered at her over the rims.

"I was talking to my neighbor," she said. "He's lived next door for about twenty-five years."

"That's probably not going to help much," Wardlow said. "Our best estimate is that the body was buried in that yard sometime between 1965 and 1972. During that time, the house was owned by a real estate investor and rented out. It had a lot of occupants. And, according to city records, it was empty for almost a year during the early seventies before the old couple bought it. Anybody could have used the backyard to dispose of a couple of bodies."

"What are you planning to try next?" Jackie asked her partner.

Wardlow exchanged another glance with Michelson. "Nothing," he said at last.

"Nothing?"

"Come on, Jackie. Unless the FBI comes up with a missing person who matches the dental files, what can we do? The neighbors don't remember anything. We have no local missing-person's reports. The trail, if there ever was one, is thirty years old. I have better things to do with my time."

"I'll bet some of those neighbors know more than they're letting on," she said. "A few of them have lived there practically forever, and they spend all their time peeking out the windows."

Wardlow leaned back in the chair and extended his legs wearily. "Well, if they know anything, they aren't talking about it."

"Oh, come on," she scoffed. "Who's going to

tell Dave Pringle anything? Just talking to the man is boring enough to put you to sleep.''

Michelson chuckled, then sobered. ''Dave Pringle is a good hard worker,'' he said firmly. ''I expect him to make a fine detective.''

''He might,'' Wardlow muttered. ''But mostly he makes me miss Kaminsky.''

Jackie patted his arm fondly, then turned to the sergeant. ''Why not let me work on the case, Sarge?''

He shook his head. ''No way. You're on official leave from duties.''

''It doesn't have to be any kind of formal thing,'' Jackie said. ''I can spend some time questioning the neighbors, and stop by the office every now and then to get debriefed. Come on, Sarge,'' she added, warming to the argument.

Michelson hesitated.

''Brian's not going to do anything with this,'' she pressed. ''I might as well have something to keep me occupied.''

He waved a hand at her bulging abdomen. ''You're soon going to have enough to keep you occupied.''

''But I'll be coming back to work in a few months. And if I have something official to do in the meantime, I won't feel so disconnected.''

The sergeant hesitated, then looked at Wardlow. ''How do you feel about this, Brian?''

''Hell, let her have the case if she's volunteering,'' the detective said promptly. ''Like Kaminsky says, we're not doing anything more with it. If she wants to wander around and have a few chats with her neighbors, it's fine with me.''

Michelson frowned. "What if the FBI turns up a match from its files?"

"Then Brian can deal with it," Jackie said. "Look, he'll stay in charge of the case. I'll just spend some time questioning the neighbors, and get my buddy Karl Widmer down at the *Sentinel* to help me look through some old newspaper files, stuff like that."

Michelson continued to hesitate.

"Please, Sarge," she said, looking at him directly.

"Why do you want to do something like this when you're on leave?"

Jackie thought about those two grinning skulls, one large and the other so tiny and fragile. Again she felt a clammy touch of fear.

"I just don't want it to be an unsolved murder," she said. "Not in my own backyard."

"Okay," Michelson said at last. "I guess you can have a look at Brian's file, and check with the neighbors. But keep it unofficial and don't use your badge, all right? And if you start building any kind of file, I'll need you to keep us briefed on a weekly basis."

She smiled and went around the desk to give him a hug.

Wardlow got to his feet, handed her the file and held the door for her. "Come on, fat lady," he said cheerfully. "If you're really taking this sucker off my hands, then I'm going to buy you some lunch."

6

Jackie and her partner went to Pizza Hut, one of their favorite lunchtime spots. He sprawled in the booth across from her, beaming.

"Hey, Kaminsky, this is just like old times. How've you been?"

"Pregnant," she said briefly, dribbling ranch dressing on her salad. "And you?"

"Not pregnant." Wardlow took a sip of coffee, then stirred in some cream. "Just scared."

"What are you scared of?"

He raised his cup again, looking a little abashed. "Getting married, I guess."

"No kidding." Jackie grinned. "Are you getting cold feet, Brian?"

"Hey, it's a big decision," he said defensively. "And my past experience hasn't made me all that optimistic about marriage."

"Chris is an entirely different woman than Sarah." Jackie thought about Wardlow's self-absorbed, greedy ex-wife who'd made his life so miserable during their recent divorce.

"I know she is." He lifted a saltshaker and held it in his hand, studying it closely. "Why do they put these little bits of rice in the salt?"

"To keep it from getting clumpy. Brian, don't change the subject."

"Is there a subject?" Wardlow smiled at the young waitress who arrived with their pizzas.

"We're talking about marriage. You were confessing what a coward you are."

"Oh, and you're not?" he scoffed. "You face life with serene confidence, I suppose. No fears about anything, not our little J.K."

"We weren't discussing me," she said, taken aback by this sudden offensive.

"Well, let's." He arched a cheerful eyebrow. "After all, you're the one who's as big as a house, about to become somebody's mother and still too cowardly to marry the daddy."

"I'm not cowardly." She chewed and swallowed a huge bite of pizza, then went on. "Why do people automatically assume that if you're pregnant, you also have to be married?"

"Because, generally speaking, it's best for a kid to have two parents."

"I know that's the party line," Jackie said, frowning at her pizza. "But I still think a kid is better off with one parent who's confident and happy, than with two people who are pulling against each other and constantly in conflict."

"You know, I've never noticed," he said with feigned innocence, "that you and Arnussen are constantly in conflict. Matter of fact, it seems to me that the two of you get along pretty well."

"That's only because we don't have to live together. God knows what would happen if we ever got married."

"You're the real coward, Kaminsky," he told her.

"Hell on wheels when you're on the job, but a lily-livered chicken in your personal life."

She thought it over, then nodded agreement. "Okay, maybe I am. But if you'd grown up with my grandmother, I'll bet you wouldn't have all that much confidence in your relationship skills, either."

"So, because your grandmother made you feel inadequate and pissed off most of the time, you can't ever commit to marriage?"

"Hey, leave me alone. You're the one who's engaged and getting cold feet."

He surprised her by reaching across the table to pat her arm. "God, I miss you, Kaminsky. The job isn't nearly as much fun without you."

"Why, Brian, that's so sweet. I hardly know what to say."

"Don't get too excited." He took another bite of pizza. "It's probably just that damn Pringle. Anybody would look good compared to that guy."

Jackie chuckled. "So you're really busy these days, are you?"

"Worse than ever. We could use about six more guys. This biker-gang thing is really labor-intensive."

"Why?"

"We're trying to initiate some kind of preemptive action," he said. "We've been rounding up criminal records, doing stakeouts and obtaining warrants on a lot of these guys to discourage them from settling in here and getting too cozy."

"Harassing them, you mean?"

"You could say that, I guess. But biker gangs are so well run nowadays that we've got to move carefully. They have ties to organized crime and access to really good lawyers.''

"They just look like cuddly old boys on Harleys,'' Jackie said.

"That's the persona they like to project, a bunch of big-bellied guys in black leather and tattoos. Kind of a joke left over from the seventies. But that image is mostly a front for an efficient criminal operation, and the bosses at the top are getting very wealthy and powerful from the drug money.''

"Scary,'' she commented.

"Yes,'' he agreed. "Really scary. The guys at the downtown office are putting a lot of manpower into holding these gangs off.''

"Well, it's about time somebody challenged them.'' Jackie wiped her mouth with a paper napkin and sighed, looking at the remaining pizza on her plate. "Lord, this tastes so good. I'd better enjoy it now, because after the baby's born I won't be able to eat spicy stuff for a while.''

"Why not?''

She smiled. "It affects the milk supply, Brian.''

"You're going to breast-feed?'' he asked, clearly startled.

"Sure. Why not? It's cheaper, it's good for the baby and you don't have to mess around with bottles all the time.''

Wardlow grinned. "Jackie Kaminsky breastfeeding. Who could ever have imagined it?''

"Go ahead,'' she said calmly. "Laugh all you want. But I intend to be a good mother to this baby.''

"I never doubted it for a minute.'' He watched

her curiously. "You really want to take that old-bones case when you're on leave, Jackie?"

"I really do. You keep forgetting," she told him, "that I haven't done any real police work since last winter. It's going to be fun interviewing people again, even if I will feel a bit like Nancy Drew doing an investigation after school."

Wardlow chuckled. "What makes you so interested in this one?"

"I don't know." Jackie picked a couple of mushrooms from the slice of pizza and ate them absently. "Something about those bones kind of got to me. It was like...I don't know." She hesitated, feeling vaguely embarrassed. "Like the skulls were talking to me."

"Talking to you?"

"I have dreams sometimes about those skulls screaming something. It scares the hell out of me while it's going on, but when I wake up I can never remember what they were saying."

Wardlow watched her. She shifted her bulk on the vinyl bench, suddenly awkward.

"Maybe you shouldn't take this on right now," he said. "It might be best if we—"

Jackie frowned at him. "Look, don't start implying that I'm some kind of hysterical pregnant lady, Brian. There's nothing wrong with me. I'm the same person I always was."

"Of course you are." He drained the last of his coffee and made eye contact with the waitress, raising the empty mug. "So, what are you going to do about having this baby? I mean, the actual birth."

"I really don't think I have to do anything," she

said dryly. "The plan is pretty much to let nature take its course."

"But if you wake up in the middle of night having labor pains, are you going to drive yourself to the hospital, or what? Chris is worried about you being all alone this close to your due date."

"That's nice of her, Brian. But there's no problem," Jackie said. "It's all been arranged."

"So what's the arrangement?"

"Paul finally had a telephone installed at the ranch. He's even wearing a beeper all day while he works. When my labor starts, I'll call him and he'll come into town right away."

"What if he doesn't get there in time?"

"It's a first baby," Jackie said calmly. "Normal labor takes ten or twelve hours."

They were silent, eating the last of their pizza.

"Brian," she said at last.

"Hmm?" He smiled at the waitress who arrived to refill their coffee cups.

"I haven't had a chance to read the whole file. Did Klein and the anthropologist say anything else about those skeletons?"

He frowned in concentration. "Well…Dr. Klein thought the girl probably had bright red hair, though that stuff with the body was so faded it looked like old grass. She would have been quite a small woman, not more than five foot two or three. Oh, and her teeth were great, hardly any cavities."

"Anything else?"

"There was a gold ring with the bones, kind of a cheap little thing with a heart shape on it. It's in the evidence locker at the station."

"Not a wedding band?"

He shook his head. "More like a kid's ring. No engraving or anything. But if she was actually wearing it, she had to be a thin woman. I got Alice to try the ring and she couldn't even fit it on her baby finger."

Involuntarily, Jackie pictured a dainty, copper-haired girl giving birth and then being hacked to pieces, her dismembered corpse dumped into a backyard grave along with her baby, who was possibly still alive....

"God," she muttered, pressing a hand to her abdomen.

"Are you okay, Kaminsky?"

"I'm fine." She smiled wanly. "But I'll sure be glad to have this baby out of here and into a crib."

"I'm not surprised."

"Brian, you were at that autopsy. Did they really think there was a possibility this wasn't her baby, that she hadn't actually given birth? It all sounds so weird."

"They didn't know. Even Dr. Klein wouldn't volunteer a guess, and you know how he's usually confident enough to go out on a limb. He said with the old pelvic injury, there was no way to know for sure if she'd carried a baby to term. But she definitely hadn't delivered vaginally."

"Did they have any idea what might have caused the old injury?"

"That stuff is all in the file. I think they said it could have been an accident, like a fall from a bicycle. But more likely it was abuse."

"Abuse?"

"Klein thought the pelvic injury was consistent with some of the autopsies he does on battered babies. If they'd survived the beating and grown up, some of those kids would have shown that kind of healed damage.''

''You mean, like somebody broke her pelvis or jerked her leg out of its socket when she was a baby?''

He shrugged. ''Something like that.''

Jackie shuddered, thinking of the discolored skull with its dirt-filled eye sockets and grinning mouth. ''The poor woman didn't have much of a life, did she?''

''Hey, don't start getting emotionally involved in this, Kaminsky,'' her partner said. ''It's thirty years old. The whole thing is ancient history.''

''I know.'' She forced herself to smile at him. ''So tell me all the rest of the news. Any juicy gossip I've been missing?''

Jackie settled in to concentrate on his chatter, putting aside the troubling mental image of the dismembered woman's corpse and that tiny, fragile skeleton lying next to it.

She got home in the early afternoon and went upstairs to change into a loose, comfortable dress and sandals. Then she stopped to look in at the baby's room, cheered by the rows of tiny garments all in readiness, the stacks of snowy diapers and drawers full of little shirts and sleepers, the bright plastic diaper pail and the mobile fixed above the crib.

''I'm going to take such good care of you,'' she told the mound under her ribs. ''You're going to have a safe, happy life. And every single day,'' she added, her face suddenly fierce with emotion, ''I'm going to hug you and tell you how much I love you."

Feeling restless, Jackie left the nursery and made her way downstairs, wincing a little with each step. Recently the baby had "dropped," settling firmly into the birthing position. This downward movement relieved pressure against her lungs and rib cage so she could breathe more easily, but made walking difficult. The weight of the fetus bore down against her pelvis so that with each step she waddled awkwardly from side to side.

Jackie went outside and sat in a wicker rocking chair on the back porch.

The afternoon was mild and still, fragrant with the scent of blossoms. Robins flitted in and out of the poplar tree by the back gate, carrying things in their beaks. She watched them with a dreamy smile, rocking slowly.

Paul had told her the birds were probably raising their babies in there, and showed her pictures of a dainty woven robin's nest with five sky-blue eggs. Jackie liked to think about the little eggs hatching, and the parents busily feeding their young within the bower of rustling leaves.

At the base of the tree her black cat stared up into the leaves, his face inscrutable. Whenever one of the robins appeared on an upper branch, he licked his chops and flicked his tail against the grass.

"Don't even think about it, kiddo," Jackie warned him. "If you ever hurt one of those nice birdies, you'll be sorry."

He turned his yellow gaze on her, then arched his back and began to claw with great energy at the trunk of the tree.

Jackie smiled and glanced over the fence, catching sight of Emma Betker in the adjoining yard.

The older woman wore a dress and sun hat and lay in a long padded chair beside a table that contained a glass of iced lemonade. A plaid shawl covered the lower portion of her body, and she'd been placed carefully so the sun fell over her shoulder, not in her face.

Eleanor, the older sister, was visible near the corner of the house, wearing denim overalls and a mannish long-sleeved shirt while she pushed some kind of wooden cart across the lawn.

Jackie watched the two women from the shadows of her porch, wondering how to approach them. Michelson had said not to use her badge or cite departmental authority, and of course she could understand why.

Still, those restrictions put her pretty much at the level of a snoopy neighbor nosing around for information. Jackie wasn't all that comfortable with such a role, especially since she'd learned during her childhood in south L.A. that it was neither wise nor safe to be overly curious about the neighbors.

Still, it might not be a bad thing in this case. She suspected there was a good chance people would provide more information to a pregnant neighbor than they might to an investigating police officer.

With sudden decision she got up and left the porch, walking across the yard to a small gate set in the picket fence that separated their two properties.

Eleanor was passing nearby with her cart, and looked up from under the brim of her straw hat. "Hello," she said.

Jackie had expected a gruff voice to emanate from

with me, Eleanor? I'd really like to know what you remember about the occupants of my house in the late sixties and early seventies.''

"Late sixties, you say?''

Eleanor cast another cautious glance at her younger sister.

Emma lay very still in the chair a few yards away, and Jackie suspected she might be straining to hear their conversation.

"I'll tell you what,'' Eleanor said at last, leaning across the fence. "Emma's just about due for her nap. Come into the house with us and I'll get her settled, and then we can talk, all right?''

"Thank you.'' Jackie moved down to open the gate that connected the two yards.

"I installed that years ago,'' Eleanor said. "At one time I was looking after both places, so it was handy to be able to come and go through the back.''

"When was that?'' Jackie asked, but the older woman didn't answer. Instead, she approached the long chair, bent to scoop her sister effortlessly into her arms and marched toward the house.

Emma clapped one hand to her head to keep the straw hat in place, and smiled at Jackie who walked along next to them.

"You're our new neighbor,'' she said.

"Yes,'' Jackie told her. "I am.''

Emma Betker was still lovely despite her age. There was an air of fragility about her, an ethereal quality, as if she were made of spun sugar that could be destroyed by a clumsy touch. This impression of vulnerability was enhanced by the contrast with her brawny sister who held her so protectively.

"And you're having a baby.'' Within the arms of

her sister, Emma's childlike blue eyes watched Jackie with guileless interest.

"Yes, I am. Almost any day now."

They reached the back door and paused. At a nod from Eleanor, Jackie reached out and held the door open, then followed the two older women into a big wood-floored kitchen. Eleanor set her sister down in a chair near the table, then went to hang their straw hats in a closet.

"When is your baby coming?" Emma asked, sitting obediently in the chair. She clasped her hands together in her lap and held her feet still, as if she were a small child.

"The baby will be here anytime now," Jackie repeated patiently.

"A baby!" Emma clapped her hands in delight. "But you must be very careful," she said, leaning across the table, her eyes wide. "Because some bad people might take your baby, you know. They might just take it away from you and then…"

Tears filled her eyes and began to trickle down her cheeks.

"That's quite enough of that." Eleanor strode across the room, gathered her sister briskly into her arms again and carried her out into the hallway. "Excuse me for a moment. I'll just get Emma settled," she told Jackie over her shoulder, "and then come right back down."

"Thank you," Jackie said. "I appreciate it very much."

She watched Eleanor's sturdy form departing, with Emma's fluffy head and little slippered feet just visible beyond, and resolved somehow to get poor Emma away from her sister for a private chat.

7

While the two sisters were gone, Jackie sat and looked around the kitchen, surprised by its beauty.

Her own decorating tastes were basically uneducated and her experience with lovely houses, except for Adrienne's, was limited to those she occasionally encountered in the course of her police work. Still, Jackie knew what she liked...a simple, uncluttered style with adornment stripped away to reveal the essential grace of the structure.

That was a perfect description of the Betker home. The kitchen was floored in dark pegged-oak hardwood, with white plastered walls and a ten-foot ceiling lined with stamped metal tiles, also painted white. The cabinets were fronted with glass, and the only color in the room came from a row of dark green patterned tiles above the counter, a collection of Delft china on an open shelf and some lush green plants, including a huge Boston fern on a wooden stand by the window.

The whole effect was cool, almost austere, yet still gracious and welcoming.

Jackie got up and went to the archway to peer into the adjoining room. It contained an oval oak dining table surrounded by ten chairs, a bow-fronted china cabinet containing antique dishes and a big couch and chairs upholstered in blue chintz and arranged in the curve of a bay window, with more plants on fern stands.

The walls here were also stark white, but covered with subtle watercolors of landscapes and flowers, all in matching frames of dark oak.

She heard Eleanor Betker's heavy tread descending the staircase, and smiled an apology when the older woman appeared in an opposite doorway.

"Sorry to snoop," Jackie said. "It's such a lovely home."

"This house is my passion," Eleanor told her calmly. "I've spent my life working to restore and maintain it. According to my research, this would be pretty much the way the parlor and dining room looked when the place was built in 1872."

"Lola told me you and Emma have lived here all your lives."

"Did she now?" Eleanor led the way back to the kitchen. "Quite the little fountain of information, your friend Lola."

"I guess she's interested in houses," Jackie said, settling at the kitchen table again. "If not, she probably wouldn't enjoy her job very much."

"Sounds like maybe she's more interested in people than houses." Eleanor yanked open the door of a big stainless-steel refrigerator, then glanced at Jackie. "Is there anything you're not allowed to have? I made a pot of iced tea this morning, but it has caffeine. And there's a bit of lemonade in here, too."

"Lemonade would be very nice," Jackie said. "Thanks so much."

She watched while the older woman filled tumblers with lemonade and iced tea, then opened a patterned tin full of cookies and carried them to the table along with the drinks.

"You're living over there all on your own?" Eleanor asked, sitting opposite her and sipping the tea.

"Yes, I am."

"Not afraid of being alone when you're so close to your due date?"

Jackie met the big woman's eyes directly. "Not too many things frighten me, Eleanor."

"Well, good for you," the neighbor said amiably. "I like a woman with some guts. Never did approve of equating weakness with femininity. That handsome blond fellow I see coming and going in the truck all the time," she said after a moment. "I take it he's your boyfriend?"

"Yes, that's the baby's father. He has a ranch out by Reardan."

Unlike most people, Eleanor didn't seem at all curious about why Jackie was living apart from her child's father.

They sipped their drinks, and for a few moments the only sound was the chirping of birds outside the window and the lazy hiss of a lawn sprinkler as water splattered against a corner of the house.

"This place is so beautiful," Jackie said again, looking around. "I love it."

"I renovated the kitchen about twelve years ago. The cabinets are new, but I think they're probably a passable replica of the originals."

Eleanor looked down at her callused hands, and Jackie wondered how much of the carpentry she'd done on her own. Almost involuntarily, she found herself liking the woman.

"Where did you get those gorgeous green tiles?" she asked.

"I painted them myself and had them glazed in a friend's kiln."

Jackie looked up at the tiles again, startled. "They're really striking," she said. "So you're an artist, too, Eleanor?"

"After a fashion. I like to putter around with some watercolors."

"Did you paint all those wonderful pictures in the living room, too?" Jackie asked.

Eleanor grinned, showing her strong white teeth. "Detective, I do believe you're gushing."

Jackie smiled back, unruffled. "Well, that just shows how impressed I am. Because I'm not normally the gushing type."

"I can see that." Eleanor studied her guest thoughtfully, then jerked a thumb over her shoulder with a mannish gesture. "The only real change I made on the lower floor was to install a modern bathroom over there in the old butler's pantry."

"You had a pantry big enough to hold a bathroom?" Jackie asked.

Eleanor chuckled. "Oh my, yes. They liked roomy pantries back in the nineteenth century. It was actually a little room situated between the kitchen and dining room, where the butler could organize and prepare his food service. I put in a bathroom and then knocked a hole in the wall to install that archway for access to the dining room."

Jackie looked at the dark oak lining the archway just behind her.

"So, this is new woodwork?" she said, marveling. "You'd never know. It's impossible to tell it from all the rest."

"I bought the oak from a house in the South Hill that was being torn down, and spent weeks trying to match the stain. It was a lot of work, but I needed a bathroom downstairs for Emma."

"Is she able to walk at all?" Jackie asked.

"After a fashion, but her osteoporosis is so severe that I'm afraid to let her climb stairs. She could break a hip or a vertebra just by shifting her weight the wrong way."

Jackie thought about the little woman with her sweet face and childlike blue eyes. "She seems like such a darling."

"Yes, she is." Eleanor glanced up, her eyes suddenly hard and watchful. "But I should probably tell you, Emma also has early-onset Alzheimer's. Some days are worse than others. It's not wise," the woman added, looking directly at Jackie, "to pay much attention to anything she says, especially about past events. Her memory can be very confused."

"Really?" Jackie said, her interest sharpening at the sense of a veiled but unmistakable warning in her neighbor's voice. "That's so sad. It must be very difficult for you."

"It's my life," Eleanor said bluntly. "Looking after this house and Emma, that's all I've got. I'd die to protect either of them."

Again her eyes met Jackie's with a cold, challenging look.

Jackie hesitated, wondering how aggressive to be with her questioning. She'd always disliked the feeling of being warned off. On the other hand, she had no desire to antagonize the woman at this point, and she could probably find out more personal details about the Betker sisters from the other neighbors.

"These are delicious cookies," she said.

"Emma made them. On rainy days I prop her up on a stool by the counter and assemble all the ingredients for her, and she spends a whole morning baking cookies. It makes her happy."

Jackie took a sip of lemonade, wishing she had her notebook with her, and reminded herself to record all of Eleanor's comments and answers as soon as she got home.

She felt a stab of pain in her back and shifted in the chair, frowning.

"Are you all right?" Eleanor asked.

"Just a little twinge. I've been having them for a week or so."

"False labor?" Eleanor asked.

"I guess so. The doctor says the baby's dropped into position, and I can expect these pains to get stronger from now on."

"When's your due date?"

"Next Friday," Jackie said.

"That means it could be anytime."

"I guess so." Jackie smiled at her neighbor. "If I have some kind of emergency, would you know how to deliver a baby?"

Again she caught that flash of white teeth. "I've delivered a baby or two in my time," Eleanor said, looking down at her big hands.

For some reason, Jackie felt a little shiver of fear and suppressed it impatiently. "Well, that's good to know," she said. "Now, about those bones in my backyard..."

"What about them?"

"The detective who's been working on the case has established that they were buried sometime after 1965."

"Of course," Eleanor said. "That was when the city trenched in the new water lines."

"That's right." Jackie watched the older woman's face carefully. "And the line ran right under the burial spot, so if the bones had been there already, they would have turned up at that time."

"Since 1965," Eleanor said thoughtfully. "Well, that puts a whole new face on the matter, doesn't it? I thought when I read the article that your bones might be a remnant of an old native burial ground, or some such thing."

"That's what John Caldwell suggested, too. But the anthropologist places the skeletons at about thirty years old."

"Skeletons?" Eleanor's hands tightened suddenly on the glass, her knuckles turning white. "There was more than one?"

"We found two skeletons." Again Jackie watched the woman closely. "A young woman and a newborn baby. For the moment the police have chosen not to include any details about the baby in reports they're giving to the media."

Eleanor got up and walked over to the sink. She leaned against the counter, staring out the window at her well-kept garden.

Jackie watched the strong back in denim coveralls, the clipped gray head and broad shoulders. "Do you have any memory of a pregnant woman living over there, Eleanor?'' she said at last.

''No.'' The woman turned around, her face composed. ''None at all.''

Eleanor poured another glass of iced tea and came back to the table.

''A lot of people lived in that house in the late sixties,'' she said. ''It was a trashy place, all kinds of strange goings-on. I complained to the police a couple of times but it never accomplished much.''

''So, you didn't notice a pregnant woman? She would have been young, quite small and thin, probably with bright red hair.''

Suddenly the woman's face contorted with a look of anguish so nakedly intense that Jackie was briefly taken aback. She watched while her neighbor struggled to control herself. Eleanor sipped repeatedly at the glass of tea, clenching and flexing her free hand.

''Eleanor?'' Jackie said at last. ''Does that description ring some kind of bell?''

The woman shook her cropped gray head and took a deep breath. ''Nothing,'' she said at last. ''Sorry. If anything comes to me, I'll let you know, all right? Now, if you'll excuse me, I have to go up and check on Emma. Sometimes she's restless during her afternoon nap and can't get herself into a comfortable position.''

She stood up in a manner that was clearly dismissive and Jackie followed suit. ''Well, thanks for your time,'' she said. ''If you should think of anything else...''

''Yes, yes, I'll let you know. Good luck with your baby.''

The woman gripped an oak chair back and waited, her face expressionless again.

Jackie lumbered toward the door and paused to smile politely, then let herself out into the shady green yard and headed back toward the gate that Eleanor had long ago installed between the two houses.

The next morning she got up and puttered around the house, overtaken by restlessness and an urge to set the place in order.

Most of her sparse belongings were already unpacked by now, except for a few cartons that remained in the basement.

Some of the boxes contained old sporting equipment and hobby supplies that Jackie intended to sort through when she had more time. The rest were full of outdated income tax forms, old service gear, outworn uniforms from her days as a patrol officer and fifteen years of notebooks that she kept out of a morbid fear she might someday be called on to supply the details of her involvement in some long-ago case.

Briefly she considered going downstairs and sorting through the boxes, then abandoned the idea, reluctant to risk the steep wooden stairs or to spend any time in the musty cellar.

Instead, she went outside into her backyard and passed a couple of hours awkwardly raking the lawn and pulling weeds from around the new bedding plants.

John Caldwell had been right, most of the petunias were already shedding their flowers. But they seemed healthy enough, and she had a ridiculous feeling of accomplishment when she looked at the array of green plants.

"Just as if I knew what I was doing," she muttered.

At noon she went inside and washed her hands, then ate a bowl of yogurt and some fruit. The phone rang, and she plodded across the kitchen to answer it.

"Hi," Paul said. "How are you?"

"Well, I'm still pregnant," she said. "If that's what you're interested in."

"I'm mildly interested. Are you getting any more of those pains?"

Jackie pressed a hand into the small of her back. "They come and go. It can't be much longer, though, or I'll burst."

He chuckled. "Well, you're sounding cheerful, at least."

"Actually, I feel great. Full of energy. I was wondering if I should drag a ladder in here and start dusting off all the lightbulbs."

"Don't even joke about it," he said darkly. "No ladders."

"Or," she teased, "I could go up on the roof and fix those loose shingles."

"I won't dignify that with a response. What are you busy with?"

"I've been working in the backyard this morning. All my new plants are doing great, Paul, but most of the flowers fell off."

"They'll come back."

"Oh, and I have a job," Jackie said. "I stopped in at the office yesterday to find out about our skeletons, and Sarge said I could do some informal questioning of the neighbors since the department doesn't have time to follow up on a thirty-year-old case.''

''How do they know for sure the bones are thirty years old?''

Jackie told him about the findings of Dr. Klein and the anthropologist, and her visit with Eleanor Betker.

''I'm sure she knows more than she's saying, Paul. You should have seen her face when I described that red-haired woman. She was practically shattered.''

''Look, try to be careful, all right?'' he said abruptly.

''What do you mean, careful? This is just a standard investigation, except that it's a few decades old.''

He was silent for a moment. ''I'll check the machine a couple of times this afternoon,'' he said. ''Don't forget to call and leave a message if anything happens.''

''I will,'' she promised. ''But I doubt that it's going to be this weekend, because I feel too good. What are you working on?''

''I'm building a new corral and loading chute. How about you?'' he asked. ''What's your plan for this afternoon?''

''I think I'll go across the street and have a chat with Mrs. Weitzel. She's another person in the neighborhood who's lived here for a long time. I'm anxious to find out what she remembers.''

Again he paused, and she could tell he was fighting the urge to remind her to be careful. Jackie felt a familiar mixture of amusement and impatience, but made no comment.

"Okay," he said at last. "Have a nice day, and I'll check on you tonight."

"Thanks, Paul."

She hung up with an odd sensation of emptiness, and brewed herself a pot of herbal tea.

It was so different these days, talking to Paul. There were no endearments anymore, and none of the teasing sexual innuendo that had once been so much fun.

"Well, what the hell do I expect?" Jackie said aloud to the cat, who sprawled on the floor near the window. "I tell the man I don't want to live with him, even though I'm having his baby. Why should I be surprised that he doesn't say sweet things to me anymore?"

The cat blinked and stirred. He had an endearing habit of sleeping upside down, flat on his back with his paws in the air. Jackie had never seen a cat do this before, but Shadow was a rugged individualist with all kinds of little quirks.

"What a life," she said to him. "You just spend the whole day following that patch of sunlight across the room, don't you?"

He rolled over and stretched, his skinny rump high in the air, then settled back into a shapeless black mass and tucked his nose under his paws. His green eyes drifted shut.

Jackie laughed aloud and drank her tea, then tidied the kitchen, took a key from the hook by the door and let herself out, heading across the street to the Weitzel residence.

It was a big square two-story house with white

vinyl siding that appeared to have been recently installed. The structure seemed plain and serviceable, not at all like the heavily adorned Betker mansion surrounded by its lush landscaping.

Jackie walked down a path to the back door, noticing that the backyard, too, looked plain and practical. A few flower beds ringed the perimeter of the yard, but most of the space was given over to raspberry bushes, rhubarb, gooseberries and a businesslike vegetable garden with rows of new plants.

She knocked at the door, which was opened almost at once.

Jackie found herself looking down at a woman not more than five feet tall, with a round, sturdy body and bright dark eyes. She had red cheeks and white hair braided into a crown on top of her head, and wore a tartan housedress, a yellow bib apron and a pair of high-top running shoes.

"Hello," Jackie said, a little startled by this apparition. "I'm Jackie Kaminsky, your new neighbor. You must be Mrs. Weitzel."

"My name is Dolly," the woman said. "Come in and have a poppy-seed roll. I just took them out of the oven."

Jackie became aware of a wonderful fragrance drifting through the back porch from somewhere inside the house. Her mouth watered.

She followed her brisk little hostess into a house that was almost comically different from the elegant Betker residence. Dolly Weitzel's tastes clearly leaned toward bright colors, plastic flowers, gingham and ruffles.

And Holstein cows, Jackie thought, dazed. There

were cows everywhere, in fridge magnets, hand towels, wall plaques and china ornaments.

"I've always liked cows," Dolly said when she noticed Jackie looking around the cluttered kitchen. "They're such nice, warmhearted animals, and they give milk every single day. I admire that kind of energy."

Dolly Weitzel also gave the impression of somebody brimming with energy. Her plump body in the high-top runners seemed almost to vibrate, as if poised for takeoff, and her eyes sparkled under the braid of white hair.

"John tells me you're with the police." She separated a couple of fresh buns from a baking pan and put them on a dish patterned with smiling cows. "I was going to ask for your help yesterday, but I didn't want to bother you when you're still moving in."

"My help?" Jackie asked. "What for?"

"I thought you might know something about picking locks." Dolly brought a plate of butter to the table, along with an assortment of homemade jams in small jars with gingham covers. "I went and locked myself out of my house again. So silly," she added, banging a fist against the tightly wound braids. "I'd forget my head if it wasn't attached."

"So, what did you do?" Jackie asked.

"I decided to climb in through one of the basement windows onto the laundry table, and wouldn't you know it," the woman said cheerfully, "I went and got stuck. There I was, hanging in space, thinking, 'Well, Dolly, you idiot, you've gone and done it now, haven't you?' And I'd probably still be there if Mike hadn't come along and hauled me out."

"Who's Mike?" Jackie asked. She had a strong feeling that she and Dolly Weitzel were going to be friends.

"He's my son." Dolly sighed. "I'm such a trial to him. He must wish he'd been born to somebody normal."

"Well, I think you'd be a perfect mother," Jackie said. "And," she added, taking another bite of fragrant poppy-seed roll spread with raspberry jam, "you're a wonderful cook, too."

The little woman beamed and held out her arm, which was disfigured by a livid bruise under the sleeve of her dress. "Look how I hurt my arm when I got stuck in that stupid window. Mike was so upset with me."

Jackie leaned over and studied the injury.

"You really should have come and asked me to help," she said. "Climbing into a basement window! What were you thinking?"

"I didn't want to be a bother," Dolly repeated. "But I'm glad you stopped in for a visit. Now I won't be afraid to ask you for favors."

"Well, I was anxious to meet you," Jackie said. "They tell me you've lived here quite a long time."

"Fifty-one years in this house," Dolly said proudly. "I came here as a bride when I was thirty-one."

"So you're...eighty-two years old?" Jackie asked in astonishment.

"Last February."

"And you're still climbing in and out of basement windows? My goodness, no wonder your son gets annoyed with you."

"Now, don't you start scolding me, too. I get

enough of that from my kids. I was thirty-one before I got married," Dolly said, "because Klaus was away in the war for six years. They took him prisoner, you see. For two years I didn't even get a letter, but I kept waiting. As soon as he came home, we got married and moved here."

Jackie listened, fascinated, waiting for more reminiscences.

But Dolly Weitzel's interest had moved on to more recent topics. "I'll bet you're here to ask me about those bones you found in your yard, right?"

"Yes," Jackie said, a little startled. "Actually, I am. You know about them?"

"Oh my, yes. Gerald told me."

"Is that one of your sons, too?"

"Gerald?" The little woman's face turned redder, and she emitted strangled sounds which Jackie recognized as laughter. "Land's sake, Gerald Pinson is almost as old as I am. He lives down the street and gives piano lessons to the neighborhood kids."

"Has he been there long?"

Dolly frowned. "About forty years," she said at last. "Gerald moved here in the late fifties, as I recall. He used to be a music teacher at the high school before he retired."

Another one to check out, Jackie thought, wondering why Dave Pringle hadn't been able to get a little more information from this group of longtime neighbors.

"So, did they find out anything about that poor man in your yard?" Dolly asked. "Do you know when he was buried, or who he was?"

Jackie repeated the story about how the police had determined the age of the bones. For the moment she said nothing about the baby's skeleton, but gave a description of the young red-haired woman in the makeshift grave.

Dolly's eyes widened. "Well, for the Lord's sake," she breathed. "You mean they killed that poor girl? They killed little Maggie?"

8

"**M**aggie?" Jackie looked at the woman sitting across the table.

"Buried in the backyard all these years," Dolly Weitzel muttered, looking shaken. "Who'd have ever thought it?"

Jackie rummaged in her shoulder bag for her notebook. "Do you mind if I take some notes?" she asked.

Dolly shook her head. "I can't believe it. Poor little Maggie."

"Do you recall her last name?"

"Maggie... Maggie..." The woman stared with narrowed eyes at a cream jug shaped like a cow. "Something short, kind of an ordinary name..."

Jackie waited patiently, her pen poised above the notepad.

"Birk!" Dolly said in triumph. "That was her name. Maggie Birk."

"And she lived in the house across the street?"

"Not for long. Poor little mite."

"Can you remember when this was?"

"Thirty years ago," Dolly said. "No," she corrected herself. "It was twenty-nine years ago. I remember because Mike turned seventeen that year and wanted to quit school and take a welding course, but we wouldn't let him because we were afraid he'd get drafted and have to go to Vietnam if he wasn't in school.''

Jackie recorded the information in her notebook, then glanced up at the bright-eyed woman with her coronet of white braids.

''Dolly, why didn't you tell any of these things to Detective Pringle the other day when he came to interview you?''

''That policeman? He never said it was Maggie buried out there.'' Dolly shook her head, toying with the gingham cover on a jar of jam. ''He just asked if I remembered who was living over there thirty years ago, and I didn't. Not until you described her.''

''Do you recall anything about Maggie's family?'' Jackie asked.

''The poor creature had no family that I know of. If she did,'' Dolly said, ''they hadn't treated her well. She walked with a limp, you know.''

''Did she?'' Jackie made a note, then waited for her hostess to continue.

''Maggie just turned up one day,'' Dolly said. ''Alban brought her home like a stray pup.''

''Alban? Do you recall the last name?''

''What was that man's last name?'' Dolly frowned, then shook her head. ''I can't remember. Alban was a thin little fellow with long hair and a scraggly beard. He looked like Jesus, you know, in all the pictures. A real hippie, Alban was.''

''And how long did he live across the street?''

''Not long. Maybe a few months before they brought Maggie home.''

''So he was married?''

"No, he had a teenage son. Just the two of them, living all on their own. That's why they wanted Maggie. Alban said they needed somebody to look after cooking and housekeeping."

"I see. How old was his son?"

"I think he was a couple of years younger than Mike. His name was Lenny." Dolly frowned. "What a nasty, ugly boy he was. My kids hated him."

"You have other children, Dolly?"

"Yes, I have a daughter Laura who's two years older than Mike. She was away at college when Maggie lived across the street. And then there's Steve and George. They were both younger. They're two years apart, all my kids," she said proudly. "Klaus was always careful about things like that."

Jackie calculated rapidly. "So your son Steve would have been about the same age as Lenny?"

"Yes, but none of my boys ever wanted much to do with him. Lenny was so weird. He didn't even go to school."

"He didn't? At fifteen?"

"Alban taught him at home by correspondence. He never said much about it, but it seemed Lenny didn't get along with the other kids at school. No wonder," Dolly said darkly.

"What did he look like?" Jackie asked.

"Lenny? He was a real heavyset boy with dark hair and a terrible complexion. The other kids hated him but they never told me why. You know what kids are like. And then one day I was delivering Steve's papers for him because he had to stay late at school for a basketball game, and I saw Lenny torturing a kitten."

"Really?"

Dolly nodded vigorously. "He was hunkered down by the back gate, so I couldn't make out what he was doing, but I heard this awful yowling. I marched over there, and when he saw me he got up and this poor little gray kitten went crawling away under the porch. I knew he'd been doing something to hurt it."

"What did you say?"

"Nothing. I hauled off and hit him with the newspaper bag. It was still almost full, so I gave him an awful whack," Dolly recalled with satisfaction.

"And what did Lenny do?"

"He swore at me. Really filthy words, things my own boys would have been in big trouble if they said anywhere around my house. Then he got up and went inside, slamming the door so hard you'd have thought it would break. I had a creepy feeling for a long time afterward, let me tell you. There was murder in that boy's eyes."

"So tell me about Maggie Birk," Jackie said after a moment.

"There's not much to tell. Alban brought her home one day and she started working for them. A good worker she was, too, even though she limped so bad."

"And you got to know her?"

"After a while. She was a timid kind of girl, but real friendly. I'd visit with her over the fence sometimes when she brought home a load of groceries. She had an old wagon and she'd haul it along the sidewalk, loaded with grocery bags."

"So you never had any idea where her home was, or her family?"

"Not a clue. I know she came in from somewhere on the bus, because she told me how Alban had found her at the bus station and offered her a job, and she was so glad because until then she didn't have any idea what she was going to do."

"Do you think she was a runaway?"

"Oh, I'm sure of it," Dolly said promptly. "She had that look, you know, like somebody who hasn't been loved. But she was a dear little thing. She could sing like an angel."

"Do you know if she was friendly at all with either of the Betkers?"

Dolly's face was suddenly guarded. "What do you mean, friendly?"

"Oh, you know," Jackie said, a little startled by the reaction. "They were next-door neighbors. I wondered if Maggie ever mentioned them visiting over the back fence, or anything like that?"

"I don't know much about Eleanor Betker, even after being neighbors for fifty-one years," Dolly said. "But I doubt that she'd ever have hurt Maggie, if that's what you're asking."

"Why not?"

"Because," Dolly said briefly, "I think she really liked the girl."

"Eleanor liked Maggie?"

"I think they were…friends." Their eyes met, and Jackie found herself wondering if the woman was as ingenuous as she seemed.

Dolly made an awkward gesture, then began to toy nervously with the cow-shaped cream jug. "Mike always says I talk too much, and he's right. But I'm so upset," she added, her face puckering. "That poor girl."

"There was obviously a specific day when Maggie disappeared from the neighborhood," Jackie said. "What did you think had happened to her?"

"Alban told me she ran away. He came home from work one day and there was a note from Maggie on the kitchen table saying she was sorry but she had to leave. He even showed me the note."

"Was it Maggie's handwriting?"

"Well, I wouldn't know for sure, but I had no reason to doubt him. Alban was a nice enough fellow, even if he did keep to himself a lot. I never could figure how he raised such an awful boy as that Lenny."

"So did you ever find out anything about Lenny's mother?"

"Not really. Alban said they'd been divorced and she wasn't fit to have custody of the boy. That was all he ever told me."

"Did he own the house, or was he renting?"

"Oh, he was just renting. A lot of people rented the house during those years. It practically drove Eleanor Betker crazy," Dolly added with obvious satisfaction, "having all that riffraff next door, messing things up and carrying on."

Jackie returned to her notebook. "So Maggie supposedly left this note and went away?"

"That's what Alban told me. Cernak!" Dolly said abruptly.

"Pardon?"

"That was his name. Alban Cernak. I knew I'd remember if I gave it a little time."

Jackie wrote down the name, then waited.

"Maggie went away, and a month or two later Alban and Lenny moved out, too. He said he had a job in Portland. But now that I think about it, he and Lenny left in a pretty big hurry. It was early July and they had a big garden in, but he went without harvesting anything.''

"So Maggie disappeared in June?'' Jackie thought about that skeleton in the backyard and Alban Cernak's freshly dug garden.

"May or June. It was spring when she left, I know that, because I remember how much she loved the lilacs. That was one of the last times she was ever in my house, when she came over to bring me a big bouquet of lilacs from their yard. What a sweet girl she was.''

Dolly's eyes filled with tears and she dabbed at them with the hem of her apron.

"Was she pregnant?'' Jackie asked.

"Maggie?'' The woman looked up, startled. "Goodness, no.''

"Are you sure?''

Dolly frowned and looked hesitant. "Well, I don't think so. She always wore baggy clothes and big loose dresses, like she was trying to hide herself, you know? Maggie was one of those girls who never wanted anybody to notice her.''

Jackie nodded.

"And she was such a tiny, skinny little thing,'' Dolly went on. "Of course, that kind don't usually show as much when they're carrying. Strange, isn't it?'' she mused. "Those scrawny ones hardly show at all, but a tall, strong girl like you can get big as a house. No offense,'' she added hastily.

Jackie grinned. "Don't worry, Dolly, there's no offense. Right now I feel as big as two houses.''

"When are you due?''

"Any minute," Jackie said.

"And they still have you running around doing police work?" Dolly asked, looking scandalized.

"This is a voluntary thing on my part," Jackie said. "The department is too busy to spend much time on a thirty-year-old murder. Since I have nothing else to do right now, I offered to talk with the neighbors."

"Well, I suppose you'd probably feel sort of responsible," Dolly said, "finding those bones right in your own backyard."

"Yes, that's exactly how I feel." Jackie smiled at her neighbor, then looked up when a knock sounded at the back door.

Dolly got up and bustled out onto the porch. "Well, look who's here," she exclaimed. "Come on in, both of you. Meet our new neighbor."

Two men came into the kitchen. One was middle-aged, shorter than average and well-built, with curly dark hair and an abdomen that still looked trim and flat under his summer-weight dress slacks. The smaller man was spare and elderly. His bearing seemed rigid, almost military, but there was a foppish look about his impeccable clothing and well-groomed silver hair.

"This is my son Mike," Dolly said, indicating the younger man who sat across the table and favored Jackie with a look of warm admiration tinged with arrogance.

He gave the impression of being the kind of person who wouldn't hesitate to hit on any woman, even one about to give birth in his mother's kitchen. Jackie smiled back at him coldly, then turned to the other man whom Dolly introduced as Gerald Pinson.

The name registered in her mind. She searched her memory, resisting the urge to glance at her notebook.

Gerald Pinson, she recalled at last, was the music teacher from up the block.

Her interest sharpened. Both the newcomers had lived in the neighborhood when Maggie Birk worked at the house across the street and met her untimely death.

"Mike works at the Ford dealership downtown," Dolly said proudly. "He's in the Million Dollar Club."

Again the man grinned at her. Mike Weitzel had good teeth and warmly tanned skin, raying away from his eyes in little creases. He wore a massive diamond-and-onyx ring on his right hand. Jackie tried without success to picture Paul wearing a ring like that.

"And Dolly tells me you're a music teacher," she said to the older man.

"Not anymore. I'm retired," Pinson's voice was mellow and rich, with a lingering trace of a British accent. "I just have a few piano students now, and the luxury of turning away the real dullards."

"I used to take flute lessons," Jackie told him, "but I was pretty much a dullard myself. I never had time to practise. Nowadays I seem to be forgetting most of what I learned."

"Jackie's a policewoman," Dolly told them. "She's a detective."

Neither man looked surprised, and Jackie realized that her occupation was already common knowledge in the neighborhood.

"So, why are you two out running around together?" Dolly asked the men.

"Gerald's shopping for a new car," Mike told his mother. "I brought a new Taurus up and took him out for a spin, then thought we'd drop by for coffee. I didn't know," he added with heavy gallantry, "that you already had such pleasant company."

"Jackie's investigating those old bones they found in her backyard," Dolly went on, "and you'll never guess who it was."

"The remains have been identified?" Pinson asked in his formal manner.

"Not officially," Jackie said, conscious of Mike Weitzel watching her with sudden intensity. "But based on our examination, plus some of the things Dolly's been telling me, I think it's safe to assume it was probably a young woman called Maggie Birk who lived in that house in the late sixties."

Mike's eyes widened, and his jaw dropped. "Maggie?" he said at last, looking from Jackie to his mother.

Gerald Pinson, too, looked shaken by the news. He said nothing, but his hands tightened on the arms of his wooden chair, and Jackie could sense the sudden tension in his body. She made a mental note to speak with Pinson privately as soon as she could arrange an interview.

"Maggie," the younger man repeated, looking dazed. "I can't believe it."

Jackie cast him a covert glance, wondering if he was faking. Something about his shock and confusion seemed oddly contrived.

"Do you remember the girl, Mr. Weitzel?" she asked.

"Call me Mike." He flashed her another smile, clearly working hard to recover his equilibrium. "After all, Jackie, we're practically neighbors, aren't we?"

Car salesmen were trained to call you by your first name, Jackie thought dispassionately. It helped to establish a sense of intimacy, and make their pitch harder to resist.

"Do you remember Maggie Birk?" she asked again.

"Vaguely." He settled back in the chair and glanced nervously at the window.

Jackie watched as Dolly handed cups of coffee to her son and the elderly neighbor. Mike reached for the coffee with his right hand, the one with the heavy gold ring. The diamonds flashed as he broke a packet of artificial sweetener into the cup and stirred it.

"But you didn't know her very well?" Jackie asked.

"Not well. In fact, I barely remember her." As he spoke, he glanced over his left shoulder at the window again.

Jackie watched him, fascinated. In behavioral psychology classes, detectives were taught how to recognize the subtle clues that indicated a witness was lying. One of the most telling was also the simplest. Right-handed people tend to glance to the right when telling the truth and to the left when consciously lying.

When Mike Weitzel denied any clear memory of Maggie Birk, he glanced consistently over his left shoulder.

Interesting, she thought, keeping her face expressionless.

But she had no desire to interview the man here in his mother's kitchen. As soon as possible she would arrange to visit him at his home or place of business, and have a private chat about his memories.

Or lack of them....

"How do you know it's Maggie?" Pinson was asking. "She lived here such a long time ago."

"We don't have a formal ID yet," Jackie repeated. "But the analysis of the skeleton matches the description of Maggie Birk."

"I'll bet Lenny killed her," Weitzel said. His voice sounded husky, as if he still struggled with some kind of powerful emotion. "God, he was a sleazy little bugger. I hated that kid."

"So, you do recall Lenny Cernak," Jackie said. "Even though you don't have much memory of Maggie Birk?"

Weitzel met her yes. "Yeah," he said coldly. "I remember Lenny, all right."

Jackie was conscious of the challenge in the man's voice, and she could sense the kind of aggressive ruthlessness that probably made him such a successful salesman.

"Well, if you don't mind," she said, getting to her feet, "maybe we could have a chat sometime? I'd be interested in more of your impressions about Lenny Cernak and his father."

"Sure," Weitzel said easily, recovering his composure. "Anytime, Jackie. Just give me a call at the office and set up an appointment, okay?"

"I'll do that."

"And while we're at it," he added with strained joviality, "maybe we can fix you up with a new car, too."

"Maybe we can." Jackie met his eyes. They were an odd shade of clear light brown, almost like a cat's, and looked incongruous in his smiling face.

She moved toward the door, putting her notebook away as she went.

"Thanks, Dolly," she said. "I'll be hoping to see you again soon. Goodbye, Mr Pinson," she added. "Would it be all right if I came over and called on you sometime as well, since you lived here when Maggie Birk did?"

"Of course," the older man said stiffly. "I'll look forward to seeing you."

Despite the courtesy of his words, Gerald Pinson looked as if reminiscing about Maggie Birk was the last thing he wanted to do.

Jackie nodded to the silent group around the kitchen table, then let herself out into the yard and headed across the street to her own house. She filled the cat's water dish and settled at her computer for a while to type up her notes and impressions, then called Wardlow to pass on the information.

"Maggie Birk?" he asked. "Would that be short for Margaret?"

"Probably." Jackie spelled the name for him. "So, have you run across Maggie anywhere in your missing-person's files?"

"Not that I can recall," he said. "Doesn't ring any bells."

"Well, I'm pretty sure she's our girl. The neighbor even mentioned her walking with a limp."

"Okay, I'll run the name and see if we come up with anything."

"While you're at it, you should also check on a guy called Alban Cernak." Jackie spelled the employer's name as well. "That was the man who hired Maggie Birk as a housekeeper. He rented this house for a while back in the late sixties."

"Look, Kaminsky," her partner said, "we're probably not going to be able to find a landlord with information on a tenant from thirty years ago. Nobody keeps records that detailed."

"They might turn up some kind of cross-reference somewhere," Jackie said. "Just see what you can find, all right?"

Wardlow sighed. "I'll check as soon as I can," he said. "But I'm not making any promises. We're up to our eyeballs here. I wish you'd have that baby and get back to work."

"Hey, I'm doing my best. Nature can't be hurried, Brian."

"So they tell me."

She twisted the phone cord, thinking. "That reminds me," she said. "My neighbor Dolly Weitzel said she had no idea Maggie Birk was pregnant. Apparently she was a thin woman, small, and if she was carrying a baby, nobody knew about it when she lived across the street. Dolly thought Maggie might have been the kind who carried without showing. Or it could have been early in her pregnancy."

"But the pathologist said the skeleton was a full-term baby."

"I know."

"Kaminsky, what are you saying? It must have

been her baby.'' Wardlow sounded puzzled. ''Because, otherwise, who the hell did it belong to?''

''I'm wondering the same thing,'' Jackie said. ''And you know what, Brian? I intend to find out.''

9

After a sparse evening meal, Jackie tidied the kitchen, then wandered outside with a book and a length of knitting.

Spokane was just a hundred miles south of the Canadian border, and the June days were long and bright. Even now, well after dinner, the sun hung far above the horizon and had only begun to cast lengthening shadows across the grass.

The backyard was flower-scented and murmurous with insect sounds, echoing with bird calls. In the big cottonwood tree near her garage, the robins continued their endless task of carrying insects to the babies in their hidden nest.

For almost an hour Jackie sat in the wicker chair on the back porch, bathed in lassitude. The baby was unmoving for the moment and she held her hands over her abdomen, cradling the heavy mound contentedly.

In John Caldwell's yard beyond the picket fence, a lawn sprinkler oscillated, sending sprays of water into the dying sun. They fell to the grass in slow cascades of broken rainbows.

She rocked and sighed, flooded suddenly with loneliness and an intense yearning for Paul.

It must be the pregnancy making her so vulnerable and clinging. Normally she enjoyed solitude and independence, but nowadays, more all the time, she wanted him near. She even craved the feeling of his strength, the knowledge that somebody was looking after things.

But this feeling was the one that terrified Jackie most of all.

Because if she came to rely on somebody else, what would happen to her security? This safe existence that she'd worked so hard to build, all of it could be snatched away without warning. Her world could vanish into the sunset without a backward glance, and she'd be left alone and crying.

Restlessly, Jackie got up and looked around for the cat. If Shadow would just come and jump onto her lap, lie cozily purring against the lump of her pregnancy, she'd feel so much better.

"Shadow?" she called. "Where are you? Here, kitty. Come and see me."

"He's over here," a voice called.

Jackie walked down into the yard. John Caldwell stood at the fence, holding a pair of pruning shears.

"The cat's on my back steps," he said.

Jackie squinted into the fading sun at Caldwell's little yellow house. She could just make out the dark smudge near the door where Shadow lay sprawled on the warm concrete. He looked drowsy and contented, his sides rising and falling rhythmically.

She felt a stab of jealousy, and a wholly irrational sorrow that brought her almost to the verge of tears.

"Nobody's faithful anymore," she told her neighbor, trying to smile. "That damn cat just goes wherever there's a warm place to sleep."

"Well, he does seem to spend more time at your

place than anywhere else," John said. "If that makes you feel better at all."

Jackie smiled.

For the first time she noticed the gentle sadness of John Caldwell's eyes.

She'd always looked on him as just a pleasant, elderly neighbor, completely bland and unobtrusive. But she was beginning to see him as an individual in his own right and to wonder about his history. Apart from his daughter he seemed to have no family at all, and she'd never seen anybody else visit at the house next door.

Caldwell appeared to sense her thoughts. He gestured with the shears toward the front of his yard where the fence ended.

"Why don't you pop over and have a cup of tea?" he asked. "I made some blueberry coffee cake for dessert tonight, and it's probably still warm."

"Everybody in this neighborhood is always offering me food," Jackie said. "If this keeps up, I'm going to weigh two hundred pounds." She patted her bulging stomach. "And the fat won't go away as easily as this weight is going to, either."

He looked slightly embarrassed, which amused her. Men of John Caldwell's generation didn't like to discuss pregnancy or childbirth, even with a woman who looked, as Dolly Weitzel had said, "big as a house."

She plodded to the end of the fence and crossed over into his yard, gazing around with pleasure.

"This place is a paradise, John," she said enviously. "Look at those shrubs and flowers! And your grass is like green velvet."

"Well, I have nothing else to do," the man told

her with a self-deprecating smile. "The yard work keeps me busy."

He went to a metal shed by the opposite fence to put away his pruning shears. Jackie stood near the steps and glared at the cat.

"You rotten two-timing son of a gun," she muttered. "I hope you're ashamed."

Shadow rolled over onto his back and waved his paws at her with an imploring look.

"No way," Jackie said. "Find someone else to rub your tummy, dammit."

He arched his back against the concrete and writhed luxuriously. Jackie chuckled and relented, bending to scratch his belly, then followed John Caldwell into the house.

It seemed to be about the same age as her own, probably dating back to the years between the two world wars when workmanship was still good but building materials were at a premium.

Caldwell's house, though, had an unadorned bachelor look. The interior was serviceable and clean but austere, almost melancholy. The only decoration came from framed Scripture texts hung on the walls, and a well-worn Bible lay open on one of the kitchen counters.

Apparently, John Caldwell favored the same reading material both indoors and out.

Jackie compared the bare walls and countertops with the gracious restoration of the Betker house, or the warm cheer of Dolly Weitzel's kitchen with its welter of Holstein cows.

Again she felt a tug of sympathy for her elderly neighbor.

"What kind of job did you do when you were

working, John?'' she asked, lowering her bulk into one of the vinyl chairs.

''I was a manager at K-Mart, retired just over four years ago.''

''Did you like working there?''

''It was a job,'' he said briefly, switching the heat on under a painted metal teakettle on the stove. ''I can't say I miss it.''

''I really like my job.'' Jackie shook her head when he took the foil wrapper from a glass baking dish on the counter. ''No cake for me, thanks,'' she said. ''I've been eating all day.''

His pink face registered mild distress. ''Are you sure?''

''I'm certain.'' Jackie smiled. ''Help yourself, but I'd prefer just a cup of tea.''

''What sort of police work do you do?'' he asked, sitting down opposite her.

''I'm a detective.''

''I believe Lola told me that, come to think of it. You'd be in plain clothes, then?''

''Yes, I am. But I was put on desk duties as soon as my pregnancy started to show. I haven't actually worked on a case for a long time. Except for this one in my own backyard,'' she added, waving a hand in the general direction of her house.

''So, have you found out any more about those old bones?''

Jackie hesitated, then decided not to mention the baby's skeleton. None of the neighbors had been told that detail as yet, except for Eleanor Betker, who seemed to have little communication with those who lived nearby. Jackie thought it might be a useful bit of information to keep to herself.

"We think the dead woman was a young house-keeper named Maggie Birk who lived in the neighborhood for a short time about thirty years ago."

He shook his head and got up to measure tea leaves into a ceramic pot. "Before my time, I'm afraid. The Gottfriedsons were already living in that house when I moved here, and I wasn't aware they ever had a housekeeper."

"No, Maggie worked for a man named Alban Cernak. He was a tenant in the house sometime before the Gottfriedsons bought it. We haven't established who it belonged to at that time."

He frowned, his pleasant face puckering with concentration, then shook his head. "Cernak? That doesn't ring any bells either. I don't believe I've ever heard the name mentioned."

"Dolly Weitzel seems to remember him quite well. Cernak had a teenage son who was apparently quite a nasty kind of boy."

Jackie watched idly while John poured boiling water into the teapot.

"Well, if Dolly didn't like him, that boy must have been really awful," John said, rummaging in an upper cabinet. "She's the sweetest, most generous person I've ever met."

"Do you know her son very well?" Jackie asked.

"Which one? Dolly has three sons."

"Mike, the car salesman."

Her neighbor grinned, and again Jackie noticed the unnatural evenness of his dentures. "That man's a real salesman, all right," he said. "Mike Weitzel keeps trying to sell cars to the whole neighborhood, and most of the time he's successful, too."

"I wouldn't doubt it. He seems pretty aggressive."

Jackie smiled her thanks when John gave her a flowered cup with an air of shy pride. The china was thin and delicate, obviously a prized possession. With a small flourish, he put matching sugar bowl and cream jug on the table.

"Oh, Mike Weitzel's aggressive, all right," he said. "I didn't know him as well as the younger two Weitzel boys because he'd already left home when I moved in here, but I seem to recall him being in some kind of trouble around that time."

"Really?" Jackie looked up with sudden interest. "What kind of trouble?"

He looked distressed. "I'm not sure. It was something that involved the police, but I don't like to repeat gossip."

"John," she said gently, "I *am* the police. I can look up this kind of information anytime I like, so you might as well tell me what you remember."

"It was some kind of assault," her neighbor said with obvious reluctance. "There was a young woman who was badly hurt, and I believe Klaus and Dolly had to pay their lawyer quite a lot to keep Mike out of prison. But I don't remember any details."

"I'll have to check it out," Jackie said thoughtfully. "Thank you, John."

He filled her cup and his own, then set the teapot on an embroidered pad in the center of the table.

"Do you know anything about Gerald Pinson?" Jackie asked. "The music teacher?"

"What about him?"

"Does he have any family?"

"Gerald's lived here a long time," Caldwell said. "And he's always lived alone, as far as I know. There's never been…anybody in his life since I've been here, at least."

Jackie noticed the sudden hesitation in the man's voice, but decided not to press for details until she'd had a chance to interview Gerald Pinson and watch his reactions.

"So, John, do you know of anybody besides the Weitzels, the Betkers and Mr. Pinson who's been here longer than you?" she asked. "Somebody who could have lived nearby when Maggie Birk was next door?"

The old man frowned and sipped his tea. "Most of them were elderly people when I moved in." He gave Jackie a wry, apologetic smile. "We've had a lot of funerals on this block over the past twenty-five years."

She nodded, again feeling a little sad. The quick passage of time, the speed with which a life passed by, was becoming more evident to her all the time, especially since her pregnancy. She pushed the feelings aside and forced herself to concentrate.

"It just occurred to me," she said, "that whoever lived in this house before you did…would have been next-door neighbors to Maggie Birk, just like the Betkers were, right?"

"Well, I suppose so," he said slowly. "Yes, of course they would have been."

"Did you happen to save any of the real estate papers? Do you know who the previous owners of your house were?"

"You know, it's not a very pleasant story," he said. "They were an older couple. Their electric power went off during an ice storm, so apparently they moved to the cellar and tried to heat the place with a gas camp stove. Other family members found them after the streets were opened again."

"Carbon monoxide poisoning?" Jackie asked.

"I'm afraid so."

She shook her head. "God, those poor people. We see that kind of thing all the time, in spite of the warnings and educational programs."

"Anyhow, I bought the house from the estate," John said. "It wasn't a big place, but my wife was dead and Lola had gone off to college by then, so I didn't see the need for anything bigger. And when I worked in the downtown K-Mart, most mornings I could walk to work."

"That's over two miles each way."

He smiled, looking more than ever like an elderly cherub. "I know, but I've always liked walking."

Jackie finished her tea and got up. "Well, I'd better head for home. Thanks for the tea, John. I'd been feeling kind of lonely," she told him, "and it was nice to chat with you."

"Drop by anytime. I'm really looking forward to seeing the...the baby," he added, his face turning bright pink, as if the mention of an unborn child was some kind of social gaffe.

Jackie laughed. "You'll be one of the baby's very first guests, John."

On the back step she paused and looked down at the drowsy cat, then at her host.

"Take him," John said in answer to the unspoken question. "By all means, take him with you. I don't even like to let him inside the house because he leaves cat hair all over. But if he stays outside, he'll get into a fight or start howling on the fence in the middle of the night.''

"Either way it'll be noisy.'' Jackie bent awkwardly and scooped the cat up. He draped himself over her arms, limp and boneless, with his paws hanging and his eyes half closed.

She laughed, feeling her spirits lift. "What a character,'' she muttered. "I never saw a cat like this in my whole life.''

"He's a strange fellow, all right.''

John stood on the back step waving as they left, his plump body silhouetted in the lighted rectangle of the door. Jackie thought of his bare, colorless kitchen, and wondered why Lola Bridges didn't do a little more to brighten her father's life. She could at least put up some pretty curtains, or buy a few things to hang on the walls and spruce up the counters.

"Poor John, his house isn't cozy like our place, Shadow,'' she muttered to the cat, letting herself in through her back door.

Already the small white house had a warm, welcoming feel. Jackie loved having all her belongings under one roof, with furniture drawn close to the fireplace and treasures displayed on the oak plate rails encircling the living room.

She switched on the gas fire and settled in one of the big chairs. Outside her window, the leaves of the mountain ash rustled and shifted against the glass like a chorus of soothing whispers.

"I love this place, Shadow,'' Jackie told the cat. She held her hands around his chest while his thin body dangled, and stared into his drowsy eyes. "I'm happy to be living here. And I have no problem at all with being alone as long as you'll make an effort to stay with me sometimes, okay?''

She shook him gently, eliciting nothing more than a bored yawn and a blink of annoyance.

Reluctantly, Jackie set the cat down and climbed the stairs to her bedroom, pleased to note that he'd decided to follow her.

She had a shower and got ready for bed, even hauled out her packed suitcase and checked it, conscious of the fact that labor could overtake her in the night, so everything had to be prepared.

Jackie woke to a beautiful morning with sunlight lying across her bed like a golden coverlet. Birds sang in the trees outside, sounding crazed with happiness.

Shadow sat on a small table in front of the window, watching the birds with rigid intensity. His only movement was an occasional lift and flick of the extreme end of his tail. Whenever a bird ventured near the glass, he emitted a low rumble of excitement, but kept his body perfectly still.

Jackie laughed and climbed out of bed, pressing a hand automatically into the small of her back as she stood erect.

"You quit looking at those poor little birdies," she scolded. "I give you Fancy Feast every time you visit. Isn't that enough for you?"

She joined him at the window to peer outside. It looked like a glorious June day, already warm though the sun was still behind the big trees in the Betker yard to the east.

Dolly Weitzel was outside edging her flower beds, wearing a comical pair of blue jeans that looked as

wide as they were long. Mike Weitzel appeared with
a wheelbarrow to carry off the lumps of sod, also
casually dressed in Bermuda shorts and an old Mar-
iners T-shirt. The man seemed more attractive than
he had in his costly, stylish work clothes. When he
paused to say something to his mother, Dolly threw
her gray head back and laughed, a peal of merriment
that Jackie could hear all the way up in her bedroom.

Eleanor Betker was outside as well, reading the
newspaper on her pillared veranda. She wore a dark
green velour jogging suit with a quilted jacket instead of the mannish denim overalls, and looked surprisingly elegant. Little Emma was barely visible in
the chair next to her sister. The smaller woman had
a selection of Barbie dolls arranged on a wrought-
iron table. She was happily dressing them in tiny
outfits, then holding each one up for her sister's approval.

On Jackie's other side, John Caldwell was out fer-
tilizing his lawn. He struggled with a rusted metal
cart that seemed to have a wobbly wheel and re-
quired constant unclogging. Jackie thought about the
beautiful, free-flowing machine invented and built
by Eleanor Betker, and wondered if she had enough
courage to ask Eleanor to loan her fertilizer cart to
the opposite neighbor.

"I've just moved in," she told the cat, "and I'm
already meddling in their lives. But somebody's got
to, kiddo. What a group. They've all lived here for
decades and barely know one another."

She went to the closet and brooded over its contents. By now, Jackie was sick of every maternity
garment she owned, though it had been such fun

when she'd first purchased and started wearing them.

She selected a pair of red shorts and a baggy white top.

"Adrienne hated all her maternity things, too," she told the cat. "Maybe we'll have a bonfire after my baby comes. It can be out here in my backyard," she went on, warming to the idea. "And we'll dance around and scream, and get rid of all our frustrations along with these ratty old outfits."

She brightened at the idea, but her smile faded when she thought of poor Adrienne who still suffered so deeply from postpartum depression. It was a hard time for that whole family.

Jackie decided to call her friend today and see if Harlan and Alex could baby-sit for a few hours while she took Adrienne out somewhere. They'd have a chance to talk privately, away from everybody else.

She hurried downstairs and brewed a pot of tea, then warmed a bagel in the microwave. When she got up to pour the tea she felt dizzy, a little unsteady on her feet, and the twinge in the small of her back was actually painful.

"Hey," she said in sudden excitement, looking at Shadow, who had followed her downstairs and now sat expectantly near his feeding dish. "Maybe this is going to be it, little kitty."

Jackie opened a tin of cat food and bent awkwardly to fill the dish. He moved over to sniff the food daintily, then began to eat while she crouched nearby to watch.

When she finally stood erect, she didn't feel anything in particular, just a bit of light-headedness and a sense of pressure in her abdomen. From outside she heard a familiar clatter as the young mail-delivery woman leaped up the veranda steps, clanked the lid of the mailbox and loped away, whistling.

Jackie went out onto the veranda and opened her mailbox to take out the bundle of letters. She paged through them rapidly.

Bills, circular, a magazine, more bills, something from the police department regarding maternity pay, but no letter from Gram.

Her grandmother had been in a snit for months, apparently annoyed that Jackie was having a baby without a father.

"Disgracing us all," she'd complained, as if a fatherless baby was far more shameful than having several of the younger cousins in jail on drug charges and assorted other felonies.

Jackie dismissed the old woman's complaints as narrow-minded and hurtful, but it still worried her when Gram stayed out of contact for too long.

She opened the mailbox again, peering inside to see if a letter had escaped the bundle of mail, and was gratified to see a white envelope lying on the metal bottom.

Jackie lifted it out and looked at it cautiously.

No postmark, no stamp, no return address. Merely the words, "Detective J. Kaminsky" in computer print on the front of a long white envelope which was unsealed.

She studied the envelope, holding it between two fingernails, and wondered if she should send it to the downtown office for scanning. But with a letter bomb, it was usually the act of unsealing that triggered the explosive device.

Carrying the rest of her mail, she took the letter inside and held it against a window. There was nothing in the envelope but a single folded piece of white paper containing a few lines of print.

"Paranoid," she muttered to the cat, who appeared in the doorway and watched her with unblinking eyes. "Totally paranoid. It's probably an invitation to some kind of neighborhood function. Maybe they have block parties here."

Holding her breath, she eased the flap open and extracted the folded piece of paper, trying not to touch it with her fingertips.

The paper unfolded and she read the lines of print which had also been generated on a computer laser printer and thus would be impossible to trace.

Detective Kaminsky, stop snooping into things that are none of your business or you will pay a great price. Maybe you'll even lose your baby. Somebody else lost her baby, you know. It was buried in your backyard along with Maggie Birk. I'm the one who killed both of them, and I enjoyed doing it. I wouldn't mind killing another baby. So back off, or you'll be very, very sorry.

The letter was signed, incongruously, "A friend." Most chilling of all was the postscript.

If you don't believe me, Jackie, check those skeletons again. I cut off one of the baby's fingers for a little souvenir. I still have it, you know.

Jackie dropped the paper on the table and felt herself swaying dizzily. An agonizing pain clamped into the small of her back. She moaned and grabbed the door frame to keep from falling.

The pain seemed to crawl through her body to the place where the baby lay. It tightened and pressed until she was unable to move, could hardly even breathe.

Finally, after what seemed like an eternity, the contraction eased. She put the letter carefully back in its envelope, using a paper napkin to handle and fold it in the unlikely event the sender had been careless enough to leave any fingerprints. After some panicky thought, she found a place at the back of an upper cabinet to hide the horrible thing, behind a row of spice jars.

But she could sense that another pain would be arriving soon, and she couldn't think any longer about letters or killers or anything else. Her only concern right now was this terrifying miracle that gripped her body, and the need to get hold of Paul as soon as possible.

10

The June warmth spread across the prairie like a blessing. Sunshine glimmered on the placid sloughs where waterfowl nested, and warmed the carpet of new grass. Buffalo beans were in flower, carpeting the hills and coulees with acres of yellow blooms. Both cattle and deer had newborns at foot, awkward and bouncy on their long slender legs.

Paul Arnussen was still building corrals. It was early morning and he worked outside digging postholes, wearing jeans and an old denim shirt that strained taut across his shoulders.

Over previous days he'd measured and laid out the proportions of his corral, marking the location for each post, then dug the holes with an auger mounted on his tractor. Now he cleaned the holes by hand and set the heavy posts in place, shoveled dirt around them and tamped them into position.

Normally he loved a job like this, something careful and precise where the finished product was serviceable and practical, but still reflected a man's good workmanship.

Today, though, all he could think about was Jackie.

As long as he could remember, Paul had hated his occasional flashes of psychic insight, and dismissed them whenever he could as the product of too much solitude and an overactive imagination.

But this morning he'd wakened thinking of her, and now he couldn't seem to get her out of his mind. He heard her laughter on the morning wind, saw her dark eyes in the centers of the wild sunflowers all around him, felt her warmth in the sun on his back.

The woman was so damn frustrating, he could hardly stand it.

All his life Paul had occupied a world where a man's value was measured by the things he built, the place he created and controlled with his two hands. Any man worth his salt could go out and make things happen.

But then he was struck down by a woman like Jackie Kaminsky, and all he could do was wait for her.

He tamped dirt around a post with unnecessary force, then straightened and looked at the young Border collie lying on a patch of grass nearby.

"It's hell, Montana," he said aloud to the dog. "Dealing with women is pure hell."

The crossbred collie lifted his head alertly when he heard his name, then settled back with his chin on his paws.

Montana had a thin, clever face, black with a white blaze running from his forehead to the tip of his nose, and one yellow eye and one blue one. The off-colored eyes gave him a fey, almost silly look, but he was a good dog with a wonderful cattle sense.

Paul paused to lift his cap and run a hand through his hair, smiling at the dog. Then he bent to work again, still thinking about Jackie.

He could hardly bear the fact that she was having

his child but still chose to live apart from him in a place of her own. Nowadays it took all his self-discipline not to start pressing her for a commitment again.

But he'd made that mistake in the past and almost lost her as a result. Remembering the pain of their separation, he grimaced and plied the handle on the digger with renewed energy.

She'd won, of course. He couldn't live without her and she knew it, so Jackie had the power to call the shots. Still, he'd resented her at first for her decision, and had maintained an emotional distance from her for most of the pregnancy.

When she bought the house, that had been the worst hurt of all. Paul had seen it as a rejection of him and his plans for a life together, an announcement on her part that she would never share her future with him, that he was doomed to be only a weekend father.

She thought he wanted that. No matter what he said, on some level, Jackie was convinced he wanted his solitude and the right to see her and the baby when it suited him. She was afraid they'd break apart if she ever moved out to the ranch.

"Shit," he muttered aloud.

At the sound of his master's voice Montana heaved himself upright and trotted over to lick Paul's hand, his tail drooping, then raced off toward the barn on some mysterious errand of his own.

In a way, Paul had to admit that Jackie had been right in her assessment, at least in the past. Part of him had been almost as terrified of commitment as she was, even though this was the only woman he could ever love and he'd always known it—since the first time he met her.

He grinned briefly, remembering the day he'd been working on a carpentry project in the city. She'd come walking across the grass to interview him as a suspect in a case she was investigating.

As soon as he laid eyes on her, he'd fallen like a ton of bricks. There was something so appealing about her tall limber body, her coppery skin, her steady dark gaze and touching air of fearlessness, all concealing a childlike vulnerability that made him want to take her in his arms and keep anybody from ever hurting her again.

But winning a woman like Jackie Kaminsky was no easy task. Paul had been sleeping with her for almost two years, they were totally sexually committed to each other and she was about to bear him a child, but sometimes he felt they were no closer to a permanent relationship than they'd ever been.

He watched the dog who came trotting back, tongue lolling, his head dropped brightly to one side.

Jackie was going to need a lot of time. She'd been through so much hell in her life.

He lifted a heavy corner post and carried it to the hole, dropping it in place with a thud, then used his level to line it up straight while he shoveled dirt carefully around it.

Ever since Jackie decided to buy the house, this had been Paul's new strategy.

He'd resolved to take it slow, not push at all, let her come around gradually to trusting and needing him, especially after the baby was born and she realized how much she wanted a father nearby to help with the responsibility.

His plan was to make himself available without blame or censure, to let Jackie call the tune, and not complain when she did. It was easier for him to do, now that he was gradually coming to understand the depths of her fear, and the damage that had been done to her by her harsh lonely childhood.

As his love grew stronger and more tender, so did his ability to hold impatience in check and allow his lover to come to him on her own terms.

But sometimes, when he caught a passing glimpse of her smile, remembered the scent of her hair or the curve of her breast, he felt a longing so intense that it left him feeling hollow and shaken.

"I'm a mess," he said ruefully to his dog. "Just a goddamn mess."

He stopped abruptly and stood erect, staring into the clouds massed along the horizon. His eyes narrowed and his face grew hard with concentration.

All at once he could hear her voice as clearly as the scraps of meadowlark song in the field nearby and the distant bellowing of the bulls. She was afraid and in pain, calling to him.

A few moments later, the beeper sounded at his belt. He cast aside the posthole digger and ran toward the house, with Montana loping at his heels. As soon as he let himself into the kitchen, Paul saw the message light blinking on the telephone.

Jackie lay in the hospital bed, her dark hair tousled on the pillow and her face drawn with anguish.

Paul bent closer and offered his hand. She squeezed so tightly that his fingers ached.

"Any other woman would scream," he mur-

mured. "Come on, Jackie. Yell a little. Be human
for a change."

Her face contorted and sweat glistened on her
cheeks. "Shut the hell up, Arnussen."

He chuckled, then wrung out a cloth in a basin of
cold water and placed it on her forehead. "Next
you'll be cursing me for doing this to you. The
woman in that other bed was swearing at her husband right until they wheeled her into the delivery
room."

"As if she had nothing at all to do with it," Jackie
said through gritted teeth. "I hate it when people
don't take responsibility for their own lives."

He removed the cloth and touched her cheek.
"That's my girl. Has the pain gone away?"

"For a minute or two." She gazed up at him.
"It's awful, Paul. Being shot in the guts was a picnic
compared to this."

"What does it feel like?"

He could see her struggling for an explanation. "I
guess it's sort of…like being in a red-hot vise. It
clamps down harder and harder, and all the time
while it's squeezing, the pain keeps twisting and
tearing at you. The worst thing of all is that I keep
being afraid I won't be able to stand the next one."

"If you can't stand it," he said calmly, "we'll
ask for the epidural."

"Like hell we will. I'm not having my baby
drugged just so I don't have to deal with a bit of
pain."

"Sweetheart," he pleaded, bending close to her,
"the epidural is standard procedure. They wouldn't
do it if there was any danger to the baby."

"I grew up in south L.A.," she said. "I've seen

too much of what drugs can do to people. Nobody's giving any drugs to my baby. Not even if I—''

Her face contorted and she arched in agony, then rolled up and whimpered in the pillow, clutching at his hand again.

"Jackie Kaminsky," he whispered, bending to draw her hair away from her ear. "You are the most stubborn woman in the world."

She shook her head in despair and he stopped talking, feeling helpless and worried. At last he stood by the bed, awkward in his denim clothes and work boots, stroking her suffering body and trying to let her feel, through his hands alone, the depths of his love and concern.

Endless hours later, as night approached and darkness gathered on the lawns beyond the hospital, they came to transfer her onto a gurney and wheel her into the delivery room.

Paul and Jackie had long since agreed that he wouldn't attend the delivery. He understood that she had a fastidious reluctance to be seen in such a state of helplessness, especially by him. Her childhood demons wouldn't allow her to show that degree of weakness. She wanted Paul to see her only when the baby had been safely delivered and she was back in control again.

Though disappointed, he yielded without argument, knowing how important it was to her. She was the one who had to endure the pain, and she had every right to do it in her own way.

Maybe he'd be allowed to watch the next one, he thought wistfully, sitting in the waiting room and paging through stacks of magazines without seeing them.

He got up and prowled around the room, then wandered down the hall to get himself a cup of luke-warm coffee from a vending machine. After a moment's thought, he punched in more coins and got a couple of chocolate bars as well, not even realizing how famished he was until he started eating them.

Paul made his way back to the waiting room, looking for a passing doctor or nurse he could buttonhole and question.

But hardly anybody was around, and the few medical personnel who strode down the hallways seemed intent on their own business. He sprawled in a vinyl couch and sipped dispiritedly at the cup of coffee.

So many things could go wrong...

But he couldn't bear to think about it. Instead, he pictured Jackie's face, her warm dark eyes and flashing smile, her touching air of cockiness and the look of shy radiance she always had when she reached sexual climax. His heart ached with love.

"Mr. Arnussen?"

He jerked erect and set the cup on a side table. A nurse in operating scrubs smiled down at him, her mask dangling around her neck.

"You can come and visit now for a few minutes, if you like."

Feeling dazed, he got up and followed the woman down the hall. At the entrance to the delivery room they met a couple of other nurses wheeling a small metal basket on wheels.

Only when they drew abreast and stopped did he realize the cot contained a baby.

"Mr. Arnussen?" one of them said. "This is your son. We're just taking him to the nursery for a bath. He's a lovely big boy."

"A boy?"

Their smiling faces danced and blurred in front of him. He held his breath and edged nearer, looking into the basket.

The baby lay there scowling, his face screwed up in comical intensity. He had a lot of thick dark hair, still streaked with dampness. While Paul watched, the infant lifted a wrinkled hand, palm out, and held it awkwardly against his cheek, then sneezed.

At the sound of that tiny sneeze, Paul was utterly lost.

"Well, hi there," he whispered, bending over the cot with tears stinging in his eyes. "Hello there, Son. How are you?"

He touched the little hand and the baby's fingers closed around his, holding tight. The face was a blend of Jackie's and his own. Even in that newborn plumpness, Paul could already make out high blunt cheekbones like his, and the same square jaw and wide-set eyes that gave such appeal to Jackie's appearance.

"What color are his eyes?" he asked one of the nurses who waited patiently nearby.

"All babies' eyes are sort of dark blue at first," she said. "But this little fellow will likely have dark eyes. Isn't he a beauty? He weighs just over nine pounds and he's twenty-three inches long."

"You're a big boy," Paul told his son, shaking the finger gently, loving the feel of the tiny hand gripping his own. "Poor Mom, no wonder she had such a hard time with you."

"Mr. Arnussen, we have to take him now," the nurse murmured apologetically. "You can see him again in a half hour or so. We'll be bringing him back to his mother's room after his bath."

Paul nodded and stood to watch as they wheeled the cart away.

"Can I see Jackie now?" he asked the nurse who'd come to fetch him.

"She's still here in the delivery room," the nurse said. "I suppose nobody would mind very much if you popped in for a couple of minutes."

He stepped gingerly through the swinging metal doors and saw Jackie lying on a tall cot near the door, her black hair a vivid splash of color in all that bright sterility. Behind her a team of nursing assistants worked under the lights in the centre of the room, cleaning up the delivery table and preparing the room for its next occupant.

Paul approached the cot and stared at her with hungry anxiety. Her face was so pale that a few unfamiliar freckles stood out in sharp relief on the bridge of her nose, and her eyes were enormous. The tousled dark hair was drenched with perspiration.

"You're so beautiful, sweetheart," he told her huskily, bending to kiss her. "Just so beautiful."

"Did you see him, Paul?"

He nodded, stroking the damp hair back from her forehead. "They had him in a little bed out in the hallway when I came in."

"Isn't he wonderful?" she asked with a drowsy smile. "Did you ever see anything so wonderful in all your life?"

"No," he told her. "I never did."

"He's got so much hair," she marveled. "And

all those perfect little fingers and toes, and big shoulders just like yours.''

"When I was looking at him, he screwed up his face and sneezed. Jackie, it was so cute."

"Oh, Paul." She gazed up at him, tears glistening in her eyes. "It's scary to love someone so much," she whispered.

"I know."

"Tell me I don't have to be afraid," she pleaded.

He understood what she was asking, and stroked her face gently. "Life has no guarantees, sweetheart," he told her. "We can only do our best to protect him, and trust that it's going to be enough."

"I didn't know it would be this way," she murmured. "I never dreamed I could feel like this."

His heart lifted with happiness and a warm surge of hope.

That tiny boy in the metal bassinet had already done what life had been unable to do for more than three decades. The child had penetrated the emotional armor that Jackie Kaminsky had built around herself, making her vulnerable to pain and love.

Paul stepped aside reluctantly when the nurse came to wheel Jackie's bed out of the delivery room.

"You can see her again in a few minutes," the nurse told him, "as soon as we get her settled in her room. And your baby will be there, too."

Paul went back to the waiting room like a man walking on air. For the first time he noticed what a nice hospital it was, so bright and cheerful, filled with smiling people who seemed to share his joy.

He'd brought a pocketful of quarters and he spent some time calling Harlan and Adrienne, Brian

Wardlow, the sergeant, even Jackie's grandmother in Los Angeles.

Far from the joy their friends expressed, the old woman sounded querulous and annoyed at being disturbed so late in the evening.

After the phone calls, he was too restless to sit and wait on the couch, so he roamed up and down the halls for half an hour until the nurse came to get him and take him to a room on the maternity ward.

Jackie was there alone, her hair combed. She wore a fresh pink hospital gown and reclined against a bank of pillows. Already her face had regained some of its color and she looked tranquil and joyous.

"Women are amazing," he said humbly, bending to kiss her. "Truly amazing."

A nurse wheeled in a bassinet. Jackie watched hungrily as the woman lifted a blue-wrapped bundle and carried it to the bed.

"Here's your little man," the nurse said, handing the baby to Jackie. "He'll be spending the night in here with you, but we'll be close by to help if there are any problems."

"Oh, Paul," Jackie breathed, gazing down at the small face in the blue wrappings. "Look at him. Isn't he marvelous?"

He moved his chair nearer. She held out the wrapped bundle, smiling.

"Are you sure?" he asked.

"I'll have lots of chances to hold him," she said when he hesitated. "Go ahead, take him."

Gingerly, Paul lifted the baby into his arms and laughed softy at the precious, substantial feel of him.

"What a big boy," he told Jackie. "Can you believe a few hours ago you were still carrying all this around inside you?''

''It's truly a miracle. Paul, it's the most awesome thing.'' She watched as he settled back in the chair again, still holding the baby. ''Did you call everybody?''

He nodded. ''Lew Michelson was out at his son's baseball banquet, but his wife said congratulations and that she'd pass on the message. Wardlow and Adrienne both said they'd stop by tomorrow to visit. And,'' he added after a brief, awkward pause, ''your grandmother sends congratulations, too.''

''Did she actually say that?'' Jackie gave him a quick, intent glance.

''Not really.'' Paul held his son close to him and kissed the warm, rounded cheek. ''She said it was about time, and maybe if you cared enough about your own family, you'd bring the baby down for a visit sometime.''

''What a mean old woman she is,'' Jackie muttered, but he could see the pain in her eyes. Mentally he cursed the unkind, self-absorbed old harridan who still had so much power to hurt, even after all these years.

''Can I see the rest of the baby?'' he asked to distract her.

''Of course,'' she said. ''I want to look at him again, too, now that we've got him to ourselves. Put him down here beside me.''

He placed the little bundle next to her on the bed and watched as she leaned over to unwrap the swaddling blanket, like someone opening a precious gift.

Her black hair fell around her face and the tenderness in her hands was so moving that he felt tears burning behind his eyelids again.

"Oh, look," she whispered, stroking the baby's little body. "Look at him, Paul."

He leaned closer, awed by the miniature perfection of his son, the broad square shoulders and long legs, the curling toes and delicate fingers with their nails like tiny pink shells.

"You did a great job, sweetheart," he said huskily, kissing her again. "You made a beautiful baby."

The little mite began to fuss, screwing his face up and turning an alarming shade of bright pink. His hands clenched and his whole body strained with effort. Jackie laughed and wrapped him in the blankets again, then lifted him in her arms and crooned softly, rocking him until he settled.

Paul watched, his heart aching with love. "Adrienne asked about the name," he ventured at last. "Have you made any decisions?"

Months ago they'd discussed names for boys and girls but Paul had told her the final choice would be hers. Afterward, they said nothing more about it. As far as he knew, she hadn't settled on a name for this child.

But now she surprised him by nodding while she smiled dreamily at the baby in her arms. "I knew as soon as I looked at him what his name was going to be," she murmured. "It's Daniel."

"Daniel," Paul said, trying out the sound. "I like that."

She looked up and met his eyes directly. "Daniel Paul Arnussen. That's his name."

His jaw dropped in astonishment. "Arnussen? You're giving him my name?"

"Why not?" Jackie said calmly. "He's your son."

A wondering joy welled up in him, an emotion so intense that he couldn't speak for a moment. He felt hope, and gratitude to the tired woman in the bed, and above all, a vast, all-encompassing love for her and the blue-wrapped bundle in her arms.

11

Jackie woke in the pale light of dawn, dragged back to consciousness by an unfamiliar sound. She blinked in confusion, wondering where she was. Her body felt sore and hollow, and her breasts throbbed with an unfamiliar pain. Dazed, she touched her abdomen and found the rounded bulk had vanished, replaced by a strange, pulpy flatness that alarmed her.

Then, gradually, she remembered the events of the day before.

Her baby had arrived. He was a healthy boy, the most beautiful child that ever existed.

She smiled and realized the sound was the baby fussing nearby. A nurse stood at the bassinet in the dim light, tending to him, murmuring softly.

"I'm awake now," Jackie said. "Does he need to be fed again?"

"Oh yes, I think he's probably getting hungry by now," the nurse said, lifting him in her arms. "This is a big boy. He's probably ready to chow down on some steak and potatoes."

Jackie laughed and heaved herself upright against the pillows, fumbling with the front of her hospital gown and the flaps on the nursing bra.

"Well, I can't offer any steak at the moment,"

she said. "So he'll just have to be happy with what's on the menu."

The nurse switched on a bedside lamp and Jackie took the baby in her arms, smiling down at him. Already he had a dear, familiar look, an expression uniquely his own. She would have been able to pick him unerringly from among a thousand newborns.

"Hello, Daniel," she murmured. "Good morning, little Danny. How are you?"

He turned pink with indignation and began to howl, flailing his arms. Jackie laughed again and put him to her breast, holding the nipple for him. He rooted around in rising panic, then fastened suddenly on her nipple and began to nurse with lusty energy.

She felt the hardness of her breasts subside with the flow of milk, and then a sense of peace and contentment.

"He's doing so well," the nurse said approvingly. "Look at him. What a boy."

Jackie smiled. "I was so afraid of this," she said. "But it's not hard at all. You just do what comes naturally."

"Of course you do," the nurse said calmly, moving toward the door. "Let him nurse for five or ten minutes on the right breast, then transfer him over if he's still hungry. Next time, we'll remember to start him on the left breast."

She went out, walking softly on her rubber-soled shoes, and left Jackie alone with the baby. He continued to nurse, eyes closed in bliss. His small mouth worked rhythmically, and his hands opened and folded like soft flower petals.

Jackie watched him, thinking about her life and

all the strange, tumultuous events that had brought her to this moment.

That poverty-stricken childhood, filled with neglect, and her troubled adolescence, her early years in the violence of the LAPD and then her struggles to advance within the ranks of the Spokane department...all of it was strangely dreamlike now.

In retrospect it seemed the only purpose of everything had been to bring her to this moment, here in the pearl-grey radiance of sunrise, holding this newborn child in her arms.

And to Paul...

She smiled, remembering his tender patience during her long hours of labor, and the look on his face when he examined his son for the first time and heard that she was giving the child his name.

"Your daddy loves us," she whispered to the baby. "He really does."

Briefly she allowed herself to think again of her own infancy and childhood, and the parents who'd abandoned her so carelessly.

Her mother had been nineteen when Jackie was born, and had left the baby with her own mother soon afterward. The girl had been pulled back irresistibly to her life of squalor and drug abuse, and had died of an overdose before Jackie's second birthday.

Jackie's father had never been on the scene. He disappeared before her birth, and she hadn't even been told who he was.

All her life Jackie had accepted these stark facts as the reality of her existence, and forbidden herself to dwell on them. But now, holding her child in her arms, remembering Paul's love and devotion, she wondered how anybody could walk away from a newborn.

What kind of people had they been?

"Nobody will ever leave you alone and scared," she told her baby in a fierce whisper. "Not as long as I have breath in my body."

He stopped nursing and fell asleep, a bit of milk dribbling down his chin. Jackie wiped it away tenderly with a tissue, then jiggled him a little. He roused and began to feed again with renewed energy.

"I love you," she told him, not even realizing she was crying until the tears began to roll down her cheeks and onto the blankets that enfolded him. "Darling little baby, I love you."

The day passed in a bewildering whirl of baby feedings, diapering instructions, meals and naps. By late afternoon she felt as if she'd been in the hospital forever, and she still had so much to learn.

How to care for the baby's bottom and the raw stump of the umbilicus, how to regulate his nursing, what kind of foods she was allowed to eat and which would be bad for the baby…

"I love it," she told Wardlow, who arrived at the end of his shift and stood by the bassinet to examine the new arrival. "It's all so much fun, Brian. And isn't he just beautiful?"

"He's a cute kid, all right." Wardlow studied the baby critically. "Lots of times newborns are just plain ugly, but this is a good-looking little guy."

"I think he looks like Paul."

Wardlow peered into the bassinet again, frowning.

"Maybe a little. But he's a lot like you, too, Kaminsky. He's already got that dogged look."

"Dogged?"

Wardlow grinned. "I'm betting this kid will be no picnic to raise. He looks stubborn as hell, just like his mommy."

She smiled back. "Brian, I'm a sweetheart, and you know it."

"Yeah," he scoffed, sprawling in a chair by the window. "Sure you are."

A nurse came in, carrying a stack of tiny disposable diapers, which she placed on a rack under the bassinet. Wardlow watched her leave, then glanced at Jackie again, lifting a rusty eyebrow.

"So, was it awful?" he asked.

"Pretty awful. It would have been a lot worse except for Paul. He stayed with me the whole time, right until they wheeled me into the delivery room. I'd have hated to go through that alone."

"You should marry that guy, Kaminsky."

She frowned. "Come on, don't you start pushing me around, too."

"As if anybody could ever push you around. Why won't you marry him?"

"Look, Brian," she said curtly. "Right now I want to be alone with the baby for a while, and get used to looking after him. I want to think about what it really means to be somebody's parent."

"And you can't do any of that if you're living with Paul?"

"Brian—"

"Never mind," he said hastily. "Forget I said anything. Have you had much company?"

"Adrienne was here for a while this afternoon."

"Yeah?" He glanced up with interest. "How's she doing?"

Jackie frowned. "Not great. She seems so sad, Brian. After all those years they spent dying to have a baby, and now she's got this gorgeous little boy and they all love him so much, but she can't seem to pull herself out of the blues."

"It's postpartum depression. Chris says she had it after Gordie was born."

Jackie thought about Wardlow's fiancée, a woman who earned her living training horses and seemed so calm and levelheaded.

"She did, really? How long did it take her to get over it?"

"Almost a year, she says. But Chris was married to that damn Stan Lewis, you know, and I doubt that he helped her very much. Adrienne's got Harlan, who's a great guy."

"That's true. I just hope she starts feeling better soon. I miss her."

Jackie was silent a moment, thinking about her friend's unhappy, withdrawn face. Finally she shook her head and waved her hand toward a lavish bouquet on the windowsill.

"And Sarge stopped by for a couple of minutes after lunch to see the baby and bring me those flowers from the substation."

"I know. He's worried about you. Lew never says much, but he really cares about you."

Jackie smiled, touched by the words. "Well, he liked the baby, too. Sarge even sat in that chair and held him for a while."

Wardlow chuckled. "I wish I'd seen that."

"And Paul will be coming in to see us again after

supper,'' Jackie went on. ''He's building corrals right now, so he can't take time off in the daytime.''

''That guy works harder than anybody I've ever met,'' Wardlow said.

''Really? I always thought you worked harder than anybody. At least to hear you tell it.''

''Go ahead, make fun of a guy who's doing your job and his own,'' her partner complained.

''Is it still busy?''

''Worse all the time,'' he said gloomily. ''Are you sure you can't come back to work next week, now that you've got this baby thing over with?''

Jackie laughed. ''No way. I get to stay home with Danny and I plan to treasure every minute of it.''

Her smile faded abruptly as she thought about the time after her maternity leave when she'd have to deliver the baby into a stranger's care. Until recently, that had been merely an abstract concept, but now it caused her actual pain.

Wardlow watched her face carefully, reading her thoughts as he often did. ''It's probably going to be easier when he gets bigger,'' he said. ''To leave him, I mean.''

''I hope so.'' She glanced out the window, then looked back at her partner. ''Brian?''

''Yeah?''

''That baby's skeleton, the one that we dug out of the backyard…''

''What about it?''

''You told me it was perfectly articulated, not dismembered or mutilated like the woman's body.''

''That's right,'' Wardlow said.

''Do you remember anything strange about it?''

''Look, I haven't been giving the case a lot of

attention, Kaminsky. We have so much going on, and your murder's more than thirty years old. It's a stone-cold trail.''

"I know. I'm just asking about the baby, that's all.''

"Well, come to think about it, maybe there was something."

His pleasant freckled face twisted with concentration while Jackie watched him closely.

"A finger," he said at last. "It was missing the little finger on the left hand. We assumed it got lost somehow while the bones were being exhumed."

A chill clutched at the pit of her stomach and crept up along her spine in shivering tendrils. "So the finger didn't look like it had been cut off?"

"No, Klein checked it over and said the joint showed no sign of trauma."

"But a baby's so..." She swallowed hard. "They're really small, Brian. You could probably just pull that finger right out of its socket and snip the skin with a knife, and there'd be no trace on the skeleton after thirty years."

He leaned forward to stare at her. "What's all this about, Kaminsky?"

"Nothing much," she said, trying to sound casual. "I got a crank letter in my mailbox yesterday, just before I went into labor."

While he continued to watch her intently, Jackie told him the gist of the note, particularly the indication that the baby's finger had been removed at the time of its death. But she downplayed the threat to herself and her own child, knowing how passionately it would upset Wardlow.

More and more, police officers were becoming the

target of personal attacks from criminals. Away from the office they endured crank calls, malicious damage to their own property and especially threats to the safety of their families—all of which added greatly to the stress of the job.

As Lew Michelson told his detectives, "It was your choice to become police officers, all of you. But you damn sure never intended to expose your family to danger in the process, and we're going to do whatever we can to protect them."

The protection, however, was woefully inadequate. Police departments around the country were stretched to the breaking point, overworked, understaffed and underfunded. Meanwhile, the criminals were better armed and more highly organized than they'd ever been.

Wardlow leaned back in his chair, staring with narrowed eyes at the bouquet of flowers on the windowsill. "We've never released information in the press about a baby's skeleton," he said at last. "Just the woman's, with a general physical description."

"I know. And when I talked with the neighbors, I only told Eleanor Betker about the baby, but none of the others."

"So she must have been the one to write your crank note," he said. "Who else would have known there was even a baby's skeleton in that hole?"

"Brian," Jackie said patiently, "it's not an issue of whether she knew about the baby. The thing is, whoever wrote that note knew about the missing finger."

"So, do you think this Betker woman is the killer?" Wardlow asked.

In the bassinet near Jackie's bed, her baby set up a small, sleepy wail, and she reached over automatically to touch him.

He subsided, hiccuping a few times, then slept again.

Jackie frowned, still patting her child absently. "I don't know. Eleanor Betker looks big and tough enough to kill somebody and chop them up with an ax. But she's a very artistic person, and really gentle with her sister. Besides, it's hard for me to believe she'd hurt a baby. Especially if it was..."

"What?" Wardlow asked when she paused.

"Well, I'm starting to wonder if that baby might have been Emma's."

"The younger sister?"

Jackie nodded. "I gather from the neighbors that Emma's always been a bit childlike, even before the Alzheimer's set in. But thirty years ago she would still have been in her mid-thirties, and probably a beautiful woman. What if she was seduced by a tradesman or some unscrupulous neighbor, and got pregnant, and Eleanor had to dispose of the baby?"

"Why kill the next-door housekeeper at the same time?" Wardlow asked.

"I don't know. Maybe Maggie found out about the pregnancy somehow, so Eleanor panicked and killed her. I really believe that woman would do anything to protect her sister."

"But, Kaminsky, this was a rage killing," he pointed out. "Even worse than the Maribel Lewis homicide. The poor girl's head and limbs were chopped off with an ax. You don't do something like that just to get a witness out of the way."

Jackie thought about Eleanor Betker's broad

shoulders and big callused hands, her air of tenderness toward poor little Emma and the unsettling hints in Dolly Weitzel's chatter about Eleanor and her feelings for the young red-headed housekeeper.

In spite of Jackie's fascination with her new baby, and the sore tiredness of her body, she still found herself anxious to get back home and consult her case notes again.

Maybe she'd see things in a different light now, after a few days away from the facts.

"So you're not scared?" Wardlow asked. "Even now that you got that letter in your mailbox?"

"Not really. People who are dangerous don't usually give advance warnings. You know that, Brian."

"We had one who did," Wardlow said grimly.

They were both silent for a moment, remembering the chilling series of letters a year earlier that had initiated such a bloody, murderous rampage.

"That was an exception," she said at last. "Even the police psychiatrist told us it was a complete aberration. Nasty letters are almost always sent by people who get their kicks out of threats, not actions. And that's how I see this one."

"Just the same, maybe I'll stop by for a visit every day or so at different times," he said at last.

Normally Jackie would have scoffed at such a suggestion. But now, with the precious bundle in its bassinet next to her, she found herself nodding thoughtfully.

"Paul's staying in town with me for the first few days," she said, "just until I've had a chance to get some rest and establish a few routines. After that," she added casually, "I guess I'll have no objections if you want to drop by and visit the baby every now and then.''

"Go on and say it, Kaminsky."

"What?"

"Say, 'I'm really, really scared, Brian, and I'm grateful for the concern you're showing for me.' C'mon, Kaminsky. You can say it."

"Up yours, Wardlow."

Wardlow chuckled and got up to peer at the baby. "Such a sweet little mommy you have, kid. A real shrinking violet."

"There's one thing that does scare me," Jackie said slowly.

"Yeah?"

"When I think about that note, and the baby's missing finger…"

She looked at the bassinet while Wardlow waited.

"What if Lenny Cernak killed Maggie," Jackie said, "and he's still living somewhere in the city under a different name? Maybe even right in the neighborhood, watching me." She hugged her arms, feeling chilled.

"How old would he be?"

"Well, about mid-forties, I guess, just like Mike Weitzel."

"But don't you think the neighbors would know this man if he moved back in?"

"You're right," Jackie said with relief. "None of them have ever forgotten that kid. They all seem to retain vivid and unfavorable memories of Lenny."

"Well, from everything you've told me, he would have been my first choice as the killer. Torturing cats is a real bad sign."

"It sure is," Jackie agreed. "Almost all serial

killers have a childhood history of cruelty to animals, don't they?''

"And it's a logical crime, too," Wardlow went on. "The kid gets the hots for the nice young housekeeper but their relationship goes bad, so he kills her and hacks her to pieces in a blind rage, then Daddy has to help to bury the evidence."

"But then where did the baby come from?" Jackie asked. "According to Dolly Weitzel, Maggie wasn't with them long enough for it to be Lenny's."

"Maybe she was pregnant when the guy hired her," Wardlow pointed out. "That could even be why she ran away. Getting pregnant out of wedlock was still a pretty big deal back in the sixties."

Jackie gave him an admiring glance. "Hey, that's not bad. You really should be a detective when you grow up."

He chuckled and touched the baby's cheek with a surprisingly gentle hand.

"I'll swing by your house as soon as you're home so I can collect that note," he said. "Maybe Claire's whiz kids down in Ident can lift some prints off it and nail your killer."

"I doubt it," she said. "Life is never that easy, Brian."

"I know, but it won't hurt to try. Hey, can I pick him up, Kaminsky?"

"Sure," she said. "He's going to be getting hungry soon, anyhow. Just be careful to support his head."

She watched as Wardlow lifted the little bundle and held it deftly.

"My sister has three kids," he said in response

to Jackie's startled glance. "I'm a pretty good uncle."

"If you think Lenny is the killer," she said abruptly, "he must also be the one who wrote the note, since the letter writer knew a crucial detail about the crime scene. But that would mean Lenny still does live in the neighborhood."

"Or he could be in contact with someone who does."

"You're right," she said, reaching for the baby. "I never thought of that."

Wardlow watched in obvious alarm as she began to fumble at the buttons on her pajama top. "Kaminsky, what are you doing?"

"I'm feeding the baby," she said. "It's time for his supper."

Wardlow looked toward the door. "Well, then," he said awkwardly, "I guess maybe I'll just…"

Jackie laughed. "You'll have to start getting used to this, Brian. It's the most natural thing in the world, you know."

"Maybe in your world," he muttered. "But in my world, it's still not the kind of thing you expect your partner to do when you stop at a traffic light. Undo her shirt and whip out a meal for the baby? I don't think so."

"I have no intention of bringing the baby to work," Jackie said calmly. "Although," she added, teasing him, "it's not such a bad idea, come to think of it. Alice and the other secretaries could baby-sit, and I'd have time to nurse him during briefings in Sarge's office."

"Kaminsky," he pleaded, standing by the door, "just let me leave, okay?"

Jackie smiled tranquilly in reply, pulling the blankets up as a shield and offering the nipple to the baby. An old hand at this by now, he began to suck greedily.

"How long will Paul be staying with you?" Wardlow asked from the door.

"Only a couple of days. He's got so much work to do at the ranch, he can't take any more time off. As it is, he'll have to commute every day to do the chores, even while he's helping me with the baby."

"Kaminsky, you should—"

"Don't say it!" She smiled to ease the brusqueness of her words. "Don't keep telling me what I should do, okay? Paul and I just have to work everything out in our own time."

"Okay. Give me a call when he moves back to the ranch, and I'll start dropping by to check on you."

"I'll do that," she said, once again surprised that she felt so little inclination to argue. "Oh, and Brian…"

"Yes?"

"Do me a big favor, okay? See what you can find out about Alban Cernak and his son, and what happened to them after they moved away. I'll breathe a whole lot easier when I'm certain Lenny isn't somewhere nearby, all grown-up and watching me."

"Okay." He took one last glance at her in the bed, where she held her nursing baby and stroked his downy head with a slow, tender hand.

"You look beautiful, Kaminsky," he said, his voice husky with emotion. "Really beautiful."

She glanced at the doorway, astonished, but he was gone before she could reply.

12

It was a few days later and Jackie was back home with her baby, settled in at the little house behind its hedge of flowering lilacs. She woke to the pale glow of predawn light and lay smiling at the window, thinking about motherhood.

Having a new baby introduced you to so many different experiences, and one of the nicest was a deep appreciation of sunrises. She'd never seen so many beautiful early mornings since her years on graveyard shifts.

Even then, Jackie had always watched the new day dawning through a mist of gritty fatigue as she'd headed home to sleep like the dead after nine hours of patrolling bars and arresting hookers.

Nowadays, during Danny's nighttime and early-morning feedings, she saw black velvet skies, star-dazzled radiance and lacy clouds across the moon, and bright new sunrises as fresh and promising as shells washed up on a summer beach.

Fatigue was still part of her life, of course. She often stumbled through her days with the numbing exhaustion of the new mother reducing her to a zombie-like, sleepwalking state. Still, it was a different sort of tiredness than she'd experienced working night shifts. And even on the worst days she felt a warm core of contentment she'd never known before.

Jackie smiled again and rolled her head on the pillow as Paul came padding into the room, bare-chested in a pair of jogging pants, carrying their son. The baby wore tiny blue terry-cloth sleepers patterned with white sea horses, and nestled contentedly in his father's brawny arms.

"He's still pretty cheerful at the moment," Paul reported. "But I think he'll be hungry soon."

"What time is it?" she asked.

"Five-thirty. He's slept more than three hours since the last feeding."

She hoisted herself up on the pillows and unfastened her nightgown. "Did you change him?"

Paul nodded and sat on the bed, still holding the baby.

"I thought I'd better do it while he was still feeling happy. This way he can nurse and drift off again, and you'll be able to go back to sleep for a while."

"Thanks, Paul." She took the baby and put him to her breast, settling back and stroking his fat cheek as he nursed.

Paul climbed into bed next to her, smoothing the covers over their legs, and turned to watch. He leaned over to kiss Jackie, then the baby, nestling his head briefly against her naked breast. She laughed and reached up with her free hand to touch his hair.

These past few days had been so pleasant. She loved having Paul around all the time, loved sharing a bed with him in such an undemanding, sexless way while both of them concentrated their attention on the baby.

If it could be like this all the time, she wouldn't even hesitate to make the commitment he wanted. But marriage was such a complicated thing, fraught with fear and danger, and the possibility of a pain too great to bear.

He sat, looking worried. "I hate to start leaving you alone so soon."

"Come on, Paul, I have to learn to take care of him by myself. And it shouldn't be too big a job for a grown-up woman who has nothing at all to do except look after one little baby."

"But you're still not strong. You just gave birth a few days ago."

"I'm strong enough," she said placidly.

"You're an amazing woman, all right." He smiled. "I love watching you with him like this. You're such a good mother."

She glanced down, touched by his words, feeling almost shy. "Do you really think so? I used to worry whether I could be a good mother to anybody, after the way I was raised."

"I know you felt that way, but none of us has to keep being the victim of an unhappy childhood."

He got out of bed, stripped off the jogging pants and padded into the bathroom, then came back out and picked up his jeans and work shirt from the rocking chair by the window.

Jackie watched him, loving the strong clean lines of his body, the long back and lean hips, the muscles flexing in his arms and thighs as he moved.

"Has Wardlow learned anything more about those skeletons in the backyard?" he asked, glancing out the window at the little flower garden.

She tensed and looked down again at the baby.

"Not much more than I've already told you. Sarge is letting me question the neighbors and start putting together a file, but there's no urgency."

Until now she'd avoided telling him about the note in the mailbox, which was presently mounted in a plastic evidence case and locked away in the nightstand, waiting for Wardlow. Briefly she was tempted to tell Paul about it in hopes that sharing the threat would make her less uneasy.

But if he knew about the note, his response would be completely disproportionate. He'd worry all the time about her and the baby, probably not be able to work, even though the anonymous letter was no doubt a crank thing.

It was somebody's obscure idea of a joke, or a plea for attention. People did things like that all the time, trying to insert themselves into police investigations simply for the vicarious thrill of being involved.

But whoever wrote that note had known the baby's finger was missing....

She pushed the thought out of her mind and smiled up at him. "I'm not getting much police work done, Paul. For these months of maternity leave, I'll just concentrate on learning to be a mommy."

"That sounds good. I love you, Jackie." Fully dressed except for his boots, he kissed her and bent to look at his drowsy son. "Is he finished?"

"I think so. He's just playing now."

"I don't blame him." Paul gave her a wolfish grin. "As I recall, those things are a whole lot of fun to play with."

She watched as he lifted the baby gently in his arms again and kissed the fluffy dark head.

"I'll put him down now and slip out," he said. "You should be able to go back to sleep for a few hours."

"Thank you." She fastened her nightgown and settled luxuriously into the bed again.

He drew the covers up around her face and bent to kiss her. "Are you sure you'll be okay, sweetheart?"

"Mmm," she said drowsily, already sinking into a delicious half sleep.

"Don't forget to call and leave a message if you need anything. Otherwise I won't phone until evening in case you're napping, okay?"

"Mmm," she murmured again, hardly aware of what he was saying. Sleep washed over her and she was lost in dreams, wandering through a sunlit landscape where birds called joyously and flowers bloomed and her son was a toddler, running along at her side, laughing and chasing butterflies.

Later the same day Jackie lay outside in the backyard, lounging in a padded chair with the baby next to her in his carriage, protected by mosquito netting. The June day was warm and languorous, richly scented with flowers.

She lifted her face to the sun, loving the warmth on her body and the feeling of being self-contained once more.

Then she sat forward to peer through the netting at her little son, who slept on his back with his arms outflung. He wore one of the combination shirt-and-underpants garments over his diaper, and looked cool and comfortable despite the afternoon heat. His small mouth pursed and relaxed with a gentle rhythm, as if he was dreaming about nursing.

She laughed, watching him, and reminded herself to tell Paul about it when he called. They'd often speculated about whether the baby dreamed, and what went through his head when he did.

Jackie settled back on the cushions, then glanced up as a couple passed along the alley. They appeared to be in their mid-forties, a tall woman with auburn hair and a stocky man wearing casual dress slacks and a linen jacket. The two strolled down the graveled back lane, deep in conversation, so well dressed and prosperous-looking that they seemed utterly incongruous among the trash cans and backyard compost bins.

Puzzled, Jackie watched until they stopped at a locked gate set into the tall wooden fence opposite her garage. Suddenly she understood their presence.

These had to be her "across-the-alley" neighbors. She'd never met or even seen the people who lived behind that big fence that faced out onto the next street. Not only were their properties separated by the fence, but also by Jackie's hedge of lilacs that had only a few breaks allowing a view of the alley.

While she watched, the man turned and peered at her through the leaves, then said something to his companion. The woman hesitated, also glancing at Jackie, then nodded and came with him toward the back gate.

They entered the yard together, smiling. The woman was thin and rather brittle, wearing a long cotton skirt and a woven tunic, both oatmeal-colored, and a rope of costly-looking amber beads.

The man was an inch or two shorter and powerfully built, with thick graying hair and a face pitted by old acne scars.

"Hello," the woman said, stopping near the baby's carriage. "We thought we should come over and introduce ourselves since we're your neighbors. I'm Carrie Turnbull and this is Bob, my husband. We were out for a walk and a cappuccino," she explained, looking increasingly nervous, "and we decided to take a shortcut through the alley because it's so warm today. But we didn't mean to startle you."

"Hello," Jackie said. "It's nice to meet you. I didn't even know who lived over there. I'm Jackie Kaminsky," she added. "And this is my son, Daniel. He's almost a week old."

Carrie Turnbull leaned closer to look at the baby with an avid expression that Jackie found inexplicably troubling.

"Oh," the woman breathed. "Look, Bob, he's such a darling, isn't he?"

The man cast Jackie a brief, apologetic glance. "We were never able to have a family," he said. "Carrie loves babies."

"I'm...sorry," Jackie murmured.

There was a brief, awkward silence while the woman continued to gaze into the carriage.

"Have you lived here long?" Jackie said at last.

"My family's been here for sixty years." Carrie straightened at last and turned away from the baby with obvious reluctance. "I inherited the house from my parents, and Bob and I moved into it about five years ago when Mother died."

"Really?" Jackie's interest sharpened. "For

some reason I thought the Betkers and the Weitzels were the only long-term residents.''

''Oh, I've never really thought of myself as part of this neighborhood,'' Carrie said. ''I was away at boarding school for most of my teen years, then I got married right out of college and moved to Portland. I didn't get to know anybody very well.''

Jackie could understand why the Turnbulls didn't fit in. There was a conspicuously prosperous air about the couple that set them apart from the other working-class residents on her side of the street, even the haughty Eleanor Betker.

She resolved to ask Adrienne about the Turnbulls next time they spoke together. Carrie and her husband had that look, as if they probably moved in the same social circles as Harlan and Adrienne. Spokane's high society was a pretty exclusive little world, and Carrie wasn't much older than Adrienne, so there was a good chance of learning more about the couple.

''I'd be so afraid if I were you,'' Carrie said, staring into the carriage again.

''Afraid?'' Jackie asked. ''Why?''

''Looking after this baby all by yourself. It's such a huge responsibility.''

The woman had thin hands, deeply tanned and glittering with rings. One of the rings was a distinctive design, a heavy, mannish-looking signet ring that seemed vaguely familiar.

Maybe Adrienne had the same ring, from some kind of sorority or service club....

She frowned, trying to remember. Carrie clutched the handle of the carriage and Jackie had to keep herself from reaching to draw the baby away.

"I'm not all by myself," she said more curtly than she'd intended. "The baby's father helps a lot."

"But so many things can happen." Carrie continued to watch the carriage with a brooding expression while her husband shifted awkwardly on his feet.

"What kind of things?" Jackie asked.

"Accident, sickness, crib death—" The woman stopped abruptly when her husband put a hand on her arm. "I'm sorry," she murmured, her face coloring. "I didn't mean to…"

"It's all right." Jackie was suddenly anxious for them to be gone. "I realize how important it is to be careful. And believe me," she added, looking directly at Carrie Turnbull, "I'm very careful."

There was a strange, chilly moment of tension while the two women stared at each other. Bob Turnbull continued to grip his wife's arm, easing her toward the gate with a polite murmur of farewell.

Jackie watched them go, frowning, then got up and wheeled the carriage into the house, anxious suddenly to get her baby inside and away from the airy openness of the backyard.

13

For the first time since her return from the hospital, Paul wasn't with her for dinner. Jackie missed him more than she cared to admit. She made herself a light meal, fed the baby and put him down, then called the ranch to talk for a while.

Paul seemed tired, but pleased that she'd phoned instead of waiting to hear from him.

Cheered by the sound of his voice, Jackie told him about the baby's day and their afternoon sunbath in the yard, and finally about meeting the neighbors from across the alley.

She omitted Carrie Turnbull's strange comments about dangers to babies. That whole conversation gave her such a creepy, uneasy feeling that she didn't even like to remember it.

"Is everything all right?" he asked with his usual quick perception.

"Sure, everything's just fine. Danny and I miss you, that's all."

"I miss you, too," he said, his voice low and husky. "Do you want me to come in tonight after I finish the chores?"

"No," she said. "By that time it wouldn't be worth the drive, especially when you have to leave so early in the morning."

"Well, I'll get caught up on the work and come tomorrow night. That's as long as I can stand not seeing the two of you, anyhow."

"I was thinking," she said with deliberate casualness, looking out the window at the new green berries of the mountain ash. "Maybe later in the month, we can come out there and stay with you for a week or so. It wouldn't be all that hard to pack up the carriage and a pile of diapers, would it?"

"Not hard at all. Jackie, I'd love that." She heard the joyous lift in his voice and smiled, then felt a tug of caution.

"I'm not talking about anything permanent," she said hastily. "Just a little holiday, that's all. Because I don't want to be away from the house too long, you know. There's so much yard work to look after."

"I know." His voice was noncommittal again. "Whatever you want to do is fine with me. Give the boy a kiss for me, all right?"

"I will. Good night, Paul."

"I love you, Jackie."

They hung up and she moved restlessly around the kitchen, picking dead leaves from the houseplants and rearranging a row of coffee mugs on a shelf.

She wandered into the living room, inexplicably saddened by the soft glow of twilight. The house seemed so quiet and empty. Jackie considered getting out her flute and doing some practising, or working on the sweater she was knitting for the baby. But she couldn't seem to settle to anything.

Finally she climbed the stairs and went into the nursery where Daniel slept in his carriage. They still weren't using the crib because he looked so tiny in that large expanse, even with the cozy bumper pads and piles of stuffed toys.

Jackie bent over to gaze at him, melting with love. He slept peacefully on his back, the handsome little face calm and reposed.

Too calm.

With a sharp clutch of terror, she bent and put her ear to his chest. His heart thumped rapidly, a steady comforting beat.

Embarrassed by her fears, Jackie straightened and turned to examine the closet.

Paul had removed the old shelves and stacked a neat pile of precut lumber in place, ready to assemble new ones. But they'd discovered a hole in the wall at the back of the closet when he'd pulled the shelves away, difficult to repair because the house was finished in lath and plaster. Finally they'd decided to buy a sheet of paneling and cover the whole back wall before installing the new shelves, but he hadn't yet found time to go back to the building supply store.

She knelt and looked at the ragged hole, about eighteen inches above the baseboard. For years it had been covered with a loose flap of wallpaper that Paul tore away along with the shelves.

"If there's really any buried treasure in your house," he'd told her with a teasing smile, "this would be a pretty good hiding place."

She stared at the small cavity in the wall, then moved closer, frowning. For a moment she fancied she could see something in the shadows, the edge of some kind of object down inside there....

Suddenly Jackie was gripped by the same kind of

chill she'd felt before in this room, a breath of evil, an irrational, shuddering terror that started at her very core and flowed out along her spine into her arms and legs with icy trickles of fear. She rocked on her knees, breathless and almost sick to her stomach.

"My God," she whispered, sitting upright on her heels until the nausea passed.

She scrambled out of the closet and looked at the baby again. He frowned in his sleep, one hand pressed awkwardly against his eye. Jackie moved the small arm and patted him, then went downstairs to get her heavy service flashlight from the back porch.

Ignoring her reluctance, she crawled into the nursery closet again and shone her flashlight down into the cavity. The beam of light illuminated the dusty laths, as well as an object made of rags and an old exercise scribbler like the kind children used in school when they learned to print.

She lifted the rags and realized they formed a stuffed doll, a Raggedy Ann with a gingham pinafore and an embroidered face, and hair made of faded orange yarn.

Jackie looked at the doll's bland smile and floppy cloth limbs, and felt another chill of sickness. She pulled out the exercise scribbler and carried it down the hall to her own room, settling in the padded rocker by the window where she liked to feed Daniel.

The paperbound book was filled almost to the back with tiny, blotted handwriting, and she recognized it as some kind of diary or journal. Briefly her years of police training made her reluctant to handle the book for fear of disturbing evidence. But the handwritten date on the front cover was January 26, 1968. Any prints on this old paper, or traces of DNA for that matter, would have long since degraded.

Jackie opened the book and read the notation on the inside cover.

My name is Maggie Birk, it said in a cramped, childlike hand. *I'm 17 years old. This is my book. I'm starting it on the bus.*

Jackie's heart began to pound with excitement. She took a deep breath and settled back in the rocker. The spell of terror and nausea had passed, and she no longer felt any sense of revulsion when she looked at the makeshift diary, or even at the smiling rag doll on her bed.

Those emotions seemed to be present only in the nursery.

Here in her own room she felt nothing but concern and protectiveness at the sight of Maggie Birk's sad little childhood relics.

Impulsively she lifted the doll and put it on her lap, cuddling it like a baby. Then she began to read. It was slow going because Maggie had crowded as many words as possible on each page, and used a cheap green ballpoint pen that had faded badly over the years.

Well, I finally did it. I ran away and I'm glad, even if it's scary to think about what's going to happen next. I kept all the money I earned from baby-sitting Andrew and put it in a sock under my mattress, and now I have enough to buy a ticket to Spokane with some left over until I get a job.

I don't even know why I picked Spokane except that my friend Josie has a grandma who lives there and Josie always visited in the summer and rode on the carousel in the park and went to feed the ducks. It sounded so pretty when she talked about it. I used to think if I could ever see that carousel, I'd be the happiest girl in the whole world. And now I will.

There was a lot of time to wait after I bought the ticket, so I got this book and decided I'd write down everything that happens to me, and then maybe I won't feel so lonesome.

It's kind of scary on the bus. There are three men with beards and dirty clothes who've been here ever since I got on in Salt Lake. I bet they're draft dodgers, going up to hide in Canada so they won't get sent to Vietnam. I'm trying not to look at them, but one is always staring at me.

I'll keep writing so he doesn't see me watching him.

I wonder what they're doing back at home. It's Friday, so Dad's probably too drunk to notice I'm gone. If anybody does, they'll think I'm baby-sitting. By the time they figure out I'm not coming home, I'll be so far away nobody will ever find me.

I wish I could have said goodbye to Mom, but she's so scared of him, she'd probably tell where I was. It's better if she doesn't know. Maybe someday I can send her a postcard and let her know I'm all right. It's funny, I've never been scared of him like she is. After he hurt me so bad when I was little, I guess I knew that was the worst he could do, so I didn't have to be scared anymore.

And now I'm gone.

I don't even hate him like I used to, because it's not Christian to feel that way toward your blood kin. Besides, all that stuff is behind me now. I'm going to have a happy new life. When I get to Spokane I'm going to find a job right away and save my money and go to college. I'll be a teacher and help little kids who live with people who hurt them.

Jackie gripped the stuffed doll in her lap, surprised to find her eyes stinging with tears.

Maggie Birk's story, though almost thirty years old, was hardly unfamiliar to her. She dealt with runaways and street kids all the time. Even Alex Gerard, the Calder's pretty foster daughter, had run away from home to escape an abusive parent.

But that had been Alex's stepfather, not her natural father.

And though the lives of those runaways weren't pretty, at least the girls didn't wind up in shallow backyard graves with their newborn babies....

She leafed forward and back through the faded green-ink pages, trying to find any mention of pregnancy. But the words were hard to decipher out of context, so it was painfully slow going.

In fact, the little bit she'd already read had taken so long that the baby was starting to fuss. Jackie looked at her watch in surprise, then locked the diary and Maggie's rag doll in the nightstand along with her handgun and the threatening note.

She went down the hall to lift the howling baby

from his carriage, holding him tenderly against her and patting his back.

"There, there," she murmured. "For goodness' sake, Danny, what's this all about?"

They still hadn't settled completely on whether to call him Daniel or Danny.

Jackie liked Daniel, but Paul said it would inevitably be shortened to Danny, so they might as well give in without a fuss. At first Jackie had resisted, but she often caught herself shortening the name, too, so Paul was probably right.

"If he becomes a whiz kid on the violin and gives a concert at Carnegie Hall when he's eleven, we can call him Daniel," Paul had said. "But if he likes to go fishing and keep an ant farm in his bedroom, he can be Danny."

"So what are you saying, Arnussen? You think Daniel sounds like a sissy?"

"No," Paul had told her amiably. "I think it sounds like a child prodigy."

Remembering, Jackie smiled and took the baby to his changing table. She removed his sodden diaper, cleaned and powdered him, then dabbed alcohol on the dried umbilical stump. It came off in her fingers, terrifying her until she looked again and saw the astonishing, rosebud perfection of the little navel underneath.

"Hey, you have a belly button, darling!" she murmured, smiling down at her son. "Look at Danny's pretty little belly button."

Somehow the healed umbilicus made the baby seem less fragile, more real and accessible to her. Jackie was seized by an urgent longing to call and tell Paul the news, but resisted.

She couldn't get in the habit of phoning every time some little thing happened in the baby's life. If she was going to be that dependent, she might as well live with the man and be done with it.

Putting a fresh diaper in place, she carried the baby down the hall to her room for his nursing. It was almost ten o'clock, so with any luck he'd sleep until one, maybe even two, allowing her the chance for a couple of hours' rest.

But after Daniel was back in his carriage and she'd gone to bed, she couldn't seem to settle. Too many things raced through her mind.

Images of Carrie Turnbull staring into the baby's carriage with such avidity, and her husband's obvious unease. And those two sad little objects in the wall cavity…

Finally she switched on the light, unlocked the nightstand and took the exercise scribbler out again, flipping to the next entry.

Tuesday, January 30, 1968

Well, my life has sure changed a whole lot since last time I wrote in this book! I haven't had a chance to write anything since Friday, so now I'll tell what happened and try to remember everything.

I got off the bus in Spokane at about nine o'clock at night. It was freezing cold and snowing, and I didn't know where to go or what to do. The bus station is right downtown, and I thought I could walk around and find a hotel, but I didn't even have a clue what direction I should go and it was snowing harder all the time.

So I decided it might be a good idea to sleep in the bus depot and look around in the morning for a place to work, a restaurant or something. That way I'd save some money, too, and not have to go out in the snow and maybe get lost. So I went to the bathroom and guess what? As if I didn't already have enough problems, I had the Curse, too!

I got some Kotex from a machine on the wall and cleaned myself up, then went back out into the waiting-room part and sort of laid down on one of the benches, covering myself with my coat. There was a sign on the wall that said No Loitering, and the man behind the desk looked at me kind of funny and seemed mad, but a lot of people came in on a bus just then and he didn't have a chance to say anything.

But I knew when they were gone he was going to come over and make me leave. By that time I was scared and ready to cry like a baby, and I had bad cramps, too. I always get them with my period, worst of all when I'm sick or upset about something.

Anyhow, I was feeling just about as miserable as a person could be, and then I looked up and Jesus was standing and watching me.

I know that sounds weird, and it isn't true, of course. It was really Alban, but I didn't know him then and he looked just like Jesus. He has these very gentle blue eyes, and long brown hair hanging onto his shoulders, and a scraggly beard, and he's thin and kind of delicate-looking but in a really manly way, if you know what I mean. Sort of like Anthony Perkins would be if he had a beard, and I've always thought he's the most beautiful man in the world.

Anyway, this Jesus-man looked at me and I looked at him, feeling like an idiot because I didn't know what to say. I was so tired and scared, I could practically see a halo around his head.

"Are you alone?" he said.

"Yes, and I'm really scared."

Well, talk about feeling stupid! I was almost crying and felt like such a baby, I could have just died right there. I was holding my Raggedy Annabel, too, and I'm sure that didn't help. He probably thought I was a complete drip.

"Have you run away?" he said. His voice was deep and really gentle, like warm honey or something. If he wasn't so old, I could fall in love with Alban just from his voice.

"Yes," I said. "And I'm not going back. Nobody can make me." As if he was going to call the police and put me on a bus to Salt Lake, or something!

But he just said, "Do you need a job?"

I sat up, still holding Annabel, and stared at him. "A job?"

"I'm looking for a housekeeper," he said. "There's only my son and me living in the house, a couple of bachelors. We need somebody to cook and do light housekeeping. Nothing heavy," he said. As if I ever cared about heavy work! "No washing windows or anything. Just a bit of laundry and tidying. We're both gone from the house all day.''

Well, I ask you.

I started thinking again that maybe he was Jesus, come to the bus station especially to drop a miracle in my lap. A minute ago I was alone and scared and had nowhere to go, and now I had a job and a place to live. I could have jumped up and kissed him, even if he was a lot too old for me.

By now I wasn't so confused and I could tell he was really old, probably about forty, because he had wrinkles around his eyes and under his beard. But that just made him seem nicer, more like a father.

A real father, not that mean son of a bitch I had to live with all my life. And I don't care if it's a bad word because that's what he is.

"My name is Alban Cernak," the man said. It's really spelled with a *C,* but he says it like it's *CH*...Churnak. "And my son's name is Lenny."

"How old is he?" I asked, getting up and putting my coat on, then following along behind him like a puppy while he carried my suitcase. Actually, it's Mom's old suitcase, the one that's ripped at one corner and needs a belt to hold it closed. I don't think she'll miss it very much. Poor Mom, she never gets to go anywhere.

"My son is fourteen. He's at home," Alban said. "You'll meet him in a few minutes."

And I did, too, worse luck. Lenny is the only bad thing about my new job, but I'll get to him soon enough. First I have to tell the rest of the story.

Alban took me outside to his car, parked down the street from the bus station. He has an old rusty Chevy Bel Aire like Uncle Sean used to drive, only blue instead of green. He put my suitcase in the back and we drove away, almost getting stuck a couple of times because the drifts were so deep and the snow kept falling and piling up along the road.

I felt a little scared then, and wondered what kind of crazy thing I was doing, riding off in a car with a complete stranger. But Alban has such a gentle face, I think anybody would trust him.

Besides, my cramps were getting worse, like they might break me in half. The doctor told Mom it's because of the way my insides are twisted from when my dad hurt me when I was little. Mom says he's sorry for doing it and that's why he drinks all the time, but I don't believe a word of it. Anyway, I was hurting too much to worry about being kidnapped, or whatever might be happening to me.

I must have made some kind of noise because Alban looked over at me like he was really worried.

"Are you all right?" he asked.

"I'm having bad cramps."

"Is it your menstrual period?"

Well, I could have died. I never heard a man ask something like that before. I was so embarrassed I didn't even know what to say!

But he was really calm, like a doctor. Of course, Alban is a doctor but I didn't know it then. "I thought you might be pregnant," he said.

"Me?" I asked. "Pregnant?"

"Yes, I wondered if you were."

"Well, I'm not."

He sort of nodded, but he had to watch out for his driving because the road was really bad. I was relieved he wasn't looking at me anymore, but I still thought he deserved to know the truth since he was giving me a job and everything.

So I told him I had an accident when I was a little girl and it sort of twisted one of my hips. That's why I wear such baggy clothes.

"But I can work hard," I told him. "And I walk with a bit of a limp but that's all. I'm fine otherwise."

He didn't seem worried, and never did ask what kind of accident, though most people do, as if it's not even rude to ask something so personal. He just smiled at me and went back to his driving, and I found myself liking him more all the time.

And no wonder. Alban is so nice!

But then we got to his house and I met Lenny, who isn't nice at all and is going to be the big problem with this wonderful new job of mine.

Jackie shifted in the bed, closing her eyes briefly to rest them after the strain of reading Maggie's faded green text. She longed for sleep, and knew Danny would wake and clamor to be fed in just a couple of hours.

But she was so anxious to find out poor doomed Maggie's impression of Lenny Cernak. And all the time she was reading the pages of girlish chatter, one question kept screaming inside her mind.

Whose baby was buried in that backyard grave?

At last she rubbed her eyes, opened the diary and began to read again, frowning with concentration.

It's Tuesday now and I have lots of time to write in here because Alban and Lenny are gone all day to the clinic. Alban is a doctor at some kind of community clinic downtown. He looks after runaways and drug addicts and prostitutes, but I'm not sure who pays him because those people sure wouldn't have any money.

Lenny doesn't go to school, and no wonder. He's so creepy, the other kids would probably kill him. Kids can be so mean. He takes lessons by correspondence and goes with Alban to the clinic in the daytime. He's supposed to be helping with cleaning and looking after patients, but I can't imagine how. If I was sick, I wouldn't want Lenny anywhere near me.

I don't even know what makes him so awful. He just is. He's fat and sloppy, and wears dirty blue jeans and great big plaid shirts. His complexion is terrible and he has greasy black hair that hangs in his face. And he's such a nasty person. You can just see it in his eyes, like he wants to hurt you and he would if he got a chance.

When he's home he sits all day and watches television, or goes down to his place in the basement and does things I don't even want to think about. One of the reasons he hates me is because Alban gave me this bedroom where Lenny used to sleep. I can understand him being mad, it's such a nice room, upstairs looking into the backyard. I told Alban I wouldn't mind having the one in the basement but he said it's better for a boy to be down there.

I'm not sure why that would be, but it doesn't bother me if that's what Alban wants. I'm just glad to have a room of my own after sharing with Connie for so many years. I'll bet Connie's glad I'm gone, too, so she can have the bed to herself. We never did get along too good, she was always Dad's pet.

It never seemed fair that he hurt me with his own hands, and then hated me because I'm twisted and walk with a limp. People shouldn't be that way.

But that's part of the stuff I don't want to think about anymore, and I won't.

So Lenny has a little corner downstairs with a bed and an old dresser with three legs and a brick to hold up the other corner. I went down there today to change the sheets and it was like a pigpen. You can't imagine the stink. He's so creepy I don't even want to think about it. Maybe all boys are awful, I wouldn't know because I only have sisters. But I don't know how someone as nice as Alban could have a son like Lenny.

Anyhow, like I said, I'll try not to think about that because except for Lenny it's a dream job. I have my own room, only have to do a bit of housework and make dinner, and otherwise I can do whatever I want with my time. Alban says if I like, maybe I could even go back to school and get my diploma next year. Then I could start studying to be a teacher!

The house is so cozy and pretty, with a fireplace in the living room and lots of nice woodwork. There's a big backyard that's filled with snow right now, but Alban says in the spring I can have a garden and grow whatever I want. I love gardens.

And I've already met some of the neighbors. Eleanor and Emma Betker are sisters who live next door in a great big mansion. Emma is so pretty, like a movie star, but I think there's something wrong with her head. Eleanor looks after her. She's a nurse, and also beautiful but sort of cold-looking.

The Weitzels live across the street in another big house. They're a perfect family. Dolly is little and plump and Klaus is big and smiles a lot, just the kind of man you'd want for a father. They have a son called Mike who's about my age and really handsome. I'm already a little bit in love with him but he probably doesn't even know I'm alive.

I'm so happy here. I feel safe for the first time in my life. It's wonderful not to be scared of Dad, and worry how much he's been drinking or what kind of mood he's in. I get to do my own work and manage things my own way, almost like I was Alban's wife and this is my own house. Of course he's too old for me. I'd much rather be married to Mike Weitzel!

But that's enough silliness, as Mom would say. I have to go make dinner because Alban and Lenny will be home soon. I think I'm going to cook a meat loaf and make some baked apples.

The diary entry ended. Jackie closed the scribbler and rubbed her eyes, then locked the old book away in her nightstand again.

She switched off the bedside lamp and lay staring up at the ceiling, trying to think.

The threatening note in her mailbox had contained details of the murder known only to the killer, unless somebody in the pathologist's office had leaked a bit of vital information. This wouldn't be unthinkable, since the hospital staff might not feel the need to be discreet about a thirty-year-old crime.

But if the note was left by the killer, it had to be somebody still living in the neighborhood who was watching Jackie's movements and knew a lot about her.

At the open window, curtains stirred in the summer breeze. She shivered and rubbed her arms, feeling chilled and lonely in the bed without Paul.

Alban Cernak must have slept in this same room. Maggie would have been down the hall in what was now the nursery, and with her arrival, sullen Lenny had been banished to the basement. Jackie thought about the dark musty cellar with its windowless room that she now used as a repository for firewood and packing boxes.

Restless and suddenly worried about the baby, she got up and hurried down the hall to the nursery. On impulse she wheeled his carriage back to her own

room and settled it by the bed, close enough to
touch.

Then, fitfully, she slept and dreamed troubled
dreams about whirling snow and entrapment in dark
hidden places, and a baby crying mournfully because nobody knew where to find its mother.

14

"I can't find any evidence these people ever existed." Wardlow cuddled the baby and smiled down at him while Jackie watched from a nearby chair.

"So Maggie Birk was never reported as a missing person?"

"She's not in any of the surviving FBI files from the sixties. Hey, look, Kaminsky. Do you see those white butterflies?"

"Yes, Brian, I see the butterflies." She shook her head, exasperated.

They were on the back porch, sipping lemonade and looking out at the sunlit yard and garden. Wardlow had his suit jacket removed, exposing the leather shoulder holster. Jackie wore a loose red cotton sundress and sandals, and the baby was dressed only in a little undershirt and diaper. The black cat drowsed at Jackie's feet.

Wardlow sighed, leaning back in the rocking chair and cuddling the baby against his shoulder, patting the tiny back. "This is nice, Kaminsky. Very domestic."

"Brian, you're making me crazy."

He glanced over at her, raising an eyebrow quizzically.

"I care about this case," Jackie said. "Even if it

is thirty years old. I want to know who killed Maggie Birk, and whose baby died with her.''

"Maybe it really was her own." He grinned at Daniel and wrapped a few strands of the baby's silky dark hair around his finger. "How come you're suddenly so sure it wasn't?"

Jackie hesitated. She hadn't told her partner about the diary, and didn't intend to until she could finish reading Maggie's whole story and learn what information it held.

But making out the cramped, green handwriting was slow going, especially when her baby needed so much care.

She felt a brief stab of guilt and suppressed it firmly. Even if she turned in the diary as evidence, Wardlow wasn't going to concentrate any more attention on it than he was doing now. He could barely keep abreast of his current responsibilities.

Besides, she reasoned, Maggie's diary was like a sort of secondhand witness interview, and she'd been authorized by the sergeant to conduct those on her own.

"You couldn't find anything about Alban Cernak, either?" she asked. "Or the downtown clinic he was supposed to work at?"

"Well, the clinic apparently existed, down on East Sprague. It was a volunteer thing operated on private funding, and they didn't check their staff credentials all that carefully. I can't find any record of Cernak being licensed as a physician with the AMA. And his name doesn't turn up in any other searches I've done."

"So he was impersonating a doctor, and then he dropped off the face of the earth?"

"It sort of looks that way. And his kid apparently never went to school, so there are no leads in that direction, either."

"Let me have the baby now, Brian. I think he's ready to fall asleep."

Wardlow yielded the baby up regretfully. Jackie put him back in his little padded lounge at her feet, where he yawned and sneezed, then dropped off to sleep almost at once.

"Well," she said, "there must be some trace of these people. You can't live a whole life and not leave any kind of paper trail."

"Speaking of paper, why don't you show me that anonymous letter, Kaminsky?"

"Okay." She went upstairs to her room and took the threatening note from the nightstand, carrying it back out to the back porch.

Wardlow read it and frowned. "Pretty ugly stuff, isn't it?"

"But you confirmed there was a finger missing from the baby's skeleton."

"Yes, there was." He put the note away in his briefcase. "So, what do you think is going on?"

"I don't know. I haven't had a chance to talk to the neighbors again, but I'm planning to interview Mike Weitzel and Eleanor Betker, and also find out more about the Turnbulls across the alley. I'm hoping Adrienne can help me with that part. They look like members of her social circle."

"So you really think whoever killed that girl is still living somewhere nearby?" He gestured toward his briefcase. "Because Sarge isn't going to like this one bit, Kaminsky."

"I know he isn't. But we all know that anonymous letter writers are almost always harmless. Besides…''

Jackie bent to tuck a light flannel blanket around her son's body, then looked up at Wardlow again.

''Brian, what kind of world will it be if the bad guys find out they can control investigations by threatening a cop's family? We can't start running scared or we'll never stop.''

''I know. You've told me that lots of times, Kaminsky.'' He sipped his lemonade. ''But that was before you had a baby.''

She set the lounge rocking slightly, and watched its gentle motion.

''Do you have any kind of security system at this place?'' her partner asked.

''Well, of course,'' she said dryly. ''I have a cop in full-time residence. What better security could anybody ask for?''

He shook his head. ''Poor Arnussen. It must be hell, dealing with a stubborn woman like you. No wonder the guy doesn't want to marry you.''

Jackie chuckled. ''Hey, speaking of marriage, how have you been feeling these days? Do you still have those cold feet?''

He stared into his glass. ''Most of the time I'm too busy to think about it. When I do, my feet are so cold I get the shakes.''

''Brian, you know that's crazy. Chris is a wonderful person.''

''So is Paul Arnussen.''

''Oh, come on.'' Her cheeks warmed with annoyance. ''The two situations are completely different.''

''I suppose they are.'' He touched the baby lounge with his toe, setting it rocking again, and cast her a teasing glance. "Chris and I haven't got a kid together."

"Look, we're not talking about me. Don't go turning this around."

He sighed and took another sip of lemonade. "I know it's crazy. I love Chris and Gordie, can't imagine being without them. It's just that old panic about actually signing on the dotted line, I guess."

"That's certainly understandable, after the way you were hurt the last time," she said. "Once burned, twice shy."

"I know, but I'm not giving in to it." He stared out at the newly dug flower bed with a brooding expression. "Chris deserves a happy bridegroom, and that's what she's going to get."

Jackie got up and dropped an arm around him, hugging him. "Well, I happen to think Chris is also getting a pretty good guy."

"Get away from me, Kaminsky!" he protested, but his smile looked pleased. "Motherhood has made you all soft and mushy. I don't think I can stand you anymore."

"Oh, come on. You love me," she said serenely. "And you can hardly wait for me to come back to work."

"Yeah," he agreed. "But I'm not proud of it."

She laughed and settled back comfortably in the deck chair, her worries evaporating for the moment in his familiar company.

Sunday, February 9, 1968

I haven't had a chance to write in here for almost two weeks, and lots of things have happened!

Best of all was that Mike Weitzel talked to me. I should really save that for last but I'm dying to write about it, so I'll tell exactly how it happened and try not to forget a single thing.

It was last Friday, when a ton of snow fell during the night, closing most of the side roads. Alban and Lenny still went to the clinic the same as always. They waded through the snowdrifts to a main road a couple of streets over where the bus was still running, but all the normal kids had a day off school because of the snow.

It stopped snowing around noon, so after I finished up the housework and found a roast to thaw for dinner, I went outside to shovel the front walk. You'd never know to look at me, but I'm really strong, and I can do heavy work like that with no problem.

Alban never said I had to shovel snow but I was hoping he'd be pleased. Lately he's started talking about moving to Portland and hinting that maybe I can go along with them, and I'd love that. After being in my own room and having charge of the house and all, I'm already spoiled. I don't want to go back to worrying about getting a job and another place to live, and I'd rather die than go home to Salt Lake.

So I keep thinking if I work really hard and try not to fight with Lenny, and Alban's happy with the job I'm doing, maybe I'll get to go along when they move.

But I don't want to think about that right

now. I'd rather talk about Mike Weitzel!

Anyhow, I was out shoveling snow and all of a sudden he turned up right across the street, shoveling their sidewalk.

Mike is so handsome. He has black hair and big shoulders, and he wears a football jacket with leather sleeves. I'll bet he's a terrific athlete, and really popular at school. I almost died when he showed up right across the street.

I didn't know what to say, so I just kept shoveling harder, and after a while he came over and said, "Hi, how are you?"

I was so scared I could hardly talk. He must have thought I was an idiot but he seemed so nice, just asked if I liked my job and how I got along with Lenny.

I told him Lenny was kind of creepy but Alban was nice, and I liked being a housekeeper and especially doing the cooking.

He said, "Are you a good cook?"

I told him I hoped so, and how I was making a roast and a banana cream pie for supper.

He said, "Maybe you'll invite me over sometime to taste your cooking. Just keep that Lenny kid away from me, okay?"

I said Lenny spent most of his time sulking down in the basement or watching TV in the living room.

"To tell the truth," he said, "it's not Lenny I'm interested in." And then he smiled in a way that made my knees knock together!

I didn't know what else to say so I started shoveling again, trying to push a huge pile of snow. He took the shovel and ran all the way down my sidewalk to clear a path, getting most of the snow out of the way for me so all I had left to do was clean around the edges.

"There," he said, handing the shovel back to me. "Now it'll be easier for you." Then he smiled again and looked so sweet, almost shy.

If I didn't know better, I'd think he likes me! But I could never put that anywhere but in my book. Saying things out loud can spoil them.

Sometimes I lie awake for hours thinking about how Mike looked, and the way he smiles and holds his head like a king. But I have to get my mind on something else, so I'll tell about the other neighbors.

I know who most of them are because Alban always talks about them when we sit in the dining room having our supper. I think he really does it just for something to say. Otherwise it's awkward because he usually makes Lenny sit at the table during suppertime. Lenny stares at his plate and watches me from under his greasy hair and never says a word, just grabs at the food and chews with his mouth open.

I hate him so much!

But I was talking about the neighbors, not creepy Lenny.

That same day, not long after Mike left, I met Gerald Pinson. He's a music teacher at the high school Mike goes to. Mr. Pinson is a funny little man, kind of prissy-looking but quite nice. He wears glasses and a big furry hat with earflaps that tie on top. I'll bet the kids at school make fun of him.

Anyhow, he came down the street while I was shoveling snow and I didn't see him until he was practically on top of me. I was singing "Four Strong Winds," which is one of my favorite songs. I always feel so sorry for the poor girl left behind, waiting for her boyfriend to send her a bus ticket so she can go and be with him, but you can tell he doesn't really want to.

All of a sudden Mr. Pinson was there in front of me, staring at me. He'd taken off his glasses and his eyes looked kind of watery. His cheeks were all pink under the fur hat.

"What's your name?" he asked.

"I'm Maggie Birk," I said.

At first I felt like saying none of your business, but I knew he was a teacher and you just don't talk rude to teachers. Besides, he seemed nice, so I didn't mind telling him my name.

"Where did you learn to sing like that, Maggie?"

Well, that was a surprise.

"I never learned," I told him. "I just always liked to sing."

"You have a marvelous voice, a gorgeous true alto. That's very rare."

When he said that, I started feeling nervous again and didn't know how to answer him, so I went back to shoveling and he kind of followed along.

"I'd love to work with you," he said. "I give music lessons at my house, you know."

As if I could ever afford music lessons!

"Oh, I wouldn't charge you anything," he said when I told him I was saving all my money to go back to school. "I'd like to work with you just for my own enjoyment. Do you think maybe you could find time to drop by in the evening sometime?"

He seemed nice enough, but the idea of going to his house at night still made me feel all creepy. I was wondering what to say, when Steve Weitzel came out of their house and walked across the street to where we were talking.

Steve is Mike's brother. He's about fifteen and not as nice as Mike though he's even more handsome. He has black hair, too, but he's thinner and taller than Mike, and has no skin problems at all. If Steve Weitzel was a girl, he'd be pretty.

When Mr. Pinson saw Steve, it was like somebody hit him. He stopped talking and looked all flustered. Steve came up to him and handed over an envelope without saying a single word.

It seemed really strange, the way he did it. I thought maybe Mr. Pinson was his teacher and he had some homework he hadn't finished or something. But Mr. Pinson seemed guilty. Quick as could be, he put the envelope away inside his coat.

"Thank you, Steven," he said, and forgot all about my singing lessons. Mr. Pinson looked like he just wanted to be gone.

"I need the money right away," Steve told him, sounding as rude as can be.

"I don't have enough with me," Mr. Pinson said. He was whispering, and looked like he might be going to cry, poor thing.

"Then go to your house and get it. I'll come with you."

I watched with my mouth hanging open while they went down the street toward Mr. Pinson's house. Once he turned and looked back over his shoulder at me, and he still seemed really nervous, maybe even scared. I keep wondering what was in that envelope.

But I wasn't finished meeting neighbours that day, because when I shoveled down to the other end of the street, Eleanor Betker came out and invited me into her house for some hot cocoa.

Now, that was an experience! But my hand is getting all cold and cramped so I'll have to tell about it tomorrow if I get enough time.

Jackie put down the book and rubbed her temples, seeing the green handwriting dancing behind her closed eyelids. She checked on Danny who still slept at her feet in his baby lounge near the chair where Wardlow had been sitting an hour earlier.

The mesmerizing stillness of the summer afternoon, the drowsy humming of insects above the flowers and the baby's placid breathing, all lulled and soothed her. She had a sense of being caught in a time warp, straddling two worlds.

The thirty-year-old events in Maggie Birk's diary seemed oddly superimposed on the present, making both of them hazy and unreal.

All those passions and secrets, hanging in the air

for three decades, shifting and changing but never really vanishing....

Jackie shook her head and got up, carrying the baby lounge inside. It was more than an hour until the next scheduled feeding, and Danny was sleeping soundly. After a brief hesitation, she went up and got the carriage, wrestling it down the narrow stairs. She put the baby on the mattress and covered him with a knitted shawl.

He stirred and wailed a couple of times, but didn't open his eyes. When she patted him and rolled the carriage back and forth, he settled almost at once.

Jackie took her key from the rack, wheeled the carriage out onto the veranda and down the steps and went back to lock the door.

On the street she paused to look around for a moment, blinking in the brilliant glare of sunlight, then started up the cracked sidewalk toward Gerald Pinson's house.

15

Pinson was outside trimming his hedge when Jackie approached with the carriage. He straightened and turned to look at her, shading his eyes with his hand.

Her neighbor wore deck shoes, pleated khaki slacks and a natty pink cotton shirt, opened to reveal a tanned, corded throat. His silver hair was combed into an old-fashioned pompadour, and sunlight flashed on the lenses of his glasses.

"Detective Kaminsky," he said, smiling. "What a nice surprise. Just out for a stroll, are you?"

"I thought the baby and I could both use some fresh air. Especially me," Jackie said. "I haven't been getting a lot of sleep at night, and I'm feeling groggy."

"Well, you certainly don't look it," he said gallantly. "You're positively radiant."

Jackie glanced up, a little startled by his look of frank admiration across the cotoneaster hedge. Somehow she'd formed the impression that Gerald Pinson was gay, and her suspicion had probably been reinforced by the passage in Maggie's diary describing his encounter with young Steven Weitzel.

But the look he gave her at the moment was one of unmistakable male appreciation, even lasciviousness. All at once Jackie was uncomfortably conscious of her bare shoulders in the cotton sundress, and the fullness of her breasts now that she was nursing the baby.

"Thank you," she said. "But I feel more like something the cat dragged in. Getting two hours of sleep at a stretch can do that to you."

He came around the hedge and out onto the sidewalk, still holding his pruning shears. "May I have the honour of seeing the new arrival?" he asked with odd formality.

"Sure," she said. "His name is Daniel."

When Pinson bent to peer into the shaded carriage, sunlight glinted sharply on the metal blades of the shears, and Jackie's stomach clenched with sudden, irrational fear.

"What a lovely baby." He stood erect to smile at her. "This child looks a lot like you."

"Do you think so?" she asked. "Except for the dark hair, I'd say he's more like his father."

"I see a lot of you around the eyes and in the shape of the jaw. A beautiful child."

Again she was aware of his concentrated male admiration, even more uncomfortable now that he stood so close to her.

"Mr. Pinson," she said curtly, "would you by any chance have a moment to chat with me? I wanted to ask you a few questions about Maggie Birk."

"I doubt that I can help you much." His smile faded abruptly, replaced by a shuttered, cautious look. "I barely remember the girl."

"Sometimes it's surprising, the little details a person remembers," Jackie said casually. "And they can be very helpful."

He paused by his front gate and made an exaggerated gesture of invitation. "By all means, Detective. I'm happy to help if I can. Welcome to my humble abode."

She wheeled the carriage up his front walk and left it at the foot of the veranda stairs, rummaging on the rack underneath to get her notebook from the diaper bag.

"Would you like me to help you lift the carriage up the stairs?" he asked.

"No, I don't think so. He's sleeping and I'd just as soon not disturb him. If it's all right with you—" Jackie waved her hand toward an attractive grouping of white-painted wicker "—I'll leave him here and we can talk here on the porch."

"Certainly. Could I bring you a cold drink or something to nibble on?"

"Thanks, but I'm fine." Jackie went up the stairs and settled in an armchair padded with yellow chintz. "I had a friend drop by earlier and we drank about a gallon of lemonade."

Pinson sat opposite her on the wicker couch, arranging the pleats in his slacks with a fussy manner, adjusting his wristwatch, touching the buttons on his shirt. Jackie realized that he was very nervous, and her interest sharpened.

But she kept her voice casual and flipped to a fresh page in the notebook, making a note of the date, time and circumstances while he watched in silence.

"Now, what do you remember about Maggie Birk?" she asked.

"Her voice," he said promptly. "I've never heard anything like it. Listening to that girl simply gave me chills."

"How did you happen to become aware of her singing voice?" Jackie asked, wondering if Maggie had ultimately decided to accept Gerald Pinson's offer of free music lessons.

The old diary, though an invaluable source of information, was also frustrating because she could only decipher it with painstaking slowness. But at least these witness statements would ultimately be confirmed or refuted by Maggie's own words.

And lies were often as useful to an investigator as the truth....

"I used to hear her when she was outside doing her work," Pinson said. "Gardening and tending the yard and so forth. But I think the very first time was in the winter soon after her arrival, when she was shoveling snow. I came along the sidewalk and heard her before she saw me. I was dumbstruck."

"What was she singing?"

He laughed, but his eyes remained cold and watchful behind the glasses. "This was thirty years ago, Detective. I haven't the faintest idea. Some kind of mawkish folk song or popular hit, I suppose. Her taste in music was uneducated, to say the least."

"Did you speak with Maggie about her singing?"

"Yes, of course. In fact, I remember asking her if she'd like some music lessons. I even offered them free of charge. It would have been lovely," he said with a sigh, "to work with that marvelous voice. What a gift the girl had."

"But she wasn't interested in singing lessons?"

"Apparently not. At any rate, she didn't leap to

take me up on the offer. Maggie Birk was really quite a common little thing,'' he added carelessly, glancing up at a hummingbird feeder suspended from the eaves. ''Amazing, isn't it, Detective, how these rare gifts are often bestowed in the most inappropriate places?''

Jackie kept her face noncommittal.

''Do you have any idea why anybody in the neighborhood might have wanted to kill Maggie Birk?'' she asked.

''I've been thinking about that ever since I learned of the unpleasant little excavation in your backyard. Obviously there must have been something going on within the household, wouldn't you say?''

''You think Alban Cernak or his son killed her?''

''Who else could have buried her in the backyard? I daresay I'd be suspicious,'' he added with a cold smile, ''if somebody arrived in my yard and started digging a grave big enough to hold a body.''

''Alban and his son were away all day at the clinic downtown,'' she said. ''I suppose that would have given a killer enough time to dispose of a body.''

He waved his hand in a curiously pettish gesture. ''I really don't like to think about it.''

''What can you tell me about the Weitzel family?'' she asked.

''The Weitzels? Surely they're not suspects?''

''I'm just trying to learn as much as possible about what the neighborhood was like thirty years ago. You seem to be fairly good friends with Mike Weitzel and his mother?''

''We've been neighbors, as you point out, for a

good many years," he said. "One does tend to become involved over time."

"Have you ever been married, Mr. Pinson?"

"I was married for a brief time in England before I emigrated. A wartime romance that didn't work out, I'm afraid."

"So that would have been..."

"More than fifty years ago," he said. "And on another continent. Hardly relevant to anything you might be investigating, Detective."

"Would you happen to have your ex-wife's current address?"

His face turned pink with annoyance. "My ex-wife has been dead for forty years. Really, I fail to see why this—"

"Can you tell me anything about Steven Weitzel?" Jackie interrupted as if he hadn't spoken.

"Steven?" His face twisted with emotion.

Jackie watched alertly and thought she detected alarm, even terror. But whatever the cause, Pinson's reaction was quickly masked.

"Yes," she said. "Steven Weitzel. Do you know him well?"

"Not at all. He's one of the younger sons. I believe he lives somewhere on the West Coast now, and has a rather squalid existence. There was a long-standing problem with drugs, as I recall."

"Really?" Jackie glanced up at her host. "I hadn't heard anything about that."

"You've only spoken with Dolly. They always try to keep the worst from her, but she's too shrewd to be fooled," Pinson added, his face softening a little. "I suspect Dolly probably knows more about her children's lives than anybody suspects."

Jackie remembered the bright-eyed, vigorous little woman. "I wouldn't doubt it."

She glanced casually at her host, thinking about those scraps of information from John Caldwell about Mike Weitzel's encounters with law enforcement when he was younger.

"Would you happen to recall any other problems with the Weitzel children while they were growing up, Mr. Pinson?"

"What kind of problems?" His tone and expression were so cold that Jackie was startled, and moved automatically a little nearer to the edge of the veranda where the baby's carriage rested just below.

But she kept her voice casual. "Well, anything dating back to when Maggie Birk lived here, I suppose. I'm trying to reconstruct an image of the neighborhood at that time, in the hopes we can maybe figure out what happened to Maggie."

"It sounds more like you're encouraging me to gossip."

"Well, I guess a lot of police work sounds like that." Jackie smiled and was relieved when Pinson smiled back. "Actually, in really cold cases like this," she went on, "we have no forensic evidence or other clues to go on. The only way for me to reconstruct the scene is through people's memories."

"And what's the relevance of the Weitzels?"

"They lived right across the street, and they had a whole houseful of kids about the same age as Maggie Birk. I'm just wondering if any traumas going on in their household might have had an effect on Maggie's life in some way."

Her host frowned and passed a well-kept hand across his forehead, unconsciously fitting a few strands of silver hair back in position. "Well, for one thing, I suppose that must have been about the same time as Laura—" Pinson stopped abruptly.

"Laura?" Jackie asked.

"The eldest Weitzel child."

Jackie flipped back through her notes. "Laura Weitzel was away at college when Maggie Birk lived across the street."

"But I seem to recall…" Pinson gave her a look of fastidious reluctance. "I suppose the whole neighborhood knew about it at the time, so somebody else will likely tell you if I don't."

"I'm sure they will." Jackie nodded in an encouraging fashion.

"Well, Laura got pregnant during her first year at college."

Pinson leaned forward. He seemed confiding, almost eager now that he'd made the decision to talk.

"Dolly and Klaus were terribly upset. They insisted she had to carry the baby to term and give it up for adoption. That was a much more common solution back in the sixties, you know."

"I suppose it was." Jackie made a note, keeping her face carefully devoid of expression. "So, did Laura Weitzel give her baby up for adoption?"

"I assume she did. But I only recall hearing that she was going to, and then nobody said another word about it. Dolly has never spoken of that baby again. All I know is that Laura came home later that summer looking frail and unhappy, but she definitely wasn't pregnant."

"And by that time, Maggie Birk had already disappeared?"

"I believe she had."

Jackie got to her feet, packed the notebook away in her diaper bag and went down to the carriage. "You've been very helpful, Mr. Pinson," she told her elderly neighbor, squinting up at him against the afternoon light. "If you recall anything else that seems significant, could you remember to let me know?"

"I'd be delighted," he said with a return of his flirtatious manner. Pinson was clearly relieved that the interview was over. "And perhaps you could drop by sometime just for a chat instead of all this police business, Detective?"

"I'll try to do that," Jackie said insincerely. She wrestled the carriage around and started off along the street toward her own house.

Daniel was awake but placid, frowning gravely at the row of stuffed toys that Paul had suspended from the hood of the carriage.

"Hi, sweetie," Jackie said to him with a quick surge of happiness. "Daddy's coming to see you tonight. He won't believe how much you've grown already."

"Talking to yourself again, Detective?" a voice said nearby.

Jackie looked up and saw John Caldwell across the hedge, raking fresh grass clippings off his lawn. Once again, despite the heat, he wore his customary long-sleeved cotton shirt and gabardine slacks held up by suspenders. His shiny bald head was bare and pink.

"You should wear a hat," Jackie told him. "That sun is awfully hot."

"Yes, it is," her neighbor agreed. "Especially when I have no hair for protection anymore. So, is this your new baby?"

"My goodness, I'm sorry," Jackie said. "He's so much the center of the world for me, I keep forgetting that not everybody has even seen him." She stood back a little from the carriage so he could get a better view. "John, meet Daniel."

Caldwell craned his neck, then trotted around to the gate and came right out onto the sidewalk so he could peer into the carriage. Wide-eyed and solemn, Daniel gazed back at him from the shadows.

"What a lovely baby," the old man breathed. He reached out toward the carriage before he noticed his grass-stained hands and drew back, giving Jackie a wistful, apologetic smile that wrenched her heart.

"I'll bring him over some evening and let you hold him," she promised.

"I'd love that." John continued to examine the baby. "I've never had any grandchildren, you know."

"Do you have other children besides Lola?"

"None."

"Oh, well," Jackie said without much conviction, "maybe she'll still get married and give you a couple of grandchildren."

Caldwell looked suddenly bleak. "I doubt it," he said.

"You know," she said lightly, "poor little Daniel doesn't have very many grandparents in his life, either, so maybe you two can adopt each other. You could be a surrogate grandfather. What do you think?''

Her neighbor's face lighted with such happiness that Jackie was touched. "I'd love that," he murmured, gazing at the baby again. "I'd really love it.''

Jackie patted his arm. "Consider it done," she said briskly. "From now on, you're Grandpa John.''

He beamed, looking shyly delighted, and she gave him an impulsive hug.

"Oh, I almost forgot," she added, gripping the handle of the carriage. "Could you tell Lola to drop by sometime when she has a minute? I got a bill for city property taxes that I don't quite understand. I thought the tax bill for this year was all settled as part of the real estate purchase.''

"I wouldn't know anything about that," he said. "But Lola will be able to help you. I'll send her over the next time she's here. She stops by almost every day.''

"Thanks, John. And now if you'll excuse us," she added, "it's almost feeding time.''

While nursing Danny, she used the time to work her way through more of Maggie's diary, holding the old scribbler in one hand and the baby in the other. She frowned at the faded greenish writing.

"I wish Maggie would get a new pen," she muttered to the baby who suckled contentedly, one hand folding and unfolding against her breast.

Jackie lifted the small hand and kissed it, then felt a brief chill when she remembered that Maggie's bones now lay in a compartment in the morgue, wrapped in a plastic body bag.

In her diary the girl seemed so real and vital that she was becoming like a living person to Jackie, another of the witnesses in this baffling case.

But thirty years ago Maggie Birk had abruptly stopped singing. She would never cook another banana cream pie, never shovel snow or play with her Raggedy Ann doll or write in a diary....

Monday, February 10, 1968

Well, I promised I'd tell about visiting the Betkers and now is a good time, because Lenny is downstairs watching TV and Alban had to go back to the clinic after supper, so I'm sitting up in my room. I really hate being alone in the house with Lenny. He's just a kid but he's still bigger than I am, and he's getting more creepy all the time.

Yesterday I was going down to take the laundry to his room and he was standing right there on the stairs so I couldn't get past, watching me from under that greasy hair. He's getting fatter and sloppier all the time, and his skin is really awful. It looks like raw hamburger and he picks at the pimples with his dirty fingernails. That turns my stomach, it really does.

Anyhow I said, "Excuse me, please," and he just repeated it after me, sort of mocking but not loud enough for Alban to hear upstairs in the kitchen. "Excuse me, please," he said in this really prissy way, but he kept staring at me until it made my skin crawl.

"I need to get by," I said, wishing I could turn around and run up the stairs again.

If you give in to a bully like Lenny, he'll make your life hell. Dad used to tell us that, and he should know because he was the biggest bully of all.

Anyhow, I tried to stand my ground, but Lenny leaned close and put his ugly face next to mine, almost touching. "I could kill you, bitch," he whispered. "I could wring your neck like a kitten and nobody would even know or care what happened to you."

My heart started beating so fast, like I was smothering. I got ready to scream for Alban, but then Lenny laughed and pushed past me. He's so fat there was hardly room for both of us on the stairs, and I hated rubbing against him while he passed. I just hated it.

When he was gone, I had to sit on the stairs for a while with my laundry basket until I could breathe again. But I still feel sick whenever I think about his skin, and his smell, and his...

Oh God, he's such an awful boy. I'd better make sure he never finds this book. I've got a good hiding place for it, in a hole I found under the wallpaper at the back of my closet. Still, who knows how much Lenny snoops around while I'm out doing errands?

I hate to think of him going through my things. Maybe I should ask Alban for a lock on my door. When Lenny talked about killing me, he really looked scary. He was even smiling, as if the idea of wringing my neck made him happy and excited.

But I won't do this. I'll think about nice things, like eating cookies with the Betker sisters. Eleanor invited me over yesterday for hot chocolate after my snow shoveling, and I've never seen such a beautiful house.

Eleanor treated me like I was a grown-up lady paying a social call. For once in my life, I really felt important. She told me to call them by their first names and took me right into the living room, which is full of paintings that Eleanor does herself when she's not working at the hospital. I couldn't believe anybody could just pick up a brush and make something so pretty.

Eleanor is tall and kind of rugged-looking, and I'll bet she'd be really beautiful if she went to any trouble.

Her sister Emma is like a flower, with soft golden hair and baby blue eyes, and as tiny as can be. She acted really strange while I was visiting. Half the time she talked in a rush like a little girl, asking me all kinds of things that weren't connected to each other. What I liked to eat and if I'd finished high school and whether I had any favorite singers, stuff like that. She kept asking things without even waiting for me to answer.

After a while she got sulky and seemed bothered that Eleanor was being so nice to me. Finally, Emma said she had something to do, and stamped off upstairs without saying goodbye. I felt bad, wondering if I'd done something to upset her, but Eleanor said her sister was just in a bad mood on account of being cooped up so long after the snowstorm.

I must admit, it was nicer after she was gone.

Eleanor and I talked about everything, and she was just wonderful to me. She acted like somebody halfway between a mother and a big sister, maybe a nice young aunt. I wouldn't really know because I only had younger sisters, and my own mom was always too beat down and scared to be much of a friend to me.

Eleanor told me all about her job at the hospital. She works in the operating room, almost like a doctor. I told her Alban was a doctor, too, and she shook her head but didn't say anything, just asked me how I liked working over there.

She was so nice, I even found myself telling her all about Lenny and how scared I am of him. She looked really upset and said she was going to talk to Alban, but I begged her not to because I just don't know what I'd do if I lost this job.

Eleanor said we could work something out, but I think she meant giving me some kind of charity and I don't want that. I intend to make my own way in the world with no help from anybody.

We talked about such a lot of things. She even asked about my limp, and I came closer to telling the truth than I usually do. She wasn't shocked or anything, she just shook her head again and looked sad, and gave me some more hot chocolate.

The only time she didn't seem nice was when I started talking about Mike Weitzel. Her face turned a little red and she said he was a violent, bad-tempered boy and I should stay away from him. I don't think that can be true because Mike is so sweet, but I didn't say anything more about him to Eleanor.

When I got up to leave and was putting my coat on in the kitchen, she helped me and then gave me a hug. Afterward, she touched my cheek and stood staring down at me so long that I started to feel a little nervous. It was sort of funny, as if she couldn't get enough of looking at me.

But I was probably imagining it, and besides, her house is so nice and she seems so interested in me. She asked me to visit again and I will as soon as I get the chance.

I think I'm going to be really happy in this new home I've found, where everybody but Lenny is nice to me!

16

It was early evening and Jackie was about to give the baby his very first tub bath. She spread a padding of towels on the kitchen counter, then filled an oval plastic tub with water and tested its temperature with her elbow, frowning in concentration.

Daniel sat beside her on the counter in his baby lounge. His small forehead creased, almost as if he knew what was about to happen and felt alarmed at the prospect.

"Hey, don't look at me like that," she muttered. "I know what I'm doing. They taught me all about this in the hospital."

But his troubled little face filled her with anxiety. Again she tested the water nervously, then arranged the soap, washcloth and baby oil.

When she lifted Daniel from the lounge a shadow fell across the kitchen floor, startling her. She whirled and saw a tall form blocking the doorway.

"Paul!" she said in delight. "I didn't expect you until later."

She couldn't recall being so happy to see him. If she hadn't been holding the baby, she would have run and thrown her arms around him—an unusual reaction for Jackie Kaminsky.

He closed the door and moved into the room, his

eyes kindling with warmth as he gazed at her and the infant in her arms. "What a nice sight," he said. "Jackie, you're beautiful."

She glanced down awkwardly at her sundress and sandals. "Oh, Paul, I'm just a mess. You can't believe how much time a baby takes up. I haven't shaved my legs since he was born."

Paul threw his head back, laughing so heartily that she found herself chuckling along with him. He reached for Daniel and she surrendered the baby gratefully, then turned back to her preparations at the kitchen counter, feeling unaccountably shy.

Paul lounged next to her, kissing the baby and nuzzling his dark hair. "What's all this?" he asked, waving a hand at the towels and other supplies.

"First bath," Jackie told him grimly. "I'm glad you came when you did. I was pretty nervous about doing this on my own."

He leaned over and kissed her bare neck. "The most macho, competent woman in the world," he teased, "all flustered over bathing a nine-pound baby."

His nearness and the feeling of his mouth on her skin surprised her with a sudden tingle of excitement and a glowing warmth that crept all through her body. According to the pregnancy books, sexual desire wasn't supposed to come back in full force until around the fifth or sixth week after delivery.

Jackie's mouth twitched with wry amusement.

Obviously the people who wrote the books hadn't been dealing with a man like Paul Arnussen....

Serenely oblivious to her reaction, he'd already placed the baby on the padding of towels and was deftly unfastening his terry-cloth sleeper.

Jackie watched his callused brown hands, moved by their tenderness.

"Hey," Paul said. "What's this?"

She moved closer, then laughed. "It's a belly button," she said proudly. "The stump dried up and came off yesterday."

Paul stared at the baby's rounded abdomen, fascinated. "What a difference it makes. He looks like a real boy now, instead of a newborn."

"Oh, he's a boy, all right," she said. "And if you don't put something over that little pink weapon of his, he'll squirt you in the eye to prove it."

Paul grinned and took the naked baby in his arms, cuddling him gently. Jackie watched them, almost dizzy with a love so complex that she could no longer separate her feelings for the man and the child.

With Paul's help she managed to bathe the slippery little body while Daniel howled in shock and outrage, his dark hair plastered wetly against his skull. They dressed him in clean blue sleepers and Jackie nursed him in the gathering twilight while Paul lay on the couch watching contentedly, his hands behind his head.

Afterward she burped Daniel and handed over the fat, drowsy baby, his small belly distended with milk.

"If you want to cuddle him for a bit," she said, feeling shy again, "I think he'll fall asleep right away."

"Okay." Paul took the baby and placed him on his broad chest, where Daniel snuggled with his diapered rump upraised like a furry blue snail.

Jackie lingered in the doorway, loving the way they looked together.

"Go upstairs," Paul told her, stroking his son's back. "I've got things under control. Spend an hour on yourself, sweetheart. Have a long hot bubble bath and shave your legs."

"God," she sighed, "that sounds wonderful. You know, Arnussen, this is actually much nicer than being a single mother."

She caught his dark, startled glance. But before he could say anything, she left the room, hurrying upstairs to run hot water into the old claw-footed tub.

After a luxurious soak and some rare time to wash her hair and fuss with personal grooming, Jackie went to bed feeling contented and revitalized.

Paul was beside her, reading, his muscular bare shoulders glowing in the lamplight. She leaned over to kiss his jaw and nuzzle the mat of hair on his chest.

"You know what? I'm feeling almost sexy," she whispered.

He lowered the book and glanced at her in surprise. "So soon?"

"Too soon," she agreed. "But I might not be able to wait for the whole six weeks."

"Now that," he said fervently, "would suit me just fine."

Jackie chuckled at his look of wolfish hunger. "It's good for me to be around you," she said. "I feel like a real person, not just somebody's mother."

"You're a great mother." He kissed the tip of her nose, then sobered. "Jackie..."

"Hmm?" She was still playing idly with the

golden hairs on his chest, wrapping them around her fingers and wondering if she and Paul had any chance of producing a blond child next time.

"Have you found out anything more about those bones in the backyard?"

"Quite a bit, actually." She told him how Dolly Weitzel had identified the missing housekeeper from thirty years earlier, about the diary hidden in the wall cavity and her interviews with the neighbors.

Briefly she was tempted to discuss the threatening note, as well. It haunted her more all the time though she tried not to think about it.

I wouldn't mind killing another baby....

She shuddered and burrowed into his arms.

"Jackie?" he murmured against her hair. "Is something wrong?"

"Listen, Paul, I think I should probably tell you something."

"Go ahead. I'm all ears."

But at that moment they were interrupted by a sleepy wail from the carriage they'd moved to the foot of their bed. Jackie raised herself on one elbow to peer at the clock.

"Almost eleven o'clock," Paul said cheerfully. "Time for a nightcap." He heaved himself out of bed and gathered the howling baby into his arms, carrying him down the hall for a diaper change before his nursing.

Long after Daniel was fed and settled, and Paul had fallen asleep as well, Jackie lay and stared at his aquiline profile in the moonlight. She felt an increasing sense of frustration with herself for the way she was handling this relationship.

Now that Paul had drawn back from her a little

and appeared, at least outwardly, content to be a visitor instead of a live-in lover, it seemed she wanted him more than she ever had.

Clearly, this man was destined to be her partner and the father of her children. Jackie's friends were probably right, it simply made good emotional and economic sense for the two of them to marry, or at least live together.

But she still couldn't make that leap. She found it impossible to picture herself giving up this house, along with her own hard-won independence, and taking Daniel out to the ranch to throw her life irretrievably together with Paul's.

Even the thought of it gave her deep chills of fear.

"Oh, shit," she murmured wearily, rolling over to stare at the ceiling.

Overcome by drowsiness, Jackie closed her eyes and waited for sleep to come. But even when she was barely conscious of her surroundings, she could still feel the man lying next to her, and kept touching him lightly with her foot for reassurance.

The next morning, Paul left for the ranch at first light. After breakfast, Jackie was outside weeding the new flower bed with Daniel sleeping nearby in his veiled carriage under the big cottonwood tree.

Above her head the two robins continued their ceaseless missions. By now Jackie could hear the nestlings clamoring to be fed, their noisy chirping silenced only briefly whenever one of the weary parents arrived with a fresh morsel.

"They're worse than you are," she told the silent carriage. "Those poor little parents are nothing but feeding machines."

Smiling, she leaned back on her heels and gazed with satisfaction at the rows of flourishing plants. The petunias looked green and healthy, and were beginning to form buds that would open soon into new flowers.

She had a brief, involuntary image of poor little Maggie's body lying under that soil for so many years, with the unknown baby next to her. Had their vital essences helped to nourish these new green plants?

Suddenly chilled, she shuddered though the sun was warm, and rubbed her bare arms nervously.

All at once somebody was looming close behind her. She jumped up to see Mike Weitzel standing near her on the grass, wearing crisp khakis and a white polo shirt, his curly hair glistening.

"Dammit!" she muttered, shaken. "Where the hell did you come from?"

"Sorry if I startled you." He watched her with obvious concern. "I knocked at the front door but there was no answer, so I just came around."

"That's okay," she said, beginning to recover her equilibrium. "I just didn't hear you coming, that's all."

For the first time she found herself wondering if she should find a way to keep her gun with her when she was outside the house.

"I thought I should drop by for a little chat, if you have time," he said.

"Why?" Jackie asked.

He met her eyes with a look of quiet challenge. "Because my mother is really upset about this Maggie Birk thing, and I'd like to see you get it over with to set her mind at rest. Besides," he added while Jackie went to get the carriage and pushed it toward the house, "I have no doubt you're wanting to talk to me, so I thought I might as well make it easy for you."

"That's very considerate." Jackie parked the carriage near the back porch and gestured toward one of the chairs.

Weitzel sat down, glancing around at the backyard. "This is really nice. You've done a whole lot of work out here."

"Paul does most of it," Jackie said. "Tending the yard helps to fill his time while I'm busy with the baby."

She found herself anxious to let Mike Weitzel know she wasn't alone here, that Paul spent a lot of time with her. The anonymous letter in her mailbox must have rattled her more than she cared to admit. And Wardlow hadn't found the time to stop by as often as he'd promised...

Weitzel cleared his throat, looking down at the big diamond ring, turning it idly on his finger. His hands were large and square, neatly manicured but still powerful-looking. Involuntarily, Jackie pictured them touching her baby and felt a deep sense of revulsion. She got up to draw the blanket higher over Danny's little sleeping body.

"So, what do you want to talk about?" she said at last, aware that she sounded brusque.

"You tell me." He gave her a brief, mirthless smile. "You're the cop."

"Okay," she said calmly. "Then let's start by finding out why you lied to me about Maggie Birk, shall we?"

His handsome face paled a little. "What do you mean by that?"

"Come on, Mike. I'm a detective. I've been trained to recognize when people are lying. You told me you had no memory of Maggie Birk living over here, but that wasn't true, was it?"

An emotion flickered across his face, possibly anger or fear, but he controlled it so quickly that Jackie couldn't tell for sure.

"Okay, you're right," he said. "That wasn't true."

"You did know her, then?"

"A little." His voice roughened. He kept staring at the diamond ring, glinting dully in the shaded light. "Maggie was kind of cute. A pitiful little thing, really, but so..." He cleared his throat. "She was so happy all the time, for no reason that I could see."

"Why did you lie about knowing her?"

He shrugged. "Why does anybody lie? It's an instinctive reaction, I guess. Somebody finds a body and it turns out to be somebody you were once involved with. Your first instinct is to protect yourself."

Not if you're innocent, Jackie thought.

She wanted to go inside and get her notebook, but was reluctant to change the tenor of their conversation when Mike Weitzel seemed to be in a confiding mood.

And she realized that part of her reluctance stemmed from the fact that she didn't want to leave her baby alone with this man, even for a minute. But it would be awkward to gather Danny up from his carriage and take him with her to get the notebook.

"You were involved with Maggie?" she said.

"Just a boy-girl kind of thing, kidding when we met on the sidewalk. Nothing serious. We were both about seventeen."

Jackie extended her legs, which looked long and silky after her bout of grooming the previous evening. She wore a tank top and cotton shorts, and was already beginning to feel trim and fast-moving again, pleasantly confident inside her body. It was a good sensation after the clumsiness and vulnerability of late pregnancy.

"Could you tell me bit about your personal life?" she asked. "Just to help me put things in context?"

"Sure, my life's an open book. What do you want to know?"

"Are you married?" Jackie asked.

"Divorced. No kids. I live in a rented house out by Indian Canyon golf course."

"That's a pretty nice location," Jackie said.

He shrugged. "I make a nice living."

"How long were you married?"

"Almost fifteen years. We sort of grew apart, mostly because I worked all the time. It was one of those cliché situations," he added cheerfully. "Right after she turned forty, she left me for her tennis coach."

"You don't seem particularly upset about it," Jackie said.

"I'm not. Kelly and I are still friends. We didn't have a messy divorce because there were no kids and I didn't mind giving her a big chunk of the money. She deserved it after putting up with me all those years. I wasn't exactly an angel myself."

"So, did she marry the tennis coach?" Jackie asked with genuine curiosity.

Marriages were on her mind a great deal these days. She found the relationships between people a lot more interesting than she once had.

Weitzel laughed and looked more at ease. "God, no! She married a dentist. Right now they're living in Mexico for six months. He's on some program where every three years he donates dental services to poor kids in developing countries."

"That's a nice thing to do."

"He's a very nice guy," Weitzel said with a mocking grin. "Kelly always did have good taste in men."

Jackie glanced across the fence. The Betker sisters were outside in their yard, where they spent so many summer days. Eleanor wore her denim overalls and pushed a lawn mower back and forth over the grass. Emma sat on the veranda, ensconced in a padded wicker chair, playing with her Barbie dolls.

While Jackie watched, Gerald Pinson came through the neighbor's front gate and walked up the path, pausing to greet Eleanor who straightened and shaded her eyes, the mower idle as she replied.

The tall woman leaned closer and said something to Pinson. He turned abruptly and looked over at the porch where Jackie sat with her guest. Pinson's face behind the glasses seemed taut, almost frightened, and he turned away immediately, climbing the veranda steps and sitting down near Emma.

"I can't figure out the relationships in this neighborhood," Jackie said. "It's really hard to understand what kind of interactions people have with each other.''

"No kidding. They're hard for *me* to figure out," Weitzel said dryly, "and I've known these people since I was born.''

Jackie gave him a quick glance but he was staring at the adjoining yard with a brooding expression.

Eleanor switched off the lawn mower and began working near her pillared veranda, raking grass clippings. Gerald Pinson continued his conversation with her, discussing lawn fertilizer in a voice loud enough to be heard next door. Their exchange seemed deliberate and artificial, as if both of them were conscious of the two people sitting nearby.

"Why do I get the impression," Jackie said idly, "that Eleanor and your friend Gerald aren't happy to see you over here?''

"Eleanor's never liked me much." He turned to her with a broad smile, and she was conscious again of his heavy-handed masculine charm. "Maybe they think we're having an affair," he suggested. "I doubt that Eleanor would approve of that.''

"Really? Why not?''

He leaned back in the chair, one arm dangling over the back, and crossed his legs. "Well, it's not exactly her style, wouldn't you agree? A male-female relationship, I mean.''

Jackie weighed this bit of information, wondering how to react.

"Not to say it wouldn't be my style," he added, glancing down at Jackie's bare legs with frank admiration.

She decided Mike Weitzel was getting far too

comfortable in this conversation, and it was time to regain the upper hand.

"So, what can you tell me about Stephanie Mulder?" she asked with deliberate casualness, and saw the quick clench of his hands, the tightening along his jaw.

Weitzel was one of those men with such a heavy beard that, in the morning sunlight, his jaw looked faintly blue even after a recent shave.

"What about her?" he said.

"Mike, we'll never get anywhere if you keep answering my questions with other questions," she said easily. "My partner tells me that in 1969, you were charged with assault on a young woman called Stephanie Mulder, and pleaded no contest so you wouldn't have to do jail time. The file's been stripped and doesn't contain much detail, so I was just wondering if you could tell me a little more about the whole case."

"For God's sake," he muttered, looking angry and startled. "Thirty years later and I still can't shake that goddamn mess."

"When you beat up on a woman," Jackie said, her voice hardening, "it does tend to follow you around."

He jerked his head erect. "I didn't beat up on her! It was a setup. Stephanie was mad at me because I wanted the relationship to be over. We slept together one last time, then had a big fight. Next day she charged me with rape. She even stabbed herself with a kitchen knife to make it look like I'd attacked her."

"But you still pleaded no contest?"

"It was going to kill my mother otherwise. She

wouldn't have been able to stand a trial. And I'd do anything,'' he added, watching Jackie's face, ''to protect my mother.''

''I see.'' Jackie leaned back in the chair and returned his gaze thoughtfully. ''You and your brothers and sister were a little hard on your mother back in those days, weren't you?''

''I suppose we were. Adolescents are never fun to raise, and we were no different.''

''What happened to your sister's baby, Mike?''

Again he looked startled and wary. ''What are you talking about? Laura has three kids.''

''But she had another one when she was in college, right? A baby born out of wedlock that she gave up for adoption.''

He gave her a look of bitterness tinged with grudging admiration. ''You really do your homework, don't you, Detective?''

''It's my job,'' she said. ''Tell me about Laura's baby.''

''I don't know anything about it, and that's the honest truth. It's something our family has never talked about. We knew she was pregnant, and that my parents insisted she have the baby and give it away. As far as my brothers and I ever knew, that was exactly what she did. When she came home that summer, she wasn't pregnant but she sat up in her room and cried all the time. The next winter she met David and got married, and settled in to have a nice life and three kids.''

''Where does she live?''

''In a suburb of Detroit. David's an executive with Ford. They're very prosperous. And it doesn't hurt me, either,'' he added, ''having a brother-in-law in the company.''

''But you've never talked with your sister about the baby she gave away?''

''Never,'' he said. ''I don't know if she even thinks about it anymore.''

Jackie glanced at the carriage. ''Oh, yes, Mike,'' she said softly. ''I'm sure your sister still thinks about that baby.''

''You could be right, I suppose. But it's certainly not a topic of family discussion.''

Jackie watched him for a moment, wondering how to penetrate the man's deliberate self-control. Except for that brief startled response when she mentioned his old assault case, she didn't feel she'd made any impact on him at all.

''So,'' she began, ''you're telling me that you and Maggie Birk were just—''

But before she could finish framing the question, they were interrupted by the sound of the side gate clicking, and the hollow thump of footsteps along the path next to the house.

17

Jackie tensed, her heart beating faster, then relaxed and settled back when Lola Bridges appeared in the sunlight near the corner of the house.

I'm so jumpy these days, it's just ridiculous, she thought. I really have to get a grip on myself.

She even wondered if her unaccustomed nervousness was part of the hormonal change associated with childbirth. The speculation made her think of Adrienne, and she reminded herself to call her friend that morning, as soon as she had a chance.

"Sorry," Lola muttered, looking awkward. "I didn't know you had company."

Mike Weitzel was examining the newcomer with a focused interest that seemed to make Lola uncomfortable. Jackie watched them idly, wondering just how well they knew each other.

John Caldwell had moved here after Mike was grown and gone, and Lola had never lived with her father in the house next door. But their parents had been neighbors for twenty-five years and Spokane wasn't such a huge city. It was reasonable to assume their paths had crossed a few times.

Mike continued to eye Lola with an absorbed, thoughtful look, as if a little surprised by her appearance. She really did look nicer than usual, Jackie thought.

The real estate saleswoman wore a summer-weight pink linen suit that flattered her plump, stocky figure, and her hair seemed less brassy, though she was still artfully made-up.

"Do you two know each other," Jackie said, "or should I be making introductions?"

"We've met," Mike replied easily. "Good morning, Lola. You look especially nice today."

Lola's cheeks reddened under the patches of cosmetic blush. "So do you," she said, but her voice seemed strained and she was clearly uncomfortable.

She hesitated by the corner of the house, looking over her shoulder as if anxious to escape.

"Dad told me you had some problems with the property taxes," she said to Jackie. "But I can come back later if you're busy."

"I was just leaving." Mike Weitzel got to his feet and glanced at Jackie. "Is that okay? The Spokane Police Department is all finished with me?"

"If I need anything more, I can always call you," she said. "And if you happen to remember anything else about the time when Maggie Birk was living here, maybe you could let me know, okay?"

"Sure." When he smiled, a gold filling flashed behind one of his eyeteeth. "Feel free to call me anytime, Detective."

He paused at the edge of the porch beside Lola.

"You too, Lola," he said. "We should fix you up with a nice new car someday soon. Realtors need to impress their clients, you know."

"If I need a new car," Lola said, "you'll be the first one I call."

But her voice sounded less confident than usual, and she avoided his eyes as he passed her. Jackie watched thoughtfully, thinking that Mike Weitzel seemed to have very complicated relationships with women.

As he left, Weitzel looked sharply over the fence at the Betker sisters and Gerald Pinson, who waved to him without expression.

For a moment his manner seemed aggressive, almost challenging. Then he disappeared around the side of the house, and Lola crossed the yard to peer into the baby carriage.

"He looks bigger already," she said over her shoulder to Jackie. "Like a real little boy, and he's barely a newborn."

"He's almost two weeks old." Jackie sighed, feeling a sudden wave of fatigue. "Time flies when you're having fun, I guess."

Lola smiled with sympathy and came to sit in the chair that Mike had recently vacated. "Is he still keeping you awake at night?"

Jackie leaned back, closing her eyes briefly and rolling her head against the chair back. "He's not too bad. He sometimes even sleeps for four hours at a stretch, but it's hard when you never get an unbroken rest. I'm reduced to having all kinds of fantasies about sleeping for twelve solid hours."

"Well, it won't be long till he sleeps through the night, will it? Not that I know very much about babies," Lola added hastily.

"I'm hoping it won't be too long." Jackie opened her eyes and smiled at her visitor.

Across the fence, Gerald Pinson and Eleanor Betker had also registered the arrival of the newcomer.

They still watched covertly from behind the veranda pillars, but didn't seem nearly as interested as they had been during her conversation with Mike Weitzel.

Finally, Eleanor set her glass aside and went down to continue raking grass clippings near the veranda while Gerald watched Emma dressing her dolls.

Jackie turned back to her guest. "Lola, how well do you know Mike Weitzel?"

"Not well at all. We know each other to say hello on the street, that's all."

"He seemed," Jackie teased, "to find you very attractive today."

Lola flushed again. "Oh, don't be silly. From what I hear, Mike Weitzel is like that with every woman he meets."

"Yeah, I've noticed the guy is quite a lady-killer, all right."

Jackie paused abruptly, a little embarrassed by her own choice of words, which seemed tactless in the extreme. But Lola appeared not to have heard and was clearly anxious to change the subject.

"About those property taxes," she said, digging into her big handbag while Jackie looked on in amusement at the plump hands sparkling with rings.

"I have the tax schedule here," Lola went on, "and a copy of the real estate offer. Now, can you recall if you..."

Seeing her visitor's discomfort, Jackie dropped the subject of Mike Weitzel and settled into a discussion of real estate fees and property taxes.

As soon as Lola was gone, she went into the house and called Adrienne to make a date for an afternoon visit, then went to get Maggie's diary before she sat down to nurse the baby.

Maggie had begun to seem more contented in the months following the tumult of her escape from home and her arrival at Alban Cernak's house. The closely written pages turned from green to blue, and became primarily a recounting of domestic trivia and the housemaid's growing fascination with handsome young Mike Weitzel from across the street.

As she read and the baby nursed placidly, Jackie's tiredness dropped away, replaced by a tense, prickly feeling which she recognized. Wardlow often laughed about this feeling, referring to "Kaminsky and her goddamn woman's instinct," but in police matters it was unfailing.

Whenever she felt this way, something was about to happen. The tension was like some kind of primitive warning to have her wits about her, to be cautious and prepared. Jackie had learned from long experience that she neglected it at her peril.

Impatiently, she skipped ahead through the diary, ignoring Maggie's recitation of household tasks and daily menus. The girl seemed fascinated by food, as if she'd never had enough to eat. From occasional references to her former life, Jackie suspected her existence back in Salt Lake City had been pretty impoverished.

No wonder Maggie thought Alban Cernak was a prince, and his modest home a kind of castle.

Jackie paused only at passages containing names she recognized, trying to analyze all of Maggie's developing relationships. In the months between February and April, the girl formed a close bond with Eleanor Betker but was a little troubled by

Emma, who seemed aloof and often childishly spiteful when Maggie visited the big house next door.

Early in April she recorded the assassination of Martin Luther King, and seemed quite distressed over it, although Jackie doubted that Maggie, with her hardscrabble Salt Lake City background, had any deep understanding of the civil rights movement and its implications for America. Warmhearted and generous as always, Maggie's concerns were mostly with "that poor man's wife and his sweet little kids."

She continued to worship Alban Cernak, recording minute details about her employer's behavior and personal appearance. His hair, though shoulder-length, was thinning on top. He had tattoos on his forearms, one shaped like a mermaid and one like a heart, which Maggie thought were completely out of character. He read the Bible and listened to opera, held a deep opposition to the war in Vietnam and was dedicated to the underprivileged people he met at his downtown clinic.

Maggie was fascinated by the man, but his attitude toward his housekeeper seemed to remain intensely proper, almost stiff. He avoided any kind of familiarity with her except for occasional bits of praise after well-cooked meals or extra work which she undertook voluntarily, like cleaning the windows.

Maggie treasured his praise, always recording it verbatim.

"Alban said the Yorkshire pudding was as fluffy as a cloud," or, "Today Alban noticed that I'd waxed all the hardwood floors. He said I was a good hardworking girl and added ten dollars to my check. He's just so nice.''

But her relationship with the sullen Lenny continued to deteriorate. By April the two young people had reached a state of open warfare. Lenny sometimes hit or slapped her when Alban was out of the house, and dared her to tell. For the most part, however, the overweight teenager remained in his basement room, "sulking and picking at his face," as Maggie expressed it.

But the girl no longer cared, because she was deeply in love.

Jackie selected a page nearer the end of the diary and settled in to read, absently patting Danny's plump little back as he nursed.

Monday, April 19, 1968

I've started keeping Raggedy Annabel in the hole in the wall along with my book. It would be just like Lenny to steal her and tear her to bits. Anything to torment me...

I feel sorry for poor Raggedy, having to spend all day in that dark hole, but at least I still get her out every night to take to bed with me. It feels nice to hold her.

Weekends are the worst, because sometimes Alban gets called down to the clinic and Lenny doesn't go along. I just hate being alone in the house with him. Mike says whenever that happens I should call and he'll come over, but I still feel awfully shy about doing that. I don't think Dolly and Klaus are happy about Mike going out with me. He's so wonderful, they probably want him to marry some smart rich girl who's going to college or something like that.

Sometimes Dolly looks at me like she wishes I was dead, which is creepy because she's usually such a nice, happy little person.

In the old days, I'd just run over to Eleanor's until Alban got back, but lately I don't like to do that, either, because Eleanor is acting so funny. She used to be really nice, hugging me and giving me things like old clothes of Emma's that fit me perfectly and look so pretty. But now she asks me about Mike all the time and warns me that men can't be trusted, and gets all red in the face.

It's almost like she's jealous, the way girls used to be at school when you got another best friend, but of course that's ridiculous. Eleanor and I haven't known each other that long, and besides, she's so much older than me. More like my mother's age, actually.

Emma acts weird, too. She's so odd most of the time, I never really know what to make of her. Nowadays she sits up in her room a lot, looking at books and making clothes for her doll collection. I can see her watching me from her window sometimes, but whenever I wave at her she drops the curtain and disappears.

I've also gone over to Gerald Pinson's once or twice on the weekend for a singing lesson, which is kind of fun. His house is really nice, and even though he seems a little creepy, when I'm there he's all business. And he certainly does think I can sing.

But last time I was there, Steven Weitzel stopped by the back door with another of those big brown envelopes, and Gerald gave him money for it.

I don't think Steve knew I was in the other room. Gerald got rid of him as soon as he could, but afterward he didn't seem interested in my singing anymore. He was all jumpy and funny-looking, and kept forgetting where we were in the song when he was playing the piano, so after a while I just left.

I'd sure love to get a peek inside one of those envelopes!

Dad always said I'm too curious, and curiosity killed the cat. He's probably right, the mean old thing. I should just stay away from Gerald Pinson's house, too.

But if I can't go anywhere, I have to stay at home with Lenny and he's so awful. He's too fat to go outside and play ball or do anything with the other kids. They even make fun of him if he's only walking down the street.

"Fatty fatty two-by-four," they call out. "Can't get through the kitchen door." If it was anybody but Lenny, I'd feel sorry for him.

Yesterday he said I'd stolen his ring, and he was going to get Alban to fire me if I didn't give it back. As if I'd want anything of his, the ugly monster! Especially not this ring, which Lenny wears all the time. It's made of gold and is shaped like four snakes that come apart, then fit back together to make a wide band. All the snakes have rubies for eyes. Sometimes I have nightmares about those red-eyed snakes coming

into my bed and crawling all over me, and I
wake up holding my dolly so hard that the poor
little thing would probably be suffocating if she
was a real baby.

Anyhow, Lenny made such a fuss about the
stupid ring that I had to stop what I was doing
and spend almost an hour looking for it. I finally found it by the laundry tub downstairs
where Monster Boy must have taken it off to
wash his hands. I didn't want to touch it so I
went upstairs and told him where it was.

"It's a good thing you decided to give it
back," he said. "You're such a little thief,
Maggie-bitch."

"And you're an ugly creep!" I yelled at him.
"I never touched your stupid ring, you freak!"

He looked like he was really going to hit me.
But Alban came into the kitchen just then, talking about what a beautiful spring day it was,
and Lenny stamped off downstairs.

Later on, after I'd finished up the dishes, I
managed to sneak away for a couple of hours
and be with Mike, which makes everything else
worthwhile. He got his father's car and I
walked a few blocks away from the house before he picked me up so nobody could tell what
we were doing. We drove out into the country,
way up along the river, and watched the sunset.

Then we got into the back seat for a while
and did what we always do. It doesn't hurt anymore and Mike is so gentle with me. He says
he loves me and wants us to be together all the
time.

I told him Alban is talking about going to

Portland very soon, maybe even next month. I'm not sure why Alban wants to move because I know he loves his job at the clinic and the house is so nice, but he just says it's a "necessary trial of life."

Alban has offered me a permanent job and said he wants me to come with them, so pretty soon Mike and I have to make a decision. I know we're both young, but we can't stand the thought of being apart. And last night I finally told him what's been happening with me. I know I'm not usually all that regular, but this time I'm really late, at least two weeks.

Oh God, I can't believe I actually wrote that down. I have to remember to hide this book very carefully! If Lenny ever found it and told Alban...

I wish I had somebody to talk to. Eleanor could help me, she's a nurse and knows all about these things, but I get the feeling she'd be really, really upset if she knew what Mike and I have been doing.

Mike was sweet as always. He hugged me and said everything would be all right, but I can tell how worried he is. Klaus and Dolly want him to stay in school because he could get drafted and be sent to Vietnam if he quits, and that would be just horrible. Alban says President Johnson has decided he won't run again in the fall, so maybe the war will end soon? I hope so.

I guess unless Mike can think of something for us to do, I'll have to talk to Alban. He's a doctor, after all, and at the clinic he works with pregnant girls all the time. But if Alban knows, he might not want to take me to Portland. And if Dolly and Klaus make Mike go away to college, I'll be all alone here.

My mind just keeps spinning round and round until I get a headache so bad I could scream. I don't know what to do! But I still believe Mike will look after me. He said he would, and I know he loves me. Mike is just so wonderful.

Jackie put the diary aside, cuddling her baby, who had fallen asleep, a trickle of milk on his chin. She wiped his face and kissed him, breathing deep of his warm powdery fragrance, then settled him in the carriage and returned to her chair, gazing out the window at the spreading mountain ash tree as she pondered.

Maggie had first suspected herself pregnant in mid-April. But she'd vanished from the neighborhood around May or June, and the newborn infant in that backyard grave had been full-term.

Had Klaus and Dolly Weitzel conspired to dispose of a troublesome influence in their son's life and an unwelcome grandchild at the same time?

Jackie tried to picture happy little Dolly Weitzel killing a baby and chopping a girl up with an ax, but her imagination boggled.

Of course, she'd never met Klaus Weitzel....

She rocked the carriage gently, resolving at the first opportunity to ask Mike what his father had been like.

As if in response to her thoughts, the phone rang

and when she answered she heard Weitzel himself at the other end of the line.

"Hi, Jackie," he said. "I'm sorry to keep bothering you."

"That's okay." Jackie looked over at the carriage, which seemed to be shifting and moving slightly. The shrill ringing of the downstairs telephone occasionally woke the baby.

"Did I interrupt anything?"

"No, the baby is asleep now. At least I hope he is." As she watched, the carriage settled slowly back into motionlessness.

"Well, I was thinking I need to talk to you again, if that's okay."

"Why?" Jackie said. "Have you remembered something else about Maggie?"

"You might say that. It—it came to me..." He paused, sounding reluctant, almost embarrassed. "I thought of it this morning when we were talking and Gerald and Eleanor were watching from the veranda, remember?"

"Mike?" she asked, puzzled by his tone.

"Look, it's nothing I can talk about over the phone. In fact, this is so goddamn incredible..." He paused again, sounding increasingly awkward.

Jackie gazed with narrowed eyes at the bulletin board fixed to the wall above the telephone.

"Two gallons of white paint, six blocks of livestock salt, penicillin tablets for the calves," Paul had written as a reminder to himself. Jackie reached out involuntarily to touch the blunt handwriting, warmed by a sudden rush of affection.

"Mike," she said abruptly, "why didn't you tell me that you and Maggie Birk were lovers?"

"What?" he asked. "I don't know what you're talking about."

"Oh, come on," Jackie said impatiently, then glanced at the carriage and lowered her voice. "First you said you didn't remember her, then you barely knew her, then it was just a casual boy-girl thing. So, tell me the truth, Mike. You were sleeping with her, and Maggie thought she was pregnant. The two of you were even talking about getting married."

"My God," he muttered, sounding shaken. "I don't know who—"

"Maggie told me herself," Jackie said bluntly.

"Maggie told you?"

"I found her old diary hidden in the back of a closet, Mike. It's been telling me all kinds of things."

He was silent so long that she thought he'd hung up. At last he said, "I couldn't marry her. My parents would have gone out of their minds. I already had my draft number by then."

"So the poor girl became a real problem to you, I suppose."

"But it wasn't... Look, can I come and see you again, Jackie? Or would you like to come over here?"

"Where are you?"

"At home out in Indian Canyon. I'll be here most of the day."

"You're not going to be at your office today?" Jackie asked.

"No, I'm taking a little time off for a change. God knows I could use a rest."

She felt a chill of alarm, a prickle along the nape of her neck. "Sorry, but it's probably easiest if you come here,'' she said casually. ''With the baby and all, you know. I'm busy this afternoon, so it'll have to be sometime in the early evening, okay?''

She could put the baby to sleep inside the house, then lock the door and sit with Weitzel on the front veranda, Jackie decided. That would be safe, in full view of the other neighbors.

Briefly she contemplated asking Paul to come in for the evening, then decided against it. If he got any idea she was feeling timid about her job or the baby's safety, he would have even more ammunition for his ongoing crusade to force her retirement from police work.

''Seven o'clock, then?'' Weitzel said.

''Sure, that sounds fine.''

''Jackie, you aren't going to believe what I have to tell you.''

''I'm not?''

''Hell no,'' Weitzel muttered darkly before he hung up. ''I hardly even believe it myself.''

18

That afternoon, Jackie and Adrienne walked side by side toward Northtown Mall, pushing their baby strollers along the shaded avenues. Both women wore shorts, sandals and tank taps, and Adrienne's face was shaded by a black silk baseball cap glistening with gold stars.

"You look better today," Jackie ventured, studying her friend's aristocratic profile.

Adrienne sighed. "I'm gradually clawing my way back. It's the most god-awful feeling, Jackie. Like falling into a deep dark pit."

"And it's all hormones?"

"Well, that's what the doctor says. I'm on some medication she claims is going to help." Adrienne frowned. "But I believe a big part of it is just me and my manic terror of motherhood."

"Wasn't this something you and Harlan have been wanting for years?"

"I guess it was." Adrienne flashed one of her old rueful smiles. "You know what they say...be very careful what you wish for, because there's a damn good chance you might get it."

"But...aren't you happy with the baby?" Jackie looked at little Matthew in the stroller. Now almost two months old, he was a chubby, blue-eyed baby with an engaging smile.

"I adore the baby. That's what makes me feel so guilty about the way I'm acting. Nobody in my house deserves to live with a bitch like me."

Jackie stopped walking and glared at her friend. "For God's sake, Rennie, stop being so hard on yourself, okay? This is postnatal depression, not some kind of crime."

"I know. I know. Don't look so fierce, Kaminsky. You're scaring me." Adrienne smiled with an awkwardness that made Jackie's heart ache.

The two women fell into step again.

"It's just that I never realized until I became a mother myself," Adrienne said, "how truly uncaring my own mother always was. I think I'm flipping out because I'm terrified it's genetic or something and I can never be different."

"But Leigh is such a wonderful mother," Jackie said, thinking of Adrienne's younger sister and her little son. "She always has been."

"That's true, but Leigh got treated differently at home right from the beginning," Adrienne said calmly. "She was a good little girl, so quiet and pretty, and Mother loved her a whole lot more than me."

Jackie thought about the complex interpersonal dynamics of the wealthy Mellon family, and of Adrienne's sister and parents.

"Families are just too hard to figure out," she said at last. "If you ever saw where I came from, Rennie, and the way I was raised, you'd think I had no business at all giving birth and trying to shape a new human being. But here I am."

"And doing great I'm sure," Adrienne said wistfully.

Jackie looked at her son's tiny body inside the stroller, his white terry-cloth sunsuit and matching socks. "I love him," she said simply. "Right now this little baby is my whole world. I can hardly imagine how I ever lived without him."

"Me, too. I think that's what will ultimately pull me out of the blues, just seeing how sweet-natured Matty is. Harlan says we probably can't mess him up no matter how inept we are."

"Babies are so great," Jackie said. "If our kids can survive our mothering, Rennie, think what strong men they'll be."

Adrienne didn't respond. Jackie glanced at her cautiously, searching for something to lighten her friend's mood.

"Hey, when we get to the mall," she said with forced cheerfulness, "let's each have a banana split, okay? We're nursing mothers. We need the calcium."

"Sounds good to me," Adrienne said absently.

"Rennie..."

"Hmm?" Adrienne bent to touch one of her son's fat pink legs, then removed his bootees.

"Do you remember anything much about 1968?" Jackie asked.

Adrienne straightened and looked at her friend, the bootees dangling from her hand. "I was six years old in 1968, just starting school. I guess I remember the standard TV images...flower children and bell-bottom pants, long hair and peace signs and love beads. That kind of stuff."

"Not me," Jackie said grimly. "I was only four

that year, about to turn five. But I still remember being terrified every night that my grandmother would be killed on the street or our apartment would be gone by morning.''

''Why?''

''It was a year after the Watts riots, and Los Angeles was still a powder keg of racial tension. Martin Luther King was assassinated in April of that year, and then they killed Bobby Kennedy in June, right in my hometown. There was so much rage and militancy down in South Central, we never knew what was going to happen from one day to the next.''

''My God.'' Adrienne looked thoughtful. ''I'd forgotten about all that. I had such a sheltered childhood, Jackie. But you were growing up in L.A., right in the middle of it, weren't you?''

''We were south of the Watts-Compton area, but the anger and violence spilled all over L.A. The summers were always hot, horrible and dangerous, but 1968 was the worst of all. I felt like a little kid living in a war zone.'' Jackie looked down at her baby again. ''I guess I was.''

''So, why are you suddenly doing all this reminiscing?''

''It's those old bones they dug out of my backyard. We've dated them to the late spring of 1968.''

Adrienne looked interested for a change, so Jackie fell into step beside her and told as much as she could comfortably divulge about the investigation, concluding with Mike Weitzel's visit to her house that morning. Adrienne listened and nodded, pushing her stroller.

''Do you know him at all?'' Jackie asked.

''Mike Weitzel? We've met a few times. I think

he has social aspirations," Adrienne said. "His ex-wife, Kelly, wanted to join the arts council, and Mike made a huge donation to get her in. But we all liked her for her own sake. She's really a nice person."

"Did Kelly Weitzel stay on in your group after their divorce?"

"For a while, but then she married Fred Alvados and they started doing this volunteer-dentist thing. Kelly even took training so she could be his chair-side assistant. They're great people."

"They sound like it." Jackie pondered for a moment. "Do you happen to know a woman called Carrie Turnbull? She lives in the big house across the alley from me, but I hardly ever see her."

Adrienne smiled, looking so much like her old self for a moment that Jackie felt a quick lift of optimism.

"Carrie? Of course I know her. She introduced me for the very first time to the joys of smoking cigarettes. It was in the bathroom at ballet class. I was eight and she was about sixteen, I believe, but already trailing clouds of scandal."

"Why?"

"Because she'd gotten pregnant a couple of years earlier, with somebody shockingly unsuitable. A teacher at the high school, or some such thing. Her parents tried to hush it up but the story got out anyhow. I thought she was wonderful."

"What was her surname at the time?"

"Kinniston," Adrienne said. "Her parents were Douglas and Angela Kinniston, and a very strait-laced couple they were, especially to have produced a daughter as wild as Carrie."

"Do you ever see her now?"

"Not at all. I'd heard that she and Bob were back in the city, but they pretty much keep to themselves. I should call her when I'm not so tired," Adrienne added, "and have a chat about old times. I always got such a kick out of Carrie."

Jackie thought about the thin, nervous woman staring avidly into Daniel's carriage. "You might find she's changed a lot."

"Really?" Adrienne gave her a quick glance. "That's too bad."

"So, what happened to her baby?"

"God knows," Adrienne said. "It was a horrible scandal back in those days. If a girl from an upper-class family got 'in trouble,' as they so charmingly put it, she went away for a trip to Europe and came back six or eight months later, and everybody carried on as if nothing had happened."

"And that's what Carrie Kinniston did?"

"As near as I recall. Though she was very thin and angry when she came home, and more rebellious than ever. She was quite a bit older than me, you have to remember, so I just heard scraps and pieces of all the gossip."

Jackie frowned, working it out in her head. "If she taught you to smoke when you were eight, and her baby was born out of wedlock a couple of years earlier, then that would have been around 1968, wouldn't it?"

"The spring of 1968," Adrienne said after a moment's thought. "I remember because it was just after Johnson declared he wouldn't run again, so Carrie's father went to work for Humphrey's campaign and our parents started spending a lot of time together. That was an election year."

"You arrogant members of the ruling class," Jackie said. "Always marking your personal milestones by political elections."

Adrienne smiled wanly. "We do tend to, don't we? Politics were always more important to my parents than eat or drink. Certainly," she added with sudden bitterness, "a whole lot more important than their children."

"Do you know anything about Carrie's husband?"

"Bob?" Adrienne shook her head. "Not much at all. Around 1971, Carrie went off to prep school somewhere in Oregon, and when she came home two years later she was married. No big wedding, no announcements, nothing. My mother said the Kinnistons were ashamed of his background and never really gave their blessing to the marriage, so Carrie and Bob didn't come home much after that."

"Until her parents died and Carrie inherited the house."

"Nothing like a hefty inheritance to bring you back home," Adrienne said.

"Do you know what Bob Turnbull does for a living, or what his shady background was?"

"Oh, I doubt that it was all that shady." Adrienne wheeled her stroller to the curb as they reached Division and waited for the lights to allow them to cross into the mall parking lot. "Angela Kinniston told my mother he was common."

"God, I despise that word," Jackie muttered. "I just hate it."

"You hate it," Adrienne said. "I grew up with

the word and the attitude, too. Dammit,'' she added moodily, watching the traffic lights. "I'm almost forty and my mother can still make me crazy. All she has to do is open her mouth.''

"Same with my grandmother,'' Jackie said. "And she's not even an aristocrat.''

Adrienne started across the street with her stroller.

"About Bob Turnbull,'' Jackie reminded her.

"Oh yes, Bob. Well, he's not cultured, but he's rich. And from what I know of him, he seems like a pretty nice guy.''

"How did he make his money?'' Jackie asked.

"Selling some kind of equipment to oil fields. I gather it's something he invented. And now he has a big contract with Boeing, too. That's one of the reasons they came back here to Spokane. In addition,'' Adrienne said grimly, "to Carrie's sentimental attachment to her ancestral home, I assume.''

Jackie was silent, digesting this information as the two women pushed their baby strollers into the multitiered coolness of the big shopping mall.

By evening she was out on her front veranda, making detailed notes about what she'd learned so far regarding Maggie Birk's final months, preparing to transfer them onto computer disk. Shadow sat on the railing nearby, washing his face with a languid paw.

Daniel was already fed, bathed and sleeping soundly inside the house behind locked doors, and Jackie had the key in the pocket of her sweatpants. When Paul had called at the end of his day's work, she told him only about her shopping trip with Adrienne, and had been careful not to mention the upcoming appointment with Mike Weitzel.

Obviously the car salesman had her a little spooked, though she couldn't say why. He certainly seemed pleasant enough, and he was nice to his mother, which should probably count for something.

Jackie thought about what Adrienne had told her that day, wondering how the bits of information about Carrie Turnbull and her husband fit into the whole story, or if that ancient gossip had any relevance at all.

She paused, biting the top of her pen and squinting at the masses of green berries on the mountain ash near the veranda.

If Carrie Turnbull had given birth in the spring of 1968, that created the possibility of another baby in the neighborhood, in addition to Sarah Weitzel's illegitimate child.

Practically an epidemic, Jackie thought.

No doubt it had something to do with the war looming over everybody, and the sense of wildness that had accompanied that threat. Also, birth control pills still weren't readily available at that time, especially for young unmarried girls.

She wrote down: "Babies: Sarah Weitzel, Carrie Turnbull. Possibly Maggie Birk or Emma Betker?" Then she stared at the paper, thinking.

Though it seemed unlikely, she couldn't abandon the thought that perhaps Emma Betker, too, had become pregnant in 1968, and that was why, as Maggie reported, the younger Betker sister spent so much time brooding and sulking in her room.

Or perhaps Maggie was delusional and really had been pregnant all along, but in total denial over her condition. Maybe she wanted so much for the baby she carried to be Mike Weitzel's child, she'd chosen to ignore the obvious signs of a much more advanced pregnancy.

Throughout the ages, women had demonstrated an infinite capacity to deceive themselves when love affairs were involved. But somehow, the image of a neurotic and delusional woman didn't square with the sunny, practical, hardworking girl who spoke from the pages of that old diary.

Jackie studied her notebook pages again, frowning in concentration.

She had the feeling, as she sometimes did at this stage in a difficult case, that she was missing something obvious. During the past few days somebody had given her a vital piece of information, or else she'd seen something that held the key to the whole case. But she couldn't put her finger on it.

She flipped back through her notebook, studying the entries she'd made during and after her interviews with each of the neighbors, and the scraps of information Wardlow had given her about the autopsy and his sketchy investigation. Nothing triggered any kind of inspiration.

Maybe after her notes were all typed up, she could see what she was missing....

She glanced at her watch and realized with a little start of astonishment that it was getting close to eight o'clock. Mike Weitzel was almost an hour late.

Jackie hugged her arms in the baggy sweatshirt and felt a sudden chill.

Was the man deliberately waiting until it was too dark to sit outside? Maybe he hoped to be invited into the house where he could be alone with her.

She got up abruptly, unlocked the front door and went in to check the baby who slept soundly in his carriage near the fireplace. Jackie studied his soft pursed lips, the dark eyebrows like tiny wings, the surprising length of his eyelashes.

It was amazing how a face could be so tender and delicate, and yet look so much like Paul's. She felt a rush of love and bent to kiss and nuzzle the baby's plump tummy under the flannelette blanket, careful not to wake him. Then she went to the phone, took Mike Weitzel's business card from her notebook and dialed his home number.

The phone rang so many times she was on the point of hanging up when it was finally answered.

"Hello," a voice said brusquely. "Who's calling, please?"

Jackie stared at the receiver in confusion. "Sarge?" she said at last. "Is that you?"

"Hello, Jackie. Are you looking for Brian? I think he's around here somewhere."

"No, I was… What are you doing there?" she said. "Did I dial a wrong number?"

"Who did you call, Jackie?"

"A guy called Mike Weitzel. He's a car salesman for the Ford dealership downtown. The man was supposed to be at my house an hour ago. At least, that's the number I thought I was calling."

"Well, you got the number right," he said grimly. "But you won't be talking to Mr. Weitzel. Ever again."

"Oh, shit," she muttered, feeling a rising dread. "What happened, Sarge?"

"Weitzel was shot this afternoon. We got the call from his dog walker about an hour ago."

"He hires somebody to walk his dog?" Jackie frowned, twisting the phone cord around her fingers.

"Yeah, the girl works for quite a few people up here in the Canyon and has keys to the houses so she can pick up the dogs if nobody's home. When she stopped in to get Weitzel's black Lab, she found the body just inside the back door."

"And you say Mike was shot?"

"Point-blank range. Somebody held a gun against his back and fired. It went right through his left chest, likely exploded his heart. The coroner's due to arrive soon."

"Did you find the slug?"

"It's still lodged in the door of the refrigerator. He's probably been dead since midafternoon, from the looks of the body."

"And nobody heard this shot?"

"We've got uniforms canvasing the houses, but this is a pretty upscale neighborhood, Jackie. Big properties with houses far apart. If people were inside their houses, or even outside mowing a lawn or something, they probably wouldn't hear a gunshot."

"Oh, hell, Sarge." She was silent a moment, thinking about Mike Weitzel's vigorous tanned body and flirtatious smile, picturing him crumpled on the kitchen floor with his heart blown to pieces.

"He's so sweet," Maggie had written in her diary. "Mike is like a little boy, even though he tries to be tough. I know he's scared of going to Vietnam and having people shoot at him…"

"Are you still there, Jackie? What exactly was your business with this guy?"

"I've been talking to him about those old bones in my backyard. Weitzel lived in the neighborhood when Maggie Birk was here, and apparently they had a…" Jackie paused, reluctant to talk about Maggie's diary before she'd finished reading it.

Once the old exercise scribbler vanished inside an evidence locker down at the police station, she'd never see it again since she wasn't officially assigned to either case.

"He and the dead girl had some kind of relationship," she said at last. "It was thirty years ago, but I still think he remembered more than he was letting on."

"So when did you last talk to him?" Michelson asked.

"This morning, about ten o'clock. He stopped in to see if the police were finding out anything. He said the case was upsetting his mother, who lives right across the street."

The sergeant paused, and Jackie could imagine the look of concentration on his broad freckled face. "So you talked to him this morning," Michelson said at last, "but he was coming back tonight to see you again. How come the second visit?"

"He called later in the morning, after he'd left, and said…" Jackie's eyes widened. "He told me he'd just remembered something that might be important. Sarge, you don't think that's why he was killed? Somebody got to him before he could tell me what he remembered?"

"So you're telling me there could be some links between these two cases? Your old bones and Mike Weitzel's murder?"

"I suppose there could be," Jackie said slowly. "It does seem like a pretty big coincidence otherwise, doesn't it?"

"Well, Wardlow's already in charge of the Maggie Birk case, so we'll likely leave him on this one, too. He'll come around to get your statement as soon as he can.''

''Tonight?'' Jackie asked.

''Oh, for sure. Nobody's going to get any sleep tonight,'' the sergeant said grimly. ''Thanks, Jackie. See you later.''

''Bye, Sarge.''

She hung up and sat picturing the buzz of activity at the murder scene.

Claire Welsh would be there by now with a crew of identification technicians, taking photographs, dusting for fingerprints and preserving the forensic evidence while uniformed officers secured the scene and homicide detectives questioned possible witnesses. The coroner would soon be arriving to bag and remove the body.

Jackie felt suddenly wistful and isolated inside the quiet little house. Wandering into the living room, she picked the notebook up and spent an hour entering all the scattered bits of data into a computer file, then went over to the carriage again to watch the baby sleep.

For once she would have liked to see Daniel wake up and howl, demanding attention. But he was unmoving beneath the covers, and the house remained so silent in the evening stillness that she could hear the murmurs and chirps of birds outside the window as they feasted on the bright new berries.

While there was a possibility that Mike Weitzel had been murdered by some jealous husband who'd never heard of Maggie Birk, Jackie had a gut feeling the two cases were connected.

She couldn't forget the note she'd found in her

mailbox the day Danny was born. With this newest development, that threat now seemed much more sinister. It had been written by somebody who knew about the missing finger on the unknown baby's skeleton, and who said he "wouldn't mind killing another baby."

Had that same person now fired a bullet into Mike Weitzel's body at point-blank range? And if so, was Jackie's newborn son also in danger?

19

Wardlow arrived less than an hour later. Danny was still sleeping, and Jackie watched the carriage nervously while she and her partner sat in the living room.

"It's just a matter of time," she told Wardlow. "He never sleeps more than four hours, and we're getting close to that."

"So we'd better hurry." Wardlow flipped open his notebook. "Tell me about your association with this guy, Kaminsky."

She described her first meeting with Mike Weitzel at his mother's house, then seeing him outside doing household chores, and finally her conversation with him that morning, as well as his subsequent phone call to make another appointment for later in the evening.

Wardlow frowned at the notes. "But you told Sarge that Weitzel had some kind of relationship with the dead girl in your yard. What makes you think so? There's no mention of it here."

Jackie gave her partner an admiring glance. "Hey, that's very good, Brian. Driving straight to the heart of the matter."

"Shut up," he told her equably. "When you

come back to work and start helping me with this stuff, you can be as patronizing as you like."

"What's Pringle doing right now?"

"He's wandering around Mike Weitzel's neighborhood and alienating possible witnesses. Just answer my question, Kaminsky."

Jackie hesitated, but after a brief struggle her police training overcame her reluctance. "I found Maggie's diary," she said at last.

Wardlow stared at her. "A diary? This dead girl left a diary?"

"It was hidden inside a hole in the wall, upstairs in the nursery."

"And it's been there all these years?" Wardlow asked, fascinated.

"It was behind a bunch of shelves that were falling apart. When Paul took them out and stripped off the wallpaper, I found this hole."

"So that would have been her room when she lived here?"

"I guess so." With disconcerting suddenness, Jackie remembered the clammy, superstitious breath of dread, that sense of hideous evil that she often felt in the upstairs room.

She gripped her hands tightly between her knees to keep them from shaking.

"And this girl talked about Mike Weitzel in her diary?"

"They were just kids," Jackie said. "And they were in love, having sex. Maggie thought she was pregnant. It was a big deal, too, because this was 1968. If Mike quit school to support her, he stood a good chance of getting shipped off to Vietnam."

Wardlow stared at her. "But Kaminsky...this all

happened thirty years ago. What relevance could it possibly have now?"

"That's what I'm trying to figure out. I'd been thinking maybe Mike Weitzel was the one who killed her to get himself out of a sticky situation, and he was getting ready to confess."

"So he called you this afternoon, telling you he'd just thought of something important?"

"That's right."

Wardlow studied his notes. "How did the guy sound during this call?"

She pondered, knowing the importance of the question. "He seemed...I don't know. Kind of baffled," she said at last. "Almost embarrassed, in a way. Maybe even a little scared."

"Why? Did anything happen while he was at your place this morning that would have triggered some kind of memory?"

"Not that I can recall. Some of the neighbors were sitting on their veranda next door, and that seemed to make him pretty tense. My real estate lady arrived just as he was leaving and they had a little skirmish about her buying a new car."

"A skirmish?"

"Two salespeople doing a mating dance," Jackie said with a brief smile. "But nobody said anything significant that I can remember offhand."

Wardlow tapped his pen on the notebook. "Nothing else you can remember?"

"Not at the moment. Sorry, Brian."

"Tell me about those neighbors out on their veranda."

Briefly Jackie described her previous conversations with Gerald Pinson and with the Betker sisters, including as much detail as she could remember.

"Have you got notes on all this?" he asked.

Jackie nodded. "I'm getting them organized and putting them all on disk."

"Sarge is going to want you to come down and do a full debriefing."

"I know," Jackie said, feeling guilty. "I should have done it earlier, but I've been so busy with the baby, learning how to fit my life into his feeding schedule. And until now," she added, "I was just working a really cold case. I'll call Sarge tomorrow."

"Okay." He closed the notebook. "Give me the diary, then, and I'll shove off. Call me right away if you think of anything else."

"Brian...can you let me keep the diary for another day?"

"Keep it?" He stared at her. "Kaminsky, you're not even involved with the case."

"Yes I am," she said. "Unofficially, I'm investigating Maggie Birk's death. Sarge told me I could."

"But now we have a guy shot to death in his kitchen, possibly related to your old bones. The whole thing just got a lot more official."

"Brian, the handwriting in this diary is really hard to make out," she pleaded. "It would take you hours to wade through it. I sit and read as many pages as I can whenever I'm nursing the baby."

"So?"

"I'm almost finished. Why not leave it with me for another day or two and let me make a report on it? You don't have time to do anything with that old diary right now anyway."

He continued to study the cover of the notebook, still tapping his pen with a rapid staccato beat.

"I really hate it when you do that," she said automatically.

Wardlow grinned at her, his tired face lighting briefly. "I know. That's why I do it."

Jackie smiled back at him, then sobered. "Have you got anything yet from the crime scene?"

"Just real preliminary stuff. Mostly conjecture, nothing positive yet. The Ident guys are still working out there."

"So tell me your conjectures."

Wardlow leaned back in the chair. "Well, I'm guessing he knew his killer."

"No sign of forced entry?"

"None at all. His body was close to the door and he even had a drink in his hand when he died."

"How do you know that?"

"Because it spilled when he fell, not before."

"So," Jackie said, "he went through the kitchen to answer the doorbell…"

"And recognized his visitor, even felt comfortable enough to turn around in a social kind of way, still holding his drink, and started leading the way into the house. As soon as he did, somebody put a gun to his back and pulled the trigger."

"Any idea what kind of gun?"

"Something pretty powerful. There were flash burns and abrasions on his back, and a good-size exit wound with ragged flesh and some pieces of bone."

Jackie nodded thoughtfully. "Sounds like a .357,

doesn't it? A small-caliber weapon wouldn't do that much exit damage.''

"I thought so, too. But if he turned his back on the guy and started walking away, still carrying a drink, he couldn't have seen the gun, right? And a .357 is pretty hard to conceal."

"Not necessarily. I've seen women carrying .357s that fit into a handbag. They're not all that common, but they do exist."

"Well, we'll know a lot more when Ballistics can get a look at the slug. They haven't dug it out of the fridge door yet."

She was silent, thinking. "If this was a powerful handgun and somebody fired it into Weitzel's back at point-blank range, the killer will most likely have some burns on his own hands, don't you think? That's something to keep in mind."

Wardlow shook his head, smiling. "Have I mentioned that I wish you'd come back to work?"

"Once or twice." She smiled at him with warm affection. "And I will, just as soon as I can. In the meantime, I'll finish with the diary, type up my notes and do what I can to help you at this end since I already know the neighbors. Okay?"

"You'll talk to Weitzel's mother and those other people who were on the veranda?"

"Sure. First thing in the morning."

"Thanks, Kaminsky," he said gratefully. "If you do some notes that I can incorporate into mine, it's going to save me a whole lot of legwork."

"Well, you know me, Brian. I always aim to please." She followed as he got to his feet and moved toward the foyer.

"Did any of his neighbors see anything?"

"Not that we can track down at this point. It's not like this nice little street you live on, Kaminsky. That neighborhood is so high-end, there's nobody at home in the afternoon on a weekday. Everybody's out working hard to pay for their big houses."

"No maids or housekeepers?"

"Not so far. Anyway, these places are pretty scattered, deliberately arranged for privacy. It's almost impossible to see the entry driveway of one house when you're inside another."

He paused with his hand on the doorknob and gave her an intent, probing look. Jackie stared back at him, knowing what he was thinking.

"Look," Wardlow said, clearing his throat. "This puts a whole new face on that threatening note you got. Have you given any thought to that?"

She shifted uncomfortably. "Yeah, it's crossed my mind."

"Damn, I was planning to stop by and check on you after you got home from the hospital. But it's been so goddamn busy down at the station, and I didn't think there was anything—"

"Look, Brian," she interrupted, "don't start getting crazy, okay? That note could have been just some kind of nasty prank."

"But whoever wrote it knew about the baby's missing finger."

"I've been thinking about that," Jackie said. "The autopsy information could have been leaked."

"How?"

"Well, what about Eleanor Betker? She worked as a nurse at the hospital for years and years, right until she retired. Maybe Eleanor has some contact inside the hospital who told her about the baby's skeleton, and she was feeling mischievous.''

"Some mischief,'' Wardlow said grimly. "Threatening to kill a baby goes well beyond mischief, don't you think? And now we have another corpse on our hands, somehow related to all this.''

"Don't worry about me,'' Jackie said. "I'm okay. I have my gun and I'm paying close attention to security. Besides, if anything starts to bother me, I can always go out to the ranch and stay with Paul for a few days until we catch this guy.''

He hesitated, still looking troubled.

"Go!'' Jackie said.

Wardlow nodded and left. She stood in the doorway hugging her arms, watching as he strode down the walk toward his unmarked police car.

Behind her the baby set up a sleepy, plaintive wail. Jackie closed the door and went inside the house to pick him up, holding him close, suddenly fierce and shaky with love.

Knowing that she had only a day or two more to keep the diary, Jackie turned quickly to the part she'd been reading earlier, where Maggie and Lenny had their bitter conflict over the missing ring. Then she skipped ahead, hoping not to miss anything important while she bypassed the mundane details of everyday life, interposed with Maggie's rhapsodic passages about Mike Weitzel.

Jackie found it deeply sad to read the girl's glowing praise of her boyfriend. Poor little Maggie had been dead for thirty years. And now that Mike Weitzel was on his way to the morgue to be processed, tagged and prepared for autopsy, his relationship with the young housemaid seemed bittersweet and melancholy.

Possibly Maggie Birk was the only person in Mike Weitzel's life who'd ever found him worthy of abject worship. In fact, Maggie had wanted her lover so much that it appeared she was prepared to indulge in some deliberate subterfuge to get him.

Late in April, Maggie confided in her diary that she'd experienced a heavy, painful menstrual period, and knew she wasn't pregnant after all. But she kept this vital information from Mike, choosing to let him believe she still could be carrying his child. In this way, she kept the pressure on him to make a break from his parents and run away with her.

"I know it's hard for him, but it's really better this way. We could go up to Canada on the bus," Maggie wrote with breathtaking, childlike optimism, "and find a little farm somewhere and grow our own food. Lots of people do. The border is only a few miles from here. And then Mike would never have to go to war and we could really have a baby. Maybe I could get pregnant right away, soon enough that he'd never know how I lied to him. Oh, I wish we could do that!"

Jackie wondered if Maggie's failure to tell the truth about her condition had ultimately cost the poor girl her life. Had young Mike Weitzel killed his lover because, cornered and desperate, he couldn't think of anything else to do?

If so, whose baby was in that makeshift grave? And how would the mystery of the housemaid's death ever be solved now that Mike, too, was dead?

Sunday, May 25, 1968

Today was another of those days when Alban goes off to the clinic and Lenny and I get left alone together. I hate it when Alban does that. Lenny is more awful all the time. He's so fat he has to waddle around the house and hardly ever goes outside. I don't know what will happen to him if he doesn't lose some weight, but he's such a pig and eats all the time—candy bars and chips and pop and anything he can get his hands on. He's so greedy, like he needs to eat as much as he can before somebody takes the food away from him.

Last week I tried again to talk privately to Alban about putting Lenny on a diet. I said I'd be willing to cook low-calorie meals and stop buying the kind of food that Lenny gobbles down all the time if it would help him lose weight.

But Alban says weight loss is a very personal decision, and until Lenny is ready to make that choice on his own, it wouldn't have any effectiveness.

"We can't exert the willpower for him," Alban said. "He has to do that himself."

Lenny's supposed to get some exercise downstairs in the basement every day, chopping wood for the fireplace, but half the time he's too lazy to do it and I wind up swinging that big heavy ax, along with all my other work, while he sits on the stairs and watches me.

The lazy creep!

I think Alban goes to the clinic all the time because he's getting things finished up. He plans to go to Portland very soon, though he won't tell us anything about it. Not even Lenny knows what his dad is planning. I asked once and Lenny told me to shut up, that Alban would let us know when it suited him.

I don't think Alban and Lenny are getting along very well. Not that anybody could get along with Monster Boy, but when I first came here they used to talk sometimes and even laugh together when they watched television. Now they barely speak. The atmosphere in the house is so awful that I hate the thought of going to Portland with them, but I don't know what else I can do.

Mike knows this is coming up, and if he can't find a way to leave his parents and look after us, I'll have no choice. I can't stay here and live in the street. But if Mike wouldn't take me away even when he still thinks I'm carrying his baby, then maybe he doesn't love me after all. I just can't believe that. I can't.

I know Mike loves me.

Anyhow, when Alban left, Lenny came upstairs and sprawled in the kitchen by the table, eating a bag of chips. He kept chewing with his mouth full and watching me wash dishes, and saying weird things. Like, for instance, he asked what I thought it would be like to die. And if I was going to murder somebody, whether I'd rather shoot them or cut them up with a knife.

It was just gross boy stuff, the same kind of thing he says all the time. Actually, this time he seemed really interested in my answers for a change, not as mean as he usually is. But I really hate watching him eat all that fattening stuff. It's like watching somebody committing suicide.

Finally I told him I had to go up to Gerald Pinson's for a music lesson and I'd be back in time to cook supper. Then I went outside.

It's so beautiful here in the spring, with all the birds chirping and the flowers starting to bloom. I wish we didn't have to leave. What I'd really like is if Alban and Lenny would go away, and Mike and I could stay in this sweet little house and raise a family. That's what I'd love most of all.

Anyhow, I went over to Mr. Pinson's house and he was so glad to see me. He looked a bit surprised since I haven't been there for a while, but he didn't say anything, just got the music out and settled down right away to work with me on a new song.

It's called "Flow Gently Sweet Afton," and it's really hard to sing. But when we were working on the song, he sat at the piano and watched me with his mouth open like I was some kind of angel. It feels good to impress somebody so much.

I was thinking that Mr. Pinson could be really nice, and kind of handsome too, in his own way. Not like Mike, more like one of those Englishmen who have a fancy title and live in a castle.

But after what I saw today, I'm never going to say anything good about Mr. Pinson, ever again!

I have to stop writing and take some few deep breaths and hug my Raggedy Annabel before I can go on, because what happened next was just so awful. Of course, it was my own fault, and I know it. Nobody made me look inside that envelope.

It was just so tempting. When he went out of the room to go to the bathroom, I saw it on his coffee table covered by a bunch of magazines. I knew right away it was one of the envelopes that Steven Weitzel gives to Mr. Pinson and gets money for.

So while he was gone, I trotted over and picked it up. I sneaked a peek inside, and I couldn't believe what I saw. It was so awful. He must be some kind of monster! I'll never, never go near him again, even on the street. When I think of all the times I've been in his house...

Anyhow, the worst part of all was that he came back and caught me with the envelope! I guess I was so horrified by those awful pictures, I just forgot everything and stood there staring at them, and didn't think about Mr. Pinson until he was standing in the doorway.

His face wasn't nice at all anymore. He looked like he wanted to kill me, but he never said anything, just walked across the room, as cold as ice, and sat down at the piano again.

"So now you know," he said. "What are you going to do about it?"

Well, I couldn't say anything at all. I dropped the envelope on the floor and ran out of the house like he was chasing me, though he hadn't made a move. He just sat there on the piano stool.

I was so upset I couldn't stand the thought of going back home to spend an hour or two with horrible Lenny, so I stopped at the Betkers instead, though I haven't been going there so much lately.

Eleanor was really nice. She hugged me and cuddled me while I cried, then made me tell what was wrong. When I finally did, she told me not to worry, that all kinds of people have strange, unpleasant sexual tastes, and that I should really feel sorry for Mr. Pinson instead of hating him.

I told her I could never, ever feel sorry for him, that I thought he was awful, and then I started to cry again. Eleanor sat down on the couch with me and held me tight, whispering to me and patting my back as if I was a little girl and she was my mother. It felt so nice. Mom never touched us much when we were growing up. And when Dad touched us, it was usually with his belt.

Emma came in while we were sitting there and saw us all cuddled together, and had a real tantrum. She shouted all kinds of things to Eleanor that I couldn't understand, and then ran upstairs, still crying and yelling. Eleanor kissed me and told me she'd be right back and I shouldn't go away, then went off to look after Emma.

But I was even more upset by having another scene, after that horrible one in Mr. Pinson's house. I got up and slipped out before Eleanor came back, and spent about two hours wandering around the streets. I didn't go home until I saw Alban's car in the driveway.

I was hoping I might see Mike while I was walking, but he's working weekends down at the gas station and hardly ever has time to be with me anymore. I'm so lonely, and I don't know what's going to happen to me next.

Jackie felt chilled and saddened by Maggie's plaintive last words. There was one more passage in the diary, dated June 3, which was close to the date of the girl's final disappearance.

But Jackie was weary after her long, eventful day, and she felt too tired to keep her eyes open any longer. Finally she set the old book aside, checked on the baby one last time, made sure her gun was loaded and available, then went upstairs to bed.

20

The following morning Jackie got up early and tended the baby. She brought him downstairs to the kitchen after his nursing and propped him on the floor in his baby lounger, while she ate a bowl of hot oatmeal with skim milk.

She looked down at his padded chair, rocking it gently with her toe. Danny gazed back, his dark eyes bright, his silky hair standing on end. He grimaced and sneezed, then rolled his head around jerkily, briefly distressed until he found his mother again, and gave her a lopsided grin.

"Danny!" she exclaimed, setting the bowl aside. "Sweetheart, you smiled at me!"

Her heart beat faster in excitement. She got down on the floor, squatting next to the padded lounge, and talked animatedly to her baby.

"Danny smiled. Yes he did. Only three weeks old and Danny gave Mommy a nice big grin, yes he did. Do it again, sweetheart. Let's practise smiling so we can surprise Daddy."

The baby rocked and puffed in his chair, then grinned, looking droll and drunken.

Jackie laughed aloud and plucked him out of the chair. She carried him around the kitchen, hugging his warm little body.

"You darling," she whispered. "Mommy's little darling. I'd like to call and tell Daddy, but you know what? I think it'll be more fun to let him see for himself when he comes to visit us tomorrow."

The baby's eyes were drooping and he scrubbed a fist against his ear, always a sign that he needed sleep. Reluctantly, Jackie put him down in his carriage, then checked to make sure the doors were locked and the cat safely out in the sun-warmed porch.

When the baby was settled, she made her way down the steep basement stairs, pausing to sit on one of the bottom steps.

Nothing much had probably changed down here in thirty years, though it had grown dingy and musty with disuse. She wondered if anybody had used the airless basement room as a sleeping place since Lenny Cernak.

No doubt many a moving carton had been stored here, along with discarded furniture and other junk. At the moment, the room contained nothing much besides Jackie's pile of unpacked boxes.

Watermarks on the concrete walls, edged with white, showed how high the floodwaters had risen on a few occasions over the years.

In the opposite corner was a stack of pine logs used for firewood. Jackie got up and approached the woodpile, standing on tiptoe to peer over it. In the cavity, she could just make out an old ax wedged against the opposite wall, its handle only dimly visible.

People always bought precut logs nowadays, so there was no need for an ax in the basement.

Jackie stared at the polished handle for a long

time, wondering why she and Wardlow hadn't thought to check this earlier. But it seemed so bizarre that the murder weapon, if that's what this ax was, still occupied its old place next to the woodpile.

Later she would call Wardlow to come and collect the ax, have it entered into evidence and examined by the lab. Nothing would come of the technician's efforts, though. Any evidence would have degraded beyond recognition after thirty years here in the damp, musty basement, which had apparently been underwater several times.

What bothered Jackie was the breathtaking arrogance of the whole thing, as if killing Maggie had been of no more significance than extinguishing the life of some annoying rodent or other pest.

Hack up the girl's body, toss her in a backyard hole and go on chopping wood.

She leaned closer, frowning. The woodpile was thick with cobwebs, but the cobwebs around the ax had been disturbed. Tattered shreds hung above the weapon like torn curtains. When she looked more closely, she could see where somebody had pressed against the dusty wood, leaning over the pile to reach for the ax.

Maybe Paul had come down here last time he was home, she told herself, trying to ease the grip of a creeping, sickening terror. She'd have to ask him about it when he came to town.

But why would Paul need an ax?

She moved back to glance upstairs at the silent carriage, then sat on the bottom step, took herself back thirty years and pretended to be Lenny. He used to sit just like this and watch Maggie chop wood, a task that he was supposed to do but bullied the housemaid into performing for him.

Jackie pictured the girl's little twisted body in the corner, dimly seen through the sparkle of dust motes illuminated by smeared windows along the foundation. Her hair would be the only fiery brightness in that shadowed place.

In Jackie's imagination, Maggie lifted the ax in a high circling arc, the polished blade flashing. She let it fall, and two neat pieces of wood rolled off the chopping block.

I'm Lenny, sitting here and watching her, Jackie told herself. I'm an adolescent boy, obese, unattractive and vicious. I hate myself and everybody else. I enjoy being cruel to weaker creatures. So how would I be feeling right now?

She dropped her head to her knees, sickened by the sudden chill of evil that invaded her body. Everything good and sweet vanished from her mind.

She felt nothing but hopelessness, entrapment, and a rage so violent that she wanted to scream, to hurt and destroy, to see blood flowing everywhere....

Jackie cried aloud and fled up the stairs, leaning over the sink for a moment in fear that she might throw up. After another long, shuddering spasm, the horrible emotions began to drain from her mind. Once again she could hear the birds singing in the mountain ash and see the rows of colorful petunias nodding in the new flower bed.

He's still here, Jackie thought, staring out at her quiet yard.

Somehow she knew this wasn't just a postnatal fantasy or the product of an overwrought imagination. It was simply the cold truth, as hard and real as the paving stones beyond her back door.

Lenny Cernak was somewhere close to her, watching her, maybe even this very minute. He knew who she was and what she was doing. But Jackie didn't have any clues to his identity. He could be anybody.

Daniel lay sleeping in his carriage, hands upflung next to his face. Jackie took his left hand and held it in her own, counting and stroking the tiny fingers until she began to feel less shaky.

After a couple of hours, she fed the baby again and put him into his snuggle-carrier for the first time, figuring that in the busy day ahead she could use some ease of movement.

The little corduroy sling was an awkward device to handle at first, but after some maneuvering, she had Danny's small weight snuggled close to her breast with only his stocking feet and his dark head protruding from the fabric pouch. She tied a bonnet on him, then slung the diaper bag over her shoulder and went to the door, gratified by the freedom of having no stroller or carriage to wrestle through gates and over curbs.

On the veranda she hesitated briefly, then turned and hurried back upstairs to her room. She loaded her handgun, put the safety on and stored the weapon carefully out of sight in the diaper bag, feeling better knowing it was there.

She went back out into the morning sunlight, locking the door behind her. Close to her breast the baby snuggled and slept in utter contentment, his bonnet askew, so he looked vaguely raffish.

Jackie straightened the bonnet, laughing down at him tenderly, then sobered as she entered Dolly Weitzel's backyard and went up to the kitchen door.

A group of people crowded the big room, all of them displaying the kind of stunned, speechless grief that Jackie had often witnessed following a violent death. Little Dolly sat very still at the head of the kitchen table. She stared out the window, her gnarled, brown-spotted hands moving and picking aimlessly amongst the cluttered ornaments.

Nobody in the room looked familiar, except Gerald Pinson. He stood somewhat apart from the group, talking in low tones to a younger, heavyset man who was startlingly like Mike Weitzel—probably one of the brothers.

Likely George, Jackie decided, since Steven Weitzel was apparently no longer in close contact with his family.

In fact, the overall family resemblance was a strong one. The pretty gray-haired woman who sat next to Dolly, murmuring to her and hugging her gently, was probably Laura Weitzel. And the young people had to be Weitzel grandchildren.

Jackie murmured her sympathies to Dolly, who gave her a vague distracted smile.

"Please, have some cookies," the old woman whispered. "Would anybody like a cup of tea? Or we could make some coffee..."

Jackie realized the automatic offers of hospitality came from a deep, deep well of sorrow, and were the only way the woman could cope with her shattering grief.

Dolly Weitzel belonged to a generation that believed if life was unbearable, you offered food.

This impression was confirmed by the significant look that Laura gave to Jackie as she stood up.

"I'll be right back," she said to her mother. "Jennifer," she added, addressing a leggy dark-haired girl of about fifteen, "sweetie, could you make another pot of coffee for Grandma, please?"

Laura Weitzel moved with Jackie past the entry to the living room, where other family members and neighbors sat around talking quietly. John Caldwell was there, Jackie noticed, but she saw no sign of the Betkers.

"You're the policewoman who lives across the street, aren't you?" Laura murmured.

"Yes, I am. And this is my son Daniel. He's asleep right now."

Laura smiled and reached out to squeeze one of the baby's little feet. Her hand was gentle and showed evidence of years of hard work. The woman's face seemed wise and rich with compassion. In fact, Laura Weitzel had a wonderful face. She would be about fifty now, Jackie calculated.

"Do the police have any idea who did this?" Laura asked. "It's so..." Her voice choked briefly. "It's just awful. My poor mother..."

Jackie touched the woman's shoulder with automatic sympathy. "We're checking all kinds of leads. In fact..." She hesitated, knowing this wasn't the appropriate time. But Laura's family would soon be going back to Michigan, so she had to ask her questions now.

"Could we sit down somewhere and have a private talk?" she said at last.

Laura stared at her, eyes wide with astonishment. "I can't...I just can't believe what you're telling me. It's all so…''

They were on a screened side porch, just beyond the hubbub of people coming to pay their respects.

As gently as possible, Jackie had told Mike Weitzel's sister about the skeleton in the backyard grave, and the murdered housemaid's long-ago connection to the man who'd just been killed.

"But you're not saying that Mike had something to do with her death?"

"I don't know," Jackie said. "I do believe the two deaths are somehow connected. Maggie Birk's and your brother's, I mean. But I'm not sure how."

"If Mike was seventeen at the time, that girl would have died almost thirty years ago. How can they possibly be connected?"

"I don't know," Jackie repeated.

Absently she patted her baby's soft diapered bottom through the corduroy fabric of the sling, searching for words.

"Laura," she began.

"Yes?"

"This is not information we've chosen to release to the public. But the fact is, there was a second skeleton in that grave."

"A second one?" Laura passed a hand over her forehead but gave no other sign of obvious discomfort. "Detective, this is so hard to—"

"It was a newborn baby," Jackie said, watching the woman closely.

"You mean, this girl was pregnant?" Laura asked, clearly horrified. "You're saying Mike—"

"No, actually, we don't believe it was Maggie Birk's child. We still have no idea where the baby came from. We only know it was buried in the back-yard at the same time as Maggie.''

''I really don't know what you want from me, Detective.''

''Laura, we've learned that you were pregnant in the spring of 1968.''

The older woman stared at Jackie, hands folded in her lap, sitting utterly still and expressionless in the padded wicker chair.

''I wonder if you could tell me what happened to the child you delivered that year,'' Jackie said.

Laura's lined face was suddenly transformed by a glow of pride and happiness. ''My baby?'' she said with a little catch in her voice. ''He's in there.''

She waved her hand toward the kitchen where a tall young man stood by the counter talking with a slender, silver-haired man who Jackie presumed to be Laura Weitzel's husband, the Ford management executive. The younger man looked to be about thirty, considerably older than the crowd of grand-children. Still, he bore the unmistakable stamp of the Weitzel family in his strong features and dark curly hair.

Confused, Jackie turned back to Laura. ''I thought you gave him up for adoption.''

''I did,'' Laura whispered, staring down at her hands, ''and it almost killed me. If David hadn't come along and fallen in love with me, I don't know what would have happened. All those years I could never forget about my lost child. Every time something would happen, like Christmas or his birthday or another baby, I'd feel so—'' Her voice caught and she stopped abruptly.

"I understand." Jackie drew her own son a little closer to her. "Believe me, Laura, I understand."

The other women tossed her a grateful, misty smile. "So last year David finally suggested that we do a search. He hired a private investigator, and just after Christmas we...found him." Laura looked up with a shining face at her long-lost son. "Isn't he wonderful?"

"He looks like a great guy," Jackie said.

"He's an aerospace engineer with Boeing. His adoptive family did such a wonderful job with him. They're just marvelous people. He's twenty-nine years old, married with two little boys. He told us he wanted to know his roots, and this summer he was going to come out and introduce himself to my mother and to Mike. But we hadn't told either of them yet, and now Mike will never..."

"I'm so sorry." Jackie got to her feet and dropped a hand on the woman's shoulder. Then she moved toward the door, where she met Gerald Pinson, also on his way out.

"Hello, Detective," he said with only a shadow of his usual heavy gallantry. "This is a dreadful thing, isn't it?"

Jackie looked at him shrewdly. "Yes, Gerald," she agreed. "It really is."

They walked together down the side path until they were out of earshot of the house. Jackie kept one hand cradled under the baby and the other on the diaper bag where her gun rested.

"By the way, Gerald," she said as he let them both out though the gate, then turned to walk up the street toward his own house.

"Yes?" He paused and glanced back at her.

"I don't know the Weitzels all that well," Jackie said casually. "Was Steven one of the people in there, by any chance?"

Again she was conscious of his careful, foppish demeanor that now seemed to be concealing a great deal of tension. He stood very still, with only his eyes darting around while he answered.

"No," he said. "As far as I understand, Steven hasn't been home for years. Only George was there."

"That's too bad," Jackie said, moving a little closer to the man, her hand covering the baby protectively. "Because you and Steven must have a lot to talk about, Gerald."

He raised his jaw, almost like a challenge. "Don't be ridiculous. What would I find to talk about with a young scoundrel like Steven Weitzel?"

"Well, for beginners, you could discuss what was in those big brown envelopes he used to give you."

The change in the man was remarkable. He seemed to crumple, to crack and shrivel before her eyes like a dried leaf thrown on a fire. The debonair facade was gone and he looked old and cornered. Malice glittered in his eyes.

"You think you're so smart," he hissed. "Such a big smart policewoman. But you can't scare me. That was thirty years ago. You can't prove anything."

"Maybe I can," Jackie said. "Maggie Birk saw what was inside one of those envelopes, didn't she, Gerald?"

"Maggie Birk was a common, trashy little snoop. She deserved whatever happened to her."

"Did she deserve to die?"

"Of course she did," he said sullenly. "But I didn't kill her, if that's what you're asking. Now get away from me. I want to go home."

He passed a trembling hand over his hair. Jackie watched him carefully, wondering how much further it would be safe to push him.

The best course of action, she decided, was to hand the man over to Wardlow and his partner along with Maggie's diary. They were now in charge of Mike Weitzel's homicide, and the two cases were looking more and more related.

"Okay, Gerald," she said. "You can go home now. But I'm sure some of my fellow detectives will want to stop by later and have a little chat with you, so don't go anywhere, all right?"

Her words were casual, but the warning was unmistakable. He gave her a look of cold loathing, then turned on his heel and marched off up the street.

Thoughtfully, Jackie watched him go, then went across to her own house to prepare lunch for herself and feed the baby.

While he nursed, she sat with her feet propped up and turned to the last passage in Maggie's diary. The handwriting was crazed and erratic, as if Maggie had been drunk or high when she composed the words.

But she hadn't, Jackie realized as she began to read. The poor girl had been frightened out of her wits.

It's horrible. It's just horrible. I can't even write down the words to tell what I saw. I close my eyes and cover them with my hands and I can still see it. And the things they said...oh, it's so awful. How could I not have known? I lived here all this time and never knew.

But now they'll kill me. They're going to come for me and kill me. I can't get away. If I jump from the window they'll see right away and catch me. They're probably waiting for me to do that.

I'm sitting on the floor by the window so my head doesn't show, and writing in here to keep from screaming. My door is locked, but they'll get in anyhow. I've never been so scared in all my life. I wet myself like a baby when I saw it happening, and now my dress is all cold and clammy but I'm too scared to get up and put fresh clothes on for fear they'll see me. I can't stand having them see me.

As Jackie read, she felt her body gripped by the same clammy terror, the breath of evil she often sensed upstairs by the nursery window.

Thirty years ago, Maggie Birk had huddled under that same window in the grip of some unimaginable horror, scribbling in her diary to keep from going mad.

Was it possible that powerful emotions could somehow endure and have a life of their own long after the people who'd experienced them were dead?

Frowning, Jackie cuddled the drowsy baby against her breast and returned to her reading.

I know they'll come for me soon, and I know they'll kill me. I'm not afraid to die. Who could go on living anyway, after what I've seen?

But I don't want them to get my diary and my Raggedy Annabel. If I hear them coming,

I'll hide my book and my dolly in the hole in the wall. Maybe someday a nice person will find them and know that I lived here, and that I wasn't a bad girl.

Maybe somebody will even find out how they killed me, and then they'll…

But Maggie's diary ended abruptly and forever with that last sentence fragment.

Jackie closed the diary and sat in the midday stillness. She stared at the tree branches beyond the window and thought about the terrified young girl crouching in her room as she waited for a violent attack.

And those she feared had obviously come for her. Maggie had time only to get the diary and her rag doll back into their hiding place, where they'd lain undisturbed for almost thirty years after the night of her murder.

But why had Alban Cernak's housemaid been killed?

What unspeakable sight had Maggie Birk witnessed? Who were the "they" she kept referring to? Not Lenny, her usual adversary, but "they."

And the most maddening question of all…whose newborn infant died that night with Maggie?

Jackie finished nursing the baby, changed his diaper and strapped him in his portable car seat. Then she lifted the diaper bag, checked the handgun again and went outside to her car. She secured the baby in the back seat and headed across town to the northwest substation, her mind still whirling with questions.

21

In the parking lot, Jackie hauled out her baby, still in his car seat, along with the diaper bag and briefcase. She hesitated briefly, then headed for the front of the police station, letting herself into the dreary little public vestibule beyond the entry doors.

The receptionist, Ginny Sharpe, was perched on her stool behind a sheet of glass heavily reinforced with wire. Alice Polson, motherly secretary to the detective staff, stood next to her. The two women appeared to be arguing over a computer program.

Jackie put the car seat and diaper bag down on a scarred wooden bench and waited for the onslaught. Alice was the first to look up and catch sight of her. Immediately she came rushing out through the connecting door, with Ginny close at her heels.

"Oh, look at him!" Alice breathed, squeezing the baby's stocking-clad foot. She bent close to the padded car seat, beaming foolishly. "Hims is a dear little manny, isn't hims? Oh, yes he is, oh yes...."

"If he responds to that kind of stuff," Jackie said grimly, "I'm sending him to bed without his supper. Hi, Ginny. How are you?"

"I'm okay, but I miss you a lot," the young receptionist said. "These guys aren't nearly as well behaved when you're not around."

"Who's been bugging you, kiddo? Give me names and badge numbers. I'll sort them out."

Ginny grinned her admiration. "Hey, I bet you would, too."

"Damn right I would." Jackie hefted the car seat again. "Is Sarge still in his office?"

Alice shook her head, went across the lobby and unlocked a door, holding it open.

"They're having a meeting in the briefing room downstairs on the Weitzel homicide," she said. "I think most everybody's down there already."

"Thanks, Alice." Still heavily burdened, Jackie edged her way through the door and into the squad room, which was deserted. Apparently the detectives were either out working or attending the homicide briefing.

"Poor Jackie, what a load. Can I help you with something?" Alice asked.

"Well, you can carry the diaper bag if you like." Jackie sighed in relief as Alice removed the weight of the big patchwork bag from her shoulder. "Thanks, Alice. But be careful," she added. "My gun's in there."

Alice apparently found this funny. She was still chuckling as they clattered down the stairs and into the briefing room, where she left the diaper bag on a chair at the rear of the room, then winked broadly at Jackie and left.

Jackie chose a table near the back, set the car seat down and rocked it gently to ensure that Daniel kept sleeping. She opened the briefcase, arranged her notes and sat down. About two dozen police officers were in the room, half of them detectives in street clothes, all with notebooks open on their knees.

Lieutenant Hatch conducted the briefing, accompanied by Sergeant Michelson who sat with him at the front of the room. Together they laid out the details on the Weitzel case, making reference to a diagram of the property and the kitchen, and another flip chart filled with colored crime-scene photos.

Jackie looked at the lurid images of Mike Weitzel sprawled on the ceramic tiles in his expensive kitchen, his life blood soaking away. No matter how many times she saw this, it was always a little more jarring when the victim was somebody she'd known personally.

She became aware of people turning to glance at her, their faces either friendly or curious when they noticed the baby in the car seat. Wardlow grinned and waved, and Michelson gave her a warm smile.

But Lieutenant Hatch worked out of the downtown office and clearly didn't appreciate babies at homicide briefings. He acknowledged Jackie's arrival with a curt nod and resumed his questioning.

"Sergeant Welsh?" he said.

Claire Welsh, the senior identification technician, stood up and consulted her notes. "We found no trace of forced entry, no prints at any entry point that haven't been cleared to family members and no sign of robbery or vandalism. The blood flow from the deceased's body was such that it completely blocked the only entry to the living room, and it was undisturbed."

"So what are you saying, Sergeant?" Michelson asked.

"We're still analyzing footwear smudges, but at this point, we have no reason to believe the assailant went farther into the house than a couple of steps inside the kitchen door where the shot was fired.''

"Thank you, Claire.'' The lieutenant looked around. "Is Detective Wardlow here?''

Jackie's partner stood up and opened his notebook. "Autopsy is later this afternoon. Detective Pringle and I will attend. We'll know more about the murder weapon when Ballistics is finished analyzing the slug we retrieved from the door of the fridge. As far as witnesses go, it's pretty much a blank. We've canvassed the neighborhood several times but nobody can remember seeing an unfamiliar vehicle in the area between noon and 6:00 p.m.''

"How did you pinpoint those times?'' one of the other detectives asked.

Wardlow glanced at Jackie. "Detective Kaminsky spoke to the deceased on the phone at 1215 hours. The dog walker arrived and found the body at about 1800 hours.''

Hatch nodded. "We'll get around to Detective Kaminsky's involvement in a few minutes. Have you turned up anything in Weitzel's business affairs or private life that might give somebody a motive?''

"Not yet,'' Wardlow said. "In business he was a pretty straight shooter, kept his promises, paid his bills on time. He was a bit of a flirt, but he seemed to stay away from married women and had no serious relationships at the moment, just a lot of women friends that he dated on a rotating basis.''

"Did all these ladies know about each other?'' Michelson asked.

"They seem to. It was a pretty casual thing. They mostly belong to the same social set. I guess single guys that age are hard to come by, and these ladies were all happy to use Mike Weitzel as an escort when they needed one. Nobody seemed to take him all that seriously.''

Except for Maggie, Jackie thought, feeling inexplicably sad. Poor little Maggie had taken Mike Weitzel very seriously....

"What about Stephanie Mulder?'' she said aloud.

"That's the complainant in a thirty-year-old assault charge against Weitzel to which he pleaded no contest,'' Wardlow told the others. "We tracked her down this morning. She's married to a serviceman and stationed in Germany at the moment. Claims she hasn't seen or heard of Mike Weitzel for decades.''

"Ex-wives?'' Hatch asked. "Kids?''

Wardlow shook his head. "Weitzel never had any kids. And the ex-wife is in Mexico on some kind of charity dentistry program. She burst into tears when we told her. Sounded genuinely fond of the guy.''

"So, there we are,'' Michelson said to the assembled group of detectives and uniformed officers. "No motive, no money troubles, no enemies. But somebody drives up to his house on a sunny June afternoon, executes the guy with a high-powered bullet in the back, then takes off without leaving a trace.''

Hatch shook his head and turned back to Wardlow. "Keep digging, Detective. We need to know everything this guy's been doing for the last five years. In the meantime,'' he added, "I think it's time we heard from Detective Kaminsky.''

At that moment the baby woke and began to fuss. Jackie tried to rock the car seat but the sleepy complaints increased. She looked around the room with an apologetic smile.

"I don't know what this fussing is all about," she told the assembled police officers. "He was fed not long ago and his diaper's clean. I guess he just doesn't like cops."

There was a general ripple of amusement and indulgent smiles that broadened into grins when Michelson strolled to the back of the room, lifted the baby from his car seat and carried him back to the front of the room, rocking him expertly.

Daniel settled almost at once and drowsed off again, his downy head nestled against the dark blue police uniform.

"Thanks, Sarge," Jackie said gratefully.

She began to read from her notebook and computer printouts, detailing the Maggie Birk case from the beginning when they'd found the old bones in her backyard flower garden, through her informal interviews with the neighbors, her receipt of the threatening note and Mike Weitzel's involvement in the case.

When she finished, the room was hushed for a moment. Then a lively murmur of conversation broke out.

Michelson nodded to Brian, who came forward and took the sleeping baby, carried him back and settled him in the car seat with Jackie's help.

"I think you can see," Michelson said, getting to his feet, "why I wanted Detective Kaminsky to address this briefing although she's officially on maternity leave for three months. Up until now she's merely been assisting Brian informally on interviews regarding the cold case. If anybody has anything to ask her about the Weitzel homicide, now's your chance."

"Did you bring the diary with you, Jackie?" Brenda Howe asked. She was a uniformed patrol officer, a pretty blonde whose formal training prior to entering law enforcement was in commercial art, but she showed signs of becoming a top-notch policewoman.

Michelson often expressed his certainty that Brenda would make detective within the next few years.

"It's here in my briefcase," Jackie said. "I'll turn it over to Brian today. It's taken me more than a week to read the whole thing."

"And what's your conclusion?" Lieutenant Hatch asked. "Was Mike Weitzel involved in the girl's death?"

"He certainly had a motive," Jackie said. "But then, so did a lot of people. And I have a feeling," she added, "that when we figure out who killed Maggie Birk thirty years ago, we're going to know who killed Mike Weitzel yesterday. In fact, I think Weitzel died because he was about to tell me something about Maggie's murder."

"Well then, let's look at the motives to kill the Birk woman." Michelson picked up a pen and turned to a new page on the flip chart.

Jackie told them about Gerald Pinson, and Maggie's frequent mention of the "big brown envelopes" that had distressed the music teacher so much.

"So, Kaminsky, did you get anything else from this guy?" her partner asked.

"Nothing definitive. Just a whole lot of bluster to hide his panic."

"Should we lean on him a bit, do you think?"

"Oh, absolutely," Jackie said without hesitation. "Send a couple of uniforms to pick him up in a patrol car and bring him down here for questioning. My guess is he'll crack like a walnut at the first show of anything official. The man's a coward and he definitely has something to hide."

She looked down at the baby, who slept peacefully in his car seat.

"You said others had motives for wanting this girl dead," Hatch said. "Who are they?"

Jackie ticked them off on her fingers. "Both Mike Weitzel and his parents, because Maggie was claiming to be pregnant and if he quit school to marry her, he'd get shipped off to Vietnam. Gerald Pinson, because she knew what was in the envelopes. Eleanor Betker seems to have been besotted with the girl and jealous of the relationship with young Weitzel. Emma Betker, on the other hand, was passionately resentful of Eleanor's fondness for Maggie. And, of course, there was a lot of hostility between Maggie and Lenny Cernak."

"Have we been able to get any kind of a line on this Alban Cernak or his son?" Hatch asked.

Wardlow shook his head. "Not a thing. The FBI search came up empty." He recounted the story of Alban Cernak's faked medical credentials.

"Anything about the clinic he was supposed to work at?"

"Nothing much, except that it did exist."

"I haven't had time yet," Jackie volunteered, "but I was planning to go see my friend Karl Widmer down at the *Spokane Sentinel,* and see if he could find any files in the newspaper morgue about that clinic. We could maybe get a line on somebody else who worked there and might still remember the Cernaks."

"Good thinking." Michelson made a note. "We'll get Detective Pringle on that angle right away. Sorry, Jackie," he added, giving her a brief smile. "But this is an active homicide investigation now and I can't have you working it."

She nodded her understanding, though she felt a sharp pang of regret. Jackie and Karl Widmer, a keenly professional journalist, had worked together on cases in the past and she enjoyed his company. She still didn't like the process of leaking police information to the press in exchange for helpful tidbits of gossip, but it was done all the time and often facilitated investigations.

"Give my regards to Karl when you see him," she said to Pringle. "Tell him I'm still waiting for him to drop over and visit the baby." The detective nodded in his solemn, humorless fashion and made a note in the pad on his knee.

"Well," Lieutenant Hatch said, "Detective Kaminsky has certainly given us some new angles to pursue. Sergeant Michelson and I will discuss all this and come up with new assignments before the end of the day. In the meantime, thanks to everybody and carry on."

The meeting broke up and Wardlow approached, looking tired, to take custody of the diary. Alice Polson reappeared with a mug of coffee and hung adoringly over the car seat.

"Alice, do you mind watching him for a few minutes?" Jackie said. "I want to talk with Brian."

"Well now, I can't think of a nicer way to spend

my coffee break,'' the secretary said, settling next
to the baby.

Jackie smiled her thanks and walked with her
partner down the basement hall to the evidence lockers.

"Brian," she said.

"Yeah?" He unlocked a door and stepped into
the room with its banks of tagged lockers.

"Can I see the ring? You told me there was a
little gold ring with the skeleton."

"Sure thing." He unlocked one of the cabinets,
inserted the diary and took out a tagged envelope.
Jackie opened it to find a tiny gold ring, small and
cheap, a heart-shape with a blue glass stone.

She tried the ring on her little finger where it
slipped only as far as the second knuckle.

"Maggie wore this," she murmured, looking
down at her hand. "What a tiny person she must
have been."

She stared at the ring, trying to capture an elusive
scrap of memory, and waved her hand impatiently
when Wardlow spoke to her.

"Damn!" she muttered at last. "I can't quite
grasp it. There's something I'm not getting and it
seems to involve a ring. Sometime in the past few
weeks, I've seen somebody wearing a ring. But I
can't remember…"

An old wooden table stood in the center of the
room. She pounded her fist against the tabletop in
frustration while Wardlow watched, clearly afraid to
speak.

Finally Jackie shook her head. "I can't get it.
Whatever it was, it's gone."

"Keep your mind off it," he suggested. "It'll come back when you least expect it."

"I know." She handed him the ring and he dropped it into the tagged envelope, made a note of the date and locked it away with Maggie's diary and the threatening note from Jackie's mailbox.

She sank into a folding metal chair at the evidence table, her chin in her hands. "I guess I'm really off the case, huh?" She tried to smile. "It was fun for a while, doing actual police work again."

Wardlow sat opposite her and patted her arm. "They can't let you be involved in an active homicide investigation while you're on official leave. But," he added, "that doesn't mean you can't still be thinking. Sarge says your instincts are infallible."

"No kidding." Jackie glowed with pleasure. "He really said that?"

"So, do you have any instincts about this case?" Wardlow asked. "Because, let me tell you, so far I'm finding the whole thing goddamn baffling. Whoever killed Mike Weitzel had means and opportunity, but no motive that I can see."

"You're right, it's all baffling. But I still have the feeling…"

Jackie brooded, staring at the bank of lockers with their wire-mesh fronts that displayed the contents. They contained a bewildering variety of objects, from bloodstained toys to plastic bags full of cocaine.

"Somebody's pretending," she said at last. "Somebody in this case is claiming to be someone they're not. The ring is a clue, but that's not it. This is a case of false identity."

"God, Kaminsky." He shook his head. "You sound like a two-bit psychic, not a police officer."

She gave him a humorless smile. "It's funny that you should say that. I've been having really weird feelings ever since I bought the house. Even before we found those bones in the backyard."

"Maybe it's something to do with being pregnant," Wardlow suggested. "Heightened sensibilities and all that. That women's intuition of yours has gone into overdrive."

"I've warned you before, Wardlow. If you keep talking about women's intuition, I'll have to hurt you."

Her partner grinned. "It's hard not to, Kaminsky. Now it seems you're not only intuitive, you're also psychic."

She ignored him, gazing absently at the cabinet containing the diary and the ring. "It's more like Maggie wants us to solve this case. If we can find the killer, she'll go away and be at peace."

Wardlow snorted.

She gave him a rueful smile.

"Okay, you're right. It sounds crazy, doesn't it?"

"Pretty crazy." He sprawled in the chair, watching her thoughtfully. "What do you mean by false identity?"

"I don't know." Jackie looked down at her hands, linked on the tabletop, and picked idly at a rough patch on one of her nails. "I keep wondering about the Betker sisters."

"What about them?"

"Well, for instance, what if Emma isn't really Emma at all? What if she's actually Maggie?"

"My God," Wardlow said. "You are going crazy."

"But that's the feeling I have about this case. Something crazy is going on."

"Like what?" he asked.

"Well, just for instance, what if Emma Betker got pregnant and Eleanor was really furious with her for besmirching the family name. They argued when the baby was born because Emma wanted to keep the kid and Eleanor wouldn't hear of it. Eleanor's a big strong woman. Maybe she killed Emma accidentally, then smothered the baby."

"And chopped her sister to pieces with an ax?"

Jackie shook her head. "I know, that part doesn't fit. But bear with me for a minute."

"I'm listening."

"Maggie saw it happen and was terrified, but she had nowhere to go. Maybe she went a little crazy. Eleanor buried the bodies in the backyard next door, then made Maggie write a note saying she was running away. Eleanor took her home and hid her away for a long time, and after a while people just believed it was Emma. Remember, Eleanor was obsessed with Maggie Birk."

"So where does Mike Weitzel fit into this scenario?"

"That's what made me think of it. He was at my place yesterday morning, looking over at the Betkers' veranda. Later, he called and said he'd realized something incredible. Maybe he twigged and Eleanor knew it, so she drove across town and killed him."

Wardlow frowned in concentration. "But Maggie

walked with a limp. Everybody knew that. They couldn't disguise it.''

"Brian, nobody ever sees Emma Betker walk. Eleanor carries her everywhere.''

He frowned, thinking, then shook his head. "It doesn't wash,'' he said at last. "I was at the girl's autopsy, remember? The pathologist said the pelvic ridge detail indicated a woman under twenty-five. Eleanor Betker's over seventy now, so Emma would have been at least in her middle thirties at that time.''

Jackie nodded reluctantly. "Okay, I guess you're right. The skeleton can't belong to Emma. But that's the kind of thing I mean, Brian. There's something weird and horrible about this case. Somebody is pretending to be something they're not.''

He watched her intently. "And whoever it is, they sent you a note saying they wouldn't mind killing another baby.''

Jackie glanced involuntarily down the hall, suddenly restless, anxious to go and find her son. But she forced herself to remain in the chair. "That was a scare tactic, I'm sure of it. Just something to warn me off. And what could be more effective for a mother than threatening her baby?''

"The baby's skeleton is the key to that case. We have to find out where it came from, if the baby really wasn't Maggie Birk's.''

"I lie awake at night,'' Jackie said, "torturing my brain over who that baby belonged to. And you know what else?''

"What?''

"I still have the feeling Lenny Cernak is somewhere nearby, watching me.''

"Really, Kaminsky?"

She gave a jerky nod. "It scares the hell out of me when I think that he might be hanging around."

"So, how do we flush him out? Have you got any suggestions for us?"

"I think you should canvas the neighborhood again. Pretend you're looking for witnesses who saw Mike Weitzel coming and going from his mother's house. But keep an eye out for any guy about the right age, and run background checks. Lenny was fourteen or fifteen at the time Maggie lived there, so he'd be in his early to mid-forties by now."

"You really think he's moved back to the neighborhood?"

She shook her head, still brooding over the evidence lockers. "Maybe he never left. I get the most awful feeling sometimes, Brian." She rubbed her arms, which were suddenly prickling with gooseflesh.

He watched her keenly. "Why don't you pack up that baby of yours and move out to Paul's ranch for a while?"

"You know what? I think I will," Jackie said abruptly, surprising herself. "In fact, I'll talk to Paul about it tonight."

"Good girl," Wardlow said. "That's one less thing for me to worry about."

They got up and started down the hall toward the briefing room, where a couple of the female officers and Claire Welsh had joined Alice in an admiring circle around Jackie's baby.

Wardlow paused in the doorway. "So, except for a broad sweep to see if we can turn up Lenny, do you think there's any point to interviewing all your neighbors again?''

She pondered, then shook her head. "Only Gerald Pinson. And the rest of the Weitzel family might know more about Mike's life than I've been able to find out. But I doubt there's much anybody could get from Eleanor Betker. Believe me, Brian, that woman is like a sphinx when she doesn't want to talk.''

22

Emma Betker lay in her lounge chair in the back-yard with her Barbie dolls spread out on her lap. Today she had two of her favorite dark-haired ones, and she was dressing them up in their evening gowns with the little glittery high heels and stylish capes.

All around her the yard was peaceful and green, with willow branches trailing onto clipped grass. The lawn sprinkler misted gently on the flower beds along the walk. Peonies spilled low over their wire cages, heavy with pink and white blossoms the size of grapefruit that filled the air with fragrance.

Ants were busy among the peony blooms, climbing the stalks and penetrating the flowers. Emma thought how wonderful it would feel to be an ant and walk right inside a flower.

But then she remembered how people stepped on ants and hurt and squashed them.

Her face clouded and she turned hastily back to her dolls. "You're going to the opera," she murmured to one of the bland plastic faces. "Both of you are going to be so pretty, and all the men will—"

She paused abruptly, frowning at her right hand. It was wrapped in a gauze bandage that encircled the palm and the back of the hand, leaving her fingers and her thumb free. A couple of the fingers had painful red welts on them.

"My hand hurts," she said, puzzled.

After a moment Emma's forehead cleared. She remembered Eleanor telling her about the kettle, how the steam had burned Emma when she was making cocoa.

Eleanor had been impatient.

"Now look what you've gone and done," she'd scolded as she taped the bandages in place. "You've burnt yourself on the kettle again. Honestly, Emma, I don't know why you keep doing these things."

Emma whimpered at the memory of her sister's tense worried face and slid farther down in the padded chair, as if to hide herself. These days it seemed that Eleanor was always upset. Emma never knew what was going to set her off.

With her undamaged left hand she smoothed a tiny white fur stole and fitted it in place on the doll's naked shoulders.

"So pretty," she whispered, feeling a little comforted, less anxious over Eleanor's moods. "You look so pretty. I'm going to sing to you now."

She began to croon in a soft, husky voice, and didn't hear the footsteps approaching until they were right upon her.

Emma looked up and saw a fearful monster hovering above her, a creature that was all black, with grotesque holes where its eyes and mouth should have been. Within the eye slits something glittered faintly, and she could see wetness and a trace of pink skin at the mouth opening.

She stared at this apparition, wordless with shock,

confused by the malevolence in those slitted eyes. Nobody was ever harsh to Emma. Ineffectually, she held up one of the pretty dolls like a peace offering, searching for words.

"Shut up," a voice snarled harshly through the mask. "Don't dare say anything, you ugly old pig, or you'll be sorry."

And then Emma saw the knife, upraised and glistening with fire in the afternoon sun. She opened her mouth and began to scream.

Jackie was in the backyard with Daniel drowsing next to her in his stroller when she heard the chorus of panicky shrieks from next door.

She'd been working on the flower bed, taking pleasure in pulling little weeds from the dampened soil, trying to get the whole of each root system.

The afternoon had seemed so pleasant since she returned from the police station. Until now, she'd actually been feeling a little embarrassed about her behavior with Wardlow after the police briefing. She'd acted like a frightened kid, even telling him she wanted to go out to the ranch with Paul.

But here in the bright sunny afternoon, all those dark fantasies seemed exaggerated, the product of an imagination unsettled by hormones and new motherhood, as her partner had suggested.

Then the screaming began and terror gripped her mind again.

Automatically Jackie threw her head up and listened intently, then sprinted toward the fence that separated the two yards.

"Oh, shit," she muttered, running back to grab the baby from his stroller.

She hurried through the little gate, carrying Daniel, who bobbed and jounced in her arms, losing his bonnet. He woke and began to howl.

When she reached the side of the house, Eleanor was already there, kneeling by her sister's chair, holding Emma in her arms. Jackie paused beside them, jiggling the screaming baby.

"What happened?" she said over his roars. "Daniel, please be quiet," she added in a lower tone. "It's all right. Mommy's sorry she scared you."

The baby hiccuped and flailed his arms, still fussing peevishly.

Eleanor glanced up, her weathered face twisted with panic. "Somebody threatened Emma. They tried to kill her, right here in the yard."

Jackie bounced the baby and looked down at Emma who sobbed convulsively, clutching her sister with thin, shaking hands.

"Did you see the attacker?" Jackie asked Eleanor, still patting the baby's bottom soothingly.

Eleanor shook her head. "I was in the kitchen peeling potatoes for dinner and keeping an eye on her through the window. But I went into the dining room to set the table and arrange some flowers, just for a little while, and then I heard her scream. I shouted back to her right away, came running outside and found her hysterical in her chair, and somebody disappearing through that hedge."

She waved her hand at a tall expense of white lilacs along the back of the property.

"Somebody?" Jackie said. "What kind of somebody? Male or female? Tall or short?"

"I was frantic with concern over Emma," the

woman said. "All I can remember is an impression of a figure dressed all in black."

Jackie shifted the baby to her hip and walked over to the hedge, looking around. "Where exactly did the intruder go through the hedge?" she asked Eleanor, who still knelt by her sister's chair.

"About ten feet to your left," Eleanor said after a brief study of the hedge. "Right there," she added as Jackie moved along to her left.

"Okay." Jackie brought a piece of landscape rock over to mark the spot, then made a mental note of the position and went out through the rear gate and into the alley. She found the point in the hedge that Eleanor had indicated, standing almost directly opposite the gate set into the high wooden fence at the back of Carrie Turnbull's property.

Gingerly she tried the Turnbulls' latch, then pushed on the gate with her shoulder. It was locked.

Still thoughtful, she carried her baby back into the Betker yard and went to stand by Emma's chair.

The woman had begun to settle a bit. She still clutched Eleanor's shoulder but her sobs had begun to subside to whimpers. Eleanor caressed her sister with long, calming strokes, then began to massage her neck and shoulders with soothing professionalism.

"May I speak to her?" Jackie said. "Right now, while the attack is still fresh in her mind?"

Eleanor sighed. "If you must."

"My concern is that she's seen the assailant," Jackie murmured. "So she could still be..."

"Yes, yes, I understand," Eleanor said hastily. She bent closer to her sister. "Emma, dear, can you talk to the lady who lives next door? The nice lady with the baby is here, remember?''

"A baby?" Emma peered up at them fearfully, then caught sight of Daniel and smiled through her tears. "Oh," she whispered. "Ellie, look at the sweet baby. They found him. He's not dead after all, isn't that nice?"

Jackie exchanged a quick glance with Eleanor, who reached out and took Daniel from her arms. With a pang of unease Jackie watched him being suspended from those big square hands, but Eleanor held him with gentle expertise and cradled him against her shoulder.

"Emma," Jackie said, kneeling by the chair, "can you remember anything about the person who frightened you just now?"

Emma frowned, her lips moving jerkily.

"Was it a man or a woman?" Jackie said.

"It was a monster. All…all black, arms and legs and everything, with slits for its eyes and mouth." Tears trickled down Emma's cheeks again.

"That sounds like a ski mask," Eleanor muttered. "You'd think people would notice somebody wearing a getup like that on such a hot day."

Jackie nodded thoughtfully. "Did the person threaten you, Emma? Did they have a weapon?"

"A knife." Emma's eyes were wide with remembered horror. "It was a great big knife. The sun made it shine like fire."

"Oh my God. Oh, poor Emma," her sister murmured, cuddling the baby and reaching with her free hand to stroke her sister's hair. "My dear little Emma."

"And then what?" Jackie asked tensely. "What happened when you saw the knife?"

"I screamed," Emma said, "and Eleanor screamed and the monster ran away."

"Nothing else?" Jackie said. "Did the attacker say anything to you?"

Emma frowned in childlike fashion and screwed her eyes up while she concentrated. "Yes! He said I had to shut up." Her face crumpled again. "And I know who it was, Ellie," she told her sister, looking tearful again. "I remembered his voice."

Eleanor and Jackie exchanged another glance. "Who was it, dear?" Eleanor said gently.

"It was Lenny. You know, Lenny Cernak, that awful boy who lives next door and says rude things to you over the fence? It was him, Ellie. He tried to hurt me with a knife."

"Emma," her sister said gently. "You're imagining things again. Lenny Cernak hasn't lived next door for thirty years."

But Jackie stood erect and stared with narrowed eyes at the silent lilac hedge. Finally, she reached out to take her baby from Eleanor's arms, holding him close and absently kissing his soft rounded cheek.

As soon as she could get away, Jackie went to her own house and called Wardlow to tell him about the attack on Emma Betker.

"What do you think?" he asked.

"Well, I think something really happened to her. She was absolutely terrified."

"Damn," he muttered, sounding harried. "So you still believe this stuff is all related?"

"I'm certain of it. Emma even volunteered the fact that it was Lenny Cernak who attacked her."

"Okay," he said. "We'll send out a couple of patrols to question them and check the scene, and I'll come by myself later in the day. I have to go to the Weitzel autopsy in a couple of minutes, then back here for an appointment with your friend Gerald Pinson. I'll interview the Betkers as soon as I have time, but it won't be until sometime in the evening."

"Brian, you should also get your people to check on the couple who live across the alley. Their names are Bob and Carrie Turnbull. Find out what they were both doing this afternoon."

"Why?"

"I'll tell you later," she said. "Oh, and one more thing…"

"What's that?"

"Do you mind if I go and talk with the Betkers again after the patrols leave? I've already asked a few questions and I'll jot down the notes right away, but I think Eleanor, in particular, might be upset enough to be a little more forthcoming today."

He hesitated, and she could imagine the grin on his freckled face when he answered.

"Hell, Kaminsky," he said. "Who am I to say you can't go next door and have a friendly chat with your neighbors?"

"Thanks a lot," she said.

Jackie fed the baby and put him to sleep in his carriage, then settled to watch as the patrol cars arrived. Uniformed police officers, under Eleanor's direction, began to inspect the yard and the alley.

There was no sign of Emma, and Jackie assumed she'd been put down for a nap in her upstairs room.

When the police had finally left and Daniel was awake again, Jackie put him in the snuggle-carrier, then went across the yard and knocked on Eleanor Betker's back door.

"That's really all I can remember," Eleanor said a half hour later. "And I've already told the police the whole story."

"I'm sorry to keep bothering you." Jackie leaned back against the couch and looked at Daniel who lay beside her on a flannelette blanket, propped against one of the big upholstered cushions.

He was gazing around the room, but when she caught his eye he smiled and kicked his feet. Jackie tickled his fat stomach.

"He seems like a bright little thing," Eleanor said from her chair.

"He's just started smiling at me. I get such a kick out of it."

Jackie pretended to be concentrating on her examination of the baby's diaper beneath his terry-cloth sunsuit.

"By the way, Eleanor," she said casually, "Can you tell me what happened to Emma's hand?"

"Her hand?" Eleanor frowned. "What are you talking about?"

"I noticed she was wearing a bandage on her right hand. I wondered how she got hurt."

"She scalded herself on the kettle while making hot chocolate," Eleanor said curtly. "Why do you ask?"

"At this point," Jackie said, steeling herself to

meet the woman's eyes, "I'm interested in anybody who's got a bandaged hand."

"Why?"

"Because whoever shot Mike Weitzel was holding the gun at such point-blank range, they'll probably have some residual flash burns on their hand."

She expected Eleanor Betker to be angry, but the woman stared at her in astonishment, then laughed with genuine amusement.

"My goodness, Detective! Do you really believe poor little Emma drove a car across town and shot that big thug in his own kitchen?"

The image seemed to tickle Eleanor. She laughed heartily, finally getting herself under control and wiping tears from her eyes.

"Sorry," she muttered. "I'm acting hysterical, I know. This has all been such a shock. But to think that Emma…" She choked and fell silent.

Jackie watched the older woman quietly. "Somebody definitely killed Mike Weitzel, and now Emma has been threatened. I'm trying to find out if she's in danger and why."

Eleanor sobered and met Jackie's gaze. "Do you believe she is, Detective?"

"Yes, I do. And I also think this whole business relates somehow to the death of Maggie Birk."

Eleanor made no response, but Jackie could see how she clenched her hands together until the knuckles whitened beneath their tan.

"I think," Jackie went on, pressing her advantage, "that Emma knows something about what happened to Maggie, and that's why she's in danger. Mike Weitzel died because of what he knew."

"All these years I thought..." Eleanor paused, biting her lip.

"You thought what?"

The weathered face twisted with pain. "Maggie disappeared. Alban had a note from her, saying she was sorry but she had to leave. He showed it to me."

"Did you recognize her writing?" Jackie asked.

The other woman gave a jerky nod. "She had distinctive handwriting, very crowded and hard to read, quite childlike."

Jackie nodded in recognition. She'd strained her eyes for a week trying to decipher that very writing.

"But I knew," Eleanor said, staring at the window, her eyes wide with remembered pain. "I knew she was dead. I could just feel it."

"How could you feel it?"

Eleanor looked back at her visitor. "I loved her so much," she said with a quiet dignity that brought an unexpected lump to Jackie's throat. "She was the love of my life. There's never been anybody else, not really. And as soon as she was gone from the world, I could tell by the emptiness in my heart."

"But," Jackie said delicately, "Maggie wasn't..."

"A lesbian?" Eleanor smiled bitterly. "Oh, it's all right, Detective, you can say the word. I won't be offended."

"Was she?" Jackie asked.

"I still have no certainty about her sexuality. Maggie was a poor little waif who'd been mistreated and abused all her life, but she responded to affection like a puppy. If somebody could have taken her in hand and given her what she needed, some security and emotional nurture, a decent education—''

Eleanor stared down at her hands.

''She was in love with Mike Weitzel,'' Jackie said.

''So she was.'' Eleanor's face darkened. ''And a lot of good it did her. That young lout was too selfish to care for any girl.''

''When I first came here to ask you about the skeleton in my backyard, and I described Maggie Birk, you said you'd never seen anybody in the neighborhood who looked like that.'' Jackie watched her hostess closely. ''Why did you lie, Eleanor?''

''Partly because I didn't want to believe you.'' Tears glistened in the woman's eyes and she brushed at them impatiently. ''In spite of my best instincts, I wanted to believe she'd actually run away and gone on to have a pleasant life somewhere. I couldn't bear to think she'd been lying so close to me all these years, forgotten under a pile of sod.''

''You say that was part of the reason,'' Jackie said. ''But right from the beginning you suspected there might have been foul play, didn't you?''

Eleanor gave a quick jerky nod.

''So, why didn't you tell somebody? Why didn't you call the police and report Maggie as a missing person?''

Eleanor gripped her hands tightly in her lap and swallowed hard. ''I was afraid...''

''Yes?'' Jackie prompted.

''I was afraid that Emma had killed her.''

''Why would you think that?''

''I knew Alban was planning to move away and

take Maggie with him, and I couldn't bear to see her go. I'd begun talking about letting her move in with us, and preparing Emma for the prospect. Emma knew I loved the girl. She was…very jealous and spiteful. She kept saying she wished Maggie Birk would die. In those years she'd begun to grow quite unstable. I worried about her all the time."

Jackie waited, her notebook open on her knee.

"That night," Eleanor went on, gazing straight ahead at the images inside her mind, "the same night that Maggie disappeared, Emma got up a few hours after she went to bed, and I heard her going out into the yard. She was a restless sleeper in those days, often wandering around in the night. Usually she just sat on the porch swing for a while, looking at the moon, then went back to bed. But on this night she was gone so long I got worried and went to look for her."

"And did you find her?"

Eleanor gave another jerky nod. "She was huddled in the back porch with mud all over her shoes…"

The woman swallowed a sob while Jackie waited.

"And," Eleanor went on, "she had blood on her nightdress. She was hysterical. She kept telling me a woman had been killed, and muttering something about a dead baby."

"What did you do?"

"I cleaned her up, gave her a sleeping pill and put her back to bed. I told her never to speak of anything she'd seen or done that night, and she never did. In fact, after that, Emma was never really what you'd call normal, ever again. It did something to her mind, which had always been fragile. Next day Alban told me Maggie had run off and showed me the note. A few days later Alban and Lenny moved away too.''

''So you never tried to get Emma to tell you what happened?''

''Later I did, but by then she had no memory of that night. Even now, from time to time, she has flashes that seem to trouble her, but nothing coherent at all. Maybe if I'd questioned her right away...''

''But you didn't?''

''I didn't want to know.'' Eleanor looked at her with fierce appeal. ''Can you understand that?''

''Yes,'' Jackie said slowly. ''I guess I can.'' She was silent for a moment. ''So you have no idea whose baby died that night?''

''None at all. There'd been quite a rash of illegitimate babies in the neighborhood during those years. Still, until you told me about the baby's skeleton in your backyard, I always thought Emma had just invented that part.''

''But you really thought she'd killed Maggie Birk and decapitated her with an ax?''

Eleanor's face turned stark white beneath the tan. ''Is that...is that how she died?''

Too late, Jackie remembered these details had never been made public. ''I'm sorry,'' she said gently. ''It was a particularly gruesome murder, I'm afraid.''

''Oh, Maggie.'' Eleanor rocked back and forth in the chair, lost in grief. ''Oh, sweet little Maggie.''

''Eleanor,'' Jackie ventured.

The older woman made an obvious effort to get herself under control.

"I don't want to alarm you," Jackie said, "but if Emma had blood on her dress that night, there's a possibility she witnessed the actual murder. And if she did, she could still be in terrible danger."

23

23

Back in her own house, Jackie surrounded a pot roast with potatoes, onions and carrots and turned on the oven. She tossed a salad and stored it in the fridge, then tried to relax by playing with the baby.

Daniel was in an amiable mood, apparently none the worse for his day of unusual activity, including all the strangers' arms and various other conveyances that had held him since breakfast.

In fact, Jackie was discovering this baby had a very definite personality of his own, and he seemed more sociable and easygoing than either of his parents. Danny's eyes brightened when he caught sight of people, his arms waved and his mouth now curved easily into the lopsided smile he'd recently mastered.

More every day, he charmed and delighted her, and touched depths of tenderness that she'd never realized she possessed.

Paul came in while she was undressing the baby for his bath. She placed the small pink body, stripped to his diaper, on a padding of towels, supporting his head and holding him around the middle so he appeared to be sitting upright.

"Look, Daniel," she murmured. "Who's here? Is this your daddy?"

Paul approached the counter, pausing to drop a kiss on Jackie's neck, then beamed down at his son. "Hi, Danny," he crooned. "Hi there, Son. Did you have a good day with Mommy?"

The baby rocked and struggled in Jackie's hands, trying to look up. His head flopped forward and his arms flailed as he sought for the origin of the big voice above him.

Jackie held her breath, waiting. The baby caught Paul's eyes and stared for a moment, then grinned drunkenly, his little face sparkling.

"Well, I'll be damned," Paul breathed in delight, reaching for his son. "He smiled at me!"

Jackie beamed proudly. "He's been doing that since yesterday morning. It's about two weeks early according to all the books. I saved it for a surprise."

Paul cradled the baby and carried him around the kitchen, singing to him while Jackie checked the meat in the oven.

"We should have enough time to give him his bath before we eat," she reported, poking at the meat. "I'm getting pretty good at bath time."

Together they set Daniel in the little oval tub. Paul held him in place while Jackie soaped his body. "You know, it almost brings tears to my eyes whenever I look at the back of his head," she murmured.

"Why?"

"I don't know. He seems so sweet and helpless. He's got no neck at all, only this little roll of fat across his shoulders, and his head, with that soft flyaway hair like some nice old guy going bald. I could just eat him up with a spoon."

Paul grinned at her over the baby's head. "I think you're bonding, sweetheart."

"Oh yeah, I'm bonding, all right," she said ruefully. "I'm so nuts about this little kid, I can hardly see straight."

When the baby was fed and settled in his carriage, and they sat together at the table eating their dinner, Jackie told Paul everything that had been happening in the neighborhood.

"Part of this I've heard before, you know," he said when she began with the recovery of the skeletons, the first autopsy results and her early interviews with the neighbors.

"I know, but I need to keep it all in sequence or I'll forget something."

When she reached the morning of Daniel's birth and her discovery of the threatening note in the mailbox, Paul's face tensed and his eyes flashed with anger.

"Go on," he said curtly as she paused. "Tell me the rest."

Jackie continued her story, right up to the police briefing that afternoon and the attack on Emma Betker in the adjoining yard.

When she finished they were both silent, staring down at their plates. Automatically Paul reached over and touched the edge of the baby carriage with a callused brown hand.

"So now what?" he asked.

"I think…" Jackie paused and cleared her throat. "I think I'd like to come out and stay at the ranch for a while," she said. "These things are happening a little too close to home."

He said nothing, but she could see the intense relief on his face.

"Look, this isn't the way it's going to be from

now on, Paul," she warned. "I'm not about to start running scared and ducking responsibility. It's just that I have no involvement in this case anymore, so there's nothing I can accomplish by staying here. And I'm not afraid for myself, but I can't send Danny away without going along, since I'm his entire food supply at the moment."

"You don't have to justify coming to the ranch," he said. "It's the most sensible thing to do. Why make apologies?"

"I hate the feeling of running away," she muttered. "Or even being warned off. And it would be really hard to leave if the Betkers were still here and I thought Emma needed my protection. But I don't even have that excuse anymore."

"Have they gone away?"

Jackie nodded. "Apparently they own a little summer cottage over by Puget Sound. Eleanor packed Emma into the car this afternoon and left an hour ago. She was really spooked."

He nodded his approval, eating quietly and glancing from time to time at the baby carriage. "Should we go tonight, too?"

Jackie thought about it, then shook her head. "I'm not worried when you're here. It's just that, when I'm alone with the baby to look after, my resources are so divided. I feel really vulnerable. There was nothing in the police manuals," she added, trying to smile, "about how to protect yourself from a potential attacker with a baby on your hip."

"Well, I have to go out to the ranch about five in the morning to turn the water on for the bulls for a few hours, then get them out again so I can pump enough for the calves. Do you want to come then?"

"Oh, God no, that's far too early. I'll put Danny down after his sunrise feeding and get our stuff packed, and you can come in and pick us up around noon when you're finished your chores. All right?"

"Sounds good." He smiled at her. "How long do you plan to stay?"

Jackie shrugged. "As long as it takes for them to solve this thing. Brian's stopping by tonight to let me know where it's going, and what they've learned about some of the other neighbors. For all I know," she added, "it could already be over. Maybe they've squeezed a full confession from somebody and Danny and I can stay right where we are."

As she spoke, Jackie realized for the first time that this was a definite possibility. She didn't know whether to feel hopeful or disappointed.

If Paul had any reaction, he kept it carefully hidden. "How about your cat?" he asked, waving a hand at the furry ball on the floor by the stove. "Will you want him to come, too?"

Jackie looked anxiously at Shadow. "Would the farm cats be mean to him? They look like such a nasty bunch of hardened criminals, that gang out there."

"Yeah, but I think Shadow is a pretty tough dude, too. He can probably hold his own in any company."

Jackie hesitated. While they watched, the raffish black tomcat rolled onto his back and tucked one furry paw under his chin, the other covering his eyes.

Paul laughed. "What a character."

"I hate to lose his trust by abandoning him," Jackie said, "after all the time I've taken to lure him into the house. He's mostly my cat now, all the time."

"Well, then," Paul said, getting up and starting to clear the table, "Shadow goes with us, too. He'll probably love having a nice holiday in the country, with lots of mice to catch."

"I'll bet he wouldn't even know what to do with a mouse. Would you, Shadow?"

The doorbell rang. Paul went to answer it while Jackie loaded the dishwasher.

"It's Brian," he said, coming back into the kitchen. "He said he'd just as soon sit out on the veranda while he fills you in."

"Okay." Jackie hesitated by the kitchen door. "This is so nice," she said, feeling almost shy. "I'm not used to having a baby-sitter."

Paul continued to clear the table. "Go on," he said calmly. "Get out of here and leave me some time alone with my son. I need to start teaching him everything I know about women."

"That'll take all of five or ten seconds," Jackie said dryly.

They laughed together. After a moment she sobered and gave him a grateful smile. "Thanks, Paul."

"What for?"

She crossed the room, put her arms around him and gave him a long, lingering kiss.

Clearly startled, he drew her closer and she could feel his rising hardness against her body. It gave her a thrill of sexual excitement, and a hungry, moist yearning that she knew would soon have to be satisfied.

"Thanks for everything," she whispered. "Everything in the world."

She turned and hurried from the kitchen before he could say anything, but she was conscious of his bemused, intent gaze on her back as she left.

On the veranda, Wardlow sprawled in one of the wicker chairs with a briefcase on the floor at his feet, tie loosely knotted and sports jacket slung over the veranda railing. He rested his feet on the railing next to the jacket, tilted the chair back and stared idly into the shadowed depths of the mountain ash tree.

"You look relaxed." Jackie settled into the adjoining chair.

"This is nice, having a peaceful little house on a quiet street." Wardlow grinned at her. "A real slice of Small Town America."

"Yeah, right. Complete with all kinds of mysteries and horrible secrets hidden just below the surface," Jackie said.

"I guess so." Wardlow squinted at the light on one of the veranda posts. Moths fluttered around the shining globe in a futile mating dance.

"Did you talk to Pinson?" Jackie asked.

"You had him pegged. The guy cracked as soon as we sat him down in the interrogation room and started the tape. Pringle and I didn't even get a chance to play good cop, bad cop with him."

Jackie chuckled at the thought of the lugubrious Dave Pringle playing any kind of cop game, then felt a quick lift of interest. "So, what did you get? Is he involved in all this?"

Wardlow rolled his head wearily on the back of the chair. "Not really. My guess is he's only got a peripheral involvement, if any. That's what he claims, and I think he's probably scared enough to tell the truth.''

''What was in the envelopes?''

''Kiddie porn,'' Wardlow said briefly. ''Gerald Pinson is strongly heterosexual and attracted to women, but also afraid of them. He's always gotten his biggest jollies from pictures of naked little girls, especially ones that are posed to be deliberately provocative. His tastes runs to seven-year-olds and younger.''

''So where did Steven Weitzel come in?''

''Steve was apparently quite the little business-man in his teenage years. He needed money to support a few bad habits of his own, so this kid paid his friends to take pictures of their younger sisters, then supplied them to Pinson.''

''That's pretty ugly.''

''No kidding,'' Wardlow said. ''And not the greatest thing to have a respectable high school music teacher involved with, either. So I'd guess that, in addition to supplying Pinson's kinky tastes, Steve also made some money in blackmail.''

''It's so much easier nowadays for perverts,'' Jackie muttered. ''They can get whatever they need through the mail or off the Internet. No need for all these shady dealings anymore.''

''A brave new world,'' Wardlow agreed.

''So that's what Maggie saw in the envelope that shocked her so much?'' Jackie said. ''Pictures of naked little girls?''

''That's what Pinson tells us. And there doesn't seem to be any reason for him to lie at this point. He was pretty broken up about it.''

"Did he kill Maggie?" Jackie asked.

"I doubt it. He denied it strenuously, and we couldn't get him to budge even though he was sweating like crazy. Claims he always believed the story that she ran away, had no knowledge of her death until the bones were dug up and had no guess as to whose baby might have been killed at the same time."

"Still, I'll bet he was pretty damn happy when Maggie vanished," Jackie said. "Especially after she got a peek into that envelope."

"He doesn't deny that her disappearance was a great relief to him."

"What about Mike Weitzel? Does Pinson have an alibi?"

"He says he was outside doing yard work all afternoon, and several of the neighbors saw him. We're checking it out."

"That's pretty thin," Jackie said, frowning, "unless somebody's able to pinpoint a time for some reason. It wouldn't take all that long to drive over to Indian Canyon and back."

Wardlow shook his head. "This old guy's a pitiful sleaze, but I don't think he's a killer."

"Anything else?" she asked.

"We've done some more routine checks into Weitzel's background and associates. Nothing yet that points to any kind of motive." He stretched his legs wearily. "We've also been trying to come up with something on Maggie Birk's childhood, but it's a complete blank. The name is so common and nobody ever reported her missing in any jurisdiction that we can find."

"That's likely the way it'll stay," Jackie said. "I

think her mother was probably relieved that Maggie got away, and she spent the rest of her life hoping she was all right.'' After a moment she shivered. ''God, I just realized the woman could still be hoping her daughter's okay. Maggie was the same age as Mike Weitzel, so her mother would likely be younger than Dolly.''

She stared at the rustling leaves of the silvered tree, brooding.

Wardlow glanced at her.

''What do you think about the attack on your neighbor lady this afternoon? It couldn't have been Pinson, because we had him in an interrogation room while it happened.''

''Did the patrols find any physical evidence?''

''Claire came out and photographed some scuff marks under the hedge where the attacker was supposed to have escaped. And a woman two doors down on the other side of the alley was taking her dog out back to do his business when she saw somebody dressed all in black walking behind a tree. She thought it was a strange outfit for such a hot day.''

Jackie's interest quickened. ''At about the same time as Emma's attack?''

''It seems that way.''

She leaned back and watched the moths that were still circling the light and flinging themselves onto its dangerous, alluring surface.

''So Emma really didn't imagine it,'' she mused. ''I never know what to make of that pair. It's like watching a folie à deux.''

''Speak English, Kaminsky.''

''Folie à deux is an intriguing concept. I learned about it at a police psychology course. It's when two people both believe the same insanity and reinforce each other's madness."

She told Wardlow about Eleanor's love for Maggie Birk and her long-held fear that her sister might have been the girl's killer.

"All these years the woman believed that and yet she never said a word to anybody?"

"Eleanor would die to protect her sister."

He stared with narrowed eyes at the porch light. "Witnesses or not, I'm still skeptical about this whole mysterious attacker. Do you really believe the Betker sisters have packed up and gone away?"

"I saw them leave. The house is dark."

"They could have come back. They could be sitting over there right now with the blinds drawn, using candles and waiting for you to be caught unawares. Do you want me to check the house?"

Jackie rubbed her arms nervously.

"If they're really hiding over there, nobody's going to answer the door and you have no probable cause to go in without a warrant. I'm sure they're gone, Brian."

"Just the same, I'd be a whole lot happier if you weren't alone here with the baby."

"I'm going to the ranch with Paul tomorrow morning. He's driving out to do the early chores, then coming back to get Danny and me. We'll stay with him until you solve this."

"Well, that's good news." Wardlow squeezed her hand. "I'm glad to hear it."

He held her hand briefly, looking down at it, then glanced up, almost shyly.

"I got over all that crap I was telling you about, Jackie."

She squeezed his hand, then withdrew hers gently and smiled. "What was that? You're always telling me some kind of crap."

"About being afraid to get married. All of a sudden it dawned on me how much I love Chris and Gordie, and how empty my life would be without them, and I thought, 'What's to be afraid of? Losing the woman would be a whole lot scarier than marrying her.' So now I'm not scared anymore."

"Well, I'm glad." Jackie reached over impulsively to hug him. "Paul and I will be so happy to dance at your wedding, Brian."

"Great," he said calmly. "And pretty soon, we'll return the favor."

Her hug turned to a punch. She drew away, pummeling him a couple more times for good measure. "You never ever miss a chance, you annoying Irishman."

"Never." He knotted his tie and reached for his jacket. "Kaminsky?"

"Yes?"

"Whose baby was it?"

"Damn, Brian, I still don't have the slightest idea. I've been wondering…"

"What?" he asked.

"It's a crazy idea, but Maggie talked in that last diary entry about seeing something so horrible she couldn't even describe it. She said 'they' were doing this awful thing and would soon be coming for her. I was wondering…" She hesitated.

"Some kind of satanism?" he asked. "Sacrificing human infants?"

"Well, it does fit, in a sort of way. There's the gruesome nature of Maggie's death, right? And that would be the kind of thing somebody would kill to keep hidden, even all these years later.''

"I'll check on it." He got to his feet and reached for the briefcase. "While we're looking up information on that clinic Alban Cernak worked at, I'll also see if I can get your buddy Karl Widmer to come up with some old newspaper reports on satanist groups in the city back around that time.''

"Okay.'' She watched him moving toward the steps. "Did you find out anything about Bob and Carrie Turnbull?"

He shook his head. "Upstanding citizens, pillars of society, very philanthropic. Bob Turnbull is a self-made man, pulled himself up by his bootstraps to become a huge success and then married well, too.''

"But have you talked with them? Do you know where both of them were when Mike Weitzel died, or if they had any connection with him?''

Wardlow gave her a keen glance. "No, but if you think I should, I'll get right on it.''

"Good." She hugged her arms. "Brian...''

"What?''

"I still have the feeling I'm forgetting something. I've seen something in the past few weeks that's the key to this whole puzzle, but it's hanging out there just beyond my reach.''

He studied her face. "You've told me that before. And when you get that feeling, you're usually right.''

"I know. If I keep trying, I'll remember it sooner or later.''

"Well, kiddo, I'll be waiting anxiously to hear from you," he said dryly.

She forced a smile, then watched him descend the steps and head for his car.

Suddenly the small hairs began to prickle on her forearms and the back of her neck. She had the feeling somebody was watching, hiding in the bushes to eavesdrop on their conversation. The summer night seemed charged with malice, alive with danger.

Normally the sensation would have outraged Jackie, made her even more fiercely determined to nail the person who was doing these things.

But now, with that precious little baby inside the house, she was fearful. She wanted urgently to wrap her son up and run away, take him to a place of safety where nothing could ever threaten him.

Jackie forced herself to stand a while longer on the step, although she felt uncomfortably exposed under the porch light in her T-shirt and shorts, with no gun at hand.

Finally she turned on her heel and went back inside the house, where Paul lay full length on the sofa, cradling the baby on his chest. Daniel had burrowed forward until his downy head rested against his father's chin. He rose and fell peacefully with the movements of Paul's rib cage. The baby was drowsy and contented, his small thumb jammed in his mouth, eyelids fluttering.

As soon as Jackie closed and locked the door, the evil images vanished and she was enclosed in warmth and safety.

24

The next morning, Jackie woke after Paul had gone. She fed and burped the baby, then settled him in his carriage again. She went back to bed and lay staring at the ceiling, thinking about everything she needed to pack.

By seven o'clock she was too restless and charged with energy to sleep anymore. She got up and had breakfast, let the cat in and started piling bags and equipment by the back door.

"It's amazing, isn't it?" she said to Shadow, who sprawled in his favorite square of sunshine near the stove. "Look how much stuff you need for one little baby. Paul and I could survive six months in the wilderness with half of this."

Shadow blinked and licked his paw, then began to swipe it energetically over his face. Jackie watched him, smiling, and felt a brief easing of the tension that had been gnawing at her for days. She could hardly wait for Paul to come back and collect them, so she could lock the door on this place and leave it behind until it felt safe again.

The doorbell rang, startling her. She went and peeked out, relieved to see Lola Bridges standing on the veranda. For the first time since Jackie had met the saleswoman, Lola wore casual clothes. She was dressed in a pair of bulging blue jeans, an old sweater and cotton gardening gloves, and carried a plastic bucket containing a trowel.

"Hi, Lola," Jackie said, opening the door.

"Hello." Lola smiled, then glanced down ruefully at her clothes. "Excuse the farmer look. I'm helping Dad plant some rosebushes."

Jackie grinned. "I'm partial to farmers, you know. What can I do for you?"

"Dad said he loaned you a sack of bonemeal when you planted your petunias, and now he's setting out these rosebushes, so we wondered if…"

Jackie slapped her forehead. "I forgot all about that stuff! Come in, I'll get it for you. It's in the back porch."

Lola followed her into the kitchen and bent to pet the cat while Jackie got the sack of plant fertilizer from a shelf in the back porch.

She returned to find Lola looking thoughtfully at the pile of luggage and baby supplies next to the door.

"Danny and I are going out to the ranch for a few days," Jackie said. "And that little boy needs a ton of supplies. Would you like a cup of tea? I was about to have one."

Lola sank gratefully into a chair. "I'd love that. Dad's busy scraping wax off the stems of his rosebushes, so I have a little time."

"Wax?" Jackie said, putting the kettle on.

"It's some kind of protective coating for shipping them. Not that I know very much about gardening," Lola added.

"Neither do I." Jackie searched for a packet of

tea. "And most all of what I know, I've learned from your father."

She put the tea bag in the pot, then raised her head when she heard a distant complaint. "Damn," she said, checking her watch. "It's not time for his feeding yet, but he often has a big messy diaper right about now."

"Oh, yuck. Better you than me," Lola said with a grimace.

Jackie laughed and moved toward the door. "Look, I'll tend to him and be down as soon as I can," she said. "Would you mind pouring that water into the teapot when it starts boiling?"

"Take your time." Lola leaned back in her chair and smiled. "I'll just sit here and commune with the cat. Dad and I hardly ever see him anymore. He seems to love you best."

Jackie left hastily to avoid further discussion of Shadow's loyalties. She ran upstairs and found that the baby had indeed filled his diaper.

"Look at you," she muttered, working quickly to clean and wash him. "Practically up to your ears."

While she was reaching for a diaper he made an additional mess, this time staining the carriage sheet as well.

She stared at him, hands on hips, while he kicked placidly. "A whole load of laundry," she said. "And on a morning when your poor mother is already too busy to turn around."

She gathered him up, sheet and all, and carried him down the hall to the bathroom to get some more washcloths.

"Lola, this is going to take a few minutes," she

called over the stair railing. "Sorry, I'll be down as soon as I can."

There was no response from the kitchen, but she could no longer hear the kettle whistling and assumed her guest was making tea.

Jackie washed the baby, slathered him with oil and powder and fitted a clean diaper in place, then dumped all the soiled things in the laundry, washed her hands and put Daniel in the middle of her bed while she hurried to change the sheets on the carriage.

By the time she went back to fetch the baby, he was drowsing off again—a welcome surprise. There was still an hour or more until his next scheduled feeding, and it looked as if he might sleep during that time and let her finish her packing.

She settled him in the carriage, covered him with a fresh blanket and went downstairs to where Lola sat in the kitchen sipping tea.

"Sorry to take so long," Jackie said ruefully, sinking into the opposite chair. "You should have seen the mess he made."

"No thanks," Lola said. "Messy diapers are definitely not my style."

Jackie poured herself a cup of tea, then looked up in surprise. "What's that noise?" she said, frowning.

"Is the baby crying again?"

Jackie shook her head. "No, I just left him sound asleep in his carriage." She strained to listen. "Besides, that sounds like it's coming from the basement, doesn't it?"

"I can't really tell. Do you think it could be the

cat? He got up and left while I was pouring water into the teapot.''

Jackie went over to the basement door, which stood open a crack. She pulled it wider. "Shadow?" she called into the depths. "Are you down there, kitty?"

This time she heard a definite yowl of pain and distress.

"What the hell?" she muttered, hurrying downstairs with Lola at her heels.

The cat had somehow become entangled in a loop of wire dangling from one of the metal support posts in the musty, littered basement. He struggled and howled, sounding increasingly anguished.

"What happened to you? What have you done, you silly cat?" Jackie knelt and tried to free him, finding it hard to see clearly through the dimness of the basement.

The scrap of wire seemed to be a heavy gauge, several thicknesses plaited together, and formed a loop that the cat had stepped into and tightened around his furry abdomen. All his frantic efforts just served to ensnare him further.

Lola knelt on the other side of the post, reaching around to help, but the cat writhed and clawed at both of them while the heavy wire coiled around their hands and impeded their efforts.

Shadow continued to hiss and scratch, sounding so pained that Jackie was increasingly concerned. She felt a loop of the wire snake tightly around one of her wrists, then the other, and looked down at her hands in confusion.

Lola took a small pair of wire cutters from the pocket of her cardigan and bent to snip the bonds that held the cat. Shadow vanished upstairs in a flash of black.

Jackie stood up, facing the post with her hands shackled around it, utterly baffled. Her wrists were trapped in a pair of heavy-duty handcuffs.

"Lola?" she said. "What's going on?"

Slowly and carefully, Lola stripped off the cotton gardening gloves and put them away in her pocket. Jackie saw the burns on the woman's right hand, painful welts that reddened her thumb and forefinger, as well as the back of her hand.

Jackie gazed stupidly at the burns, knowing what they were but unable to put the information together in her mind. Then she saw Lola's left hand and the ring that she wore on her smallest finger.

For what seemed like hours, Jackie stood manacled to the post, staring at that gold ring. This was the detail that had nagged so long at the back of her mind. Lola had been wearing the ring since their first meeting, but it was one of many on the woman's pudgy hands, and Jackie had never made a particular note of the design.

It was made up of four golden snakes intertwined to form a wide band. All the snakes had rubies for their eyes.

"Jesus," she whispered.

Lola stood back, watching her calmly.

"Hey, unlock these cuffs," Jackie said, trying to keep her voice level and persuasive. "Come on, Lola. Whatever's going on here, you don't want to get into any more trouble. Just unlock the cuffs and we'll go upstairs and talk about it."

Lola stared back in silence. Her lip curled with

contempt, and Jackie was stunned by the depths of malice and cruelty in the woman's eyes.

"That was Lenny Cernak's ring," Jackie said, gesturing with her shackled right hand toward the golden serpents. "You must have known him."

"Oh yes." Lola smiled unpleasantly. "I knew him, all right. I've known him all my life."

Jackie felt a quick surge of panic but suppressed it firmly. She had to stay calm and talk her way through this, because Danny was sleeping upstairs in his carriage.

"You've known Lenny all your life?"

Lola sat down on the basement steps, still watching Jackie with an intent expression. She reached into her other pocket and took out a small silver revolver, holding it reflectively in her palm.

Jackie stared at the weapon in grim fascination, knowing this was probably the gun that had killed Mike Weitzel. It looked small and innocuous, almost like a toy. But the hollow shells it fired were inch-long, copper-plated instruments of death.

"I could kill you right now," Lola said, squinting at the barrel of the gun.

Jackie bit her lip, wishing she could see the woman's face more clearly.

"You don't want to kill me, Lola," she said. "Let's talk about what's been going on here. Is Lenny Cernak still living in the neighborhood?"

"God, you're so stupid," Lola jeered. "I thought you were supposed to be such a big smart cop, but you're just pitiful."

"Then tell me what I'm missing," Jackie said. "Tell me what you know that I don't."

"My father was always very religious," Lola said

after a long, charged silence. "You do know that much, don't you?"

Jackie nodded jerkily, thinking about John Caldwell's well-worn Bible and the framed Scripture texts on the walls in his house.

"Yes," she said. "I know that John's a very religious man."

She wondered if Caldwell was still outside in his rose garden and would hear if she screamed, then decided it was too risky. Lola had a gun and she'd probably used it recently. Jackie's best chance was to remain quiet and soothing and try to keep the woman talking.

"After my mother went away," Lola said in a monotone, "my father was attracted to me. I was twelve years old, starting to get little breasts. He couldn't leave me alone."

"He assaulted you?" Jackie said in disbelief. "Your father did?"

"Yes, and then he was horrified with himself. He felt so awful, he wanted to cut his hands off. He tried to make sure it would never happen again."

A sickening suspicion began to form in Jackie's mind. She suppressed her revulsion, trying to think.

"What did your father do to keep himself from touching you, Lola?"

"I'd always been a tomboy, and after that he encouraged me. He dressed me like a boy and changed my name, and pretended I wasn't a girl at all."

It was all becoming clear to Jackie, and more horribly bizarre than she could have imagined.

"He changed your name," she repeated. "He called you Lenny."

"It worked for a while," Lola said in that same

expressionless tone. "I think for a year or two we both believed I was Lenny, and he didn't touch me. As long as everybody thought I was a boy, he wasn't tempted. But then everything changed."

Jackie remembered Maggie's diary and her frequent observation that Lenny was getting "fatter and fatter." Suddenly she understood everything.

"Was it your father's baby?" she asked, trying to picture mild-mannered, sanctimonious John Caldwell having sex with his young daughter.

Lola gave a sharp bark of laughter. "Oh no. He never went that far, although we both knew he wanted to." She stared at the gun in her hands. "It was three boys in a vacant lot downtown. They picked on me, thinking I was a boy, and chased me and pushed me down. One of them started hitting me and realized I was a girl. Then all three of them raped me. A few months later we found out I was pregnant." Lola shuddered. "It was so horrible, having that thing growing inside me."

"Why didn't you have an abortion? Your father worked at a clinic, didn't he?"

Lola's mouth twisted. "I told you, he's a very religious man. My father believes abortion is a sin. He said the baby was a gift from God and we had to raise it, but we could never, ever let anybody know that it was mine."

"How did he propose to keep that a secret?"

"He got Maggie and brought her home, telling everybody we needed a housekeeper."

"But why?" Jackie asked. "Where did Maggie come into it?"

"God, you're a stupid bitch." Lola stared at her, then shook her head. "He knew we couldn't stay in

Spokane if I had the baby, but he loved that job at the clinic and he never wanted to leave. They actually believed he was a doctor, even though he just had some training as an ambulance attendant, nothing more.''

"So, what was the plan?"

"When it was time for the baby to be born, he was going to take a two-month leave of absence from the clinic for a training course. We'd go to Portland, taking Maggie with us. Then he'd dump her somewhere and let her make her own way home to Salt Lake City or wherever she wanted to go. He'd deliver my baby himself, and after two months, we'd come back here. He'd tell everybody at the clinic that it was Maggie's baby but she'd gone away to school and left it for us to look after, and she was going to come back for it soon."

"So that was why he needed Maggie, right from the beginning," Jackie said. "He wanted to pretend it was her baby."

"Of course."

"And you were supposed to go on being disguised as Lenny?"

Lola nodded. "Just for a little while longer, he said. Then I could go away to a private high school and on to college, and nobody ever had to know what we'd done."

"But that was crazy."

"Of course he was crazy," Lola said thoughtfully, as if they were discussing a stranger. "I see that now. But he wanted that baby so much it didn't matter how many lies we had to tell. He just couldn't stand having anybody know what he'd done to me that made him need to turn me into a boy. Once you start up with a big lie like that, you have to keep on.''

''What went wrong?''

''The baby came a month early. I was downstairs in my room having it, with my father there to help. The thing was just starting to come out when Maggie brought down some laundry. She looked through the door and saw us.''

Jackie tried to imagine how shocking and horrible this would have been for Maggie Birk.

To see the ''boy'' she'd always known as Lenny lying down there in the musty basement giving birth to a child, and Alban Cernak hovering over the bed with his hands drenched in blood…

The poor girl must have thought she was living in a nightmare.

No wonder she'd cowered up there in the room under the window, scribbling in her diary to keep herself calm, wondering when they would be coming for her and what they were going to do.

''Who killed her?'' Jackie asked.

''I did. As soon as the baby came, I told my father to go upstairs and get Maggie. He made her write a note saying she was running away. Then he brought her here to the basement. She kept shaking and screaming, and he punched her so she'd be quiet. She fell down. I got up and started hitting her with the ax.''

''Right after you'd given birth?'' Jackie said.

''I was crazed. It hurt so much and I hated everybody. I hated those boys for what they'd done to me, and my father for saying we had to keep the baby, and stupid Maggie for seeing it and messing up everything. I just kept hitting her, thinking how much I hated everybody. I can still remember," Lola added reflectively, "how good it felt to hit her."

"You hacked her to pieces." Jackie looked at the plump middle-aged woman sitting on the steps in her blue jeans and cardigan.

"And then I smothered the baby," Lola continued in the same matter-of-fact tone. "My father tried to stop me but I was out of my mind by then, covered with blood, screaming."

She looked down at the gun again. "It was so much easier to kill the baby. I just held my hand over its mouth and nose until it died."

"Did you really keep one of its fingers?"

"I twisted off the little finger. I wanted to have something to prove that it really happened, I guess. I put it in some alcohol and it shriveled up like a little chicken claw. I still have it."

Jackie took a deep breath and battled a wave of nausea. "So, what happened next?" she asked, knowing that Lola planned to kill her or she'd never be telling all this.

If only she could somehow keep the woman talking until Paul came and prevent her from thinking about Daniel in his carriage upstairs...

Keep sleeping, darling, Jackie thought urgently. Please, please don't wake up and cry.

"My father put Maggie's pieces on a tarp along with the baby and took them outside in the backyard, then came back to find a shovel. Emma Betker was wandering around in the dark like a sleepwalker and found them. We watched her from the house. I was going to kill her, too, but he wouldn't let me. He said Eleanor would never believe anything Emma said after we had the bodies safely buried."

"But Emma had blood on her dress when she went home."

"Did she?" Lola glanced up, looking mildly curious. "We didn't know that, or I would have killed her for sure. Why didn't Eleanor ever say anything about it?"

"She was afraid Emma was the one who'd killed Maggie, because she was jealous of her."

"The ugly old dyke." Lola gave another harsh burst of laughter and got to her feet, moving up a couple of stairs. "No wonder she had a guilty conscience, the way she chased after Maggie."

"How long did you and your father live in the house afterward?" Jackie asked.

"Not long. We waited a couple of weeks so it wouldn't look suspicious," Lola said. "Then we moved away. He hated giving up that job at the clinic, but I couldn't stand living here anymore. I made him leave."

Jackie strained surreptitiously to see her watch, wondering how soon Paul would be coming. "Then why did your father move back here?" she said, unnerved by the tone of desperation she could hear creeping into her own voice.

I wouldn't mind killing another baby, Lola had said in her warning note.

"He was obsessed by what we'd done. He kept worrying somebody would dig up the backyard and find those bodies, and he wanted to move back so he could stand guard over them. I tried to stop him, but for once in his life he wouldn't listen to me. After a few years he had to come back and nothing would stop him."

"Why didn't he move into this house, then?"

"It wasn't available. That old couple was living here, but the house next door was for sale. My father gave himself a different name, got a new job, shaved off his beard, cut his hair and wore long-sleeved shirts all the time so the tattoos on his arms wouldn't show. I was away at school by then, and nobody ever recognized him. He's lived over there all these years, watching the backyard to keep it safe."

The woman began to mount the stairs again.

"Lola, wait," Jackie called. "Why did you kill Mike Weitzel?"

Lola was near the top of the stairs. Her voice drifted down from the shadows. "That day when he was here talking to you and I came around the corner, I knew he recognized me. All the times we'd met before he'd never made the connection, but you had him thinking about Maggie and all that old stuff, and I could just see when it dawned on him. I had to keep him from telling you."

Jackie remembered Weitzel's hushed tone when he said he had something fantastic to tell her. No wonder he'd been reluctant to discuss it over the phone.

"Now, stop talking to me," Lola added peevishly. "I have things to do."

"But when did you—"

"Shut up," Lola yelled. Again she bent to peer at Jackie through the sparkling dust motes. "I tried to tell you not to buy this place. Every time it's been for sale, my father's made friends with the neighbors and recommended me as the salesperson, and I've been careful about who bought it. But you were so stubborn. You deserve whatever happens to you."

Jackie struggled vainly, pulling on the handcuffs until her wrists were chafed and raw.

She held her breath and listened while Lola trudged up the rest of the stairs. Her footsteps moved around for a while in the kitchen and back porch, then went outside. Jackie sagged against the post, limp with relief.

The woman hadn't gone up to the second floor. Daniel was safe in his carriage for the moment.

She heard a car start up and drive off. As soon as the sound of the engine died away, she began to scream.

"Help!" she shouted, wondering how far her voice would carry. The Betkers were gone from next door and Dolly Weitzel was alone in her house across the street, locked away in her grief. "Somebody, come and help me!"

John Caldwell, or Alban Cernak, was her only hope. But, Jackie realized with a sudden chill, he probably knew everything that was going on. He was so completely under Lola's control, no doubt he was sitting next door, refusing to pay any attention to her shouts.

She frowned, trying to understand why Lola had gone away and left her and Daniel unharmed. Maybe, like so many killers, the woman was going off to kill herself after her orgy of confession. She'd had that look when she sat fondling the gun.

Wherever Lola had gone, Paul would be here soon, and then the baby would be safe.

Jackie only had to a wait a couple of hours and try to stay calm.

Then she smelled the smoke, curling down the

stairs through the open door, and heard the greedy crackle of flames.

Her eyes widened in horror.

"Fire," she screamed. "Help me, somebody! Oh, God, Danny!"

Sobbing and yelling, she strained against the harsh metal until her shoulders ached and blood ran down her wrists. Fire mounted beyond the stairwell and the basement slowly filled up with smoke.

25

By midmorning, Paul was ready to turn the bulls
out of the watering pen so he could let the calves
in.

Getting the bulls to leave the corral was always a
risky business. At this time of year they were heavy,
sleek and belligerent, and the ones that weren't out
with the cows had been confined because of sore
hooves or other painful problems that made them
even more testy and unpredictable.

Many a rancher had been killed in his own corral
by an injured bull that had suddenly gone mad and
charged at him without warning.

Paul edged around the perimeter of the pen, waving a stock whip. He kept one hand on the fence
and a wary eye on a big black Angus, the worst of
the lot. The bull had wicked close-set eyes, fleshy
forequarters and a threatening bellow, and he could
move with fearful speed on his short legs.

"Go on, get!" Paul yelled. "Get out of here, all
of you."

The bulls milled and stumbled. They pawed the
ground, raising clouds of dust in the pen, and he
could smell their rank, musky scent.

Suddenly he stopped and gripped the whip, thinking of Jackie. As vividly as if she were there beside

him, he could see her face and hear her voice calling to him. Her eyes were big and dark, full of entreaty.

Paul smiled with pleasure, glanced at his watch and gently flicked a couple of the Hereford bulls into position, urging them along toward the open gate.

Today, in just a couple of hours, she was coming to the ranch and bringing the baby. For a little while at least, Paul Arnussen was going to have his whole family together under his own roof. He felt more optimistic than he ever had since he'd first met this difficult, fiercely independent woman he loved.

Paul knew, of course, that she was only coming to the ranch because she feared for the baby's safety, and when the danger had passed she'd probably want to leave again. Still, he took comfort from the fact that she'd chosen to come to him, and that her love for the child had brought her to this decision.

It boded well for the future. Maybe if Jackie realized how pleasant life was at the ranch and how good it would be for their son...

He paused again and frowned, one hand clinging to the fence.

Her image was more insistent in his mind. He began to feel a little sick, the way he often did when he got one of the paranormal flashes that he hated.

"Jackie?" he said aloud, raising his head. "Are you all right?"

The prairie wind snatched the words from his mouth and carried them away.

Suddenly Paul's head filled up with terror, like dark wings beating inside his mind. He sensed entrapment, fear, panic, a feeling of being underground and in smothering darkness.

Sore wrists, blood and struggle, ragged gasps of smoky breath.

And Jackie, terrified, calling him.

He left the bulls in the watering pen, left the whip on the ground, left everything—and ran for his truck.

By the time he careened off the freeway and through the city to pull up in front of her little house, almost half an hour had passed, and he was sweating with fear and nausea. His hands felt slick and damp on the steering wheel.

Jackie's neighborhood looked serenely detached in the midmorning stillness. The houses on both sides of her, that Victorian mansion belonging to the Betker sisters and John Caldwell's little cottage, both had a deserted air. The big white house across the street was also silent and still.

Nobody was outside running around, nobody seemed to be in any kind of panic. Paul felt briefly reassured. Then he saw a finger of flame licking out through the opened kitchen window. At the same time he heard the distant wail of a siren.

He flung himself from his truck and ran in through the back door, heading for the basement where he knew instinctively he was going to find her. Inside the kitchen he encountered a wall of smoke, thick and choking. He yanked a curtain from its rod and covered his face, then stumbled down the basement steps.

Lower in the house the air was a little better, but he had to peer around, his eyes stinging, before he saw her hanging limply against the metal post. Her hands ran with blood and her shoulders heaved.

"Jackie," he shouted.

She raised her smeared face and looked at him. "Get the baby!" she screamed, entreating him with her trapped, bloody hands as he hurried toward her. "Paul, get the baby! He's upstairs...."

He hesitated for an anguished moment, glancing upward in despair. Then he studied the handcuffs that bound her and tried to think.

The cuffs were heavy-gauge stainless steel, almost impossible to sever even with a good pair of bolt-cutters. He had no tool in the truck that would be effective. A hacksaw would take too much time.

In the movies, Paul thought bitterly, they'd just take an ax and slice through the chain. But in real life, such a thing was impossible. He'd take her hands off for sure before he severed those cuffs.

He hesitated for another couple of seconds, then took a set of pliers from the tool pouch at his belt, locked it onto the turn mechanism of the support post and began to loosen it, putting all his strength into the effort.

"Be ready to run!" he shouted to Jackie. "This thing will come down on our heads!"

"The baby!" she yelled, looking almost too weak to stand. "Leave me and get the baby!"

He ignored her, struggling awkwardly with his hands over his head to loosen the bolt. Finally it began to give. Paul backed up and took a couple of short runs at the metal post, shoulder first, jarring himself with the pain.

On the third pass it fell to one side, wobbling crazily. He wrenched the post off its base, pulled it through the handcuffs, grasped Jackie and sprinted for the stairs just as the living-room floor caved in behind them and a great rush of heat clawed at their backs.

Paul stumbled out through the fiery kitchen and into the backyard with Jackie in his arms. They fell together on the lawn and he rolled on top of her to smother the little flames that had broken out in their clothes.

Behind them the house was ablaze, with flames licking from all the windows and shooting through the roof. A couple of fire trucks and police cars had arrived at the scene, disgorging men onto the lawn. They unrolled hoses and rushed forward, shouting.

"My baby's in there," Jackie screamed, struggling to her feet. Her face was blackened, her hands still manacled and bloody. "Danny!"

Paul had already left her and was running back toward the house. He got as far as the door when he was tackled by two burly firemen. He shook them off, as if they were children, and wrestled his way forward again. It took two more men to restrain him. Paul struggled wildly in their grasp and felt the bitter salt tears running into his mouth.

"You can't go in there, man," one of the fire-fighters said, his young face wretched with sympathy. "You just can't go in there."

Dazed and disbelieving, Jackie knelt on the lawn watching as Paul struggled with the firemen. At last she understood and slumped onto the grass, seized by an anguish so intense, it felt as if her insides were being ripped out.

"Danny," she cried, her face burrowed into the prickly grass, her hands clawing at the dirt. "Danny, Danny, Danny."

She was conscious, vaguely, of various things happening.

Paul came back and sat on the grass beside her. He gathered her into his arms and rocked her, and she could see the pale streaks on his face where tears continued to wash through the blackened soot.

Wordlessly, she huddled against him.

One of the firemen came over with a gleaming instrument that snapped the handcuff chain like a toy. Jackie still had the metal bracelets on her wrists, tender against her chafed and bleeding skin, but she wasn't even aware of the pain.

Her entire consciousness was centered on an agony so fierce, nothing else could penetrate.

Wardlow and Michelson appeared through the stinging mists of smoke and approached them. Wardlow knelt nearby and had a brief conversation with Paul. Jackie knew they were talking about the baby because Paul kept her head pressed against him, his hands covering her ears so she couldn't hear.

"Jackie," Wardlow said after a moment, bending close to her. "Who did this, honey? Do you know who cuffed you and set the fire?"

She rocked her head against Paul's charred shirtfront, nodding.

"It was Lola," she whispered, and Wardlow leaned nearer to make out what she was saying "From next door." She gestured feebly at the adjoining house. "She killed everybody."

Wardlow and Michelson got up and disappeared. Jackie burrowed into Paul's arms again.

The house was totally engulfed by now. Windows and doors twisted into crazy shapes, dark outlines against a sea of orange, and then vanished one by one.

"Don't look at it," Paul whispered hoarsely, trying to cover her eyes with his grimy hands. "Darling, don't watch."

She pushed his hands away and stared at the house, dry-eyed, wondering when the tears would come and ease the terrible knot of grief in her chest. Surely this agony was too great to bear.

A person had to die of a pain like this, she thought with weary detachment. Because how was it possible to go on living?

Suddenly she felt Paul stiffen. He got slowly to his feet, lifting Jackie with him, and held her in the circle of his arms, staring intently at something over her head.

"My God," he whispered. "Dear God…"

Jackie turned numbly to follow his gaze. Her eyes stung and took a long time to focus. She saw Wardlow through a mist of smoke, stumbling toward them from the house next door. In his arms he carried a blanket-wrapped bundle and his freckled face streamed with tears.

Jackie faltered toward him, her hands shaking.

Wardlow delivered the bundle into her arms. It was clean and sweet, moving warmly in her arms. She looked down to see her son's face. The baby was indignant, howling with outrage. His cheeks were red and mottled, his eyes screwed shut, small hands flailing.

"Danny," she whispered stupidly. "Danny, it's you. It's really you."

Then at last the tears came, dropping off her

cheeks and making sooty little marks on the flannel blanket.

"The guy had him next door," Wardlow said, looking dazed. "He was carrying him around, trying to stop him crying. The old man seemed pretty vague, but he was taking good care of the baby. He kept saying, 'I went and got him as soon as she left.'"

Wardlow hesitated, looking at Jackie.

"The old guy said he wasn't going to stop her from doing what she had to, but he couldn't let her kill another baby."

Jackie sobbed aloud, holding her precious bundle. She sat on the grass, rocking him and crooning, her cheeks still wet with tears.

Word of the baby's safe reappearance spread amongst the firefighters, who glanced in their direction with blackened faces creased by happy grins.

Paul sat beside Jackie and reached out a shaking hand to stroke the baby's soft rounded cheek.

"Hold us, Paul," she said fiercely. "Hold us and never let us go."

He put his arms around both of them and rocked them. Jackie was vividly conscious of the muscular hardness of his body curved against hers. She felt more alive and enclosed in love, more richly cherished and blessed than she'd ever been in her life.

With a final shudder and roar, the little house collapsed in a shower of sparks. The air was hot on their faces as they huddled together, sheltering their child.

___ Epilogue ___

Jackie sat at a mullioned second-floor window, gazing down into the autumn splendor of the big yard. Heavy bronze chrysanthemums nodded in the garden, flanked by a colorful display of petunias and dahlias. The grass was freshly clipped, so smooth and flawless that it looked artificial. The edge of a ribboned bower was visible near the corner of the patio, but she turned her eyes away quickly and concentrated on the flowers again, watching a bee hovering above the blossoms. Its striped body and legs were dusty with pollen.

Briefly she wondered if John Caldwell was enjoying this lovely fall day. Her former neighbor was still in a detention home for elderly offenders, undergoing psychological assessment to determine if he was fit to stand trial for his part in those long-ago deaths of Maggie Birk and his own newborn grandchild.

Wardlow had gone a couple of times to interview the old man, and told Jackie he seemed vague and disoriented, content to sit on a bench in the sun and watch the gardeners.

"He'll never come home again," Wardlow had said. "He'll get old and die in one of those places, Jackie, and I don't think he'll mind a bit. The guilt's been eating him up for thirty years. Now he feels he can rest and start paying his debt to society.''

Jackie shifted in the chair and frowned at her manicured fingernails. There was a chip in the polish on one thumb. She examined it anxiously, then clenched her hands into fists, thinking about Lola Bridges.

The real estate saleswoman was at another assessment facility, but had already been pronounced sane and would stand trial on three counts of homicide and two counts of attempted murder.

Despite police debriefings and trauma counseling, Jackie still couldn't bring herself to think very often about the day of the fire more than two months ago, and her anguish when she'd believed Daniel was still inside the burning house.

Restlessly she got to her feet and moved closer to the window, peering out.

Almost everybody she knew had begun to gather on the lawn below. Wardlow and Chris held hands and looked like a blissful newly married couple. Karl Widmer, Jackie's friend in the local press corps, stood at the edge of the patio, hawklike and handsome in a gray sports jacket. He held a champagne glass and chatted with Leigh Mellon, Adrienne's pretty blond sister, while Leigh's small son played croquet with Alex on the lawn.

Even Lew Michelson was there, sturdy and red-faced in a dark blue dress suit, with his shy little wife at his side.

Jackie moved away to study her reflection in the mirror. She wore a trim, knee-length sheath of heavy cream-colored silk, with a mandarin collar and satin frogs adorning the bodice. The pale shimmer of fabric brought a warm flush to her cheeks and made her hair and eyes look even darker.

"Beautiful," Adrienne said behind her, opening the door quietly and coming in. "You're just so beautiful, honey."

Adrienne wore a suit of bronze silk and looked slim and stylish. Her eyes were suspiciously moist.

"Are you okay?" Jackie asked.

Her friend came nearer to adjust one of the satin fasteners on Jackie's dress. "Hey, I should be the one asking you that question," she murmured. "But yes, I'm fine."

"Really?" Jackie looked at her searchingly.

"Really," Adrienne said. "The medication is finally beginning to work. All those dark clouds are lifting and life is worth living again. Every day I feel a little better."

"Oh, Rennie, I'm so glad." Impulsively, Jackie hugged her friend, and they stood close together for a long moment.

Adrienne was the first to draw away. "Hey, come on, we can't do this, Kaminsky. I'll get you all mussed. How do you feel?"

"Surprisingly good," Jackie confessed. "I always thought by this point I'd be getting ready to take my gun and blast my way out of the place, but instead I feel perfectly calm."

"Wasn't it a great idea to use my mother's house? The backyard is just gorgeous. Jackie, you should see the flowers down there."

"I've been peeking out the window, but I can only catch the edge of the bower from here."

"Well, it's a setting fit for a princess."

"Some princess." Jackie grimaced, then glanced

cautiously at her friend. "Rennie, how's my family behaving?"

"They're being perfect angels. Joey and Carmelo are telling Harlan how to fix that funny noise in his Mercedes. Very sharp dressers, those two guys," she added with a grin.

"And Gram? Is she drunk yet?"

"Your grandmother is drinking nonalcoholic punch and having a lovely chat with my mother."

Jackie couldn't picture her garrulous, sharp-tongued grandmother having any kind of conversation with elegant Barbara Mellon. Her stomach tightened with anxiety. "What in God's name could those two be talking about?"

"Knitting," Adrienne said calmly. "Last time I passed by, they were moving from woven patterns to cable stitches and pom-poms. Look," she added, squeezing Jackie's hand, "stop worrying. Everything's going just fine."

"And Danny? Where's my baby?"

Adrienne gave her a placid, secretive smile. "You'll see."

Jackie looked again at her chipped thumbnail, then at her watch.

Five more minutes.

"Are you really fine with all this, sweetie?" Adrienne asked. "No doubts or fears, after all that time you kept resisting?"

Jackie nodded. "I realize now I was crazy to be so scared. But it took that awful moment when I thought everything was gone. My house, and all my stuff, and my..." Her voice faltered. "My baby..."

Adrienne leaned over and stroked Jackie's shoulder until she was able to continue.

"I think it takes a revelation like that, when you know you've lost everything," Jackie said, "to understand how foolish it is to govern your life by the fear of loss. Life is so short and fragile. I want to start celebrating the good things I have, not waste time brooding about all the bad things that might happen."

"Amen," Adrienne murmured.

The two women sat down for a moment in silence while the swirl of merriment grew louder on the manicured lawn below the window.

"And the commute from the ranch won't bother you when you have to go back to work?"

Jackie shrugged. "It's twenty miles. Just about long enough for me to get my thoughts in order before work, that's all."

"But you were always so worried about living out in the country and keeping your job."

"That was just an excuse to keep from facing up to reality," Jackie said frankly. "Paul's going to put a house trailer on the ranch. We'll hire a live-in nanny to look after the baby and the house while I'm at work. It'll be great, actually. I'll come home every night to a happy baby and a home-cooked meal."

"And Paul," Adrienne said.

"And Paul," Jackie echoed, feeling a sudden surge of love so intense that her body could scarcely contain her joy.

The door opened and Harlan popped his head inside. "Ready, ladies?"

Jackie got to her feet and made a few nervous adjustments to her dress and hemline.

"Oh, come on," Adrienne said. "You look gorgeous. Here's your bouquet. Make sure Leigh's the one who catches it, okay? I like the look of that newspaperman she's been chatting with.''

Jackie took the beribboned arrangement of baby's breath and yellow roses, and moved out into the upper foyer to take Harlan's arm.

Alex stood there holding a padded wicker basket festooned with ribbons. Three-month-old Daniel lay against the cushions, beaming and resplendent in a tiny white tux complete with gold bow tie.

He laughed and kicked in delight when he saw his mother, and Jackie touched his fat cheek gently, hoping she wouldn't cry and smear her makeup.

The strains of organ music drifted up from the foyer. Alex started downstairs with her baby basket, followed by Adrienne. Then Jackie descended slowly on Harlan's arm, down the Mellons' curved staircase and out through the double doors of the great hall, conscious of a mass of expectant faces gathered near an outdoor bower.

Wardlow's cheerful freckled countenance and Michelson's broad, beaming smile. Her cousins Joey and Carmelo, looking dazzled by their surroundings. Gram's wrinkled face and shrewd, unsmiling appraisal of her granddaughter's appearance. Leigh Mellon and her little son, still next to Karl Widmer. Other friends and co-workers from the police force.

Alice, the department secretary, and Ginny, the substation receptionist, were both crying openly and wiping at tears as Jackie passed down the aisle.

And finally, at the front, waiting by the altar among a riot of autumn flowers, was Paul.

He stood half a head taller than any man in the garden, wearing a well-fitted gray tux, his smooth blond hair gleaming softly in the autumn sunlight. When he turned and watched Jackie approach on Harlan's arm, his dark eyes kindled with admiration and a love that wrapped close around her, full of warmth and strength.

She smiled at him, and moved forward to take his hand.

EXPOSÉ

LAURA VAN WORMER

In *Any Given Moment* Laura Van Wormer revealed the secrets of the talent industry.

In *Talk* she took us behind the scenes of television news.

Now Laura Van Wormer reveals the secrets of the high-end tabloid magazine business... where more than a few people are willing to kill for a juicy exposé

EXPOSÉ

On sale mid-July 1999 wherever hardcover novels are sold.